Praise for THE KING'S ELITE, *1ˢᵗ edition*

"A Captivating Story"

If we could teach today's youth one character trait which would it be? Some may say 'humility' and others 'courage,' but one character trait that is often left to be learned the hard way is forgiveness.

In THE KING'S ELITE, author John Kay exemplifies the importance of forgiveness through a captivating story complete with swords and sorcerers.

After reading THE KING'S ELITE, the reader will be left wondering, "Will I choose to learn the art of forgiveness?"

—TERRY DELANEY
Book Review editor
ChristianBookNotes.com

THE KING'S ELITE

III

THE KING'S ELITE &

THE PRINCE OF
ITIHASIA

‡

J. Elliott Kay

BorderStone Press, LLC
2016

First Edition

The King's Elite & The Prince of Itihasia

BOOK 3 *of* THE KING'S ELITE

Author: J. Elliott Kay

Cover, maps, and interior artwork: D. Ellen Ingle

© 2016

www.borderstonepress.com

Published by BorderStone Press, LLC
Brian R. Mooney, PO Box 1383, Mountain Home, AR 72654

BORDERSTONE PRESS, LLC publishes this volume as a document of critical, theological, historical and/or literary interest and does not necessarily endorse or promote all of the views or statements herein.

ISBN: 978-1-936670-24-6

Library of Congress Control Number: 2016931813

City of Aversace

CONTENTS

Deep within my mind,
nestled carefully in my imagination
lies one of many kingdoms from one of many lands.

Feel free to explore this imaginary kingdom,
fill any drab voids you may find
with your own colorful cognitions.

No need to be concerned with the details of the world,
the layout of the land,
or the religion of the people.

Still, there is much to consider.

Nothing can exist without
some fiber of significance.
The story of this kingdom is simple and profound,
tragic and uplifting,
dark, yet whole.

As the story teller,
you will learn from me
everything you must know
for the story to begin and conclude
with full meaning.

After all, what is a story
without a moral?

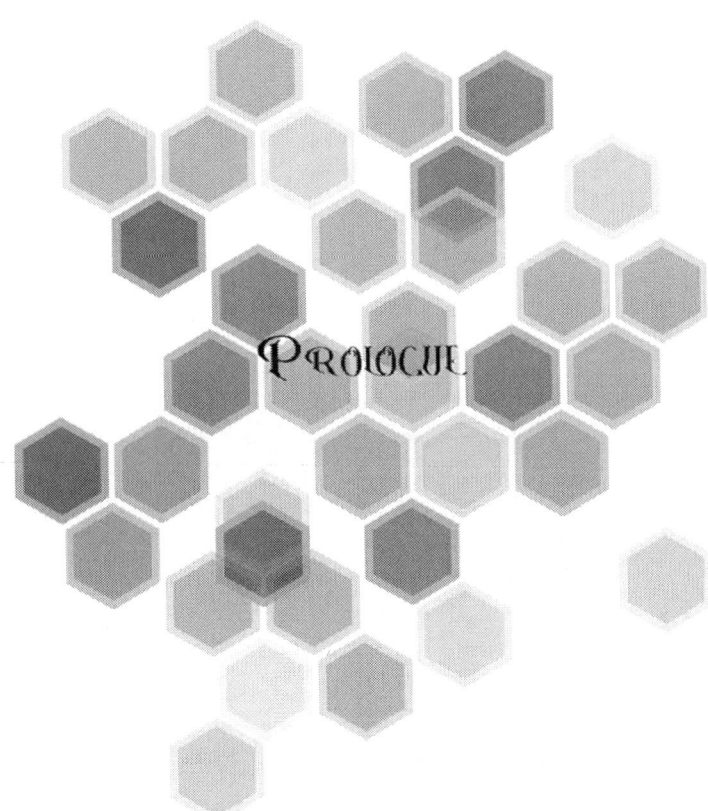

PROLOGUE

PROLOGUE

To the Prince of Itihasia,
Much has changed since you first inquired about my identity. I have no doubt you find it hard to place your faith in my wisdom. There have been setbacks to my plans, but consider this; we knew these days would come, and we've always known the odds were against us. You would never have believed me had I told you where we would be in this world. You must look past our present circumstances and realize how far we've come. Remember, it is I that brought us here.

Word has come to me that you've made a significant sacrifice for the guild. Know that such actions do not go unnoticed. I can empathize with you. I too have sacrificed much for the Greater Good. Do not be discouraged, soon our efforts will come to fruition. Elaborate plans, brawn and dumb luck won't be rewarded in this fight. The victory belongs to the one who has learned to adapt and react accordingly. Cunning, my friend, will win the day.

The board was set years ago, yet the game continues. Only a few pieces remain. Though the enemy may control the board, you're the hidden ace in my sleeve. You must accept your role and trust me to safely move you into position. Wait for my signal, then strike with all of your cunning and might. With your resourcefulness and my intuition, we may yet see the king's armies fall. Then, as promised, you may claim your rightful place as supreme ruler of the land.
For the Greater Good,
The Ebon Crow

CHAPTER ONE

THE LAST SOLACE

CHAPTER ONE

THE LAST SOLACE

FREJA PARTED THE foliage of a patch of wildflowers. She breathed in the aroma. The scene was a paradox within itself. A cloudless, blue sky held the sun in place. It beamed over the fields like a halo. Crisp winds batted the trees and their leaves with gentle pats. The sun's warmth complimented the cool breeze.

"What do you see?" A voice whispered.

"It's a beautiful day." Freja whispered back. She plucked a flower and held it to her nose. She breathed in.

"Do you see a way around?"

Freja rolled the stem between her fingers, noting each characteristic. The colors where vibrant, the leaves patterned, and the scent fresh. It simply belonged. The valley's edge was its home. It was beautiful.

"Freja! Is there a way?"

Freja's eyes narrowed. She reluctantly focused her gaze past the flowers. Instead of rolling fields dotted with yellow wildflowers, Freja saw trampled grass and wagon ruts filled with mud. Where the air should be brisk and clear, hot smoke and ash billowed across the plain. Instead of the songs of birds, iron clanged in preparation for war. The once verdant field now laid in ruin as the Itihasian army gathered and grew like an ominous storm; and in its eye stood Averlace, bracing for impact.

All paths were blocked. Averlace was alone, surrounded by her enemies.

"I don't see a way, Bratheon," Freja said. She took one last sniff of the flower. She crawled backward on all fours and vanished under the brush. The prickly bushes and undergrowth ignored her passing as she gracefully weaved between their thorns and vines. Her brother was where she left him, reclined against an old oak, drawing in shallow breaths.

"There is no way," Freja said. She sounded relieved.

"We don't have a choice," Bratheon said. "We have to get in the city."

"If the purpose was to warn them, then we are too late," Freja said. "It's not worth our lives to deliver news that tells them nothing."

"They don't know the extent!" Bratheon said. "Besides, we can't stay in these woods forever."

"Why not?" Freja tied her hair back. "We know no other way of life. We'll last longer in the wild than in Averlace's streets, especially with it under siege. I can care for you out here." She crushed the wildflower in her hands then spat on the broken petals. The tacky mixture expanded into a gummy ball as she rolled it between her fingers.

"The woods are no longer our home," Bratheon said.

A long wooden staff leaned against the oak. He reached for it, but winced and recoiled.

"The woods are our home. I won't accept anything else," she said. "Let me see it."

Bratheon turned to his side. An arrowhead pierced his back, just under his right rib. Freja stuffed the medicinal herb into the wound.

"Any better?" Bratheon said through a labored breath.

"It needs to come out."

"More reason for us to get to the city."

"More reason for us to stay in the woods," Freja said. "You need to accept that we're too late. We can't do anything for these people. Had we arrived a few days earlier, then perhaps, but that isn't the case. That arrow in your back may be our salvation. Had it not slowed you down we would have arrived before the Itihasians—Doomed with the rest of Averlace."

Bratheon batted Freja's hand away. "This is greater than us. The king must know more is on the way."

"Of course this is greater than—" Freja bit her lip. She ducked down and scanned the woods then whispered. "I have our way of life in mind. Is Averlace's degenerate way of life worth the cost? We are the last of what's left—"

"You think I am unaware of that?" Bratheon said. "You're not the only one hurting. Nor the only one who has lost. If you're concerned about preserving our magic, then hiding in the woods until we are dead and forgotten is not the solution to our problem. This city is."

"Father said they abandoned Manaism years ago. They will despise us, possibly even threaten. We aren't even sure they would open the gates for us. Even if they are receptive to us, what difference would our arrival make? What good will it do to risk our lives to warn them of a danger that is now at their doorsteps?"

"It may make all the difference in the world. They may be counting on reinforcements, and support, to wait out the siege, but I don't see how it may be possible now. Help isn't coming. King Alderman must know this. The more the king knows, the better decisions he will make."

Freja folded her arms. "I still don't think the people of this kingdom are worth the risk."

"Really? ...Mother and Father would be really proud to hear that." Bratheon bared his weight on his staff and heaved himself to his feet. "They didn't have us grow in magic so we could learn to value ourselves over others."

"They didn't want us to waste our gifts for ungrateful people either. Averlace fears people like us."

"By the way you are talking, I wouldn't blame them." Bratheon reached for his horse's reins.

"You're going anyway, aren't you?"

"It's the selfless thing to do."

"The 'selfless thing to do' is what killed Mother and Father. It's what put that arrow in your side."

"Is that so?" Bratheon licked his lips and glared at his sister. "Who is being ungrateful now?"

"I'm just trying to save you!" Freja's eyes reddened. Tears trickled down her face. "You are all I have left now."

Bratheon reached for Freja and pulled her in. She carefully wrapped her arms around him, mindful of his wound.

"Freja," Bratheon brushed a wisp of hair behind her ear. "When the world takes from us, it is natural to want to withdraw and withhold. But we can't. We must continue to give of ourselves. We must always be truly selfless. The world is the way it is because it has forgotten. It needs us. We can't hide in the wild forever."

Freja clinched her brother's cloak and pulled it to her cheeks. She listened for the songbirds, the babbling brooks and the wind's hushed breath. The wild was her solace, but even its untamed presence could hardly be felt. War had come, leaving a wake of death and destruction. Bratheon was right. If there *is* any hope for the land, it is behind Averlace's walls.

Bratheon swayed as he held on to his staff. Freja braced him against her shoulder.

"How am I going to get you past the enemy and inside the city?" She lowered him back to the ground.

Bratheon forced a smile. "Let's be realistic... I was doomed the moment I was hit fleeing the glade."

"Stop it. I can heal you. I just need time."

"Freja listen to me."

"No, stop it. You listen to me! You came for me! I wouldn't be here without you. That's how it's been. That's how it will be. If I am riding for the castle I won't be riding alone."

"That's not what I intended."

"You are coming with me?"

"Of course I am."

"Then what did you mean?"

Bratheon brushed her hair and kissed her head. "Just promise me you will keep riding for the gate no matter what happens."

"If you can promise me you won't give me a reason to stop."

Bratheon laughed. "I can do better than that... I know of a reason to keep riding."

Freja smiled and shook her head. She clinched her eyes to fight her tears. "You are reminding me of Father... Heavens, you can be so sappy."

"Then you know what I was about to say?"

Freja nodded.

"And you believe it?"

"I do," Freja said as she wiped her tears. She observed the woods and thought of home. Even if she were to return, it would never be as it was. "I do believe it..."

"Then let's do this... not for us."

Freja's lips parted from a timid smile,

"...For the Greater Good."

CHAPTER TWO

THE RIDERS OF EVERTIDE

CHAPTER TWO

THE RIDERS OF EVERTIDE

WHEN THE ENEMY army sounds the retreat, then you may wear your ring.

King Alderman's words haunted Bruan's memory. What first sounded as a herald to new beginnings now seemed a hopeless dream.

Put that in your pocket. It may be in your possession now, but it must still be earned.

Bruan tumbled the ring in his hand. He felt on top of the world that night. King Alderman declared him Captain of the Wall. After the battle at Manadon Gate, anything seemed possible. Bruan envisioned the Itihasian army retreating as their advances failed to breach the walls. Their mighty war machines would break against Averlace's defenses. Enemy morale would fall as it challenged the courage and determination of Bruan's men. All due to his leadership...

Recent days painted a much bleaker future for Averlace. Itihasian numbers increased throughout the day and into the night. Averlace had been outnumbered three to one, but as the nights passed, the odds continued to grow against their favor.

"Ten to one," Bruan mumbled to himself. He pulled his hand from his pocket, leaving the ring behind. He stood from his chair where he kept watch and leaned over one of the wall's crenels. The enemy showed no signs of aggression. They were still setting camp. After a week of reinforcements they grew and expanded their perimeter around the city. Long caravans brought supplies, ending Bruan's hope. *Averlace won't outlast the siege.* The enemy needed to only wait. It was Averlace's next move, and there was nothing that could be done.

Bruan looked down the northern wall. It was the longest portion of Averlace's defenses and consequently, the weakest. The enemy knew it too. Throughout the night the Itihasian's shifted the strength of their army from the western side to the north. Bruan wanted two men at each merlon, but the king denied the request. It would pull too many men from the other walls.

"Captain," a giant of a man saluted Bruan. It was Barret. Dark circles shadowed his eyes. He handed Bruan a brown letter. "The stores, sir. As you asked."

Bruan looked the paper over. The numbers were better than he had hoped. "There is some good news," Bruan forced a smile. Barret nodded.

"We are fortunate the farmlands were evacuated when they were. Many lives were saved, and the harvests, though early, were brought with them. An uncanny sense of the enemy's motives."

"Our king is a wise leader."

Bruan raised an eyebrow. "Cunning, perhaps." He involuntarily reached for his ring. "The wisdom comes from his council." Bruan folded the letter and shrugged. "Forgive me...Give this to the quartermaster. The information is for him."

"He's already seen it, sir. He believes we have enough food to last for three months. Of course our water is fine. We're blessed to have our river run through the city."

"Until they poison it," Bruan said. "Inform him then that each man on the wall is to receive a full ration on their watch. I want them strong. Alert. They will need some incentive to fulfill their shifts."

"Defending their homes isn't incentive enough, sir?"

"It is for now, but... Time is against us. It weakens resolve and morale. Men will start to question orders. They will grow angry and discontent."

"Not with our captain," Barret said. "The men talk about you all the time. Saving the king in the field and all. Few men have the honor of saving the king's life, much less surviving it. To think you have done it twice now... Some call you the Aegis of the Elite."

Bruan looked away. Had Barret forgotten who Bruan was? What he had done? Bruan wanted to lash out, but he thought better of it. Morale was low enough. Rumors of the captain of the wall chastising soldiers for singing his praise would be worse than the arrival of an entire Itihasian legion.

He had thought the king's grace would rid him of his guilt. It would have, had Davrian not received the same honor. Worse yet, Davrian wore the signet ring without proving himself. Bruan was guilty of treason, but Davrian's trespasses far outweighed Bruan's single act. Still, at least the guild master sat in a prison cell.

Bruan looked across the northern fields and studied the enemy. There were so many of them.

When the enemy army sounds the retreat, then you may wear your ring.

"What about our arms?" Bruan said.

"Our fletchers are hard at work. We shot nearly all our arrows during the battle. Down to just a couple hundred between the three gatehouses."

"And now?"

"Each house has fifteen hundred, sir."

"That's hardly enough."

"With our reserves and volunteers on the wall, we have almost enough swords for each hand. We are better off with our armaments. Every head now has a leather cap and we have a cuirass for most."

"I want each man carrying something, a dueling sword if need be. We can't have unarmed men on the wall. The enemy knows we are weak enough."

"I'll let the quartermaster know at once," Barret said.

"You handle it," Bruan said. "I'm making you Lieutenant."

"Sir?" Barret fought to hide a smile.

"Find a man for each wall to tally the numbers. I want to know how many come each night. Where they shift their numbers. The number of supply wagons. Keep reporting to me every six hours."

"Yes, sir."

"This wall is too easy a target. The hill of Carper's Vale must be cleared. Assemble a team of engineers. Have them ready to work as soon as I have the king's permission to clear the land. The hill is high enough for a ballista to defend every wall but the south. The heavens know the north side will need it."

"Consider it done."

"And one more thing, Lieutenant."

"Sir?"

"We must do what we can to keep morale high."

"Yes, sir," Barret said, his smile easier to hide now. "Armaments, quarter reports, clear Carper's Vale and high morale."

Bruan saluted his new Lieutenant and watched as the hulking man ran down the ramparts. He looked across Averlace. It was hopeless. At any moment the enemy could storm the walls, and he couldn't find a weapon for every man.

"Aegis of the Elite," Bruan muttered to himself. It had a nice ring to it. Was it true? He turned from the city and gazed across the fields filled with enemy soldiers. Defending the city against such numbers was an impossible task. Yet the king gave him the responsibility to lead the city's defenses. Was it a step of faith, or an act of desperation?

Bruan reached for the ring in his pocket again. He didn't survive the battle at Manadon Gate for nothing. He slipped the ring on his finger and held it up. Just like he had to believe before that there was hope for redemption, he must believe there was hope for Averlace.

As Bruan admired the ring, his eye caught a glimpse of a rising dust cloud.

He leaned out, peering in the distance. After a moment he made out an armed cavalry rushing the road.

"To arms," Bruan cried. "To arms. To arms."

The ramparts stirred to life. Curses and prayers were exchanged as orders directed the men. Bells rang to alarm soldiers to the north wall. The men worked just as Bruan's drills had trained them. Within a minute Bruan heard news from every gatehouse. While the north was reinforced, the other walls raised banners and lit torches, anything to make the enemy believe more men were present. Spearmen rushed the gatehouse to brace the gate and serve as the first line of defense should it fail.

As per drill, Bruan climbed to the top of the barbican guarding the gatehouse. There he waited for his archers massing atop the ramparts. Illiott was with them. An old veteran named Ingran led them. Ingran lined the archers along the wall, all within range of the gate.

"I'm assuming they're armored," Bruan told Illiott. "Have your men wait until the enemy is upon the gate."

"Cavalry only?" Illiott said. "Against our walls?"

"They may be escorting a smaller force. Sappers perhaps."

"It makes no sense. They know our walls are formidable. They took many losses at Manadon. Why risk a single cavalry unit while the rest of their armies stay behind?"

"I don't know. We can't prepare for the unknown. Get to Ingran and be ready to leave for another wall. Have them hold their fire unless the enemy is attacking. They may be hoping to draw several volleys just to deplete—"

Bruan was interrupted by a thunderous crack of lightning. The bolt fell from the clear sky and struck in the rising cloud of dust. Though hundreds of yards away the men felt a pounding wind as thunder rolled across the valley.

Bruan's mouth hung ajar. Illiott was speechless. Both held a hand over their eyes and checked the sky.

"What was that?" Bruan said.

The soldiers cried out. Their eyes fixed on the clear sky.

"They come wielding magics!" A man shouted, his voice panicked.

Bruan looked through the machicolations' murder holes onto his spearmen below. They shifted around and nervously exchanged glances. They hadn't seen the lightning, only felt and heard the thunder.

Bruan pulled a man away from the wall and stood in the soldier's place. He leaned out and stared at the rising dust. Nothing. The cloud stirred down the road. It had to be cavalry, nothing else could move as fast.

Another crack of lightning exploded into the cloud. Illiott jumped with a start. For a brief second, the lightning illuminated the cavalry's silhouettes. Bruan thought his eyes deceived him.

"Did anyone else see that?" Bruan called out.

"Aye, captain." Barret called out. "Horsemen riding in the cloud of thunder."

"How many?"

"Two, sir."

Bruan rubbed his eyes, confused. Only two riders made for his walls, surrounded by what appeared to be a thunderstorm. Were they enemy manaists? Powerful enough that two could level a city's defenses?

"Ingran!" Bruan called out. "Have your men fire as soon as they are in range. Don't allow them a chance to speak."

"Captain," Barret yelled. "They are leading the charge. The rest of the cavalry rides behind."

Bruan looked for black flags on the southern and eastern walls. They hadn't been drawn. The enemy only moved at the north.

Illiott and the archers waited patiently for the enemy to come within range. The killing ground for a volley was a hundred yards out, but with only three arrows per man, each shot would have to be precise. They would have to wait until the enemy was close.

"Archers ready," Ingran yelled out.

A strong wind from the north blew against the ramparts. By now the two riders could easily be made out. Bruan counted twenty cavalrymen behind. Red Itihasian banners flapped above their heads. From what Bruan could see, none of them wore armor.

"Fire!" Illiott gave the command and a hundred arrows flew from the wall. Most of the volley blew wayward as it flew against the wind. Only a few arrows kept course. The lead rider waved their hand. Illiott and his men watched in astonishment as the black shafts of their arrows turned to thinner, green stems and their fletching to petals. The deadly hail of arrows transformed to a rain of flowers.

The wind blew harder, kicking up a blinding storm of dust. It howled over the ramparts with a deafening roar. Illiott covered his eyes and ears as best he could and hid behind a merlon for cover. A voice carried in the wind's violent buffets, audible, and clear as the sky just moments before.

"Let us in!" a chorus of childlike voices called. "Let us in! Let us in!"

It wasn't like anything Bruan had seen before. The wind blew with the force of a hurricane, knocking and pushing men from their posts. The green gatehouse banners tore from their halyards. Bruan watched as his men scurried from the ramparts and ran for cover. Others cowered as lightning thundered overhead. He hoisted himself up to look over the wall, but the wind pushed him back down. Barret was blown off his feet.

"Let us in! Let us in! He can't hold them off much longer," The voices howled. With another crack of lightning, the wind stopped as quickly as it began.

Bruan lifted his head above the merlon he hid behind. He couldn't see the two riders, but the rest of the cavalry stayed out of the archers' range.

"Captain, below!" Barret pointed through one of the murder holes. The two riders waited at the gate. A young woman and a wounded man, slumped over his horse.

"Open the gates," she shouted. "Hurry."

Bruan looked back at the cavalry. Their steel armor and uniformed cloaks could not be mistaken, they were Itihasian horsemen for sure. The girl and her companion looked different. Battered, weakened... desperate. Were the Itihasians after them?

The leader of the Itihasian horsemen rode out and circled his men. He waved a short lance and shouted to the walls.

"On your feet," Bruan yelled to his men. "Stay wary." He helped Barret up. "Keep your eye on them. Shout for me if they ride for the gate."

Bruan left the barbican and descended a ladder to ground level. Athan met him near the gate, his short swords in hand.

The dust from the wind had yet to settle. Bruan weaved his way through the spearmen guarding the portcullis. He followed a young girl's voice as it continued to call out. The same voice in the wind.

"What's going on?" Athan said as he coughed. "What's happening up there?"

Bruan didn't answer. He blindly made his way to the portcullis.

"Let us in. They are coming," the woman continued to cry. "Captain."

Bruan looked to the ceiling of the gatehouse and saw Barret peering through.

"The Itihasian's are riding for the gate!"

Bruan saw the young lady, her arms reaching through the portcullis's iron grating. Her eyes were wide with fear.

"Let us in. Please."

"Ride you fools!" Bruan shouted as he waved the riders away. "The enemy is upon us. We won't open this gate."

The woman shouted her defiance. She backed from the gate and stared at the ground. She raised her arms. The iron began to quake and moan.

"Freja," the male rider called out. "Stop."

A frightened soldier threw his spear at Freja. As it left his hand, the spear turned to sand.

Bruan stepped back. The portcullis bulged towards the mysterious riders. The gatehouse shook.

"Freja, stop," the man cried out. He hopped from his horse. Hunched over, he hobbled to the woman. He whispered in her ear.

"Fire!"

Ingran gave the command to his archers. Bruan saw the field dot with arrows. Few riders fell. The rest continued their charge.

"Get them out of there," Barret shouted.

Bruan looked past the couple. The Itihasians were closing fast. He had to decide.

"Please, let us in," the man said, his voice calm. "We can help you."

Bruan cursed. The wind, thunder; the arrows to flowers, a spear to sand. Could they be Averlace's salvation, or would he be allowing another threat into the city? He looked at the bent portcullis. Terrible power... Yet she stopped.

"Open the gate," Bruan ordered. "Hurry."

Clanking chains rattled above their heads and dust fell from the ceiling as the iron gate lifted. It rose a foot then stopped with a fierce screech. Bruan looked up. The damage had been done. The bend in the iron kept it from rising farther.

"Hurry crawl under," Bruan said.

Freja dropped to her knees and scrambled under the gate. Her brother was less fortunate. He scooted under, but his chest wouldn't fit.

"Bratheon," Freja shouted. She concentrated on the iron and extended her hands, trying to bend it back. Arrows continued to rain down from the ramparts above. It wasn't enough. The enemy made it under the gatehouse.

"Stop the manaist!" The leader shouted.

Despite the chaos Freja kept her focus. The iron moaned and bent back, but it was too late. The Itihasians were upon her brother.

Bratheon pointed to the soldiers. Another clap of thunder erupted just behind the men, disorienting them. One managed to lift his lance, but a stone fell on his head from the murder holes above. Freja worked to align the gate, but it was useless. She dropped beside Bratheon and dug her fingers in the ground. Bruan dropped his sword and went to help, scrapping the dirt away, digging for each inch for Bratheon to fit. He wasn't getting anywhere. Bruan looked for anything to use as a shovel, but noticed Freja wasn't digging. The soil around her fingers darkened. Before his eyes Bruan watched the earth turn to a muddy pool. Bratheon started sinking.

More riders made it inside the gatehouse. Averlace's men held the Itihasians as long as they could, but it wasn't enough. Bratheon's scream broke Freja's focus. She looked up to see a sword piercing his back.

Freja rose and with a terrifying calmness extended her arms to the enemy soldiers. A torrent of fire flashed from her fingers. Bruan looked on in horror as the enemy screamed. He reached through the mud and pulled Bratheon under the gate.

Freja closed and lowered her hands. The fire stopped and the portcullis dropped to the ground. She went to her brother and pressed on his wound.

Piles of smoldering ash were all that remained of the enemy. Bruan looked at the charred ceiling in disbelief.

"Where can I take him?" Feja said.

"...Who are you?" Bruan said.

"Where can I take him?" Freja shouted. "He needs help."

"Right..." Bruan stepped back. "...He needs help." He turned to his men. All stepped away from the manaists.

"Take him to Mandel," he ordered two soldiers. "Hurry."

The two men heaved Bratheon from the ground. They made it several yards until another man stopped them with a litter. They laid Bratheon down and carried him to the surgeon. Freja followed, sobbing and trembling.

Illiott climbed from the ramparts and met Athan and Bruan. Together the three stared at the scene.

"What happened here?" Illiott said.

"I was hoping you would be able to tell me," Bruan said. He picked up his sword, still lying near the puddle of mud.

CHAPTER THREE

LETTERS AND LIES

CHAPTER THREE

LETTERS AND LIES

KING ALDERMAN studied a city map with his officials. He stood dressed for war, with a breastplate bearing his emblem, a rearing stag. Oiled leather epaulets rested on his shoulders and his war hammer leaned against the table. Dark bags circled his eyes. He missed his bed, but he wouldn't dare rest in his chambers with the enemy at his doorsteps. Valice insisted he stay with her, but he wouldn't have it. The king must be with his men, he had told her.

Alderman had just fallen asleep when he heard the first boom. The siege machines have begun their work, he thought. Within seconds he was armed and ready to ride out. He couldn't believe it when his men told him it was only thunder.

Still, there was trouble at the northern gate. Alderman cursed himself for trying to sleep. There was too much to be done. The storehouse needed to be rationed, as well as the river water. Averlace prided itself on the Nana River. Its crystal clear water ran deep through the city with depths reaching close to fifty feet. It had to be monitored now. The Itihasians needed only to poison its source to avoid war altogether. The source... that was another matter. The river's dam was a little over a mile north of the city, out of their reach now. Destroying the dam would direct the water away from the city. It had to be secured, but how?

Bruan found King Alderman mulling over the map. Alderman looked to the captain with sunken eyes. He pursed his lips, bracing for ill news. Bruan didn't have to wait to be asked.

"The wall stands."

"Causalities?" Alderman said.

"None."

Alderman's shoulders dropped, his eyes wandered. "That is good news. You don't seem relieved."

"It is only a matter of time, your Majesty. They are only gauging our strength."

Alderman sat in a chair and leaned on the table. He motioned for Bruan to join him. "There is something else?"

Bruan nodded.

"Leave us," Alderman ordered his officials.

"That's not necessary, your Majesty. The whole city knows by now."

"Knows what?"

"It wasn't an attack on the gates. The Itihasians were chasing riders—Manaist riders from Evertide."

Alderman looked from his map. "Manaists? Did they make it?"

"Yes. The enemy was stopped at the gate. Though the portcullis needs repair."

"What's the concern? The gate is closed is it not?"

"It is. But it's the manaists that concern me, Your Majesty."

Alderman leaned back in his chair and stroked his chin. "Magic is legal now, captain. We have defended our enemy's enemy with no cost to ourselves. A victory is a victory, is it not?"

"It's their magic. They called down lighting against the Itihasians—Summoned wind strong enough to knock my men from the ramparts."

"So this is the storm I heard earlier..."

Bruan continued, "The girl changed—"

"A girl?"

"Yes, a young woman. With the power to change arrows to wildflowers, and a spear to sand! She nearly ripped the portcullis from the gatehouse. She changed the earth to a muddy pool right before my eyes. The most terrible was the fire from her hands. Within seconds she incinerated twenty or more men and their mounts."

"Twenty?" Alderman's face came alive. He didn't know whether to be thrilled or concerned. "Fire, thunder and wind... It's just like the stories we've heard. You said there are two?"

"The brother of the young lady was badly wounded. The surgeon, Mandel, believes he will pull through."

"And now they are safe behind our walls..." Alderman mused. "Has Fadrien and Illiott talked to them?"

"I sent word out for Fadrien to meet them. Illiott saw everything."

"What about the city?

"Scared sir." Bruan pursed his lips. "Scared of the siege, the Syndicate, and now these manaists."

"They fought against the Itihasians did they not? What do we have to fear?" Alderman said.

"Your Highness... Had you seen their power—I didn't know what to do. I wanted to keep them out, but the next thing I knew I was fighting to help them in."

Alderman tapped his chin. "You are sure of what you saw."

"I assure you. Ask any man at the north gatehouse."

"And the Itihasians pursued them to our walls... Do you expect them to attack tonight?"

"I don't believe so, your Majesty. Though I wasn't expecting anything that has happened so far today." Bruan sat down and pointed to the map. "The enemy is still moving the bulk of their strength to the north. They are unorganized. Their herds of cattle were still at the forefront of their southern encampment. They are in no position to attack with all of their strength at this point. If they attack tonight, we will hold."

"For now," Alderman said.

Bruan shuddered at Alderman's voice. The king seemed to be at a loss.

"What do you propose I do with these manaists?" Alderman said.

"Wait for Fadrien and Illiott to speak with them," Bruan said. "I know nothing of magic. My concern is defending the wall." Bruan tapped his knuckles against the city map. He gave Alderman a solemn look. "How long do you think we have?"

Alderman blew out a steady sigh. "Our rations will outlast us, but... More are coming. They continue to grow, we are only weakening. Morale will be the first to go... I've yet to hear from the Marquise. I fear help isn't coming. We are all we have."

"Perhaps help arrived," Bruan said.

"We will see."

"You don't trust the manaists?"

Alderman crossed his arms. His eyes kept a loose gaze on the map. "We may not even need their magic. Can you imagine the enemy's fear? To have two riders divide their camp with a summoned storm then cast fire from the gates? Now the power they could not stop has reinforced our walls. What do you suppose Kvrual is thinking?"

"I have no idea. I wouldn't know what to do."

"Neither does he. You said it yourself, he is unorganized. His army isn't ready. We must use this time wisely."

"So what would you have me do during this lull?" Bruan said.

"Nothing for now. I want them to sit idle. Nothing kills the resolve of an army faster than an indecisive commander. We have another enemy within our walls that must be eliminated."

"The Syndicate?" Bruan said.

King Alderman nodded. "It is time for the guild master to uphold his promises."

*   *   *

Loud raspy knocks woke Kit. He stumbled in the dark across his living room and patted the door for its handle. The door rattled with impatient knocks.

"What are you doing, sleeping at this hour?" Lyle shouted from outside.

Kit groaned. "What are you doing... awake at this hour?" He opened the door to find a blurry mass of colors waiting on his doorstep. He shielded his eyes from the sun, allowing them time to adjust before opening them further.

"You're still sleeping?" Lyle said.

"Was..."

"Great heavens! Only you could sleep while the city lies under siege. And the thunder! Who could have slept through that?"

"It's light outside..."

"Why wouldn't it be?"

"Because it wasn't just moments ago?"

"Moments ago?" Lyle pushed the door fully open. "It's nearly noon."

"Good... Still some morning left to sleep in."

"Not hardly. Give me a hand."

Kit rubbed his eyes and tried to focus. "What is this... A wheelbarrow?"

"All of my belongings. Well, the ones I can't live without," Lyle lifted on the handles and pushed.

Kit blinked. "What are you doing?"

"Moving in."

"Moving in? What's wrong with your home?"

"It belongs to Josie, Adeline and their parents for the time being."

"What's wrong with their home?"

"What is wrong with you?" Lyle swerved the wheelbarrow over Kit's foot as he pushed it through the door. He spoke over Kit's curses.

"Their home is too close to the eastern wall. I wanted them safe from harm. Even if it survives the siege they will be in the soldiers' way."

"I'd rather the whole family move in here than share a roof with you again."

"They wouldn't," Lyle said. "There is no way they could handle your latrine."

"Oh, here we go. Haven't moved in yet and you've already brought that up."

"Most livestock have better hygiene than you, Kit."

"Listen, I can hardly be blamed for your misfortune. You assumed that bucket was fit for bathing."

"It was on your kitchen table!"

"See, there you go again. I never said that was my kitchen table."

Lyle shook his head. He stopped mid-room, his eyes scanned the scene. Rotting food trailed from the door to Kit's bed. Clothing, blankets and rags were strewn from one corner to the next. A tree had been planted in the fireplace to catch the rain. A cauldron sat on the hearth with a charred log sticking out, Kit's makeshift fire.

"Where did you come by all of these clothes?"

"They're Josie's," Kit said.

"What?"

"No, No. It's not like that. It's what's left of her wardrobe from the theater. Costumes I've yet to return."

"Seriously, Kit. How do you live with yourself? ...How am I going to live with you? Does Josie know about your... lifestyle?"

"Oh she loves my style," Kit smiled. "I admit this place could use a feminine touch, but I guess that is why you are moving in."

Lyle pretended he didn't hear. "Where am I sleeping?"

"Wherever you can find space. I'll help make you some room."

"What were you doing up so late anyways?" Lyle said as he grabbed clothes and collected them by the armful.

"Working."

"On what?"

"Another performance."

Lyle dropped the clothes on Kit's bed and gave an incredulous look. "Another performance? What do you mean?"

"Another play, you could say."

"Kit, the theater is gone."

"I'm not stupid, of coarse it's gone."

"Well you didn't know it was daylight outside."

"True, but a theater is for the audience. A true performer needs no stage."

Lyle rolled his eyes. "What is it for? Where will it be?"

"It is for Averlace," Kit said, his smile exaggerated.

"Averlace needs another man on the wall. Not a mad man scribbling plays in the middle of the night."

"Well I disagree. Art has its uses during times like these. Besides, you know I am practically useless with a sword." Kit pointed to his head, still bandaged from the attack in Havenwood. "To be honest, your words hurt."

"I apologize," Lyle said. "Truly. Forgive my callousness."

Kit sat at his table. "There is nothing to forgive. You've been through a lot. I'd be rough around the edges too if I were you."

Lyle said nothing. He made space for his belongings. Kit's home had no available drawers or closets. He grabbed an empty crate for his books and packed a cooking pot with his linens which he sat near a pile of pillows he would use as a bed.

Kit broke the uncomfortable silence. "What did Adeline say?"

"How is that head of yours? You took a nasty hit."

"My head is fine. Don't avoid the question. What did Adeline say to you?"

"About what?"

"When you offered your home to her?"

Lyle wadded up a towel and tossed it to the ground. "Adeline and I aren't speaking."

"What? Is something wrong? She's mad at you?"

"No. Nothing is wrong. I... I'm just avoiding her."

"Avoiding her? Why? She needs us! The siege is terrifying enough. They just lost their theater, now their home. You should be with her."

"It's not that simple, Kit."

A single knock tapped the door, interrupting Kit's protest. Kit rose and walked to his doorsteps and found two letters bound together. The first was addressed to Kit. He stuck it in his pocket and read the other. Kit looked for the courier, but he was no where to be seen.

"Lyle? You've lived with me for a matter of minutes and already you are receiving mail at my home."

Lyle's brow scrunched. "Funny. How would anyone know I am here now?"

Kit shrugged his shoulders. "That's not what I would be concerned about."

"What do you mean? Who is it from?"

Kit flashed the letter to Lyle and pointed to a black bird stamped on the back. "The Ebon Crow."

"The Ebon Crow?" Lyle jumped to his feet. "Finally, a connection with this Crow fellow. Maybe now we can learn more about this sponsor Davrian speaks so highly of." Lyle ripped the letter open. "Honestly, Kit, I am not concerned in the least bit. We'll figure out how he got the letter here. You should know by now this sort of thing energizes me."

"I wasn't talking about the letter," Kit said. He pointed to Lyle's linens. "I'm afraid that pot may not be as clean as you assumed."

CHAPTER FOUR

VISIONS AND PROMISES

CHAPTER FOUR

VISIONS AND PROMISES

LIGHT PARTED THE cell's darkness with a bright slit. It widened as Athan pushed the door open. Davrian lied on his back, arms folded on his chest and feet together. The guildmaster's eyes were wide open.

"On your feet," Athan said. Bruan walked in the cell, his sword drawn. Behind him entered King Alderman.

Davrian stood and brushed his clothes free of dirt. "Welcome, Your Majesty."

"You have some promises to fulfill, Guildmaster," the king said.

"That I do," Davrian smirked. "I was beginning to wonder when you'd come. For sounding so urgent, you have taken your time."

"Where's the rest of your Syndicate?" King Alderman folded his arms.

"There, now that's how I like it. Straightforward and precise," Davrian turned away and ran his finger along the wall's cracks. "It depends. To be honest, I am not sure how many remain. I've been out of touch. Nearly had a mutiny on my hands. In fact, it's safe to say it's no longer my guild. It belongs to the Itihasians."

"We aren't talking about the Itihasians; I'm here about the Syndicate. Where are they hiding?"

"I'm trying to tell you, I don't know."

Alderman fought to hide a smile. "A mutiny? It's starting to make sense. If you can't lead them, then you will help us finish them."

"You could say that, your Majesty," Davrian said. "Though this room may be the safest place right now, especially with you having some use for me."

"I'm not sure that's the case," Alderman said. "You admitted not knowing where to find the Syndicate."

"I may not know where they are, but I know where to start looking."

"Where is that?"

"Deserters. Anyone wanting to leave a city under siege would be foolish... Unless they had somewhere to go—Someone waiting for them."

"And we need your help controlling our deserters?" Athan said.

"You're better off knowing why they are leaving. Anyone willing to abandon the city now must have ties with the Itihasians, and only the Syndicate has connections with the farlanders."

"So there are connections with the Syndicate and the Itihasians?" Alderman said.

"Unfortunately," Davrian said. "As you well know, these Itihasians tend to work their way into just about anything."

"This mutiny... you were losing power to the Itihasians?" King Alderman said.

"Indeed. To their commander Kvrual."

"How long have you been working with the Itihasians?"

"Never," Davrian said.

"Don't lie to me," Alderman's lips tightened into a glower. "We know of Sullion, the one Owin executed. He was a member of your guild. Now a whole army of these foreigners are at my doorstep. I am going to find out why they are here, and I don't think I'll be surprised to find you in the middle of it all."

"Why they're here? You really don't know?" Davrian shook his head. A crooked smile flashed his teeth with a short laugh. "You're either more clueless than I'd imagined, or brilliant at playing dumb."

Athan's sword scraped from its sheath. "You're speaking to the king, or have you forgotten?"

Alderman waved Athan off. "I don't care for this man's respect, I just want his answers." Alderman locked eyes with Davrian. "Now tell me, why have the Itihasians come? Is it something more than a conquest?"

"Indeed," Davrian said.

"Then what is it?"

"I'm not sure you will believe me. Besides—"

"I'll decide if I believe you or not," Alderman stormed. "Enough of the games! I won't be toyed with. I've met your demands. I made you a member of the Elite. It's time to fulfill your end of the deal."

"I have everything I need." Davrian bowed. "I stand ready to serve, Your Majesty. We best get started. The enemy will no doubt make their demands in the next day or so."

"What is it then? What do they want?"

"Riches," an unsettling smiled crept across Davrian's face. "Averlace has wealth long forgotten."

"Riches? They've come to plunder?"

"Like I was about to say—It matters not. You are in no position to meet their demands. Your only hope now is to make sure you have no enemies on this side of the wall. That is something I can help you with."

"How are you going to help us find the Syndicate?"

"That may take some time for me to decide. The Syndicate is good at moving from one place to the next. It is something I taught them well. Lucky for you, I know all of the tricks. I'll need ink, a pen, a map of the city and information from the streets. A lantern wouldn't hurt either. It may take me a day or so to find the rest of my guild, but I will. By then you should have heard from Kvrual. You will see that I speak the truth."

"The truth," Alderman grunted. "How have you come by this information?"

"Information is my job, Your Majesty," Davrian said.

"You've had past dealings with the Itihasians?"

Davrian ran his fingers through his long silver hair. "Like I said, they were trying to get involved. They saw my guild as a potential tool for their campaign against your kingdom. I refused them membership."

"So gracious of you," Alderman said. "I would thank you, but I know better. Didn't want any competition controlling your guild?"

"Absolutely," Davrian said. "The Syndicate is mine. I built it from the ground up. It was designed for a specific purpose. Only I am fit to lead."

"Then why was Sullion allowed in the guild?"

"Sullion was... a treaty. A means to satisfy the guild's sponsors."

"Sponsors? Like the Ebon Crow?"

"Yes. Many of whom were starting to favor the Itihasian's proposed vision for the guild. I allowed Sullion to join to get them off my back."

"And what vision was that?"

Davrian laughed. "Treasure, riches. Wealth and power beyond imagination. You see, those deserters I told you of, that is what they desire. They are Syndicate members fleeing the city in hopes of the Itihasian promise of wealth and power. The Itihasians, I'd imagine, would be more than glad to take them in."

"So the Syndicate will flee to ally themselves with the Itihasians in hopes for treasure and power... And I am sure you offered a much more honorable vision for the guild," King Alderman said. "What, pray tell, could that possibly be?"

"Why, the Great—"

"The Greater Good," Bruan answered for Davrian. He looked to the king. "I couldn't stand to hear him say it one more time."

Davrian chuckled. "Some things are hard to forget, aren't they captain?" He looked to the king. "Bring me the items I requested and I'll get to work. You'll see in the next day or so that I am right. Kvrual will be asking for you. You'll see then... You will see."

* * *

Athan closed Davrian's cell door and locked it. Across the hall King Alderman and the rest of the Elite gathered around a table. The officer's detention cells had been emptied. Davrian was the only prisoner. The empty cells had been converted to the military headquarters with new offices for managing the siege. With Davrian as an integral part of the Elite's information, Alderman requested the room across the guild master's cell serve as the Elite's new meeting room. It was safer to meet near Davrian than to transport him from one meeting to the next.

The rest of the Elite overheard Alderman speak with Davrian from the hallway. "He is right," Eamon said as the men sat. "Davrian was often in a power struggle with the Itihasians. I was there when Kvrual declared himself guildmaster. That was the first I heard of someone else trying to win over the guild. Apparently it wasn't the last. Many left Davrian in favor for the Itihasians, but the vast majority stayed loyal."

"Davrian was set up wasn't he?" Alderman said. "When we first caught him, he was betrayed by an inside man? Did you have anything to do with that?"

"No," Eamon said. "If I had to guess, I'd say it was Guile's doing. Perhaps Sullion and the Itihasians were behind it too."

Alderman cleared his throat. He looked to Lyle and Kit across the table. "Davrian asked for information from the streets. Do either of you two know what it is he's looking for, or will we need to go back and ask?"

"He is looking for signs, not people," Lyle said. "Things we would consider banal and mundane. Something as simple as a blue apron draped in a home's window sill with a potted flower resting on top. We would have to ask what sign he is looking for; but whatever it is, it's a signal that determines which hideout is currently in use."

Alderman sighed, "You mean I have to go back in there and ask?"

"I will speak to him myself," Kit said. "Alone."

Lyle thought for a moment. Kit noted his brother's tense shoulders.

"What for?" Lyle said.

"He has you... compromised," Kit said.

Lyle folded his arms. His thoughts raced to Erisa lying dead in his arms. "Perhaps you're right," Lyle said.

"I can handle Davrian just fine," Kit said.

"Recruit whatever help you may need," Alderman said. "I am sure Captain Bruan can spare a few swords for more eyes on the streets."

"As you wish, your Majesty," Bruan said.

"Speaking of the wall, I am curious to hear from you Fadrien. Have you had a chance to speak with the riders?" Alderman said.

"Briefly. The girl was still quite distressed when I met her. Her brother was unconscious, but Mandel says the young man is doing remarkably well. As soon as he wakes I will bring my students to meet them. The girl, Freja, seemed comforted to know we have a school of Manaism."

"Were they trying to escape from the enemy? Why did they ride for the city?" Eamon asked.

"To help," Illiott said. "The girl told us her brother wanted to help Averlace fight the siege. They are fortunate they were able to make it through. It's a miracle really."

Alderman fidgeted in his chair. "Can they be trusted?"

"I don't see why not," Illiott said. "An enemy of our enemy is our friend, are they not?"

Alderman gave a contemplative grunt. "Are they? Lighting from a clear sky, deafening wind strong enough to knock a man off the ramparts, changing a spear to sand, fire hot enough to leave the enemy in ashes—It all sounds similar to the nightmares of our past. The wise King Astrannax banned magic years ago. After hearing your stories, I am reminded why."

"Yet you lifted the ban, Your Highness," Illiott said. "Don't regret your decision. These riders may save us. Think of what we can learn from them."

"That's why I'm concerned," Alderman said.

"I can assure you the school won't tolerate the practice of black magic," Fadrien said. "To be fair, I do find the magic used a bit concerning. The girl incinerated nearly twenty men and their horses. From what we know of Manaism, that power came from anger."

Alderman lower his head. "Who have we allowed into our city? ...Am I the only one concerned here?"

"No," Fadrien said. "Do we still have your trust? Illiott and I will handle this. These people aren't monsters, just two young people trying to escape with their lives."

Alderman nodded. "You understand my concerns. I will trust your discernment."

"Yes, your Majesty. I can't help but feel optimistic. These two may be exactly what Averlace needed," Fadrien said.

"Again, I'll leave it all in your capable hands," Alderman said. "Is there anything else before we dismiss?"

"Deserters," Bruan said. "I haven't seen or heard of anyone trying to leave the city; but if such an event were to arise, what would you have me do?"

"It is treason, Captain Bruan. The law calls for death. For now arrest anyone who tries to leave. They will stand before me under trial."

Bruan lowered his head, "As you wish."

"There is another issue, your Majesty," Lyle said. He pulled a small paper from his pocket. "I received a letter from The Ebon Crow earlier this morning. It is short, no less alarming. It reads, 'Davrian will soon need my trust. Follow him wherever he leads you, and you will see the end of the Syndicate.'"

Eamon and Athan stirred in their chairs. Fadrien tapped his chin. King Alderman stared at the letter, his face without expression.

"What do you make of it?" Alderman said.

"Kit and I don't know," Lyle said. "It raises many questions. How did The Ebon Crow know where to find me in order to deliver the letter? How does he know about Davrian? I received this letter hours before your conversation with the guildmaster. There is no way this Crow fellow could have known we are working with Davrian."

"Unless he can look into the future," Illiott said.

Lyle nodded in agreement. The room fell silent.

"A manaist? Involved with the Syndicate?" Alderman said.

"Gredulous," Eamon said. "He isn't quite as powerful as he would like others to believe, but he can look into the future."

"Yes, I know," Illiott said. "I hired him to tell me my fortune once."

"It brought us nothing but grief and chaos," Bruan said. "Throw the letter away. It can't be trusted."

"I agree," Fadrien said. "Besides, Gredulous is out of our reach. We must deal with the here and now."

"What about Davrian?" Kit said. "Should we confront him about the letter?"

"I say we leave Davrian out of this. The less he knows the less likely he will be able to trick us into something," Bruan said.

"That logic could work against us," Lyle said. "Davrian may be of better aide the more he learns. The real question is what are these men's intentions? I believed the Ebon Crow worked against Davrian, but the letter suggests they may be working together."

"What do you propose?" Alderman said.

"Nothing. Times like this require us to act, not react. We had a plan before I read this letter, I suggest we stick to it. We need to learn more and make the best decisions we can in the mean time. Only time will reveal Ebon Crow's identity and more importantly, his intentions."

Chapter Five

BALLADS, LILACS, AND CHAMBERPOTS

CHAPTER FIVE

BALLADS, LILACS AND CHAMBERPOTS

JOSIE PLOPPED HERSELF in a chair, exhausted. Moving her parents into Lyle's home took longer than expected. It was the first time in months her mother had stepped outside. Both parents struggled to make the walk. Soldiers, off duty, offered to help, but the fight at the northern wall called them to positions.

Josie and Adeline waited until Lyle and Kit could help move. It had taken all day.

Josie massaged her head and closed her eyes. The past week had been too much. Her theater gone; Picus' army revealed as invading Itihasians; the city under siege; her parents' health failing; moving homes, and now her sister's heart broken. It was too much. She rested her head on Lyle's table. She about fell asleep when she heard notes plucked from a lute.

Adeline tried to hold Lyle's lute, play and read music all at the same time. She always wanted to know how to play, and through the years she would get short lessons from the brothers. She knew enough to amuse herself, though it was her dream to accompany her own voice.

Adeline's fingers fumbled along the instrument's neck as she attempted to play *The Lily*. The strings buzzed against the frets; her hair fell over the strings. Adeline threw her hair behind her shoulders, only to have it fall in her way again. Defeated, she laid Lyle's lute across her lap and rested her face in her hands. Tears flowed. She felt Josie's warm hands gather her hair.

"Why don't you try again?" Josie said as she tied Adeline's hair into a ponytail. "I don't think I've ever seen you give up so easily. Usually you're the one encouraging me."

"It's just a song," Adeline said. "I've never been cut out to play an instrument."

"You're starting to sound like me."

"We need to know our limits. My talent is in acting and singing."

Josie joined Adeline on the couch. "This has nothing to do with music or acting. I know this face. I wore it one night alone in my auditorium."

A wispy laugh escaped Adeline's lips. "You were pitiful. Moping around for Kit. You thought you lost him forever."

"You don't look any different."

"Things are different... Kit has feelings for you. I have no one. I'm going to die an old maid."

"Lyle is more complicated," Josie said as she played with Adeline's hair. "I think you just need to give him some time and space."

"No need to tell me that."

"I didn't mean it like that. I know you've been sensitive to his past."

"No, not that. I mean you're right. I need to give him time and space. It's just he has already asked it of me."

"What do you mean?"

"Oh, this is embarrassing."

"Say it," Josie gave a light tug on Adeline's hair.

"The day of the battle, just before Lyle and Kit rode out. Lyle told me goodbye. He... I thought he was going to kiss me, but I was wrong."

"Adeline, I'm sorry."

"I told him I loved him too." Tears welled in Adeline's eyes. Her face scrunched and reddened. "Everything is wrong now. Mum didn't even know where we were most of the day. She is so bad off. Dad—"

Josie hushed her sister. She wanted to say everything would turn out fine, but even she found it hard to believe. Kit had a way of making her feel better. If he wasn't making her laugh, he was assuring and encouraging, or simply holding her. There was nothing he could do about her ailing parents or burned theater, but he was always beside her. He didn't have to be beside her. He chose to be. Somehow it made life's trials easier to bear. Poor Adeline didn't have that.

Adeline broke into a silent cry. Josie pulled her sister's head onto her shoulder. She could feel Adeline's warm tears. She wished she knew what to say, but nothing ever came to mind. Crying along and sharing the pain was the only way she knew to help.

*   *   *

Lyle and Kit walked side by side through Bollarow's streets. Bollarow made up Averlace's largest and oldest housing district. Wooden, two story homes with steep roofs and shuttered windows crowded the cobblestone streets. As the city grew with new additions such as Carper's Vale and the growing artisan district, the homes in Bollarow deteriorated over time. Few referred to the area as Bollarow any longer. Most simply called it the Slums. Bollarow lived up to its epithet, making it a perfect stomping ground for the Syndicate.

"So what are we looking for?" Lyle said. "Blue aprons again?"

Kit rolled his eyes. "That was a terrible night."

"You should have listened more closely to Erisa's directions."

"I can't help it if Hue and Akron sounds like blue apron," Kit said.

"You spent all night looking for a blue apron," Lyle laughed. "Erisa and I waited for hours on you outside of Hue and Akron's. I was worried sick."

"It was our first lead on a Syndicate hideout, wasn't it?" Kit said.

"It was. And the night I fell for Erisa," Lyle said. "You know I often wonder why she helped us that night. It is evident to me now that she was already working with the Syndicate by that point. Still she led us straight to those thieves. We never would have found them in that pantry."

"Everything about her has been a puzzle," Kit said. "Who knows, maybe those thieves were used just so she could build our trust. Davrian probably wanted her to spy on us."

"No. That can't be the case. Think of all of the criminals she helped us find over the years."

"But then why betray us? Why leave you?"

"She was never with me to begin with," Lyle said. "It was all an act."

"Yet she died in your arms, after you kissed her," Kit said. "Davrian told you about her curse on you. Death after love's next kiss."

"So then why curse me if she loved me?"

"She wanted you for herself."

"Then why leave me?" Lyle stuffed his hands in his pocket. "What are we looking for?"

"Lilacs," Kit said. Unsure what to say, or if anything needed to be said at all.

"That's it?" Lyle said. "It's nearly summer. Lilacs are blooming everywhere."

"Davrian told me to look for Lilacs in the window sills... Have you ever thought about confronting him about it?"

"About Erisa?"

"No the lilacs—Of course Erisa."

"What's the point? He wouldn't give me an honest answer. Even if he did, what good would it do now?"

"Closure."

"It's done. I'm moving on," Lyle said.

"Are you?"

"Kit, she wasn't the woman I thought I married. It's that simple. Sure, she loved me—She must've for her curse to be fulfilled. But, it wasn't the type of love I had for her. Like you said, she wanted me for herself. It wasn't true love. I was... a possession. Nothing more."

"She harbored a lot of anger and hate. Which is why the Syndicate was so appealing to her," Kit said.

Lyle nodded. "So lilacs..."

"In a window sill. That includes nearly every home this time of year," Kit said.

"Just like all Syndicate signs, it must be subtle enough to blend in with the rest, yet different enough to stand out for someone who knows what they are looking for."

"What are we looking for other than lilacs?" Kit said, his eyes scanning every window on the street.

"You know—For someone secretly working for the Syndicate... We sure found a lot of Syndicate members with Erisa. You think she would have steered us away."

"Moving right along aren't we?" Kit said.

"Don't you think that is peculiar?"

"Of course I do! I've always thought it strange. You are just now asking about it?"

"I should look into it. Perhaps if I confronted Davrian about her involvement in helping us route out his guild, I could find some closure."

"Is that not what I just suggested? Do you ever listen to me?"

"I do, all the time. I just can't let you know that. It will get to your head."

"You never give me credit for anything."

"That's not true. I still praise your escape from Davrian's Tomb."

"Right, but you manage to water it down somehow. Like when you whine that I made you believe I was dead for a whole day. You can never just say, 'Kit that was great,' and leave it at that. You always have to bring something else up."

"Look!" Lyle pointed to a butcher shop window. "A chamberpot!"

"See! There you go again. You could thank me for keeping you in my home, instead you had to bring up your spoiled linens. Even though you didn't take the time to inspect the pot, you—"

"No," Lyle shushed Kit. "Look."

Kit followed Lyle's finger to the butcher shop. In the center of its window sill sat a clay pot with lilac shoots toppling over its brim as a bouquet. He studied the window and flowers. "I don't see it," he said. "It's in a chamberpot, but is that so unusual? I have a sapling planted in mine and it's sitting in my chimney."

"Any resemblance to you further qualifies its peculiarity," Lyle said. "It's not the chamberpot alone. The shop is closed, and it's only midday. He should be at his busiest."

"He may not have much to sell. The siege has cut off access to our livestock."

"Let's have a closer look. Keep your eyes peeled. If this is serving as a Syndicate hideout, then we aren't the only ones interested in this shop."

Kit started to gag on the air as they approached the window. He brought the collar of his shirt over his nose. Lyle stuck his head through the window. No one was inside.

"Hello?" Lyle called out. "Anyone here?"

"Try the door," Kit said through his shirt.

Lyle pushed the handle. "It's locked."

"Look," Kit waved Lyle back to the window. He pointed in the dark towards the ceiling. Green slabs of meat hung from the rafters.

"That meat was prepped and ready to be salted," Lyle said. "Instead it's been left to rot."

"Perhaps the owner abandoned the shop in fear of the siege?" Kit said. "These shops usually have root cellars underground. He and his family could be hiding below."

"Yet someone recently took the time to place fresh lilacs," Lyle said.

"To cover the smell?"

"No, the stench is too strong. Even if it were the reason, why use a chamberpot?"

"Is this the building Davrian is looking for?"

"I believe so." Lyle looked to the neighboring shops. To the left was a tannery and the right an apothecary. A couple doors down a baker loaded his cart, headed for Manadon Square. All the shops were seeing business.

"The place seems lively enough." Kit said. "Should we ask someone about the missing butcher?"

Lyle shook his head, "No. If this shop is serving as a hideout, then without a doubt we are being watched. I don't want anyone getting suspicious. If we ask the wrong person the right question, it could spook the Syndicate into abandoning their current cycle of hideouts. Let's get back and tell Davrian what we found. I have a feeling it's what he is looking for."

CHAPTER SIX

PRECARIOUS POWER

CHAPTER SIX

PRECARIOUS POWER

REJA CRINGED AT the rag in her hands. She wrung it out into a bowl. To her horror the clean water turned a cloudy red. So much blood. Poor Bratheon's blood. She knew best not to look at the floor. Her feet kept slipping on the slick marble, even after Mandel poured sand under the table.

Bratheon's bleeding stopped, but it took longer than Freja had hoped. It was Mandel and his student, Lurie, who had saved Bratheon. She had hoped to avoid the archaic practice of medicine, but it was the simple needle and a course horse hair that accomplished what her magic could not. Her lips curled and quivered as she ran her hand over his stitches. It would scar. Magic would have closed the wound within an instant and healed beautifully.

Let him rest, were the instructions Mandel left her. Rest took time and time played cruel jokes, but there was nothing Freja could do for her brother. She threw the bloody rag into the bowl and ran her finger down his back. Nothing happened. Why couldn't she help him? If Bratheon was awake he would know what to do. He needed her now, but she was alone. No one else could give him the help he needed.

Let him rest.

Freja pulled a chair to the table holding her brother. She fell into it, exhausted. She rested her head on the table and caught sight of the bloody floor.

"I'm sorry," Freja shouted. Her voice cracked as it dissolved into sobs. "I'm sorry."

*   *   *

"Go ahead and open it," Fadrien said to Illiott.

"It's locked," Illiott said.

"The infirmary, locked?" Fadrien peeked through the nearby window. "He's pulled the curtains. Give it another knock. Surely he's in there."

Illiott raised his hand. The door's slide window opened.

"Go away!" Mandel growled. "They're under my care now!" The view window slid back.

Illiott gave Fadrien a puzzled look. He tapped the door.

"I'll send for the night watch!" The old man's voice cracked.

"I'm here with the king's councilman, Fadrien. We must speak with you," Illiott said.

Mandel slid the window back open. He stood on his toes but only the tops of his bushy eyebrows made it to the window. "Fadrien?"

"We must speak to the riders!" Fadrien said.

"Not now you won't. The girl finally fell asleep. The boy's critical."

"It's a matter of grave importance."

"What's important is keeping these two safe. Had a mob at my doorstep, demanding to meet them—peeking through my windows. Some shouting curses, others praise."

"The king must know if they are a threat."

"Of course they're not!" Mandel said.

"How can you be so sure?" Illiott said. "They are incredibly powerful. The girl killed—"

"I've heard the stories. Had she wanted to do the same to us she would have done so by now. Use your head! You're as dumb as those meddling about here earlier today."

"The king ordered us to speak with her," Fadrien said.

"I've spoken to her. The poor girl is scared lifeless. She's harmless. Come back tomorrow."

"What would I tell the king?" Fadrien said.

Mandel's bushy eyebrows disappeared from the view window. Chains and locks rattled. He pushed the door open, his white apron bloodied top to bottom.

"She cried herself to sleep," he said. "Lurie tried to calm her, but there was nothing she could say. Apparently the girl claims she knows how to heal her brother, but she can't."

"She can't?" Illiott said.

Mandel shrugged his shoulders. "Say's she can't cast her magic now—Too angry or something the likes. Lurie and I haven't seen the girl do anything peculiar. She's just like the rest of us. She fought for her life—Fought for her brother. She's upset and it's no wonder why after today. If it's any condolence to you, I'd be more concerned if she was acting normal. Leave her be. Come back tomorrow."

Fadrien and Illiott exchanged glances. Mandel wasn't one to dismiss anything of significance. He understood the risk of harboring powerful strangers.

"You are responsible for them," Illiott said.

"Of course I am!" Mandel snorted. "Think I need a boy like you to remind me?"

"Thank you for your time," Fadrien said. "I'll tell the king all you've said. Your word is trusted. Is there anything we can do for you?"

"Send for a guard. You won't be the last to visit tonight. Seems the whole kingdom is interested in these two," Mandel said as he shut the door.

Illiott folded his arms. "That's what we fear."

*   *   *

Valice ran her fingers through her hair, working out the braids. She forced herself to look in the mirror. It was as she feared. Dark bags circled her eyes. Her skin was pale and lifeless.

It had been a long day. Since the siege, she took on many of Rhett's responsibilities; meetings with the city provost and field messor at noon, then with the beadle concerned with deserters. All the while she conducted herself with grace and confidence, assuring everyone she passed Averlace is 'well, strong and secure.'

"Well, strong and secure," she muttered again under breath, trying to convince herself it was true.

"You look beautiful."

Valice turned around. Rhett leaned against the doorway. His shoulders slumped, his face dark and haggard.

"You look terrible," she said with a smirk. Her eyes were more sympathetic.

"How's Vance?"

"Asleep. He was asking for you before they took him to bed."

"Was he?" Rhett smiled. His thoughts drifted to home. Life used to be simple, then he married. Life was balanced, then he became a father. It was then a joy, then he became king. Now it was a struggle, with the kingdom under siege.

Valice watched her husband drift. "Are you alright?"

Rhett's head snapped to attention. "No. I'm not."

"I know better than to ask what's wrong," Valice said, her fingers still working out braids. "So… What's changed?"

"Changed?"

"What's different? This isn't the first war you've faced. You've quelled rebellions, hunted the Syndicate. Is a siege any different?"

Rhett walked to his queen and held her shoulders. He gently started rubbing them; their eyes met in the mirror. "If only my men would speak so plainly to me as you do."

"It's because you intimidate them. I know better," she smiled.

Rhett's eyes darted away. "I'm afraid I may have made a mistake."

"Wouldn't be the first."

Rhett didn't laugh. "A grave mistake."

"I told you not to allow Davrian into the circle."

"No, not that. It's Fadrien, Illiott and the school. I wonder if I shouldn't have lifted the ban on magic."

"Is that what's on your mind? There are a countless number of concerns we face and you are worrying about the school? Is it the riders?" Valice said as she turned to face him.

"We can't control people with such power."

"Control? …You are thinking years ahead, of policies and principles. What about now? Can the manaists help us?"

"That is my hope, but are they worth the risk?"

"You said it yourself. We can't control people with such power. You are worrying about things beyond your control."

"You've heard about the riders?" he said.

"I have."

"Even if they mean well, should one person have so much power?"

"Power to do what? Kill twenty men?" Her brow raised. "You have the same power... You may not summon fire from your hands, but have you not killed as many men on the battlefield? What difference does it make?"

"I can be stopped."

"They can't?"

"It goes beyond these two riders."

"Like I said. You are worried about the future. We have to survive now. By whatever means."

"Not whatever means... Our ancestors banished Manaism. They thought it an evil thing."

"It's a tool used by evil people, just like any other weapon. It can also be used for good. That's why you built the school. You have faith in your people. Magic will be used for good again," Valice said.

"Perhaps I was naïve."

"Perhaps you are losing sight of your own vision for Averlace?"

"It's not that simple," Rhett said. "I understand now the lure of magic's more destructive powers. Even if we defeat the enemy with magic, are we dooming ourselves to repeat our terrible history?"

Valice wrapped her hands around his waist. "I don't believe that is a kingdom's future when their ruler asks such questions. You are too intentional. It won't come to that."

"My good intentions... Owin might still be with us if not for my 'good intentions.'"

Valice shook her head. "You are not responsible for Owin. He made his choice. Can you not focus on the good?"

Rhett scoffed. "Not with my kingdom under attack. All I see is war and death."

"There is courage, loyalty, and love too," Valice said. "Don't overlook the valor of our people. They will prove to you they are ready for magic."

Rhett kissed the top of her head. "By winning the war without it?"

"Can we? Can we win without magic?"

"It would prove we don't crave magic's power," Rhett said.

"And that we are truly a courageous, loyal, loving people." Valice's lips parted with a warm smile. She reached over her shoulder and held his hand.

Rhett nodded. "More reason for Averlace to win the war without magic."

"That's not what I meant," Valice said.

"Their magic has served its purpose. The enemy has a new respect for us. They won't charge our wall without looking overhead for the next crack of thunder or wall of fire."

"So what will you do with the riders?"

"If they are truly our allies then they will respect my wishes."

Valice lowered her hand. "So you won't accept their help?"

"I won't accept their magic," Rhett said. "Not until Averlace is ready for it."

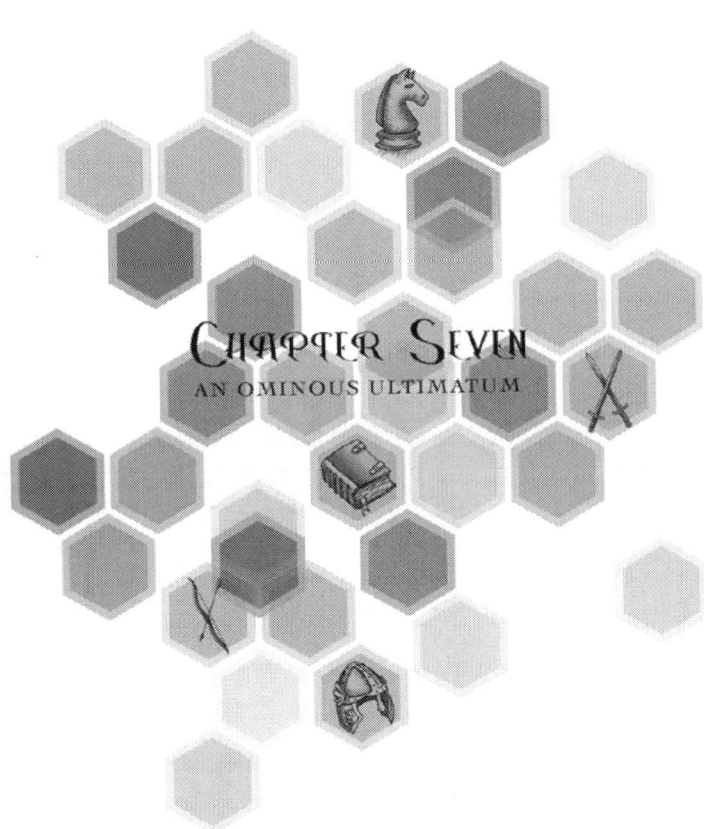

CHAPTER SEVEN
AN OMINOUS ULTIMATUM

CHAPTER SEVEN

AN OMINOUS ULTIMATUM

RUAN CLIMBED THE ladder to the top of the ramparts. He rushed by his men, all standing silent and reticent. He made his way to the gatehouse and found Barret standing over the center crenellation.

"There Captain," Barret pointed. "Just to the right of the hills leading into the meadow."

Bruan held his hand above his eyes. Two men waited under a banner, seated at a table. Four armed soldiers stood behind them.

"They asked for the king?" Bruan looked to Barret.

"Yes, sir. A lone rider approached our wall and called for a parley. Your orders?"

"Keep the reserves off the walls, but have them at the ready. The councilman and I will meet them. It will undoubtedly be a waste of time."

"The councilman? They asked for the king. It could be a trap. Perhaps another should join you."

"Surely, they don't think we're stupid. They will have to come within range of our archers if they want to talk to me." Bruan winked. "Don't worry. I'll bring a few companions along. If these Itihasians try anything funny, they won't live long enough to laugh about it."

* * *

Illiott watched from the wall as Bruan, Athan, Eamon and Fadrien rode to the Itihasian emissaries. Per Bruan's orders, he shot a flaming arrow ahead of his companions. It landed in a clearing on top of a hill, a hundred yards from the wall. Bruan and the others rode to the flame then waited. The message was clear, if the enemy wanted to talk, they would have to come perilously close to the wall.

The emissaries left their table behind and walked the distance. The Itihasians dipped in and out of sight as they walked the hills and through the tall grass.

"They seem annoyed to have to leave their table," Athan said.

"They were expecting us to sign a treaty," Fadrien said.

"They shouldn't have bothered," Athan said.

"Why carry it so far only to leave it behind?" Eamon laughed.

"No wonder it is taking them so long to stage a siege; they are trying to furnish the entire field," Athan laughed.

"Quiet," Bruan said. "Keep your eyes sharp. They are expecting to meet with the king. There is no telling how they will react. They may try to cut us down."

Athan rested his hands on the pommels of his swords. "Perhaps, Illiott should have ridden out with us."

"We'll be fine," Bruan said.

"Take your hands from your swords," Fadrien said.

The four Itihasians stopped a few yards from the Elite. A tall, old man in a red, silken robe led the way. He leaned on an escort. The four guards followed behind. The old man was bald except for a few stray strands of hair that flapped in the wind.

He had a thin, gray beard and his eyes were framed with deep wrinkles and bushy eyebrows. His escort carried a pair of bladed weapons. He too wore a thin beard braided with clinking jewels and trinkets. The emissary's hand never left the guard.

"Well met," the old farlander called out, his voice deep and resonate.

Bruan didn't answer. He kept his arms crossed; his eyes held the enemy in an icy stare.

"You've fought gallantly, Your Majesty," the old man said. "But surely you have come to respect the might of our army. Even now we have the strength to overrun your walls. Still we grow. It is time to surrender. Think of the lives of your people." The old man's voice trailed off. He looked on the Averlacians, confused by their silence.

"Will you not speak?"

"You've come to ask for our surrender?" Bruan said.

"We have come, Your Highness, to make peace. We have—"

"How dare you insult our king by mistaking him for a mere captain?" Bruan shouted.

"My apologies, Captain. Please tell me, which of you is the king, so that I may address him appropriately?" The old man called out.

"Do you think our king wishes to entertain an audience of his enemy? An enemy that encroached the gates at the cost of our people's blood. An enemy who brazenly surrounded our city in the name of peace? Our king stands now from his keep, peering down on you like the vermin you are!" Bruan pounded his chest with his fist. "I am speaking for His Majesty," he bellowed. "If you wish to speak to King Alderman, you will have to come through me and every sword on my wall."

The man paused. "Then who is it that speaks in the king's place?"

"I am Bruan, Captain of the wall, member of the Elite and Aegis of the King."

The old man jerked his arm free from his guard. His face scrunched with the anger he suppressed. "Captain Bruan, does your king cower before the might of Itihasia? Does he have his soldiers not only do the fighting for him, but the negotiating as well?"

"Give me your name and what business you've called me from my wall to discuss?" Bruan said.

"My name is Sgoravon. I'm here to discuss the terms of your surrender."

Bruan stepped into his stirrups. "You have wasted our time. Go back to your camp and tell your commander that he will have to meet King Alderman inside the keep if he wishes to discuss any terms of surrender."

"That is precisely what I plan to do, Bruan," the guard with two bladed weapons hissed. He stepped before Sgoravon. "My name is Kvrual. Unlike your king, I have the courage to make demands face to face with my enemy. Itihasia isn't interested in this kingdom. The people and this land, it's all worthless. The value lies within. We are here for the power hidden behind your walls—The manaist treasure you hide from the rest of the world. We won't leave until we have it and the one powerful enough to wield it."

"Treasure?" Bruan stifled a laugh.

Kvrual's face strained, there was no humor in eyes. "The manaist treasure. We are here to claim it. Give it to us and no more blood will be shed."

"What treasure?" Bruan said.

Fadrien paused, unsure how to respond. In his hours of study, he never read anything that implied of a hidden treasure. It wasn't rare years ago to find a magical artifact, but most had been melted down, sold to traveling merchants or destroyed in fear of its power.

"Averlace has no manaist treasure. And who do you speak of? The one powerful enough to wield it?" Fadrien said.

Kvrual cocked his head. "Playing me as a fool won't get you anywhere. I am speaking of the refuge your kingdom hides from us. Our prince! His father calls for him."

"Your prince?" Fadrien said. He shot Bruan a curious glance. "I am afraid you are mistaken, Commander. We are not harboring any refuges from Itihasia. Much less a prince."

"You have a day to give him up and to grant us safe passage to the manaist treasure. If our demands have not been met by midday tomorrow, we will claim the treasure ourselves and will raze the city until our prince is returned to us."

"If your forces march against our walls they will be destroyed," Bruan said.

"The power your men faced yesterday is but a taste of what our manaists are capable of," Fadrien said, hoping the commander couldn't see past his bluff.

Kvrual's lips broke into an eerie smile. "Your manaists don't even know what they have, nor do you know of the threat that made it into your city. You have more enemies than allies and a coward as a king. If you want to protect your people you better do what you believe to be best and take matters into your own hands."

Kvrual turned his back to Bruan. Sgoravon pointed to the table they left behind and pulled a paper from his robe.

"Mruav," Sgoravon called out to one of his armed soldiers. "Take this to the king's councilman."

Eamon, Athan and Bruan eyed the hulking man. Mruav sensed the Averlacian's tension and pulled his sword from its sheath. He jabbed it into the ground before walking to Fadrien. It didn't make Athan feel any better.

Mruav towered over his companions. He wore leather gloves with brass plating that covered his knuckles. His arms were long and powerful with dozens of scars giving testament to his experience in battle. Like the rest of the Itihasians, he wore beads in his beard and was dressed in a silken shirt.

Bruan could tell the Itihasian was no less deadly without his sword. He slid his feet from his stirrups and directed his horse beside Fadrien. He drew his sword, careful not to draw any attention.

"Bring the Prince of Itihasia by mid day tomorrow, along with this treaty bearing your king's seal," Sgoravon said as Mruav handed the paper to Fadrien.

"I'll take that," Bruan said, extending his arm between the two.

Mruav looked back to the other soldiers and muttered, "Des skil theac cec bel ontro'vo." They laughed as Mruav turned to Bruan, "Look for me, Averlacian. I'll be the one to pour your blood."

Sgoravon chuckled and reached for Kvrual's hand. Mruav and the others followed while keeping their eyes on Bruan. The Itihasians disappeared behind the rolling hills. Only then did Bruan let down his guard.

Fadrien rolled the treaty neatly and looked to Bruan. "Manaist treasure?"

"Are you not familiar with it?" Athan said.

"I'm not. I haven't heard of such a thing, even in rumors or myths. It must be the wealth that Davrian mentioned... But that's not what concerns me," Fadrien said. "Who's this Prince of Itihasia?"

"Have they really come all this way to claim a treasure we've never heard of and a prince we haven't seen?" Bruan said.

"Haven't seen?" Eamon said. "You don't think it could be the riders?"

"The riders?" Fadrien said. "...They both displayed frightening power. Perhaps it is the young man."

"Why were they running from the Itihasians?" Athan said.

"Let's hurry back," Fadrien said. "There is nothing we can figure out here. I hate there is so much we don't know. Worst yet, Davrian seems to be ahead in the game. How did he know about their demands of the treasure?"

"Yet he is offering to help," Bruan said. "He may be the only one with the answers we need, and he knows it."

"But we can't trust him," Fadrien said.

Bruan looked at the Itihasian army and sighed. "I don't know if we have a choice."

CHAPTER EIGHT
MYTHS, LEGENDS, AND SECRETS

CHAPTER EIGHT

MYTHS, LEGENDS AND SECRETS

LURIE LEANED OVER the well and looked down. Being close to the river, Mandel's well stayed full, but she couldn't see the water reflecting back. She unwound most of the rope until she heard her bucket smack the water. Could it be they neared the bottom? The well had been in use all day, filling vats in preparation for the siege or to store in case the river was tainted.

Lurie pulled up a full bucket. For the first time in her life water was precious. Just a few nights ago the world seemed so promising. She was studying at Fadrien's school of magic, earning Mandel's confidence as his apprentice, befriending the Captain of the Wall. She rested the bucket on the well; her eyes looked up to the stars, then back to the city wall.

A wounded prisoner to leader of the city's defenses, she thought. *I wonder if he even thinks of me now?* Lurie chuckled at herself. In the middle of a siege and still she wondered about Bruan. She poured water into her bucket, taking only enough needed to clean Mandel's floors. Behind her three men approached. Startled, she dropped the water.

"Can I help you?" she said.

"Easy," one of the men said. He was one of the Elite. Her school master Fadrien and Captain Bruan were with him.

"I didn't mean to scare you," Athan said. He picked up the bucket to refill.

"We need to speak with the manaists," Bruan said.

"Captain Bruan, what a surprise. I was just thinking of you." Lurie turned away. She could feel her cheeks reddening. She reached for something, anything to do, but Athan beat her to the well's pulley. "I was wondering about... your recovery."

"I'm fine," Bruan said. "Haven't had the time to think about it really."

"Well, you seem to be moving along wonderfully. I guess that means everything's healed." Lurie smiled, hoping her words weren't as awkward to hear as they were to say.

"It appears so," Bruan said. He cleared his throat. "We're here to speak to the manaists. Can you take us to them?"

"One is critical. I can't wake him now. Perhaps you could speak with them later?"

"Can we speak with the girl?" Bruan said.

"It's urgent, dear," said Fadrien.

"Right... I will take you to them, though I doubt Freja will be in the mood to talk. She's been through too much these past two days."

"We all have," Bruan said. "I'm afraid it will only get worse."

"I'll be sensitive," Fadrien assured Lurie. He held his hand out for her to lead the way. Athan followed, carrying Lurie's bucket.

They found Freja resting her head next to Bratheon. The place looked like a butcher's shop. Blood dripped from the table. Freja was covered with it. Her back shuddered with heavy sobs.

"Freja?" Lurie patted the girl's shoulder. "What's wrong?"

Freja moaned. She struggled to take a full breath between her sobs. "I'm what's wrong. It's me! I'm in the wrong. Always." Freja jerked her head up. Bratheon's blood was caked on her face. Her eyes were crazed with anger.

An uneasy feeling settled over Bruan. He reached for his sword and waved Fadrien back to the door.

"Whoa, calm down. Lurie wrapped her arms around Freja and held the girl's bloodied head to her shoulder, rocking her. "Your brother is hurt, but he will be fine. It will take time, but he will heal."

"I should have saved him."

"You have saved him," Lurie said.

"No, I made it worse." Freja clinched at Lurie's arms. "I always make things worse!"

Bruan feared no man. Magic he could face; he even heard his prophecy without fear, but the sight of Freja, covered in her brother's blood, was unnatural. Someone so young should not be filled with such anger. It reminded him of Illiott and his reckless actions. In his rage Illiott unknowingly aided the Syndicate and started a terrible series of prophecies that nearly destroyed the king and his men. This girl's anger was the same, yet she had power, and Bruan had seen what she could do.

"Perhaps she was right," Bruan whispered to Fadrien. "Maybe we should come back later."

"No," Fadrien said. "I must speak with her tonight. Lurie will calm her down."

"I don't think Lurie understands how dangerous this girl is," Bruan said.

"Which is why she may be able to calm the girl."

Bruan watched as Lurie rocked and shushed Freja. She ran her fingers through the girl's hair, assuring her all would be fine. Freja loosened her grip on Lurie's sleeves. Her sobs softened to sniffles. Bruan's hand moved from his sword.

"He will make it. He will make it," Lurie whispered in Freja's ear.

Freja lifted and nodded her head. She wiped her tears.

Lurie tilted her head, her eyebrows raised. "Are you alright?"

"Yeah," Freja nodded.

"Your brother will be fine. You saved him."

"He will not be pleased with me when he wakes up."

"What do you mean?" Lurie looked to Freja then to Bruan.

"He... I um. I misbehaved," Freja said with a nervous laugh. "That's what he would have said."

"I don't understand, Freja."

"I don't think you would."

"Try me," Lurie said.

Freja studied Lurie's eyes. She stood up and walked to the head of the table. Despite Bratheon's terrible wounds, he slept with a smile.

"What did you give him?"

"Mandel calls it Dwale; it's a variant. He uses it normally for surgeries. It is a paralytic as well as anesthetic."

"I'm not sure why I asked. I don't know what any of that means..." Freja said. "He looks peaceful."

"Why would he be disappointed in you?"

Freja ran her fingers through Bratheon's hair. Lurie resigned to Freja avoiding the question.

"Freja, these men here would like to talk to you."

"I'm not talking to them," Freja looked to Bruan. "He is the one who wouldn't let us in. I have nothing to say to him. He angered me. He is the reason why I had to resort to violence. It's his fault. Not mine."

"Freja, Captain Bruan here helped you past the gate. He is a nice man. You should talk to him. I think they need your help."

"I wouldn't have killed those men if he had opened the gate."

Fadrien walked to the table. "Freja, are you sorry you had to use your magic against those men? Do you think your brother will be disappointed to hear you harmed those men?"

"You wouldn't understand. You can't understand us. Everyone here is so different."

"Freja, you have a code don't you? As a manaist you weren't supposed to harm anyone with your magic were you?"

"No," Freja said with tears in her eyes. "How did you know?"

"I understand manaists are supposed to have selfless hearts with high regard for peace."

"You are a manaist?" Freja said

"I am learning. So is Lurie here. We have a lot to learn though. That is why I need your help."

"You will have to wait for my brother. He knows more than I."

"We may not have that long dear," Fadrien said. "It's just a few a questions."

"Please, I'd rather just be left alone right now."

"Freja, I wish I could wait, but you may be the only one who can help this city right now."

"I will not fight a war for you!" Freja said.

"No, no, of course not. I would never ask that of you," Fadrien said. "I want peace. I want to avoid war. I believe you can help me with that."

"Would that please Bratheon?" Lurie said. "Think of how proud that would make him."

Freja's eyes darted between Lurie, Fadrien and Bruan. "What is it you want?"

"Just some questions answered, like where are you from?"

"We are from Evertide," Freja said.

"Why are you here?"

Freja tried to swallow. Her face contorted in pain and anger. She started to cry. "We lost everything. This army destroyed our home. Our parents are dead. I wanted to run away, northward. Bratheon wanted to come here and warn Averlace of the invading army. We argued. I told him I would rather stay and hide in Evertide than to ride for Averlace. I forced him to stay. We hid in the woods until they found me. Bratheon saved me, but he was shot as we escaped. They chased us all day though the woods. That is when I agreed to run for Averlace. He wanted to help, but we were too late. The army beat us here."

"I'm sorry about your parents," Fadrien came to Freja's side and rested his hand on her shoulder.

"They were good people," Freja continued between her sniffles. "They were manaists. We lived away from town so that we could practice in secrecy. My family and a few others have lived that way for generations, ever since magic was forbidden. They started teaching us at thirteen. Bratheon nearly completed their schooling..."

"And you?"

"I studied Manaism for only four years... until they came. But even then I was behind. Father said I had an aptitude for controlling magic, but that I struggled with controlling my heart." Freja turned away from Bratheon and cupped her face. "That's why I couldn't help him."

Lurie joined them and put her arm around Freja. "You helped him Freja. He wouldn't be here without you."

"I could have healed him," Freja cried. "I wanted to, but I couldn't."

"Oh I see," Fadrien said. He leaned forward and found her eyes behind her matted hair. A warm smile parted his thin beard. "You are blaming yourself for not being able to heal him?"

Freja nodded. "I was too angry. I could have closed his wounds, but I—"

"Freja, he will pull through," Lurie said. "Don't blame yourself. You did what you could when you could. You can't expect any more from yourself."

"It's just that I have always struggled with my anger."

"We all struggle with something," Fadrien said. "What matters is that we know when we do wrong so that we can learn from our mistakes. That way we can help ourselves and the ones we love. Which is precisely what you are doing."

Freja wiped her nose on her sleeve. "Thank you. Both of you. Talking does help. We haven't talked to anyone for days."

"I'm so sorry about everything you and your brother have been through," Lurie said.

Fadrien patted her on the shoulder again and hugged her. "You are with friends now. We will care for you. I'm sure Lurie here we be more than glad to help you get cleaned up. Mandel will look after your brother—He's in good hands."

"Is that all?" Freja said.

"No, I'm afraid not. There is much more we need to know, but perhaps we can finish tomorrow, when you are feeling better."

"No, we came here to help. Let me help. I'm feeling better already, promise."

"Very well." Fadrien led her to a neighboring room and sat her down at a clean table. Lurie draped a blanket over Freja's shoulders and offered her a ladle of water. Bruan joined them. Freja stared at the stalwart captain, her eyes unsure, yet forgiving.

Fadrien held his hands and leaned over the table. "Freja, what did your family tell you about Averlace?"

"Nothing good. They said the people here hated magic and those who practiced it. Manaism was illegal here. That is why we lived in hiding, with other families who practiced."

"Is there anything else?" Bruan said.

"I don't know what you are asking. We never came here or wanted to for that matter. To me Averlace was a terrible place because no one practiced good magic. To be honest, you have surprised me. I thought everyone here was evil and selfish. When I think of Averlace I don't think of its rich history with Manaism, I think of its troubles with crime and the Syndicate."

"What is Averlace's rich history?" Fadrien said. "Do you know any?"

"Not really. Bratheon could tell you more."

"Nothing?"

"Well, nothing other than the obvious. Stuff everyone knows."

"Like what?"

"That there was a great war between the good and evil manaists. That everyone knew magic before, but after the war everyone feared it. So it was made illegal. Now no one is allowed to use magic. After the war the king of Averlace had the arbiters hide all of the manastone and magically imbued weapons underneath the city."

"Wait, what?" Bruan said.

"There was a war—"

"No the part about the weapons and manastone," Fadrien said.

"All of the weapons used in the great war were sealed away so no one would ever use them again, along with the books. Father said there are thousands of urns filled to the brim of manastone."

"Where did you hear about this?"

"From my father."

"Did he ever say where it was? Do you have a book or any more information about this... treasure?"

"Why?"

"I've never heard of such a thing, and would like to know more about it," Fadrien said.

"But why? How could you have never heard about it? Everyone knows the story."

"The enemy has demanded that we give it to them, but we don't know where it is. We didn't even know we had it."

"But how could you *not* know?" Freja said.

"Averlace has forgotten much of its history, mainly due to our fear and ignorance. Many consider our magical heritage a dark blot that should be forgotten, or they at least pretend it never existed. If what you say is true..."

"Father was right," Freja said. "He used the same words to describe you... fearful and ignorant. I promise you it's true."

"How can you be so sure?" Bruan said.

"Because my father said so. He was never wrong before."

Bruan crossed his arms. "He also told you everyone here is greedy and self-centered. Was he right about that as well?"

Freja stared at Bruan before answering. "I hope not. Still, I find it hard to believe that no one here is familiar with the hidden manaist armory."

"Do you know where to find it?" Fadrien said.

"All I know is that it is hidden underneath the city."

"Underneath the city? Where could that be?" Fadrien said.

"The sewers?" Bruan said, hoping he was wrong.

"Possibly," Fadrien said. "There are the tunnels the Syndicate used like the one boarded up in the school. They may be a place to start looking."

"There is something else we need to ask," Bruan said. "What do you know about the Prince of Itihasia?"

"The prince?" Freja said. "Itihasia? As in the enemy?"

Fadrien nodded. "Have you heard of him?"

"No, I haven't."

"Nothing?" Bruan raised a suspecting eye. "You—"

Fadrien waved his hand, silencing Bruan. Fadrien could see Bruan's distrust, but he wasn't going to press the issue. Lyle and Kit would have to talk to the girl. Perhaps they could sense if she was hiding anything.

"Thank you, Freja. I will leave you alone. I hope the best for your brother, though I am sure he will be fine with you by his side. I've learned a lot from you. I hope you won't mind if I return."

Freja shook her head. "Of all the people in this city, there is no one here who has at least heard of the hidden armory?"

"Illiott may know," Fadrien said. "Though surely he would have said something by now if he knew anything of it. His father dabbled with Manaism before it was made legal. That was years ago, and Illiott was very young then. He will be the first one I will ask."

"And I know of one I will ask," Bruan said. "...One who is quite familiar with the tunnels."

CHAPTER NINE

WAR'S PRELUDE

CHAPTER NINE

WAR'S PRELUDE

IT WAS A MOONLESS night. Bruan fumbled his way through the streets. He cursed himself for ordering the city lights extinguished. At the barrack's entrance Bruan felt for the door, realizing the lack of light did more harm than good. For the moment, opening a door seemed more important than offering light for the Itihasian's catapults to target. After several blind pats he found the door's handle. He pushed it open only to find the hall darker than the streets save for the faint glow of light from underneath Davrian's cell door.

Bruan gathered the cell key from his belt and quietly slid it into the lock. In a single motion he turned the key and opened the door. Part of him hoped to catch the guild master in the middle of a suspicious act, perhaps working towards one of his hidden schemes. Bruan instead found Davrian sound asleep. In the center of his room a lone lantern burned, surrounded by stacks of paper each bearing a portion of the city map. Bruan scanned the papers for signs of the city tunnels. Arrows pointed from one building to the next, but he couldn't decipher their meaning. He almost woke Davrian for questioning when he noticed a small letter at the guild master's feet.

The letter was sealed in black wax. Stamped below the wax was a black bird. It hadn't been opened. The letter lay inches from the door, slipped in during the night. Bruan tucked it into his pocket. He searched the floor for anything else of interest. There were only the maps, scattered around the lantern, ink well and quills. Davrian stirred on his cot. Bruan reached to awaken him, but thought against it. He stepped out and quietly locked the door behind him.

Bruan broke the seal and knelt at the bottom of the door. He held the letter up to the cell's escaping light. It was indeed addressed to Davrian. Bruan wanted to read the letter, but with only a few hours before the Itihasian deadline, every minute counted. He stuffed the letter in his pocket and made for the king's throne room.

*   *   *

The night's clear sky gave way to a spectacular sunrise. Eamon peered from the Manadon gatehouse barbican, welcoming the sun. The western field was empty. Only rutted trails and trampled earth remained as evidence of the invading army. For a moment he could pretend the Itihasians were no more, but he knew better. He knew not to look northward.

It had been the longest night Eamon could remember. Dotted lines of torchlight moved northward from the western fields as the Itihasians prepared for their attack. Eamon fought the urge to count the lights and focused on searching for sappers. The worst had been listening to the enemy's ceaseless war cries and battle songs. Bonfires sprang sporadically across the enemy camps. As the deadline neared, Eamon couldn't tell if the enemy was celebrating or gearing towards war.

As the situation grew more uncertain Bruan moved the bulk of Averlace's defense to the north wall, leaving Eamon and a few others to watch the west barbican. At the first sign of aggression, they were to strike the gatehouse bells for help. The sun's breaking light signaled the end of the night, proving the Itihasians would honor their deadline. Even if it was just another six hours, Eamon was relieved.

"Stand straight," Athan said. He found Eamon leaning against the wall, his elbows resting on the merlon.

"Morning," Eamon said with a lazy salute. He noted his brother's rigid posture, stern eyes and light step. Eamon straightened his back, but his head hung heavy.

Athan looked to the north. He slowly filled his lungs with the cool air then released a labored sigh. "At dusk they looked more like cattle—Scattered all about the plains...Somehow the night transformed them into an army."

Eamon didn't know what to say. Athan had hoped the Itihasians would never mount to a serious threat. It was a fool's hope.

"Able to sleep?" Eamon said.

"The best I could. Thank you, by the way."

Eamon's head tilted back with a silent chuckle. "I didn't take your watch for your sake. I wanted an alert officer in the morning." Without thinking, Eamon leaned against a merlon.

"Up," Athan said.

"Right, right."

"Don't take it personally," Athan whispered. "It sets a bad example."

"You're right. Not sure I'm cut out for a soldier's life." Eamon gave a faint smile.

"You mean the Syndicate wasn't concerned with discipline, rules and standards?" Athan forced a laugh. "I figured a little discipline would have rubbed off during your time with Davrian."

"I know you jest, but you would be surprised," Eamon said. "Though nothing like military life, Davrian had a peculiar taste for conduct."

"Oh?"

Eamon stretched out his arms. "It made little sense; he would tolerate the most destructive behavior, while at times he dismissed members I assumed he would have rewarded. Take wearing black for example."

"Was there a punishment for wearing another color?" Athan said.

"A fine. We couldn't wear any color other than black. Yet he would laugh when one slit another member's throat."

"And now we have him working for us," Athan said. "I don't know how I feel about it all."

"I've been meaning to ask you."

Athan folded his arms. "King Alderman doesn't like it either. He sees Davrian as a necessary risk. I trust his judgment."

"Do you?" Eamon said. "You trust he's made the best decision each time."

"I didn't say that. I trust he always has the best intentions."

"The best intentions... Good intentions never solved a problem, but they can pave a path of woes."

Athan raised his eyebrow.

"You're familiar with the proverb?" Eamon said.

"No, just wondering how you came up with it," Athan smiled.

Eamon turned from the wall, grateful to think of something other than the invaders. "It was another one of Davrian's odd requirements."

"What is that?"

"Manaist proverbs. We had to memorize several of them."

"Those thugs didn't mind the reading?"

"None of us knew where he came up with the stuff. I'd imagine some would have been concerned had they known they were learning manaist teachings, but most wouldn't have cared anyway. Besides, it wasn't until I started classes with Illiott and Fadrien that I made the connection. The idea of the Greater Good—Straight from one of those Manaist books."

"Does Fadrien know this?"

"I don't know."

"You should tell him, Lyle and Kit too. The more they know the better."

"I will, as soon as I leave my post... and find some sleep."

"That would be now," Athan said, "though sleep will have to wait. I'm here to relieve you. The King called a meeting. Apparently Bruan found something in Davrian's cell. From the sound of it, they'll need your help questioning Davrian."

"I don't know what I can do to help. Davrian told us nothing. I honestly know little about his schemes, or where to find the remaining members."

"Give yourself some credit. You have a better idea than most..." Athan stepped to the wall and scanned the western field. The catapults lined the northern plain. "Do you believe the Syndicate is still the main threat?"

"Perhaps," Eamon said. "Why do you ask?"

"It seems fighting crime serves us little while the city is under siege."

"So you are questioning King Alderman?"

"No, it's... I understand his reasoning. He doesn't want any enemies on this side of the wall. I just can't imagine the Syndicate being a significant threat any longer. Were there strong connections between the Syndicate and the Itihasians?"

"The meeting you raided, when you captured Harrot, Carrick and the others, that was when I saw an Itihasian for the first time."

"Kvrual?" Athan said, remembering the blow the Itihasian commander delivered to his head.

"Yeah, Davrian didn't care for him. There was no partnership there."

"Davrian cares for no one," Athan said.

"Well, this was different. I've seen Davrian face his enemies. It's always with a smack of confidence. You get the feeling Davrian already knows how he is going to defeat them. That wasn't the case with Kvrual. Kvrual was a piece of the puzzle that Davrian didn't know where to place."

"So you don't think they are working together?"

"No."

"Then isn't that more reason to let the Syndicate be for now? We can't afford sending men on a manhunt, we need every sword on the wall we can get."

"The worst thing we could do is forget about Davrian," Eamon said. "That's exactly what he wants."

"Then why would he join the Elite? It still puzzles me."

"You and everyone else. If I had to guess, I'd say we are over thinking it. He is saving his own skin—Simple as that. That's what he did with Erisa—Left her. He left me too. He knows the end is near; he wants to be in prison when the enemy comes. If the Itihasians see him as an enemy of their enemy, perhaps they will have mercy on him. It's the same reason why he offers to help eliminate the Syndicate. He is looking for a way out."

Athan shook his head. "I still don't understand why the Syndicate is a threat without Davrian."

"Because the few that remain are still organized. Perhaps not as strong as it once was, but they could prove to be a valuable asset to the Itihasians, which is why this hidden treasure concerns me."

"And you said you wouldn't be any help. Did I not say that you know more than you think?" Athan said.

"We'll see... Are you not coming to meet with the Elite?"

"I've already been briefed. It's my shift on the wall. Besides, I have some planning to do."

"Planning? Something I can help you with?"

"Oh, just the day. Banal things. Nothing to concern yourself with. Enjoy some time off the wall while you have it."

"If that's possible... I'll be back before too long."

"Get some rest."

"Will do," Eamon said. He fidgeted in place, his eyes lost in thought. He leaned against the merlon.

"You should go," Athan said. "You may not have another opportunity to rest before—"

"They attack?"

Athan nodded his head. "Are you alright?"

"It's just funny to me."

"What is?"

"The things people choose to talk about. Here we are together after years of separation, keeping watch over an enemy that will surely overcome us. It could be the last time we speak together. Who knows?...What do we talk about?—The Syndicate, making plans, getting some sleep."

"You're talking like we will never see each other again."

"It's a possibility."

"Well, that's true, but—Why so dismal all of a sudden? No one should live fearing the worst. You can't live like that."

"I have lived like that! Ever since Melchoir's murder."

Athan scowled. "Must you bring that up? Do I owe you another apology?"

"No, it's not that."

"Then what is it?

"I don't know." Eamon picked at his hands, his face went blank. "I guess I just wanted more. I used to believe there was nothing for me. There was only finishing off Davrian. But then, in one day, I find my brother and Davrian is captured. Life took a turn for the better, but... Well, in several hours this city may be leveled and the Itihasians will breach our walls. I guess it wasn't meant to last... I am glad to have found you before all is over—That's all, it just needed to be said."

"This isn't over," Athan said. "Now I'm not foolish enough to believe life owes me anything, but I have to believe we were reunited for something more than just... to die on the wall together. You are here because we need you."

Eamon nodded, but Athan could tell something still troubled him. For the past four days they'd been inseparable until last night's watch. Even so, Athan felt distant. Perhaps Eamon felt the same way.

Eamon made for the ladder leading down from the ramparts. "Be careful. I'll try to be back before noon."

"Eamon," Athan said. "I don't know where we would be without your help. I wish you could give yourself some credit."

Eamon scrunched and cocked his head. "You know, I had a chance to kill him—Davrian. I was going to curse him, instead I blessed him. I wonder... where we would be had I done things differently."

"We all have things we wish we could have done differently," Athan said. "Sparing a man's life is nothing to regret.

"I don't regret it. I did what I believed to be the right thing to do. I just hope it was indeed the right thing."

Athan nodded. "Either way, I'm proud of you."

Eamon smiled, unsure what to say. "Take care of yourself."

Athan watched Eamon descend out of sight. He faced the western plain, peering at the edge of Havenwood forest. A single tent stood on the southern side of the Numen River. Athan strained his eyes to count what he believed to be horses tied to a post. It was too far to tell.

"Planning," Athan scoffed at his own words. "He will kill me when he finds out." He looked back to the ladder Eamon climbed down. *Perhaps I should tell him now?* he thought.

Shouts came from below the ramparts. Athan thought nothing of it at first, but more voices joined in on the commotion. A heated argument soon erupted. Athan looked down to see Eamon and another guard surrounded by a small mob of townspeople.

"Open the gate!" The mob's leader shouted. He brandished a large butcher's cleaver. The crowd shouted in agreement. Several held hammers and small knives. One man carried a long pike.

"The gate is to be kept shut—King's orders," Eamon said.

"We are done with Alderman!" a voice cried out.

"He'll have us wait and do nothing!" another said.

"We're all going to be slaughtered. I'd rather take my chances fleeing than wait for them to crawl over our walls!"

"Open the gate!"

The townspeople closed in on Eamon and the guard. The guard tried to stand his ground, but the man with the pike pushed him aside. One of the townsmen started up the gatehouse ladder. Eamon grabbed and twisted the man's arm.

"Gammon?" The man with the pike made towards Eamon. "It's me, Garth."

The name brought Eamon back to his days running with the Syndicate. He recognized Garth and the man with the cleaver, Mort. The man he held was Edwin. The three of them worked together for years under Guile's leadership, back before Davrian started the guild.

"No need for games." Edwin said. "Word has it that the enemy attacks at noon today."

"And Davrian is captured," Mort added. "It's all over. Kvrual is waiting for us on the other side."

"No one is to leave without the king's permission," Eamon shouted.

"The king's permission?" Garth said. "You can't be serious? Everything we've worked for is now for the taking. We need to join Kvrual before he crushes us with the rest of Averlace."

Eamon released Edwin's arm and pushed him back to the crowd. "I've always been loyal to the king." Eamon drew his sword. "I won't open the gate for you."

"Fine, don't come. Just let us leave. No one here will know you let us go, save for him," Garth pointed to the guard. "I can take care of that for you if you'd like."

The crowd closed in. "Athan!" Eamon shouted. "The gate."

A large hand grabbed Eamon's neck. He felt Mort's cleaver press against his throat.

"You shouldn't have done that." Mort said. "Open the gate!" He shouted to the guard. "Hurry, or I'll carve another mouth into this one here. We'll see how well he screams for help then."

A stone from above crushed Mort's head. His body collapsed onto Eamon, forcing him to the ground. Eamon saw his brother through a murder hole. Athan straddled the ladder and rode it down. The guard beside Eamon drew his sword and batted Garth's pike away. Athan cut his way through the crowd before Eamon was on his feet. Edwin and the rest of the mob dispersed, vanishing into the artisan district. Moments later the street filled with guards from the north wall.

Athan held Garth at sword point. Two others lay dead beside Mort.

"What took you so long?" Eamon said, hands trembling.

"I raised the king's banner for reinforcements, didn't think I could take them all," Athan said. He pointed to the king's banner.

Eamon saw the green banner with Alderman's black stag flying at full mast. The gatehouse guard bound Garth's hands.

"Are you alright?" Athan said.

"I'm fine, thanks." Eamon ran his hand along his cheek, dabbing at the blood. "It looks worse than it is. I was hoping we had a little longer before the action started today."

Athan's mouth straightened into an uncertain smile. "I'll take this one to see ole Gavain in prison. Inform Alderman about the rest of the deserters."

"Davrian was right," Eamon said. "The Syndicate is trying to flee."

Athan looked to Mort's body. "I wonder what else he said is true."

CHAPTER TEN
HISTORY LONG FORGOTTEN

CHAPTER TEN

HISTORY LONG FORGOTTEN

EAMON PUSHED THE barracks door open. Shouting carried down the hall. It was Alderman, the meeting had started. Eamon stopped at the door. Across the hall Davrian's cell was left open. Eamon peeked in and found hand drawings of Averlace covered the floor. Each paper containing a small section of the city in fine detail. Carper's Vale, the artisan's district, Manadon Square, Bollarow, and even the keep's courtyards were drawn in near perfect proportion. The pages were placed side by side to form a greater map of all of Averlace. Notes were scribbled beside homes, businesses and random landmarks. Eamon recognized a portion of Davrian's work. They were Syndicate escape routes, a series of stops to make depending on the day of the week.

Each guild member was assigned a group. It was their responsibility to memorize their group's sequence of stops. In the case of an emergency, the group would follow their series of hiding places until Davrian deemed it safe and lowered the warning. It kept the Syndicate on the move and organized.

Eamon stared at the map. Davrian copied it all by memory in stunning detail. Not only had he recalled the layout of the city well enough to draft an accurate map, he also remembered the twisting web of routes for more than fifty groups.

Alderman's voice thundered. The door to the meeting room whined and moaned as Eamon pushed it open, drawing the attention of everyone inside.

Eamon first noticed Davrian seated alone in the corner of the room with his cuffed hands resting on his knees. His head hung low as he stared at the floor. Lyle, Kit and Fadrien were seated on the far end of the table. Illiott and Bruan sat across from them on the edge of their chairs. Their eyes darted to Eamon then back to King Alderman who stood by the table's side, out of breath and red faced.

Eamon pulled a chair beside Bruan, careful not to disturb the meeting. It didn't matter, Alderman's voice drowned out any noise. The king continued without missing a beat.

"You were right when you predicted the Itihasian demands," Alderman glared to Davrian. "They've drug their ragtag army from the other side of the world to claim a treasure we've never heard of—And they demand that we give up their missing prince. But what you failed to mention was your existing ties to the Ebon Crow."

"Existing ties?" Davrian said. "He wants me dead."

"You lie." Alderman folded his arms. "You've been more trouble to me than I even realized. Had I known what you would bring upon this kingdom... I would have stuck you myself when first given the chance."

"But you didn't, Your Majesty," Davrian said.

Alderman pulled his war hammer free from its sling. He pushed a chair aside and made for Davrian.

Davrian raised his hands, "And that might just be your saving grace."

"Is it?" Alderman stormed. "You—My saving grace? You dare lie to me while I have evidence against you?"

Davrian scrunched his eyes. "Evidence?"

Alderman waved for Lyle to stand.

Lyle brushed his brown hair aside. "I have here a letter Captain Bruan recovered from Davrian's cell. The letter was sealed in wax, unopened."

"It was on the floor just beside his scribbled maps. Must have been slipped underneath during the night," Bruan said. "I found it first thing this morning when I checked on him. It's a letter from the Ebon Crow."

Davrian reclined in his chair, his fingers drummed across his lips.

"When you're ready," Alderman motioned for Lyle to being.

Lyle unfolded the letter and snapped it open with a flick of his wrist. He took subtle glances at Davrian as he read.

> To the inglorious Master of the Guild,
> Call me a fool, but I thought you would have learned by now. It seems as though your first imprisonment wasn't a good enough lesson for you. Now here you are. Locked up again. I was ready to wash my hands of you, but then a thought crossed my mind. I dismissed it at first but the prospect proved irresistible. I believe I have a plan that even your incompetency can handle. Best of all your part can be played from your cell and when successful, the payoff will benefit the both of us. There are two things you must do.
> The Syndicate must be destroyed; it's now a liability. I am afraid the guild has too many trails that could lead the Elite to discovering my identity. I assume it

being your guild you will need some incentive to work towards its demise. Consider this; destroy the remaining Syndicate members, and I'll reward you with a quarter of the Manaist treasure. As for your second task, you must help the king locate the treasure. I would be a fool to think you had come this far without having the pieces of the puzzle. Solve it, and tell me of the treasure's whereabouts. Once the treasure is in my possession I will negotiate your freedom with King Alderman.

There is more to be done, trust me to provide you with adequate resources to see the job finished. Do not fail me, guild master. Greatness awaits us.

The Ebon Crow

Davrian scoffed at the final line.

Eamon glanced at the guild master then looked to Bruan.

"You are sure he didn't have a chance to read it?"

"I doubt it. I woke him up when I entered. I saw the letter first and picked it up before he was even off his cot. The seal was unbroken."

"We are fortunate to have found this," Eamon said.

"Indeed. What do you think of it?" Bruan said.

"I know nothing of the Ebon Crow. I was involved with the Syndicate for years until I first heard of him."

"But he wanted to get rid of Davrian?"

"According to Davrian, yes... A while back, Guile claimed he was working for the Ebon Crow directly, and that he was to replace Davrian as the guild master. There was another after Davrian's job. While at the meeting in Carrick's house, Kvrual also announced he was going to start leading the Syndicate.

Davrian assumed Kvrual was aided by the Ebon Crow. So yes, in light of all I know, it's safe to assume the Ebon Crow wanted to get rid of Davrian."

"But now he wants to work with Davrian. Why the change of plans?" Bruan said.

"I haven't the faintest idea," Eamon shrugged. The room fell silent. The men exchanged looks, waiting for the other to speak.

Davrian cleared his throat, "Is no one interested in what I have to say?"

"No." Lyle said.

Davrian smiled, "That's a shame. Why even bother bringing me here."

"You have no idea what's going on. You weren't expecting a letter from the Ebon Crow. You are just as puzzled as the rest of us," Kit said.

"No, you are wrong," Davrian said. "If anything it's all the more clear to me." Davrian shot a devious glance to King Alderman. "Even if I had found the letter before Bruan, I would still have shared it with you all."

"Oh, please," Illiott said. "You're just trying to save face. You had an opportunity to work against the king without us knowing it. You would have taken it had Bruan not found that letter."

"To save face?" Davrian laughed. "Because I am the most popular man in the room? I've offended everyone here. Saving face is not my priority."

"What is then?" Lyle said.

"Taking down the Syndicate. Did we not agree that I will help you do just that? The Ebon Crow has now asked me to do the same, and it is understandable why. The longer the

Syndicate operates, the greater chance of his identity being discovered. Also, the fewer members there are, the more of the Manaist treasure he gets to keep. This letter changes nothing. If anything, we may have an ally where we once had an enemy. I don't know what he meant when he said 'adequate resources,' but it can only help us round up the Syndicate. We are fortunate that the Ebon Crow misunderstands me. He wrongfully assumes I want to keep the Syndicate. I admit that I wish things could remain as they were, but now that the Itihasians have swayed most of the remaining members against me, I would rather the guild go down than for it to be led by another."

"Especially Kvrual?" Eamon said.

Davrian cringed at the Itihasian commander's name. "Him, or Guile."

"You are up to something, Davrian, ever since you asked to join the Elite. Do you really think we believe you are this defeated? That you are petty enough to destroy the guild simply because you no longer control it?" Lyle said.

"We are all defeated, Lyle!" Davrian said. "Your city is surrounded by an invading army with orders to attack at noon. My guild is divided, those loyal to me are hiding, imprisoned or dead. The rest are doing what they can inside this city's walls to help your enemy raze your defenses. Destroying what's left of the guild is helping me, I admit it. The promise of a share in the treasure is alluring to me as well. But I believe the king is the greatest benefactor here. Now the Ebon Crow believes he has me in a vulnerable position. He wanted me gone, which is why he enlisted Guile and Kvrual to oust me. But he too is desperate, and is offering me a way out. Fortunately for you, that means I must assist the king. We are fortunate the Ebon Crow and King Alderman wish the same thing."

Alderman eyed Davrian, "The end of the Syndicate..."

Davrian leaned back into his chair. "You are wise to realize your greatest threat is the Syndicate. For that I am flattered."

"So you will continue on, destroying your own guild in hopes that the Ebon Crow will follow through on his promise to negotiate your release?" Alderman said.

"If it means the end of the Syndicate before someone else takes control of it, yes," Davrian said.

"What makes you believe I will ever release you?"

"All I know is that the Ebon Crow can be awfully persuasive," Davrian said.

"What about the manaist treasure?" Bruan said. "What do we know of it?"

Alderman looked to Fadrien and Illiott. "Have you two learned anything else about the manaist treasure?"

Fadrien shook his head. "Not enough to claim it exists, but the manaist riders were familiar with the story. They believe the treasure is here, hidden under the city."

"If it helps, your Majesty, I believe it is under the city as well," Davrian said.

"What do you know of the treasure?" Fadrien said.

"Only myths and rumors," Davrian said.

"If this is all true, then how is it that the rest of the world is familiar with the treasure, yet no one within this city knows more than rumors of its existence?" Bruan said.

"When Manaism was outlawed, many who practiced it fled the kingdom. They brought with them stories of the once glorious and powerful city of Averlace and its magical treasures to all corners of the world. While the world told tales of magical treasure, talk of it in Averlace was squelched. Magic was forbidden and to be forgotten," Fadrien said.

"What if it isn't real?" Lyle said. "What if there is no treasure and the Itihasians are here to conquer something we can not give? Is it all a bunch of fairy tales blown to legendary proportions?"

"Regardless, we must still search for it," Illiott said. "If we find it then it could be used against our enemies."

"Use it against the enemy?" Alderman's voice rattled.

"Why not?" Bruan said. "If it's as powerful as the riders believe, the Itihasians would be no match for us."

"But is it safe?" Alderman said.

Bruan laughed. "I'd hope not. That's what makes a weapon lethal is it not?"

Alderman folded his arms. "You find my question humorous?"

"No, Sire," Bruan lowered his head.

"If there is a treasure powerful enough to destroy the enemy, my first question as king is not *how* to use the manaist power, but *should* we? What danger would we subject ourselves to if we armed ourselves with magical weapons we don't know how to use? I'll make this very clear," Alderman rose from his chair. "This manaist treasure changes nothing. Nothing! We will continue to defend Averlace as planned. I will not rest our hopes on unfound treasure."

"What if it were to be found?" Davrian said.

"More reason to defend the city!" Alderman barked. "Have you all forgotten? I believed the use of magic would help us destroy the Syndicate. It nearly destroyed us instead. We didn't have the wisdom to decipher our prophecies. Magic destroyed your wife in prison did it not?"

"My past wife," Lyle mumbled.

"Not well trained. It backfired against her. A lesson for all of us. That is why I opened the school. We will first learn to use magic as it was intended. If we were to find a powerful horde of magical treasure, we won't use it until we have people adequately trained."

"Yes, Your Majesty," Fadrien said.

"Furthermore, there is no hope in finding the treasure before midday. We must do what we can now to hinder the Syndicate from helping the Itihasians. I agree that the mysteries of the Manaist treasure must be solved, but it will have to wait for now. "

"That may not be necessary," Davrian said.

"Is that so?" Alderman said. "Should I have you prioritize for me now too?"

"There is a series of tunnels under this city," Davrian said coolly. "You all know this, but you have forgotten."

"What does that have to do with anything?" Alderman said.

Davrian sat back in his chair, "These tunnels make up an integral portion of Averlace's history—History long forgotten. Their walls are lined with towering columns, intricate reliefs and colorful frescoes depicting the city's past. Some of the ceilings are twenty feet with spans thirty feet across. Many of these tunnels have since been incorporated into a sewer system, some were flooded in the process."

"What are you talking about?" Illiott said.

"An opportunity to work towards both objectives," Davrian grinned. "The Syndicate has not forgotten the tunnels. A select few of us used them daily, to hide or travel undercover from one end of the city to the next. There is even an exit that led outside of the city. Perhaps the secrets of the treasure can be found there. More importantly though, it would be a perfect way for the Syndicate to sneak in the enemy."

"You aren't talking about the tunnels that once connected the granary and the hidden Syndicate hideout underground?" Fadrien said.

"I am. They lead straight to them."

"The school rests on top of that tunnel. The entrance is boarded up," Illiott said.

Davrian stifled a laugh. "The school, yes but there are many more. There's the palace library, the neighboring courtyards, the smithy shops along the river, the stables, and nearly every home in Carper's Vale to Bollarow. They are all connected and many more," Davrian said. "But only one leads past the walls, I can lead you to it. It must be sealed before the Syndicate shows the passage to the enemy."

"Impossible," Illiott said. "Surely we would know if such a place exists."

"You lie," Eamon said. "If there are tunnels like that, then why didn't you use them when you led Thad and I out after the raid on Carrick's house?"

"Because Guile was after us too. No doubt he was waiting there for us."

"Then how come I never learned of the tunnels?" Eamon said.

"Just like the Run, it was a need-to-know basis. Only guild leaders and a few sponsors knew of the deep tunnels," Davrian said.

"If there are Syndicate trying to help the Itihasians, and they are inside our walls; then how are they communicating?" Fadrien said.

"They aren't," Davrian said. "But it's not the Syndicate inside the walls you should worry about."

"Guile," Eamon said. "We left him in the Itihasian camp."

"But wasn't he a prisoner?" Illiott said. "And I was under the impression Guile and Kvrual weren't getting along."

"Well, I wasn't getting along with the Elite, but here I am, working for the crown," Davrian said. "Guile's in a similar position. Working for Kvrual may be the only option he has right now."

"He is to find Kvrual a way into the city in exchange for control of the guild?" Lyle said.

Davrian chortled, "I wouldn't be surprised if that was their terms."

"How big of a tunnel are we talking about?" King Alderman said. "I can't imagine a tunnel twenty feet tall going unnoticed."

"The one leading to the plain is just large enough for a single man to crawl through. But it leads to a vast chamber, which would be a perfect staging area for an army to mount a surprise attack on the city."

"Then it should be small enough for us to easily block," Bruan said.

"But only if we get there before they do," Davrian said.

"And you know how to find it?" King Alderman said.

"I do," Davrian smiled.

"It's a trap," Illiott said.

"Oh I would come armed. I wouldn't be surprised if we find some resistance," Davrian said.

Bruan looked to Fadrien. "This seems to align with what Freja told us last night."

Fadrien nodded. "She said the treasure was hidden under the city. The correlations between the two claims is... exhilarating. The way he describes the tunnels' size and design with frescoes of Averlacian history—I can hardly imagine what wonders we may find."

"Or dangers," Davrian added.

Alderman stood from his chair and pointed to Bruan. "Assemble a small party to escort Davrian to this tunnel. Find it, seal it and search for other tunnels that the enemy could use against us. For now I'll manage the walls myself."

"There is only one tunnel leading outside. You'll only waste your time if you search for more," Davrian said.

Alderman ignored the guild master.

"As you wish your Majesty," Bruan said. "We will search for others."

"Then get started immediately. I want that tunnel sealed by noon. Search for any signs of the Syndicate. Is there anything else?" Alderman looked to his men. Fadrien shook his head, and Lyle gathered the letter from the table.

"Your Majesty, a small group of rabble rousers gathered at Manadon Gate. They tried to force their way out, but they were stopped," Eamon said.

"Rabble rousers?" Alderman said.

"They demanded to be released, claiming they would rather take their chances negotiating with the Itihasians than die behind the walls."

"Were they arrested?"

"We have one of them sir. Another three were killed. Six or seven escaped us."

"Where they with the Syndicate?" Davrian said.

"They were. I recognized several of them."

"Are you sure?" Illiott said.

"Yes, I am sure." Eamon pointed to the cut on his cheek. "It's hard to forget the face of a man who threatened me with a cleaver."

"A butcher's cleaver?" Lyle said.

"Yes, why? Is that important?" Eamon said.

"Davrian sent Kit and I on a hunt for any building with a specific sign or symbol. By finding the certain criteria, in this case lilacs in a window sill, we could locate a hideout that is currently in use."

"The Bollarow butcher shop happened to have a lilac bouquet in its window. It was also abandoned," Kit said.

"Any idea how long?" Davrian asked.

"Based on the condition of the hanging meat, I'd say two days." Lyle looked to Kit to confer.

"I would bolster each gate." Davrian said. "Keeping the Syndicate in this city until you can capture them is of the upmost importance. As far as our trip to the tunnel. It begins with the Bollarow butcher shop."

"See to it, Captain Bruan," Alderman said. "I'll let you decide what arrangements are necessary. Any future dealings with deserters must be handled discretely, yet quickly. Others may mistake these traitors as cowardly townspeople. It could spread fear. We can't afford for people to lose faith."

"Any leads on the Prince of Itihasia?" Lyle said.

Fadrien cleared his throat. "When Bruan, Athan and I visited the manaist riders last night, I asked the girl if she had ever heard of the Prince of Itihasia. She said she knew nothing about him."

"I think she is lying," Bruan said.

"You think it's her brother?" Lyle said.

"I think you and Kit need to speak with her."

"It will have to wait," Alderman said. "Knowing who the Prince of Itihasia is changes nothing. Even if we had him, we would never give him up to the enemy along with this treasure they seek. Find the tunnel."

The king rose to dismiss the meeting. The rest of the Elite raised their hands. Bruan reached in his pocket with his free hand and clasped his ring. Alderman's hand felt bare without his own signet ring. He glanced at Davrian who stared on with a poised grin.

"Brace yourselves men," Alderman said. "Remain steadfast with courage and confidence in yourself and faith in others. As long as I'm on the throne I will see to it that Averlace is served by the bravest and brightest. So long as I have the Elite, Averlace will have hope. Long live the Elite," Alderman said.

"Long live the King," the men said in unison. Davrian loudest of all.

Chapter Eleven
THE ASTRANNAXIAN TUNNELS

CHAPTER ELEVEN

THE ASTRANNAXIAN TUNNELS

THE BUTCHER SHOP door broke off its hinges with ease. Bruan stepped over the splintered wood. Athan and Illiott followed close behind, their weapons drawn. The first floor circled around a flight of stairs that led to an upper level. They weaved around the rotting meat hung from the ceiling, careful not to make a sound. Athan and Illiott checked the corners as Bruan walked the center.

"I'll say it this one last time," Bruan shouted into the darkness. "Come out now with your hands up. Any sudden moves and I'll cut you down."

No one answered.

A rattling sound clanked against the floor. Bruan swung his blade before him. Illiott nearly lost his drawn arrow. It was Davrian, rushing in even though Eamon pulled back on his chains. Lyle, Kit and Fadrien waited outside.

"Like I said, there's no one here," Davrian said. "We are wasting time."

"Forgive our lack of trust," Athan said. He sheathed his sword and pointed to a long counter that ran alongside the inner wall. Below it were a set of hinges nailed to the floor boards.

"A root cellar," Athan said.

"Perfect," Davrian dropped to his knees and pried his fingers under the seam. Despite the cuffs around his wrists, he lifted the door open. Another set of stairs winded down to a muddy hole. The rotting smell grew worse as they descended the moldy steps. It was a dead end. A pile of cabinets stacked on top of each other cluttered the room's center. Across the room an old hutch leaned into a wall. Dried mud caked its sides. Its feet had been sawed off, leaving it flush with the earth.

"There," Davrian pointed to the hutch. "Behind it."

Bruan, Athan, Eamon and Illiott pushed on one side, but the hutch wouldn't budge.

"It's sunk into the mud," Illiott said.

"It's too heavy," Bruan said.

"Empty it out," Kit said. He pulled the doors open but recoiled and jumped away with a loud cry.

"What's wrong?" Lyle grabbed Kit and looked him over. "Are you hurt?"

"A trap? Fadrien said.

Athan peeked inside. He squinted his eyes and looked away. "No," he said.

Fadrien brought his lamp close, illuminating the grizzly scene and the source of the foul stench. Two bodies had been crammed inside. A mother and her child.

The men stood solemn, forgetting why they were even in the butcher's cellar.

"It's the butcher's wife and daughter," Fadrien said, horrified.

"Mort," Davrian said. "The butcher's name was Mort."

"Butcher indeed," Kit said. "He should be drawn and quartered."

"He's dead," Athan said. "He was one of the one's trying to flee the city earlier this morning."

"Funny," Kit spat. "I don't feel any better."

"What would possess a man to do such a thing?" Fadrien said.

"Why don't you ask him?" Lyle pushed Davrian to the ground. "It's his guild, his responsibility. I say he cleans it up."

"We don't have time to provide the dignity they deserve," Bruan said. "I'll have one of my men send word. We must press on."

Lyle watched Bruan and several guards remove the woman and child. He fumed in anger as he listened to Davrian direct Athan and Eamon to destroy the hutch. With a few heavy blows, it collapsed and crumbled under the wall's weight, causing a small avalanche of dirt and mud. After the dust settled, the men could see a small tunnel and hear the faintest sound of rushing water.

"This should connect us with a sewer that drains into the main gallery. From there it will be a short walk to the tunnel that leads outside. It's not far." Davrian said. "Just follow the water."

Bruan handed every third man a lit torch. He then joined Davrian and the two led the way into the cramped tunnel. Athan, Eamon, Fadrien and a small contingent of guards followed. Lyle waited and watched Bruan's men wrap the bodies in long white sheets.

Lyle had to look away. "I don't know if I can continue." he said to Kit.

"Is it Davrian?"

Lyle nodded. "Just like Erisa...I saw her when I looked on that poor mother and her child. All of this destruction for Davrian's 'Greater Good.'"

Kit new something needed to be said, but what? He hoped Lyle had moved on, but Erisa's death changed Lyle. A part of him died with her that night.

"Did you noticed how smug he looked when he saw them?"

"I didn't," Kit said.

"It was the same look when he heard that Erisa died..."

"I'm sorry Lyle."

"Hear me, brother. Before this is over, Davrian will pay for all he's done."

*   *   *

Davrian sloshed his way through knee deep mud. The walls grew narrow farther into the tunnel. The tunnel turned to the right and its ceiling dropped, forcing the party to crawl on their hands. Fadrien dropped his torch, losing it forever in the sludge.

"Not what I imagined when I first heard of carved reliefs and colorful frescoes depicting our kingdom's history," Fadrien said.

Davrian chuckled. "I'm sorry to disappoint you councilman. This is my first time trekking through the Bollarow tunnels. I suppose I shouldn't be surprised to find them in this condition. We have only a short distance left until things get more comfortable."

Without Fadrien's torch between them, Athan and Eamon kept stumbling over the councilman. Fadrien felt his way around, relying on Bruan's torch light three men down. The tunnel would go black in tight corners. Fadrien's hands and face were covered in spider webs and the smell of rat assaulted his nose. He bumped his head against the ceiling.

Fadrien felt around for Eamon, but he could only feel the muddy wall and more spider webs. He was about to panic but then concentrated on the sound of rushing water ahead.

"This way." Davrian called out.

Athan led Fadrien to the smallest crack yet. Fadrien reached ahead for Eamon's cloak. A few feet farther Fadrien could see the light from Bruan's torch. The rushing water he heard was now a roar. The ceiling lifted off Fadrien's head and the walls widened out. After a few moments, Fadrien's eyes adjusted to the torchlight.

"This here, gentlemen, is the Numen river," Davrian said. "It will lead us the rest of the way. Oh, and as promised—Your frescoes, councilman." With his cuffed hands Davrian pointed back to the tunnel.

"Unbelievable," Fadrien said. He took a torch from one of the guards and held it to the wall.

Vibrant color flickered in the torchlight. The stone glittered with images just as Davrian described. Past kings ruling over Averlace, manaists casting spells before a panel of arbiters, and even the palace library being built were a few events Fadrien recognized. There were countless more unfamiliar to the learned councilman. The wall continued on past the torchlight's glow. Even the floor was impressive. Marble and granite stone lined the river with pedestals displaying sculpted busts of heroic figures.

"Look," Illiott called to Fadrien. He pointed to the muddy tunnel. "The floor is spotless. No dirt, or anything. We didn't even leave a trail."

Fadrien looked at the soles of his filthy shoes. "Impossible."

"You'll find a lot of peculiarities in these halls," Davrian said. "Most harmless, some terrifying."

"Terrifying?" Athan said.

"Quite terrifying," Davrian said. "I had an officer in the guild I wanted to reward. He was one of my most trusted crime lords. I found a home down here that I knew he would appreciate. He stayed in it for one night. We never saw him again... but we heard him. When he went missing we searched for him, starting at his new home. He screamed for us to come and help him, that he was trapped. We followed his voice to his bedroom, but we never saw him. Still he called for us to help. He claimed he could see us, but we couldn't see him."

"What did you do?" Eamon said.

"I knew there was magic still lingering under the city. Perhaps an old spell cast years ago to protect the home. We concluded that maybe he was trapped inside the walls. We tried busting him out, but with each strike against the wall he screamed in pain. We were hurting him. It was like he had become part of the home. There was nothing we could do. We left him. After some time he stopped calling out for help."

Kit shuddered.

"Magic protecting the home?" Fadrien said. "Only black magic could produce something so horrific... Consumed by the wall?" Fadrien stepped back from the frescoes, they had lost their charm, but their mysteries further intrigued him.

"There are spells everywhere here. Some perhaps thousands of years old. Others only a hundred or so. Remember that Averlace wanted to protect itself from its own magic. I believe that home had a spell on it to protect it from unwanted visitors. These halls may have similar spells. Don't let your guard down."

Davrian led them alongside the river. The marbled road showed no signs of wear. It connected to smaller streets that were divided into blocks, just like the city above. Shops and homes were carved out of the cavern's walls. Bridges crossed the river every few hundred feet. Statues guarded the abutments, presumably heroes and notable figures.

"This is a whole city," Bruan said.

"This is Averlace," Davrian said. "The city you know above was nothing but farmland. The keep was built to protect the main entrance into the city, but today it is used as the library."

"How do you know this?" Fadrien said.

"I've spent a lot of time down here hiding, councilman. To keep my mind occupied, I'd admire the walls and do my best at interpreting their meaning."

"Have you found any manaist relics down here?" Illiott said.

"Plenty," Davrian said. "Some I've hated to part with. But like I've said, you must be careful. I wouldn't grab the first thing that strikes your fancy."

"Your sword," Lyle called out. "The one with stones set in its hilt; you found it down here didn't you?"

"I did. You know, I never thanked you for giving it back to me," Davrian said.

Lyle thought back to the fateful moment on the balcony. The king was saved, the Syndicate was falling apart. Davrian had lost everything.

Stay where you are Lyle, or I will kill her.

Lyle would never forget the look in Erisa's eyes when Davrian held his knife to her throat. Lyle kicked Davrian's sword away for her freedom, but she followed her guild master over the balcony's ledge.

"Where is it now?" Lyle said. He refused to dwell on Erisa.

"The Itihasians have it. Took it from me when I was captured. No doubt it has fueled their lust for the manaist treasure."

"It came from the treasure?" Illiott said.

"No. To be honest I don't know where it came from. It was a gift to me, from one of my men. He found it in one of the homes here. Do you think I would be leading you down here if I already knew the treasure's whereabouts?"

"You would have been long gone with your riches instead of sorting out this mess with your guild," Illiott said.

Davrian tapped the side of his nose, "I imagine things being a bit different if that were the case."

The marble road ended with a final bridge crossing the river. They had come to the end of the cavern. Davrian led the party over the bridge then stopped. The Numen rushed underneath into a frothy whirlpool where the water emptied deeper into the earth.

"Interesting, no?" Davrian said.

The men could barely hear him over the river's roar. They saw Davrian pointing to the end of the cavern. Rising from the pool stood a magnificent relief carved in the wall. It was a stag with its head lowered to the water as if taking a drink. Massive antlers covered the wall's entire span. Where the other reliefs were more shallow in depth, the stag jutted out several feet, standing nearly free from the wall.

"How incredible," Fadrien gasped.

"Much like the stag on Alderman's banners," Lyle said.

Kit leaned on the bridge's railing for a better view. "It's identical. Imagine it as a silhouette, it shares the same antlers."

"It'd be interesting to learn why he chose the image for his banner," Lyle said.

"Family heraldry?"

"Then judging by this relief, King Alderman would come from a prominent family. This stag is the central feature of the city. I wonder—"

Kit paused. He raised his hands from the bridge's stone railing then patted it again. "Did anyone else feel that?"

"Feel what?" Illiott said.

"Shaking," Kit said.

Lyle felt the railing. His eyes curiously scanned above. He was just about to pull away when he felt it tremble. "The earth is shaking."

"I feel it too," Athan said.

Dust and small rocks fell from the ceiling. The cavern rumbled once then stopped.

"Should we clear the bridge?" Fadrien said.

"Not a bad idea," Lyle said.

"An earthquake?" Illiott said.

Kit kept his hand on the bridge railing, "I don't know."

The cavern rumbled again. More dust and rock fell from the ceiling. The rumbling grew louder and fiercer as it continued. Bruan yelled for everyone to clear the bridge. By the time they made it across the rumbling stopped."

"What's going on?" one of Bruan's soldiers said.

"Magic?" cried another.

"Where have you taken us?" Bruan shook Davrian.

"I am not familiar with anything like this," Davrian said.

"We must leave," another soldier said. "Before it comes down on us."

The rumbling started again, louder than before.

"Your torch," Davrian held his hand out to Bruan. "We need to hurry. The tunnel leading outside is just ahead."

Bruan first refused but reluctantly obliged when a large boulder fell from the ceiling into the river. Davrian grabbed the torch and led the men to the other side of the cavern. He stopped just outside a small building, the first of an entire district of merchant homes and shops. They scaled alongside the building with their backs pressed against its outer wall. The rising dust clouded the air. Davrian's torch bobbed up and down like a hazy globe as he ran.

"Stay with me," Bruan shouted over the rumbling.

The cavern quaked and moaned. Davrian darted off the main marble road onto an alleyway between more deserted shops and homes. Bruan struggled to keep up with the guild master who ran and navigated the streets with an accustomed familiarity. He kept glancing back to make sure no one was left behind.

Lyle and Kit brought up the rear of the line. The group moved quickly between the buildings with only the hazy torchlight bouncing off the alleyway corners to follow. They almost caught up with Eamon and Athan but a building collapsed, blocking their way.

"Wait up," Lyle shouted. It was no use. The deafening sound of falling rock drowned out his voice. He continued to shout.

"That way," Kit pointed to a glow of light reflecting from another alley.

The brothers ran to the light only to find an abandoned torch. It was Davrian's.

"He's gone," Kit said.

"No he's not," Lyle said. "He can't have made it too far with his shackles."

"He managed to outrun us with those shackles," Kit said.

Lyle took the torch. They were standing at an intersection of four roads.

"There's no telling where he is," Kit said. "And where are the others?"

"Stop and think. He can't be far. Panicking won't help us."

"I'm not one to panic—And I am thinking. He..." Kit looked up. "It stopped?"

"The rumbling?" Lyle said.

"Yeah. It stopped as fast as it began."

The cavern was quiet again save the river's roar, now muffled by the surrounding buildings.

"Davrian!" a voice shouted. It was Bruan.

"Over here," Lyle called out.

Bruan followed Lyle's voice and the party reunited at the four road intersection.

"We lost Davrian," Bruan said. "He left us."

"He can't be far we can find him," Lyle said.

"We can't stay here," Illiott said. "The whole cave is about to come down on us."

"Where do you suppose we go?" Athan said. "What's to keep us from walking into some magic spell down here again? If we aren't careful we may bring down the cave on our own."

The cave rumbled again like thunder, distant yet powerful. The source of the sound moved closer until it seemed directly overhead, growing from a low rumble to a series of pounding blows.

"That's no magic," Lyle said.

"What is it then? An earthquake?" Illiott said.

"It's the siege," Lyle said, his voice heavy. "It has started."

"Catapults?" Kit said.

"We will have to find the tunnel without him," Bruan said. "It must be sealed before the enemy can sneak in."

"It was all a lie," Athan said. "There's no tunnel."

"But he was honest about the city underneath," Fadrien said.

"The most convincing lies have a grain of truth," Eamon said. "He wanted to lose us down here. It's always been his plan.

"We have to get out and help," Illiott said. "I can't imagine what it's like up there.

"I might be able to lead us back the way we came," Kit said. "I made a note of everything we passed just for this reason."

Lyle ruffled Kit's hair. "At least someone's thinking."

"That won't be necessary," Davrian's voice called out from the center of the intersection.

The men waved their torches around, looking for the voice. Davrian emerged from the road, pushing an iron grate aside.

"Where have you been?" Bruan seized Davrian by the shoulders. "What's the meaning of this?"

"This is the tunnel. It's part of an aqueduct system for when the Numen River overflows. It leads outside of the cave and waters the farmlands—Well, it used too, until most of the water was directed for the sewers we use now."

"What were you doing down there?" Bruan said.

"We found your torch a few houses down," Lyle said.

"Under every home's doorstep you will find a small drain. They all lead to the aqueduct system I just described. I crawled in there to see if water was running through. It's still dry. As for that particular home, it belongs to Guile. He claimed it for himself years ago. I wanted to see if he had been here recently. Turns out he has."

"What, how do you know?"

"A note. I found it on his table in plain sight."

"The Ebon Crow?" Lyle said.

Davrian nodded. He handed Lyle the note. "Best to read it now."

"There's no time. The siege has begun. We must get above ground," Bruan said.

"I agree, but you wouldn't believe me if I just told you. Read it." Davrian said.

Lyle snatched the paper from Davrian and leaned towards Kit's torch. His eyes scrolled down the letter then darted back to the others.

"They're trying to destroy Davrian's Tomb," Lyle said.

"Who is?"

"Kvrual," Lyle said.

"Why?" Illiott said. "How?"

"The siege, right now!" Lyle said over another pounding boom.

"In hopes to release prisoners, cause panic and chaos," Bruan said.

"To be more specific, I believe he hopes to get more Syndicate out on the streets," Davrian said. "This letter was left for anyone lucky enough to make it here."

"They would know to come here to look for directions?" Lyle said.

"Yes," Davrian said.

"What does it tell them to do?" Kit said.

"Remain here until Guile returns. He'll then lead everyone in an escape from the city," Lyle said.

"How?"

"It doesn't say."

"I am assuming Guile plans to lead the survivors through the tunnels." Davrian said. "You and your brother did well in identifying the butcher shop as a hideout. Apparently we came early. We must be careful on our way out. They may be gathering as we speak."

"This seems all too convenient," Bruan said. "Why do I have a sinking suspension the Syndicate is waiting to strike at the butcher's shop? From there they could easily bring you back to Kvrual."

"Are you suggesting I set this up?" Davrian said. "You do remember I want to avoid Kvrual?"

"I'm saying we put too much faith in the Ebon Crow's letters," Bruan said.

"I see... If it assures you any, I believe I am too valuable of an asset for the Ebon Crow to throw away to the Itihasians. He needs me to lead you to the Syndicate. He won't risk a chance for the Itihasians to capture me."

"I'm starting to think I might just give them the chance," Lyle said.

"Then I better make it worth your while to keep me," Davrian said.

"How about you start by not disappearing again," Bruan said.

Another boom quaked overhead.

"I believe I can manage that," Davrian said.

"And how about a suggestion on plugging the aqueduct?"

"I believe I can deliver on that as well," Davrian smiled. "Follow me. Torch please?"

Bruan said nothing. He pushed Davrian ahead of the group. The guild master led them through a winding series of turns. They made their way back on the main marble road that ran on both the river's sides. Davrian shared what he knew about the underground city of Averlace as they trekked through, pointing to various buildings and features. He was interrupted every so often from the siege's pounding attacks. Bruan urged him to quicken the pace. Davrian took them to the opposite end of the cavern in a near sprint. The road's final bend revealed their destination, the Numen Falls.

Fadrien huffed and wheezed. He bent over, out of breath. "What now?"

Davrian gazed at the river. His eyes went to a blank stare. He held his hands out to its mist. "They say the will of the Numen River determines the fate of those who drink its water."

"What now?' Fadrien repeated.

"I heard you councilman." Davrian pursed his lips. "Obviously, this is where the Numen enters the city. It is here I believe we can control the river."

"How?"

Davrian pointed to a podium with a relief carved around its stand. Three circular engravings were cut into its surface. Each shared the same inverted design inside. Fadrien studied the engravings for a moment. He cocked his head then snapped his fingers. "Oh the medallions! It's the same design."

"I hope you brought yours," Davrian said.

"Of course." Fadrien pulled his medallion free from his neck. He was about to place it in the far left engraving, but Davrian grabbed his arm.

"I don't know what will happen. We should be careful."

"What did you think would happen? Why bring us here?" Illiott said.

"It will redirect the water, that I am sure. I just don't know how, or where."

"Do it," Bruan said. "We've wasted enough time."

Fadrien placed a medallion in the inlet. The red stone in the center setting glowed. Illiott pushed his way through the men for a better view, his eyes fixed on the glow. They waited, but nothing happened.

"Try another," Illiott said.

"No, leave it be," Davrian said. He held a finger to his lips and shushed the men. A faint clanking sound came from the ceiling. As the clanking grew the men could hear water rushing from underneath the marble road.

Davrian ran to a nearby home and lifted the doorstep's grate. A satisfied smile parted his mouth. "Water is running through. We're directing water through the aqueduct. You may take your medallion back, councilman."

Fadrien retrieved his medallion. Water still rushed through. Davrian had the others check the homes and the road's main drains. Fadrien lifted the grate of a nearby home, a strong current flowed through. He dipped his hands into the cool water.

"Water here," Bruan's voice carried from a few doors down.

"Same," Athan said.

Fadrien lowered his grate. Did every home have running water? What else could his medallion control?

"That should do it," Davrian said. "No one can crawl through with all of the combined water."

"What do the others do?" Illiott pointed to the stone podium.

"I am not sure, but we have what we want now. Best to leave it be. If we survive this war, you can fiddle with everything down here to your heart's desire."

"Are we done here?" Athan said.

"We are," Davrian said.

"Seemed too easy," Illiott said.

"Take easy when you can," Davrian said. "That's hardly ever the case down here."

"The king instructed us to search for other tunnels leading outside," Bruan said.

Davrian looked to the aqueduct. "I can assure you, there is only one."

"I assure you, guild master, your word isn't enough."

"When will it be captain? I've led you this far. Everything has been as I promised."

"It'll take more than one expedition to earn my trust."

"What would I gain at this point from keeping a secret tunnel? Think about what you lose for wasting time down here searching for a tunnel you will never find. You'll spend weeks here until you are satisfied with your search. Even then you wouldn't have explored every nook and cranny."

"What do you have to gain? Perhaps another way out?"

"Would I not have taken that tunnel by now? You would still be finding your way out of here had I not come back to you. The only way out of this city now is through the gates. If we get back soon, we can hunt down what's left of my guild now that I know there's nowhere to hide."

"As much as I hate to admit it, I believe he is telling the truth," Lyle whispered to Bruan.

"You know he is up to something."

"I do, but escape isn't part of his plan. Nor is helping the enemy into the city. We need to head back."

"What if he is right about Guile?" Kit said. "We need to find him before he can aid the enemy."

All eyes were on Bruan. He didn't mind the pressure, it helped him make decisions. It was making the same mistake twice that Bruan feared most of all. Davrian will not fool him again.

"Let's move on," his eyes narrowed on Davrian. "Keep your eyes sharp. No telling what we may run into."

The cavern rumbled.

"You're going to have to trust me at some point, Captain," Davrian said. "Hopefully before it's too late."

CHAPTER TWELVE
SMOKE AND FLAME

CHAPTER TWELVE

SMOKE AND FLAME

ILLIOTT VOLUNTEERED to scout ahead. Athan and Eamon waited at the end of the tunnel, ready to dash into the butcher's cellar. Eamon held his breath and listened for footsteps and voices. He watched Illiott creep onto the stairs and gooseneck to the floor above.

"I don't hear anyone," Eamon said.

"We should move," Bruan said. "We are wasting time. I need to be on the wall."

Illiott leapt out of sight, silent as a cat. He was gone for a brief moment, then jumped back to the steps, landing with a rough thud.

"No, one's here."

Bruan cursed and stomped into the cellar, casting all caution aside. Another heavy thud crashed in the distance. Smoke filled the first floor, pouring through the windows. Fadrien was the first to step outside. Soldiers ordered civilians to seek shelter in the lowest level of their homes. Bruan led the others out of the butcher shop.

"Back inside," a soldier yelled to the councilman.

Fadrien was hardly recognizable. His white robe was ruined, soiled from the shoulders down. Gray patches of dried clay dotted his face and mud dripped from his beard. Only his back was spared from crawling the tunnels.

"He's with me," Bruan said. The soldier watched as Athan, Eamon and the others exited the building, each filthier than the one before.

"What's the situation?" Bruan said.

"I've heard the enemy's ranks are formed. It's only a matter of time until they march against our walls. The catapults have started to fire."

From the street Braun saw columns of black smoke rising above the rooftops.

"They've attacked from the North?"

"Yes sir," the soldier said. "Manadon Square and the Artisan District were hit hardest."

Bruan cursed. "I'll take Davrian back to the barracks. Athan, take Eamon and go to the western wall. Fly the banners for reinforcements if need be, though don't count on any men from the north wall. With the bulk of the enemy force attacking the north, I can't afford to send men—"

"Bruan, we've been through this," Athan shouted. "The men know what to do."

"I'll take Fadrien to the keep then meet you with the rest of the archers on the wall," Illiott said.

Bruan nodded and drew his sword. "Good luck gentlemen. Let us serve our king well this day. Long live the King!"

* * *

Lyle and Kit ran for Manadon road. The artisan district suffered only a few small fires. One boulder reached the edge of a river mill, knocking the water wheel off its shaft. Smaller rocks landed in the wheat fields to little effect. The smoke columns must have been from Manadon Street. Lyle's home was just on the edge of Manadon, beside Doyle's Inn. Kit counted three smoke columns. As they neared Lyle's home, they could tell the fires were close to Josie and Adeline. Kit feared the worse.

"Perhaps we should move the girls back to their original home?" Kit said to Lyle.

Lyle said nothing. It wouldn't help. He could tell when Kit feigned optimism. Agreeing with him would only make it worse. He ran faster for Manadon Street. Once they crossed the Numen and passed the last shop on smithy row, Lyle could see the fire.

"It's Davrian's Tomb!" Lyle bent over to catch his breath.

Two dark pillars of smoke and ash rose over the burning rubble. The top half of the tower had fallen onto the decking at street level. The old tower was a complete loss.

Kit ran past Lyle. The fire in Davrian's Tomb didn't ease his fear. Another smoke cloud rose across the street. Lyle forced himself up and chased after Kit. He lost his brother in a crowd, fighting the flames. Lyle could still make out Kit's voice over the roaring fire and the yelling townspeople.

"Josie! Josie! Where are you?"

Lyle followed Kit's voice to Doyle's Inn. Smoke rose in the back. Lyle's heart sank.

"Josie!" Kit cried.

Lyle worked his way to the back of Doyle's Inn. The back half was engulfed in flames. Another twenty feet, and the fiery boulder would have smashed into Lyle's home. He ran to his door and nearly collided with Kit who was carrying Josie's mother in his arms.

"Help them with Caren," Kit cried. "They can't breathe in there."

Lyle ran in and found the girls carrying their father, Caren. Smoke poured in through the windows making it nearly impossible to see, much less breathe. Lyle hauled the man over his shoulders and followed Kit to a clearing. He laid Caren beside his wife, Esra.

Kit embraced Josie. She buried her face in his neck. Lyle could hear both of them crying. Adeline offered her mother a ladle of water. Her hands trembled as she fought to keep the ladle steady.

"Allow me," Lyle said. "Are you alright?"

"I am," Adeline said. She dabbed at her face with her sleeve.

"Your parents?"

"We are fine... Just scared."

"I can't imagine."

"The tower was the first hit. We started carrying my parents downstairs once we realized we were under attack. We didn't make it far when the inn was hit. I thought it was your house; it was so loud."

"Are you sure you're fine?"

"Yeah. Thank you." Adeline closed her eyes and took a deep breath. Everyone was safe, for now. She brushed her mother's hair back as Lyle held the ladle for her to drink.

"She's getting worse. She hasn't said a word today, even with all that's happened."

"She is fortunate to have you," Lyle said.

"We are fortunate to have you," Adeline said. Though her hands trembled, her eyes were more confident.

Lyle turned away, "What are we going to do with those two?" He pointed to Kit and Josie. "I've never seen him so scared before."

"They are perfect," Adeline said. She took a deep breath and scooted next to her mother. "They're coming aren't they? The Itihasians?"

Lyle nodded. "I need to move you farther from the wall. Perhaps Kit's home."

"Have you ever seen a couple so comfortable with each other?" Adeline nodded towards Kit and Josie. "So sure of what they have... Look at them; it's like a fairy tale. There they are embraced in the midst of a war. Kit in his rugged, mud stained garb, Josie untarnished and beaming. The wind picks up her hair and blows the smoke away... Just like a painting. Everything around them is wrong, yet they're content with each other."

"It does seem perfect when you put it like that."

"Why is it that a relationship comes so naturally for some couples, while others have to work just to survive, and even harder to thrive? Especially when you know no couple loves less than the other?"

Lyle felt a lump growing in his throat. He couldn't look at Adeline.

"Thank you for coming for us," Adeline said. She squeezed Lyle's hand and moved to check on her father.

Lyle looked to Kit and Josie. They were still embraced. Kit was whispering in her ear and played with her hair. Adeline was right, they seemed made for each other. As much as he fought it, he felt his eyes drawn to Adeline.

Why do others have to work just to survive?

Lyle closed his eyes. Now was not the time to be distracted by a girl. The enemy would most certainly follow the barrage with an attack.

"Kit, we need to help with the fire. It's close enough to spread to the house."

"We can't leave Caren and Esra outside," Kit said.

"We'll be fine," Josie said. "We'll take them to your place."

Kit kissed her hand. "When the attacks start again, make for the farm house next door. Hayden has a root cellar there."

"We'll be fine."

"We'll be back once the fire is under control."

Kit kissed Josie's cheek. Lyle was waiting with a bucket in each hand and heavy sack cloths draped over his shoulder. Neighbors and street watchers were already helping the innkeeper, Doyle, fight the flames. Women and children kept the adjacent buildings wet while the men fought the fire. Lyle and Kit dunked their sack cloths in water and wrapped it around their chests. They joined the townsmen as they pushed against the burning walls with pikes and pitchforks, forcing the building to collapse inward as it burned. It was an hour until the fire was safely contained.

Lyle splashed his face with water. "That could have easily been my home."

Kit said nothing. He nodded and drank from a bucket.

"My thanks," a voice said from behind.

Lyle and Kit turned around to see Doyle. He leaned on his pitch fork and stared at his inn.

"I'm sorry for you loss," Lyle said.

"Don't be," Doyle coughed. "It's just a building... First the Kettle and Dove and now my inn. At least no one was inside. Can't say the same for the prison. I heard one of the guards say the warden was crushed under the stone."

"Gavain?"

Doyle nodded his head. "Along with most of the prisoners. That's why it took the guards so long to show up here. We might've saved the inn had more help arrived in time."

"Any idea how many escaped?" Kit said.

"Three or four, the guards said. Told me to keep an eye out for them. Apparently one of them is missing an arm—Should be easy to spot around here."

"Harrot..." Lyle said. "Davrian's right hand man."

"Wasn't that the hand Harrot lost? Does he still keep the title?" Kit nudged Lyle. Lyle wasn't laughing.

"Thank you," Lyle said. "Again, I'm sorry, if your family needs a place to stay, my home is available. The girls are moving to Kit's."

"I'm indebted to you," Doyle said. He picked up his pitchfork and started sifting through the rubble for salvage. It reminded Lyle of doing the same for Josie's theater a few days before.

The Kettle and Dove's ruins were next door. The ground and foundation was still black from the fire. Four burning boulders covered in pitch had landed in its lot. Lyle looked around. Between the inn, the Kettle and Dove, Manadon Street and the area surrounding Davrian's Tomb, Lyle and Kit counted over a hundred burning boulders.

"This was the only area to be attacked, besides a few stray rocks that landed in the Artisan District," Lyle said.

"What are you thinking?" Kit said.

"They were aiming for a specific target."

"You don't think they were trying to set the whole city ablaze?"

"No, their attacks would have been more spread out. They were trying to attack the prison. I'm afraid the note Davrian found from the Ebon Crow was right. Davrian's Tomb was the target."

"Why? Just for the hope of releasing prisoners?"

Lyle nodded, his eyes still scanning the street and fires.

"That shouldn't come as a surprise," Kit said. "Releasing prisoners on a besieged city is an age old tactic."

"But why not more key positions? The barracks, stables, mills, farms, or even the wall itself? But more importantly, if they wanted to release prisoners, how did the foreign enemy know which building to attack?"

"You think Guile told them?" Kit said.

"I believe so," Lyle said. "If what Davrian says is true, then we are fortunate to have sealed the only entrance."

"And if Davrian has been lying?"

"Then there is a plan set and fully in motion... And I have no idea what it could be. Davrian is playing a game, and I am losing. I must do better, but I have no more leads."

"Perhaps it's not as complicated as you think. What if Davrian is trying to help and is telling the truth?"

"Impossible. Don't write off what we know of him. He is a traitor and a liar. He has driven good people to make horrible choices."

"You're right," Kit said. "Unfortunately, you're always right. What do we do now?"

"Hope the wall holds... Get the girls settled in your place."

"The wall will hold," Kit smiled. "Bruan and Athan will see to it. They'll do their job. We need to do ours."

"I agree," Lyle said. "I'm tired of making guesses. It's time to figure out what Davrian is up to."

"Where do you suppose we begin?"

"Guile," Lyle said.

"Sounds like a waste of time. We don't know where he is," Kit said. "He'll be impossible to find."

Lyle smiled and pointed to Davrian's Tomb. "Impossible to find? Guile, maybe so. Harrot, the one-handed prisoner? Not so much."

CHAPTER THIRTEEN
RISING BANNERS

CHAPTER THIRTEEN

RISING BANNERS

BARRET LOOKED through a spyglass. Behind the Itihasian siege machines footmen, heavily armored with skull helms and plated mantles, made ranks. Each carried quivers holding no more than three bolts.

Bruan ordered a quarter of his men to tend to fires, clear roads and move any wounded. All of the reports came in; the damage done to the city wasn't extensive. Davrian's Tomb and the inn were destroyed, leaving Manadon blocked with rubble. A few crofts and a mill in the artisan district received minor damage. Carper's Vale lost a few homes, but the area would soon be cleared to make room for Averlace's ballistae. The wall and each gatehouse was spared.

The western gate blasted its horn. An ominous boom carried over the city. Traditionally the horns sounded the beginning of the summer solstice festival, a time of celebration and merrymaking. Today it promised war. Barret raised his spyglass and held his breath.

"They're moving the line north of the gatehouse," he told Bruan. "The gatehouse is flying their yellow banner."

Bruan grabbed the spyglass and scanned the field. Footmen advanced alone in five ranks, leaving behind their assault towers.

"Have the men hold their fire." Bruan ordered Barret. "Fire only when they have a shot. The enemy will try to establish a position closer to the wall to serve as a staging area for their assault towers. Let them get comfortable first before you order the first volley."

Bruan ran for the western gatehouse along the wall's rampart. The men were scared. The skirmish with the manaist riders, and the Battle for Manadon Gate were victories for Averlace, but unconvincing ones. The riders were unpredictable and powerful, wielding devastating attacks with their magic. King Alderman's cavalry had caught the enemy off guard while fighting for the gate, plus the wall deterred the enemy from over-running the Elite.

The siege was different. Now Averlace was at the mercy of the enemy catapults, which waited to launch fire and stone safely behind their infantry. Averlace did not have the strength to meet the enemy on the field. Their only hope was to outlast the Itihasians.

Illiott ran with the archers to answer the gatehouse's yellow banner. They were four-hundred strong, designed to move from wall to wall at a moment's notice. They had been trained to line behind the ramparts and send volleys overhead. The leader was Ingran, a hunter who lived alone in Havenwood. Bruan first offered the position to Illiott, but the schoolmaster declined suggesting Ingran instead.

Ingran served the marquis, patrolling the borderlands with Illiott's father. The man had little patience for others, and his rigid demeanor made him unpopular with the men; but none could argue against his leadership. He named the unit the Falconeers, in honor of his family's crest.

Ingran gave the order to draw bows. Illiott notched an arrow and waited. The soldiers on the wall looked nervous. A sound like a continuous wave breaking against the shore grew. Soon war cries could be made out. The enemy was close; still Ingran held his hand up. The seasoned veteran waited for his order. Grappling hooks toppled over the wall. Captain Bruan stepped out from the gatehouse barbican and waved his sword.

"Volley!"

"Volley!" Ingran repeated to his men.

Illiott launched his arrow with hundreds of others. The men on the wall cheered as they watched the enemy fall.

"Volley!" Bruan shouted, waving his sword in a circle.

"Volley!" Ingran cried.

The Falconeers let their arrows go, though in sporadic succession. Again the men cheered, but the cries of the enemy were louder. Illiott wished he could see. A tinkering sound came from behind the wall. Illiott looked to the rooftops. Short black bolts dotted the thatched roofs. Smoke started to rise.

Bruan rose again from the wall, shield over his head. "Volley!"

"Volley!"

No cheers followed the Falconeer's arrows. Men fell from the ramparts. Illiott looked on in horror as they toppled over, their bodies pierced with black bolts. The Averlacians held their positions.

Soldiers threw stones or blocked incoming shots with shields while boys hid behind the merlons, handing rocks and debris to empty hands. A red flag rose above the barbican, calling for reinforcements. The enemy was now at the wall.

"To the wall," Ingran called out. "Fire at will!"

Illiott ran into the barbican to fight beside Bruan. The captain was reaching through a murder hole to pull out a burning bolt stuck outside.

"They have no way to climb the wall. Stay low and fight the fires!" Bruan shouted.

Illiott peeked between two wooden planks. The Itihasians brought wooden shields that were carried by teams of two. The shields were long enough for six men to hide behind for cover. Their crossbowmen advanced to the wall's base and fired.

A bolt thudded into the barbican's wooden side. Illiott reached out and pulled it free as bolts landed around his arm. An enemy archer stepped from his shield to take a shot. Illiott lined his arrow up to his target, but Bruan knocked him down. A bolt flew into the barbican, just missing Illiott's head.

"Stay down!" Bruan yelled. "There's too many of them. They're hoping to pick us off."

The Averlacians hunkered down, subjecting themselves to fire. It never seemed to end. Bolts lined the gatehouse and barbican from top to bottom. Illiott went to pull another bolt out and saw the purpose behind the attack. The nearest tower north of the gatehouse was covered with troops climbing up the embedded bolts.

"They're climbing the walls!" Illiott pointed.

Bruan briefly looked out the barbican. A hand reached for his neck and tried to pull him down. Illiott stabbed the man's arm with an arrow. Bruan punched his attacker, sending the man to the ground.

More invaders scaled the wall and towers. The defenders threw everything available; rubble, barrels, glass, broken bolts. It wouldn't be enough.

"Swords!" Bruan cried. His command was relayed along the wall.

The men drew their swords while the defenders continued to throw what they could find. A few Itihasians made it over the wall, but were cut down. A horn sounded in the field. The remaining enemy retreated to their mobile barriers. The Falconeers took advantage of the retreat and answered with a continuous fire. Only a few were skilled enough to find their mark.

"Cease fire!" Ingran ordered his men.

The command gave Illiott enough courage to peek out from the barbican which just moments ago would have meant certain death. Hundreds of bolts dotted the exterior wall.

"They're retreating." Illiott said.

"For now," Bruan rubbed his neck. "They'll be back."

Shouts of celebration lifted from the ramparts as Averlace watched the enemy fall back to camp.

Bruan broke a smoldering bolt from the wall. He held it to his eye and looked down its shaft. "That was only a small skirmish. They are probing our defense," he said as he tossed the bolt aside. "They won't be so quick to retreat next time."

* * *

"Bray?" Freja patted her brother's cheek. "Wake up. These two young men are going to help move you."

Bratheon opened his eyes. "Time to move?"

Freja smiled; it was the first she heard him respond. Yesterday he opened his eyes. She had shouted and jumped all around his table then; she wanted to do the same now.

Two boys held a litter beside Bratheon's table. They were first ordered to man the wall, but Mandel requested them for their strength. Bratheon was the first of many men to be moved; it would be an impossible task for Mandel and Lurie alone. The old physician needed more help. Bruan had refused.

Freja scooted Bratheon off the edge in a hurry. He grimaced and reached for his back. Freja checked the bandage below his right shoulder. An amber red patch blotted its center. The bleeding was slowing, but it still needed to be changed. It would have to wait. The two boys carried Bratheon to the next room where Mandel had prepared as many beds as could be found. Bratheon wrapped his arms around Freja's neck as she pulled him from the litter onto a bed.

"What's happening?" he said.

"The war's begun. It's time to move you on."

"What happened?"

"You were hurt... again. But you are doing so well now," Freja said.

"We made it?"

Freja nodded. I need to leave you for now. I promised Mandel I would help."

"Mandel?"

"The man taking care of you. He saved your life."

Freja's smile straightened. There was a time when she could have done more for Bratheon. She had closed deeper wounds in Evertide, but that was a different time when she was near everyone and everything she loved. No one wronged her, or had taken what was most important. Since her parents' death and the destruction of her home, hatred was all she felt, and her magic suffered for it. Before she believed hate was something you were or were not, but now she understood what her mother taught—Everyone is capable of evil, repressing it isn't enough; it must be replaced with love.

Her inability to heal Bratheon was the first time Freja realized she was capable of hatred. She had changed so much since Evertide, but how could she learn to love in the midst of a war? How do you love an enemy?

The cries and moans of wounded men brought Freja back to the hospital room. Lurie struggled to hold a thrashing man on Mandel's table. A broken bolt jutted from his chest.

"My iron!" Mandel called.

Freja told Bratheon she loved him, but he had already fallen back asleep. She ran to the small fire and pulled a cauter rod from the coals. Mandel pulled the bolt free from the man's chest.

"Pull these out," he held the bolt to Lurie. "They're not barbed. Keep pressure on the wound until I can seal it." Mandel grabbed the glowing red cauter from Freja and pressed it against the man's wound. Smoke and the stench of burned flesh wafted up to Freja as the man yelled. He kicked and squirmed on the table. Freja looked away. The young man's eyes rolled back into his head.

"Hurry, move him and keep him covered," Mandel instructed one of the litter boys. The other boy brought the next soldier to Mandel's table. A similar bolt had struck his leg. Mandel looked the man over and shook his head.

"He can wait. Move him to a bed. Keep them coming."

Freja looked outside. A line of twenty to thirty men ran from the hospital to the Numen River's edge. Most suffered from the enemy's bolts, some had burns from fighting fires and a few others had broken bones or minor injuries. Mandel could never see them all.

"Go to the line," Lurie said to Freja. "Have them organize the line with the most urgent at the front."

Freja froze. The line of injured soldiers was daunting. How could she help these men? Healing with magic came naturally to her, at least it used to. Medicine was different. Where would she begin? She recognized some from the gate when she begged them to raise the portcullis. None had moved to help her in her time of need. They were just as her parents said. The city of Averlace was filled with selfish and fearful people; magic could not survive in such a climate.

Still, Freja thought, *someone had compassion.* Bratheon was alive because someone else cared. *There is love here... I can help these people.*

Freja rolled her sleeves and made for the front of the line. The first soldier was propped against the door unconscious, a friend held him upright. Two bolts pierced his back.

"He's gone," the man told her.

There was nothing she could do. Her courage and will to help met and clashed with defeat and hopelessness. She moved to the next man without saying a word. A bloodied hand grabbed her arm.

"Help," an older man said. His voice wavered.

Freja looked him over. Blood ran down his shoulder to his hand. His other hand lay in his lap, severely burned. Down the line women offered water to the soldiers. Freja ripped a piece of her shirt then dunked it in a water basin. She wrapped the rag around one man's hand and sent him to the back of the line.

Next she saw another soldier unconscious on a woman's lap; the look on her face said it was his wife.

"Bolt hit his head while fighting the fire," the woman said. "Fortunately it hit his helm. Burned his hands bad, but he finally fell asleep while we waited."

"Wake him," Freja said. "He shouldn't sleep if he took a hard hit to the head."

"But he was in so much pain," the woman said, her eyes heavy.

Freja ripped off another piece of her shirt and dipped it in the water. She wrapped it around the man's hands and lightly smacked his cheeks. He woke up and grimaced.

"Take him down the line," Freja said. There was hurt in the woman's eyes, but understanding too. Freja had no words; there was only the next man.

She ran into the hospital and grabbed a sheet from one of the beds. She ripped it as she walked back to the line.

So many more.

The next man needed help immediately. A bolt pierced and broke his collar bone. Any closer and it would have severed his neck. Two friends carried him from the wall and both stayed with him until help arrived. His skin was pale and sweaty. Shouts came from Mandel's operating table, no doubt the cauter iron.

"He will be with you soon," Freja said, her voice trembling. "Don't move him," she told the others.

A weeping mother was next. In her arms laid her son, just years above ten. Freja looked down. The boy's legs were mangled. Freja's stomach churned as the mother told how the boy fell from the ramparts reaching for a burning bolt and landed before a speeding wagon.

"He was with his father," the mother said. "Eldric saved him."

Freja looked to the next man; he was awake but labored to breathe. Small cuts ran across his face and bruises spotted his skin. Freja didn't have to ask. The man had been trampled by a team of horses while rescuing his son. She looked down to the next soldier in line. More bolts, more blood; and most unsettling was the helpless loved ones doing what they could for their wounded soldiers. Freja couldn't take it. She knew how each mother and wife felt. Memories of Bratheon's torn and broken body flashed in her mind. There was nothing she could do then, her heart was filled with hatred. Her magic was limited to devastating fire and overwhelming wind. Now her heart broke.

"Help me," the mother cried, her voice broke.

Freja didn't know what to say. She wanted to run away, but her knees gave way and she fell to the ground beside the boy's purple and blue legs. With a shaky hand she reached for the mother.

"I'm sorry," Freja said. She clasped the woman's hand.

The mother's grip was tense and desperate. Freja held it, doing what little she could to comfort. The small act brought peace. Tears streamed down the woman's face.

"We'll be alright," the woman said. She brushed her son's hair back and kissed his forehead. "Thank you," she said to Freja.

The woman's posture straightened and her voice steadied. Her fear vanished.

Freja looked to her hands. Her mother had the gift of encouragement. Did she have the same? If she could encourage the mother by her touch, can she heal again?

She touched the father's legs. The man coughed and wheezed. He spat out some blood, but soon after drew in a deep breath. A puzzled look came over him, but there was relief.

"What's happening?" He said.

Freja jumped to her feet. She wanted to scream for joy. She quickly dropped back to her knees and rubbed the boy's legs. He stopped whimpering to his mother and watched in amazement as his legs took back their form and color. His mother shouted.

Freja left the family to their shock and bewilderment. She crawled to the man with a broken collar bone. With one hand on his forehead and the other pushing the bolt free, the man's body restored itself to its original form. His friends looked on, unsure whether to praise the girl or cower in fear.

Minutes later, Mandel's litter boys came for the next man. They stopped at the door. The street from Mandel's makeshift hospital to the Numan River pulsed with riotous celebration. Men in bloodied garments danced with one another. Other's lifted Freja above the gathering crowd.

"I said next man!" Mandel shouted as he stepped out. He dropped his smoking cauter iron. His jaw hung ajar. "What is this?"

Lurie and the litter boys were without an answer.

"They're healed?" Lurie said.

Freja struggled against the crowd and made her way to the bewildered physician. She knelt down beside the dead soldier against the door. His friend never left him. The friend looked to Freja, his eyes hopeful. The crowd died down and held its breath as she touched the man's face. Nothing. Unwilling to lose, Freja closed her eyes and held the man's face with both hands and concentrated. She thought of his friend's love and imagined the dead man's family. Still nothing happened.

The man's friend lowered her hands free. "It's alright." He said. He pursed his lips and held his mouth, bracing himself for reality. His friend was dead, and nothing was bringing him back.

Despite the twenty or so men she healed, Freja was crushed by the man's death.

"It was his time," the friend said to her.

Silence hung in the air. The crowd, unsure whether to weep or rejoice, parted.

"I'm sorry," Mandel said as he took Freja by the arm and led her inside. "Is there anything you can do for the others?"

Freja nodded. She followed Mandel to a room full of empty beds, save three. Two still writhed from their cauterized wounds. The other, her brother, slept sound asleep. She ran to the first two beds and healed the men. The writhing and moaning stopped in an instant.

Lurie, the two litter boys, Mandel and his patients looked on as Freja approached her brother's bed. Freja couldn't compose herself as she held her brother's hand. She stroked his arm and gently played with his hair. Bratheon awoke. His eyes opened and his lips parted in a knowing smile.

"I'm so sorry," she said. "I should have listened. I could have healed you sooner. You've been through so much."

Bratheon shushed his sister and hugged her. His forgiving touch was healing in of itself. Freja melted in her brother's arms.

Lurie watched on in silence. She tugged on Mandel's sleeve and whispered in his ear. "We must find Fadrien and Illiott. They have to know about this."

Mandel nodded. "Go, but give them some time. She deserves it."

CHAPTER FOURTEEN
THE ARBITER'S CONCLAVE

CHAPTER FOURTEEN

THE ARBITER'S CONCLAVE

NALINDA SHOOK out the cramps in her hands. At her feet laid hundreds of school books. Fadrien feared if the enemy took the city, the books would be burned, stolen, or worse yet, read. With Nalinda's help the two cleared a nook in the passageway hidden below the school. There they stacked as many books as they could. Illiott promised to brick and mortar its entrance.

"I believe the fighting has stopped," Nalinda said, wiping sweat from her brow. "It's gone quiet."

"The walls have held," Fadrien said, his voice trailed off in thought as he stared at his books. He picked up another, blew the dust off its cover and placed it on top of the others.

"You don't think we can win?" Nalinda said.

Fadrien held the book up and shook his head. "There is so much here. Such rich history. These riders from Evertide have given us a glimpse of what the people of Averlace are capable of... but I fear the knowledge is lost in these books. Now I'm forced to seal them away from our enemy. Possibly forever."

"What book is that?"

Fadrien rubbed the last of the dust off with his sleeve. *"Identifying Malice: A Precautionary Introduction to Black Magic."*

"Have you read it?" Nalinda said.

"No," Fadrien said. "He tossed the book onto the stack."

"I'm sure between you and Illiott, Manaism and Averlace's heritage is safe. You two have worked tirelessly to learn what you can. Think of all—"

"We have barely scratched the surface," Fadrien said. His eyes reddened.

Nalinda lowered her head. She reached for the next book, but Fadrien's hand stopped her.

"I'm sorry." He squeezed her hand. "Your words were kind. You are wrong though. The future of Manaism depends on you, Lurie, Eamon and Illiott. All I can do is help you start the journey."

"I believe you already have," Nalinda smiled. "It won't end here." Nalinda patted the wall of books. "Once the war is over, I'll tear down this wall for the next generation of students."

Fadrien lifted the last pile of books and began stacking them. "That pleases me greatly... I have no doubt that you will. Now let's get out of this musty hall and breathe some fresh air. Perhaps that's the culprit for my foul mood."

Together the two climbed the steps back into the school. Nalinda lowered the trap door then turned to find a young man waiting in one of the school desks.

"Corwin?" Fadrien said. "What brings you here?"

"I have a message and delivery for you, councilman," Corwin said. "I apologize for the delay, but my courier has been called to the wall. The parcel says it's urgent."

"Who's it from?"

"I don't know. I found it on my desk," Corwin said. He stood, bowed then made for the door. "Illiott found me on my way here. Says to wait for him. He too has something urgent to share with you."

"Who's he?" Nalinda waited to ask after Corwin left.

"The king's head servant. Replaced the traitor Womack."

"Young to have such a position."

"Indeed. He was Womack's apprentice."

"Is that so? No one finds that odd?"

"Odd?"

"How do we know if he is with the Syndicate or not?"

"Corwin? No, you misunderstand. I know the boy's family; honest people. He was never party to Womack's dealings with the Syndicate. Corwin hasn't the nerve for such things. Even so, I'd wager Davrian would have pointed him out to the Elite by now."

"You assume Davrian is honest?"

"I'm afraid I can't speak of it dear. It's best you stay out of the Elite's business. I assure you we are doing everything possible." Fadrien reached for the box wrapped in a blue thin cloth. "Let's see what this is all about."

Tied in with the cloth was a folded letter with *Urgent* written on it. Fadrien started to read aloud, then stopped. He had hoped the box would distract Nalinda from prying into Elite business; the package would do the exact opposite.

"What is it?" Nalinda asked.

Fadrien folded the letter and tucked the package under his arm. A puzzled expression flashed across his face. "I'm sorry, dear. Now is not the time or place." Fadrien could feel Nalinda's disappointment, and he was thankful she didn't press the issue. She went to close the door Corwin left open, but instead widened it.

"Master Fadrien, there's a crowd of people outside."

Fadrien looked over Nalinda's shoulder. Manadon Square was filled with onlookers, mostly women and children. In the center of the crowd, Illiott led a young couple to the school steps.

"What's going on?" Fadrien said to Illiott. He stepped aside as a tall young man ducked his head to enter. Freja, the manaist rider, followed. Fadrien's eyes darted back to the young man. He hadn't recognized him. Was he the girl's brother? The same one clinging to life on Mandel's table?

"Impossible..."

Illiott raised his eyebrows as he closed the door on the snooping crowd. "He isn't the only one. She's healed over twenty others as well. The whole city knows."

"Healed? How?" Fadrien walked to Bratheon, staring at the rider as if he were a specter.

Bratheon cocked his head to the side. "How?"

"How did you heal him?" Fadrien looked to Freja.

Freja shrugged her shoulders, unsure how to answer. "I chose to."

"Chose?"

"I chose to heal him and imagined it. My love for him fueled the spell."

"By all that is good..." Fadrien said. "He was nearly dead. And you've healed others from the battle?"

"You should have seen the soldiers," Illiott said. "She mended broken bones, sealed wounds and restored burnt flesh. All in a matter of minutes."

Fadrien's eyes went blank as he took it all in. "I'm sorry, I haven't introduced myself. I am Fadrien, and this is one of my students, Nalinda. This is our school of magic. I assume you have met Illiott; he is the headmaster here. I had the pleasure of meeting your sister earlier while you were still..." Fadrien shook his head, trying to grasp the truth.

"Do you know what this means for Averlace? ... For our school?" Illiott grabbed Freja's shoulders and shook her like a trophy. "You've saved lives. Think of how many more you will save—how many we can all save, once we learn from you."

"You're here to teach us?" Nalinda said, clasping Freja's hands.

"We are here to help," Freja said, walking out of Illiott's hold.

"I don't understand," Nalinda said. "You say all you had to do is imagine the spell. That's exactly what Master Fadrien and Illiott have taught, but we have yet to conjure a spell. What are we doing wrong?"

"Not wasting any time are you?" Bratheon said.

"The enemy isn't," Illiott said. "We are close; we are so close to understanding Manaism. I can feel it. It's been my hope to learn in order to defend Averlace. As the enemy gathered around our walls my hope faded. Then you two arrived, blasting your way through the enemy, and now you've healed our wounded."

"And now you wish to learn the same power?" Bratheon looked Illiott over. The two were about the same age. *How could one so young be the headmaster of the school... a school unable to cast a spell?* Illiott looked all too eager to learn Manaism. The glow in Illiott's eyes when he described the riders 'blasting through the enemy' troubled Bratheon.

"You wonder why you can't cast a spell?" Bratheon looked to Nalinda, "It could be any number of things, but the root of the problem is always the heart. Having a selfless heart is hard, even toward a loved one. To maintain a heart of love, even during a time of war and death... harder still."

"A selfless heart." Illiott rubbed his chin. "Even during a time of war and death." He thought of Sullion and the day the Itihasian murdered his mother and father. How could he love someone who had no love of their own? He then remembered the day he tried to kill Sullion in Davrian's Tomb. He would have had he not been stopped. He looked to Freja.

"So, it was with a selfless heart when you healed the people today. What about the day you commanded the wind to blow back an entire volley of arrows, called thunder from the sky, turned shafts of wood to harmless flowers, and summoned a torrent of fire?"

Freja smiled as Illiott boasted about her healing, but her pride vanished at the mentioning of fire.

"The lightning storm was Bratheon's work. As for the fire... That was my mistake," Freja said.

"Mistake?" Illiott said.

"It was fueled by malice and hatred. It's what my heart wanted for my enemy."

"Yet you saved a loved one in doing so. Was it not an act of love?"

"No," Bratheon said. "It was not."

"I don't understand," Illiott said.

"Imagine a manaist and his loved one were cornered by a thief. The thief threatens to rob and kill the manaist. Unknowing to the thief, the manaist laid a trap. If he were to walk into the trap, it will most certainly kill him. The question is, how does the manaist protect his loved one, while showing love to his enemy?"

Again Illiott thought of Sullion. His fists tightened. How could Bratheon even suggest that Illiott love his parents' murderer?

"Impossible," Illiott said. "You can't love a man like that."

"That is why you fail to understand Manaism," Bratheon said with a short, mused laugh. "The greatest difference between love and hate is that love can sustain itself, hate cannot. Eventually, hatred will destroy itself."

"So how does one love his enemy?"

"It's a choice. Love is always a choice. Going back to my story, the cornered manaist shows love to his enemy by not directly destroying him. In his heart he wishes the best for the thief; that his enemy will choose a selfless life of his own. Not only would such a redeeming decision remove the manaist and his loved one from danger, but it will also provide the thief with a more fulfilling life of his own. So he warns the thief by saying, 'If you take another step towards me, you will be destroyed.'

"The thief now has a choice to make. He can continue on his path of selfishness, or repent and walk away. If he chooses to press his attack, it is his own hatred that will destroy him, not the manaist's trap. If he chooses to walk away, it is the manaist's mercy and love that gives the robber a second chance to lead an honest life. Love was giving the robber a choice. Hatred is deciding yourself to destroy your enemy."

"Like the men I killed under the gatehouse," Freja said.

Bratheon wrapped his arm around Freja and nodded. "Freja was filled with hatred. That is why she could not heal me. Her heart was clouded."

"Must she give them a choice?" Nalinda said. "It's unlikely the enemy was willing to discuss different options. She had to act to save you."

"I admit my story is a perfect scenario. I know reality is much less forgiving. The story teaches the importance of the condition of your heart. Acting in love does not always end with a peaceful resolution. It can mean the end of the enemy, or the end of you."

"So you are saying she could have done the same action, but in love?" Nalinda said.

"It is possible."

Freja took a deep breath. "I doubt I would have though. Had my heart been filled with good and love, I probably would have thought of a more peaceful alternative."

"Love..." Illiott said, his voice strict. "Choosing the selfless path."

"Mastering Manaism is first mastering the heart," Fadrien said.

"Yes, proven by an act of sacrifice," Bratheon said. "That is why manastone is required in order to cast a spell."

"You used manastone to cast your spells?" Nalinda said.

"I did," Bratheon said as he opened a pouch tied to his belt. In it a fine red powder glittered. "Freja used a bracelet she wears."

Freja held out her wrist. Around it was a twisted, thin vine. Its leaves long withered away, but the stem retained a verdant glow. "It was my mothers," she said. "Infused with manastone."

"Manastone must be used in order to cast a spell. Some believed it is symbolic of the sacrifices one must make in order to love. Freja's bracelet will only last so long, until it must be infused with manastone again," Bratheon said.

"How long will it last?" Nalinda said. She held out her hand, hoping Freja would let her see.

"That depends on the power of the spell. The greater the spell, the greater the cost," Freja said.

"Manastone is precious," Bratheon added. "A manaist must be wise as to when he should spend it. Harvesting manastone is a laborious task, and it comes from only one area."

"The mines," Fadrien said. "North of Evertide."

"That is why the Itihasians began their invasion there," Bratheon said.

"That bracelet," Illiott said as he exchanged a questioning look to Fadrien. The councilman gave an approving nod. "It is infused with manastone. Does it share any similarities with this?" Illiott pulled the arbiter's medallion from under his tunic.

Bratheon and Freja gasped. The medallion needed no introduction.

"How did you find this?" Bratheon said.

"It was my father's."

"And this was given to me by King Alderman," Fadrien revealed his own. "We have another, hidden safely."

"Three?" Bratheon's expression revealed his amazement. "You have three of the five?"

"You know of these?" Fadrien said.

"I know they are extremely powerful. That only five of the most powerful and deserving manaists were allowed to carry them. They were judges."

"Called arbiters, correct?" Fadrien said.

"Yes and if you read closely, they read *For the Giving and the Taking*."

"We've noticed," Illiott said, annoyed. He wanted to know the meaning, but didn't want to risk looking so ignorant.

"Do you know where the other two are?" Freja said.

"No," Fadrien said.

"I assumed, with them being so powerful, they all were buried with the rest of the Manaist treasure. It concerns me that two are unaccounted for. Hopefully they are indeed hidden with the rest of the treasure," Bratheon said.

"What makes them so powerful?" Nalinda said.

"They don't need to be infused ever again. They have an infinite amount of energy. In the wrong hands, they could wreak havoc."

"Why create a medallion with so much power?"

"I am not sure," Bratheon said. "But I am sure the manaists of the time had their reasons."

Bratheon eyed Illiott. The headmaster looked entranced by the medallion's unlimited power. The twos' eyes met.

"You don't like it that I have this in my possession?" Illiott said.

Bratheon said nothing.

"Let me guess. You doubt 'the condition of my heart.' Because I don't love the man who murdered my parents?" Illiott snarled. He tucked the medallion back under his tunic's collar.

"I didn't say that," Bratheon said.

"Then what are you saying?"

"There is a great deal of maturity required to own such a... a weapon."

"I see, and I am not fit to own it. Let me guess who you might have in mind—"

Fadrien stood between the two men. "Illiott that's enough."

Bratheon waved his hand, "You misunderstand me, headmaster."

"Well, I am not sure how I could have loved Sullion the day he died. To be honest, I still sleep better each night knowing my parents have been avenged. And know this. I have nothing but love for Averlace... Why is it I cannot defend her with magic? I just came from the wall... I willed for the enemy bolts to wither away before they struck my men, just as Freja had done... Still the men with me fell. Was that not love?"

"I don't know," Bratheon said. "I don't know the condition of your heart."

"The condition—" Illiott gritted his teeth. "I want peace for Averlace."

"But at what cost? Ten-thousand dead Itihasians?"

"If that is indeed the wergild. Where does love stand for such a price? I would gladly pay it, especially if I had the power to call thunder and lightning from the sky. If you are so loving and willing to help, why not destroy the enemy while they camp?"

"Have you not been listening, headmaster?" Bratheon said.

"Every word—It's not good enough for you to be one of the few with such incredible power. You have to flaunt your heart's perfect condition. Say no more, I know who you are. The powerful one—Able to wield the manaist treasure... The enemy is looking for you aren't they, Prince of Itihasia?"

"Illiott!" Fadrien held his arm out. His eyes relentlessly peered at the headmaster. "These people may be the only ones to help us. Can you not show them the respect they deserve?"

Illiott turned away and cursed under his breath. He stormed between Freja and Bratheon towards the underground passageway.

"Forgive him," Fadrien said. "He spoke out of turn. The battle weighs heavy on his mind. Give him time."

"What did he mean by Prince of Itihasia?" Bratheon said.

"Is it related to what you asked me last night?" Freja said.

"It is," Fadrien said.

"We are not with the enemy!" Bratheon said.

"Nor is the Prince of Itihasia," Fadrien said. "Listen, I need you two to be honest with me. If you really are the prince, we need to know. The enemy has demanded that we give him up. They believe we are harboring him."

"What if I am this prince?" Bratheon said. "Once you find him, will you give him to the enemy?"

"We don't want to give him to the enemy. If he is the only one powerful enough to find or use the treasure, then it would be disastrous to give him up."

Bratheon folded his arms and looked to Freja. The two stared at each other.

"You're still denying it?" Fadrien said.

"I don't even know who or what the Prince of Itihasia is," Bratheon said. "My sister and I are from Evertide. We are refugees. The Itihasians invaded our home and killed our family and friends. What makes you believe I am who the Itihasians seek?"

"They claimed he had enough magical power to wield the hidden treasure. If what you say is true, it is quite a coincidence that the two of you show up before the enemy made their demands. Especially considering the manner in which you arrived."

"This explains your headmaster's behavior then," Bratheon said.

"Like I said, you will have to forgive him."

"Illiott believes we alone have the power to wipe out the enemy?" Freja said.

"Do you?" Fadrien said.

"No," Bratheon was horrified by the question. "That would require a tremendous amount of hatred—even if it were against our enemy."

"But if I understand what you are saying... It could be done with a tremendous act of love?"

"I suppose, but I will be honest with you. That reasoning is why my sister hesitated when coming to aid Averlace. You are seduced by the wonders and benefits of Manaism, but haven't given much thought of the sacrifice needed to perform magic."

"Love is sacrificial," Freja said. "For love to be sincere, you must be willing to pay the cost."

"Cost? As in manastone?" Nalinda said.

Freja widened her eyes and shook her head. "How does one explain?" She looked to her brother.

"I doubt we have the time tonight. I must go to Illiott," Fadrien said. "Can you help us? Teach us what you know."

"You already know what must be done," Freja said. "I can sense it; you just lack the courage to act."

Fadrien lowered his head and cleared his throat. He glanced back to the steps leading to Illiott and the stacked books waiting to be hidden.

Nalinda had never seen Fadrien so solemn. "What about me? Can you teach me? Lurie and Eamon too?"

"I believe so, but I will say that I won't teach here until your headmaster leaves the school. Though he intends to do well, it is by a path of violence and vengeance—A quick and disastrous way to cast powerful spells." Bratheon expected Fadrien to protest, but the councilman nodded.

"I understand. I will speak with him."

Bratheon gave an incredulous laugh. "That simple? He will leave so easily?"

Fadrien slanted his eyes. "I said I will speak with him. You misunderstand him."

"We've come to help Averlace. I'm sure by now you've seen how Manaism can help; it may possibly win the war. It can however, just as well destroy Averlace if taught to the wrong people. You will have to trust our judgment as to who we believe is fit to learn."

"Trust is something Illiott and I are quite familiar with... Though I understand your concern, it is my hope you will come around."

"Few have greater love or devotion for Averlace than Illiott," Nalinda said.

"That I have no reason to doubt... but what about his hatred for the enemy?"

Fadrien crossed his arms and held his chin. Illiott had been one to take drastic measures in the past. He nearly killed Sullion with a chain, sought to condemn Bruan with prophecies, and unknowingly participated in an attack against the captain and king. Bratheon was right, but how would Illiott respond? He was eager to follow his father's footsteps as a manaist. Removing Illiott from the school he helped start would only exacerbate his anger.

Fadrien sighed. He didn't want to talk about Illiott any longer, at least not with Bratheon and Freja.

"Do you two have a place to stay?"

"We've been staying at the infirmary," Freja said.

"Not the coziest place," Nalinda said.

"You are more than welcome to stay at the school if you find it would be more accommodating to your needs," Fadrien said.

Freja shook her head. "I think for now it'd be best for me to stay with Mandel and Lurie. I will be of more help there."

"Thank you for your offer," Bratheon bowed.

"Ask if you need of anything. Despite the siege we still meet in the afternoon, so long as everyone is available. Please stop by then," Fadrien said. "Also, I will arrange a time for you two to meet with the king and the Elite during their next meeting. If you are sincere in helping Averlace, you will attend. Now, if you'll excuse me."

Bratheon and Freja bowed and followed Nalinda out. Fadrien grabbed the letter and package Corwin delivered. He waited for the door to close, then tore the wrapping off. Inside was a book with a ragged cover, just like the rest in the school.

"*The Arbiter's Conclave*," Fadrien read aloud. He held the letter up. On the back he found the familiar black bird stamped below the wax seal. Farvré jumped on the table to inspect the box.

"Do I dare?" Fadrien said to Farvré. He took a deep breath and broke the wax seal.

> *Words fail to express how thrilled I was to learn of the new school. I too am an enthusiast of the lost art of Manaism. Please accept this book from my own library as a token of my sincerity in pledging to be a dedicated sponsor. I believe you will find it most helpful in your future studies. For the Greater Good,*
> *The Ebon Crow*

Fadrien opened the book. He read the preface, which included a summary of the book's subject; a detailed account of the arbiters, their role as judges and manaist representatives to the king, and the power bestowed to them through the great medallions they carried.

Fadrien closed his eyes and massaged his head. To have received the book about the arbiters and their medallions just moments after learning the extent of their power from Bratheon was uncanny.

"Who are we dealing with?" Fadrien muttered to Farvré. "Whether friend or foe, I'm afraid the Ebon Crow is beyond us."

Fadrien looked back to the tunnel entrance. He could hear Illiott mixing a pail of mortar to seal the books.

"Illiott," Fadrien called out. His fingers ran across the book's title. "I'm afraid I have something you need to see."

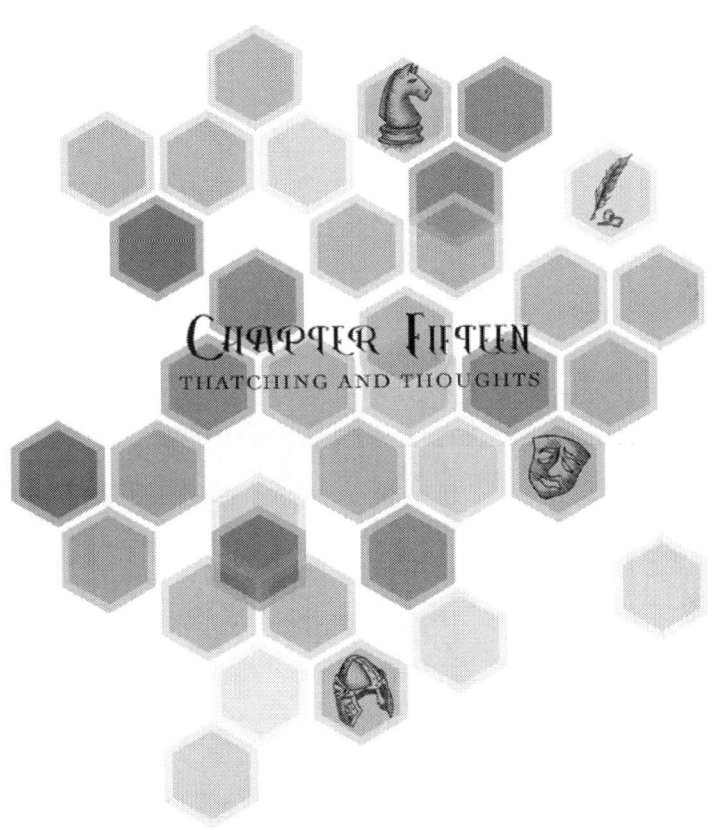

CHAPTER FIFTEEN

THATCHING AND THOUGHTS

CHAPTER FIFTEEN

THATCHING AND THOUGHTS

GRAY CLOUDS with silver tops and dark bellies rolled across the sky. In the west Lyle saw rain drizzle over the fields. The wind was slow, affording him time to run to his abandoned home before it pushed the thunderheads over Averlace. With a little luck, he could make it back with the tools needed to patch Kit's leaky roof. It was a project that needed proper attention years ago, but Lyle never bothered to help his brother who seemed just as content with or without a dripping ceiling. Housing Josie, Adeline and their parents provided a more pressing incentive.

Lyle looked to the western wall as he ran the streets. Before he never paid any attention to the guards or banners. Now it was the first thing he noticed each time he stepped outside. The guards seemed lax and Alderman's green banners with the black stag flapped in the wind. All was well, for now.

Pots, pans, barrels and vats lined the homes and stores along the street, hoping to catch the coming rain. Workers scrambled outside the saw mill, hammering makeshift troughs together to collect water for fighting fires.

Fire, Lyle thought. That's why the enemy waits. Suddenly the storm seemed less menacing and he slowed from a run to a pondering jaunt. Lyle took the time to be alone, to have his thoughts all to himself. He couldn't think of the last time he enjoyed a quiet morning. So much has happened. Between the invasion, Davrian joining the Elite, the Evertide riders, Ebon Crow's involvement and the hidden city below, Lyle found himself confused, overwhelmed and lost.

Confusion was a familiar feeling to Lyle. To him it was a necessary component to solving a mystery. It pushed him to seek options and information. Being overwhelmed was nothing new as well. Stress kept him focused. The sense of urgency kept him hard pressed and determined. Feeling lost, however, was intolerable. Lyle was accustomed to not having all the answers, but not knowing where to start... was that how defeat felt?

Lyle breathed the warm wind. The scent of summer rain cleared his mind. This was what he needed, a time to process. A time to put the pieces together. There were too many unanswered questions and too little information. If he could consolidate the problems, then he could find a place to start.

"Davrian," Lyle muttered to himself. Why join the Elite? He claimed it was to destroy the Syndicate. Why would he do that? To clear his name, or to serve Ebon Crow in hopes that the sponsor would follow through on his word?

Who was the Ebon Crow? Can we trust him? Davrian claims he doesn't know who it is, yet he has a great deal of faith that the Ebon Crow will fulfill his promises. Can the Ebon Crow persuade King Alderman to release Davrian once the Syndicate is eliminated?

Davrian speculated that the Ebon Crow wanted the Syndicate gone to brush away any trails that may have lead to his identity. There was also the manaist treasure. Maybe the Ebon Crow wanted a greater portion for himself, that was why he wanted to eliminate the Syndicate. Or it could be a combination of both? Why would the Ebon Crow be interested in the treasure? To sell it for profit? To use it? Is he a manaist?

The treasure... Did it really exist? *We have to assume it does. Two days ago I didn't believe Davrian's claims of an underground magical city. He was right. What else is the guild master right about? Can we trust him?*

Thunder rumbled in the distance. The storm clouds tumbled over the field and the wind blew harder. Soot and ash from the Kettle and Dove wafted up and clouded the street. Lyle brought his shirt over his mouth as he walked through the gray and brown cloud. He thought of the night Erisa was captured, her ankle broken. Davrian abandoned her to the flames.

She trusted him... *Erisa believed in his cause. Are we falling in the same trap? Why is it, despite all of his atrocities, I still feel compelled to trust him? Did Erisa get what she deserved? Even in prison she said Davrian isn't who I think he is. Is Davrian plotting another scheme, or is he the key to destroying the Syndicate and the Itihasians?*

The Itihasians... *An invading army seeking a treasure we have long forgotten. Is magic as wonderful and powerful as we imagine? How could we have forgotten so quickly? Why is it feared so?*

A raindrop splattered on Lyle's nose just as he opened his door. The house reeked of smoke, otherwise there was no damage. It was quiet, except for the tapping rain on the shingled roof. Lyle was tempted to stay and enjoy the storm, but Kit's home needed more than thatched patching to stay dry. Work in the rain would give him time to think, so long as Kit didn't try to help.

Lyle kept unused shingles under his staircase. There were more than enough for the job. He grabbed his satchel of tools and was just about to leave when he noticed the envelope. It was hiding under his satchel. It was the letter from the Ebon Crow. Bruan had told him to burn it. Lyle nearly did, but he kept it as evidence out of habit. He picked it up and read it again. He looked it over, hoping to catch something he had missed before.

Lyle,

Davrian will soon need your trust. Follow him wherever he leads you, and you will see the end of the Syndicate.

The Ebon Crow

Lyle squinted his eyes. The rain was now a heavy fall. He needed to get back; still he couldn't stop thinking of the letter and the Ebon Crow.

Whoever the Ebon Crow was, he obviously knew the Elite would have issues trusting Davrian. Then again, who wouldn't? Anyone who knew Davrian wouldn't trust him. Why risk writing such a letter to the Elite? But it wasn't addressed to the Elite. *The letter was written to me.*

How did he know that I would personally have reason not to trust Davrian? The Ebon Crow must know who I am. That explains how the letter found me at Kit's house. But no one knew I was moving in with my brother except for...

"Kit," Lyle said aloud. "But he was asleep when I first came. He didn't know I was moving in until moments before the letter arrived."

Lyle laughed at the thought of Kit being the Ebon Crow.

"Now that would be the greatest act of all time," Lyle said.

Adeline, Josie and their parents were the others that knew I was moving, but I'd believe Kit was the Ebon Crow before any of them. Still how did the Ebon Crow know unless he has magical capabilities? Perhaps it is Gredulous... *He is the only manaist I know with enough power to look into the future.* The new riders from Evertide were possibly powerful enough. There was also the Prince of Itihasia, supposedly powerful enough to wield the manaist treasure. The Prince and Ebon Crow both had reasons to keep a hidden identity. Perhaps they were both one and the same?

Lyle folded the letter and tapped it against his lips, "Is the Ebon Crow also the Prince of Itihasia?" He stuffed the letter in his satchel and stepped into the rain. Kit's roof would have to wait.

*   *   *

Bruan could hear Davrian's door banging before he stepped foot in the barracks.

"He's been at it all morning, Captain," Barret said as he led Bruan to Davrian's cell. "He's been calling your name."

Bruan drew his sword. "Open it."

Barret opened the door. Davrian was on his back with both feet in the air, ready to deliver another kick, like a child throwing a tantrum.

"What's the meaning of this?" Bruan said.

Davrian smiled. "I'm hungry."

"You'd have me come from the wall to—"

"Oh, please, I'm not that petty," Davrian said as he tapped one of his maps. "May I have a moment with the captain in private?"

Bruan cursed and sheathed his sword. "Give us a minute," he said to Barret who bowed and closed the door.

"Rough day on the wall? It's raining is it not? Makes for a miserable watch I'd imagine."

"It's keeping the enemy in their tents and their catapults silent. Most of my men are asleep in the towers."

"Sounds like you may have time to focus on other matters?"

"Not for idle chat with prisoners..."

Davrian smiled. "You can't forget about Guile. I know where you can find him. He's meeting with what's left of the Syndicate tonight.

"Where?"

"Back at the butcher shop."

"How do you know this?"

"Thinking... I get to do a lot of it in here."

"Why would Guile go back to the butcher's? Surely he knows we've been through there," Bruan said.

"Tonight marks the end of the three day cycle. He will return, along with any Syndicate. From there they will try to escape the city."

"But we sealed their exit."

"I said they will try to escape," Davrian said. "There is too much water flowing out for anyone to crawl in, but if one has the will and fortitude, they might be able to hold their breath long enough to ride the water out."

"And if they're not at the butcher's?"

"Then we will look at Guile's home in Old Averlace."

"We?" Bruan laughed.

"You will need me," Davrian said.

"I need you in here."

"No, Bruan you must go. Guile will be there I promise. We must capture him."

"I never said I wasn't going, just that you aren't coming along. You forget yourself, Davrian. You are a prisoner. One I still don't trust."

Davrian jumped to his feet. His chains went taut, holding his arms and legs in place. "Listen to me."

"You're not coming."

"Listen to me!" Davrian said. "Hopefully, you can remember Guile's home. He most certainly will make a run for it once he sees you. Guile can't escape."

"He won't," Bruan said.

"More importantly, remember how I've helped you. When you have captured Guile, remember me. Know that you can trust me."

"I do trust you," Bruan said. "I trust you to lie and self serve."

Davrian's face strained. "This war for the treasure... it is only going to grow darker, and more desperate. You will have to trust me if this kingdom is to survive. I am your key. Remember that... Then I will earn your trust."

"What do you mean? Key?"

"All in good time," Davrian smiled.

Bruan shook his head and reached for the door. "You play your games then wonder why we can't trust you."

"My games?" Davrian laughed, "That's precisely why you must trust me."

Bruan shook his head as he stepped out. He locked the cell, Davrian was still laughing. It was the same laugh as when they were imprisoned together in Davrian's Tomb. Confident.

Bruan stumbled away from the door. He looked down to see Barret unconscious. Bruan drew his sword.

"Who's there?" Bruan's eyes darted from one end of the hall to the other. He checked Barret over and found a large knot on the back of his head.

"Come now, on your feet." Bruan propped Barret against the wall. "What happened?"

Barret batted his eyes. "I... don't know."

"You didn't see anyone?"

Barret shook his head.

Torches lined the hall. Barret was attacked in a brightly lit area. At their feet Bruan noticed a letter. His throat tightened as he flipped it over. The black crow stamped on the back confirmed his fear.

> *To the infamous Captain of the Wall. The trap has been set. Follow the one-armed man from the Artisan District well to the Bollarow butcher shop. You'll find the last remnants of the Syndicate there, waiting for me to lead them out of the city. Hopefully, you'll be ready to disappoint them.*
> *The Ebon Crow*

The outside door creaked open. Bruan dropped the letter and spun with his sword. It was Lyle.

"Everything alright?" Lyle said, looking at Barret.

"Another letter," Bruan said. "Barret took a hit while I was with Davrian. The Ebon Crow was here. He left this letter."

Bruan handed Lyle the letter. Barret was young, but no fool. To be surprised and attacked like this was alarming. Whoever delivered the letter was skilled, yet they spared Barret's life. So was the Ebon Crow trustworthy?

"What do you think?" Bruan asked Lyle.

Lyle looked to Barret. "Able to get up?"

"I believe so sir," Barret said.

"The captain and I need a moment in private."

"The last time I heard that, somebody bopped me on the back of the head."

"Then don't wander far," Lyle said as he offered Barret a hand.

Barret stood on his feet and braced himself against the wall. After a few steps he walked on without any need of assistance.

"I came to question Davrian, but this says enough," Lyle tapped on the letter.

"I'll inform the king," Bruan said.

"No," Lyle said. "I don't think that is a good idea."

"Why not?"

"He won't like it that we are acting on a tip from the Ebon Crow. The letter says to keep a low profile. Alderman will have us march a small army to Bollarow."

"I don't think I would do it any differently. There's no telling how many Syndicate will be there."

"The letter says 'last remnants', I doubt there will be many, besides I'm not suggesting we go it alone; just that we use a little more finesse. We'll follow the one-handed man like it suggests, scope out the scene and plan accordingly."

"You may feel comfortable improvising, but I do not," Bruan said. "We don't know how much time we'll have. This may be our last chance to catch the rest of the Syndicate. We can't waste this opportunity."

"That is why I suggest we do exactly as the Ebon Crow wants. Something tells me we can trust the Ebon Crow. For whatever reason, he is going through incredible lengths to see the Syndicate eliminated. His letters appear out of thin air and seem to find us no matter where we are. The information is accurate; he is always a step ahead of us. He has proven he is someone not to be trifled with—It's all planned out. We just need to show up and do what is asked of us."

"You have that much faith in the Ebon Crow?"

"Just a gut feeling," Lyle smiled.

"I'm gambling the chance of capturing the rest of the Syndicate on a gut feeling?"

"That's how I've always done it before."

"No, that's your brother talking. You've always used your head."

"True, but then again, Kit is the one who's never been wrong."

"Shouldn't we at least get the rest of the Elite involved?" Bruan said.

"No. We must keep a low profile."

"I agree that we shouldn't tell the king, but I'm not going after the rest of the Syndicate alone. I'll have Barret bring some men and wait behind the apothecary across the street."

"Are you trusting this letter or not?" Lyle said. "You trust it enough to believe there will be a one-handed man to follow and that there will be a gathering of Syndicate at the butcher shop. Why not trust him further?"

"This doesn't sound like a trap to you?" Bruan said.

"Whoever wrote this letter knows we aren't dumb. He's well aware that he is asking you to trust a letter that sounds like a setup. Why would he expect you to go alone to single-handedly arrest a group of Syndicate unless he had a plan? The Ebon Crow will see this done."

"How can you be so sure? And don't give me that gut feeling nonsense."

"Because Davrian trusts the Ebon Crow," Lyle said. "Davrian believes that if he can help us finish off the Syndicate then the Ebon Crow will negotiate his release with King Alderman. I don't know their history together, but Davrian has learned to trust the Ebon Crow's word."

"Even if this works out, you can't possibly believe the Ebon Crow and Davrian are working towards the greater good for all of Averlace. We are being used."

"But it may keep us alive for another day," Lyle said. "Their schemes will rise to the surface before too long, we'll just have to be ready by then."

Bruan sighed. "Where will you be during all of this?"

"Close enough to witness what happens," Lyle smiled. "Don't worry, I'll be sure to pass your story on in song."

"Fair enough, just revise my past a little. You know, less betrayal and more heroics."

"Bruan, our past only defines us once we're dead. Until then it's the here and now. So far I'd say, your story has the makings of a legend."

"Hopefully it won't end tonight, alone with the Syndicate."

"I'll be there," Lyle said. "Stay sharp and we'll get through this."

"Thank you," Bruan said. "Your words encouraged me."

"I meant it, Captain." Lyle said. He clapped Bruan on the shoulders and made for the outside door. "Now let's finish off the Syndicate."

* * *

Eamon tossed his gloves to the floor and kicked off his boots. He couldn't unfasten his sword fast enough. Never had his bed been more inviting. Never again would he offer to take Athan's watch. Sleep proved harder to find than he anticipated. Since he last slept, Eamon watched the west wall twice, explored the underground city of Old Averlace, cleared roads from the barrage and defended against the first attack. Eamon tried counting the hours since he last slept, but numbers couldn't keep his attention, he couldn't even remember walking home.

Eamon threw a log on the fire then collapsed in his bed. He didn't even bother finding a blanket. Despite his heavy eyes he kept jerking up from his bed. At first he saw the silhouettes of the enemy darting across his room, like the Itihasians in the northern plains, but a second glance revealed they were only shadows flickering from the hearth's glow.

Eamon turned his head to face away from the fire and adjusted his pillow. Instead of plush feathers, his hand crumbled a paper envelope. He held it up to catch the fire's light. The fine writing was hard to make out in the dark, but after a moment he recognized his own name. A shadow raced across the paper.

Eamon turned around. A dark figure dashed for the door, it crashed into the table and scrambled outside. Eamon reached for his sword, but couldn't find it.

"Who's there?" Eamon cried. His hands scurried across the floor. Feeling for his scabbard.

The figure was gone. Eamon found his sword under his bed and raised it towards the door. His hand still grasped the envelope. He closed the door and bolted the lock. As tired as he was the letter couldn't wait. He sat on the hearth and read, keeping an eye on his door.

When he finished reading he tossed another log on his fire. His mind wouldn't allow any sleep. It raced with thoughts. The Ebon Crow had paid him a visit, leaving behind a specific list of instructions.

CHAPTER SIXTEEN
THE FORGOTTEN PROPHECY

CHAPTER SIXTEEN

THE FORGOTTEN PROPHECY

RUAN COULDN'T believe what he was doing. It was one thing to stand before the enemy army with trusted men by his side. Alone in Averlace's dark alleyways was different, and the rain didn't make it any better. At least the Bollarow well, where the Ebon Crow instructed him to wait, was in the center of a crossway. He could see anyone approach, but the one-armed man was nowhere in sight. Bruan casually looked over his shoulder. Lyle was talking to a man, more than likely the apothecary store owner. They stood together under the apothecary's eves, talking and watching the rain.

Bruan did just as Lyle instructed. He bent down and dropped a bucket deep into the well. Just act normal, Lyle had said. Bruan drank the water out of his hand and scanned the area. Nobody. Only Lyle and the man at the apothecary. The actor seemed too involved in his conversation to have an eye on Bruan as promised.

This is stupid, Bruan thought. *Chasing Syndicate with my head down in the well—Just waiting for a knife in the back.* Rusty hinges sang from behind. The apothecary door opened. An older woman walked to the well with an empty bucket.

"Excuse me, Captain," the woman said. She dunked her bucket into the water.

Bruan looked around. She was alone. Still, he needed to move her along.

"Let me give you a hand," Bruan said. "You shouldn't be out here alone, this late in the rain."

"It's the least I could do," she said. "Poor man needed water." She pointed back to the apothecary. Bruan saw another man in the window.

"One of your soldiers, sir," she said. "Wounded yesterday on the wall."

"Allow me," Bruan pulled her bucket from the water. He was about to walk it back to the soldier, but Lyle waved him down to stop.

Bruan looked closer at the soldier behind the window. His left arm was in a sling. It was Harrot. Bruan held out the bucket.

"Thank you, but can you carry it for me?" she smiled. "It's too heavy for me and the poor man lost his arm in battle. It may do him some good to see you."

"Oh, I think I better not." Bruan looked to Lyle for direction.

"He wanted me to ask," she said. "Please come see him."

Bruan started walking. Lyle didn't move. Neither knew what to do. Harrot stepped out and met Bruan at the door. With his good hand Harrot dipped a ladle in the water.

"Thank you," he said to the woman. "You too, Captain." He took a sip and nodded for Bruan to follow.

Bruan looked back to Lyle, but the actor was gone.

"Just a quick word. From one cellmate to the other," Harrot smiled. He turned Bruan towards the well and reached in his cloak. Bruan stepped back and reached for his sword. Harrot's hand returned with a black cloak.

"Follow me," Harrot said.

"What is going on?" Bruan said.

"We are doing what we are told. I'm meeting you and you're following me."

"You got a letter too?" Bruan said.

"I did."

"Where are you taking me?"

"To the last gathering. But I wouldn't ask any more questions if I were you. You already know all I know."

"Why are you helping the Ebon Crow?"

"Ha," Harrot threw the cloak into Bruan's arms. "Because it's all the Syndicate has ever known. If we want to live, we do what the Ebon Crow says."

"I thought you followed Davrian."

"We do, but where do you think he gets all of his bright ideas?"

Bruan wrapped the cloak over his shoulders. *This isn't happening*, Bruan thought. *What if I am caught? The king may think I'm collaborating with the Syndicate again.*

"I'm taking quite a risk following you, Harrot."

"And I'm not? How was I supposed to know you weren't going to arrest me?"

Bruan shook his head.

"I wasn't... But let me tell you something about the Ebon Crow. He preys off other's needs. Desperation will bring anyone together. He knows that... He knows neither one of us will betray the other because we need each other."

"What is it you need?"

"An arm," Harrot laughed. "...You're still the fool I first met back in Davrian's Tomb if you think I'd tell you that. You don't know what I need for the same reason I don't know what you're after. It keeps us working together."

"You don't know why I'm here?"

Harrot shook his head. "All I know is that the Ebon Crow fulfills his promises. You will learn that too... You will come to respect it, and it will keep you alive."

"So the Ebon Crow is good?"

"Well, that depends on who you ask. I'd tell you yes. He has done a great deal of good for me and the Syndicate, but then again he has done some good for my enemies as well... Let's just say the Ebon Crow is good to himself."

"And you're comfortable trusting someone like that?"

"Aren't you?"

"I'm afraid I don't have a choice," Bruan said.

"And that's how it all works. The Ebon Crow is a mastermind."

Harrot stopped walking. He hid his nose under his sleeve. The smell of rotting meat met Bruan at the butcher shop's doorstep.

"Here we are," Harrot said. "For your own good, I wouldn't follow me any longer."

The door creaked open before Bruan could object.

A man with thin, greasy hair peeked out. He turned away and muttered behind the door. Bruan could hear several voices laughing and cheering. The man returned.

"Harrot? Edwin said he saw you crawl out of the prison, but none of us thought you could make it here."

"So little faith, Garth," Harrot said as he leaned into the door. It creaked open. "I have the Captain with me."

Bruan stopped. Only one foot in the door and Harrot already ratted him out. He turned to run, but ran into a man who had snuck up behind. He wore a hood and covered his face with a black veil. A faded red cape was draped over his shoulders.

"Captain Bruan? Cold feet already?" the man said. His icy voice demanded every man's attention. "Now's your only chance to leave Averlace, but the way out isn't through this door." He held Bruan's shoulder.

Garth looked past Bruan to the man with the black veil. "Who are you?"

The men stood silent, unable to move. Edwin and Garth looked to each other.

"Guile!" Edwin called down to the cellar. "Get over here."

Garth looked to Bruan then back to the hooded man. "You're not...?"

"The Ebon Crow," Guile said as he parted between Edwin and Garth. He held his hand out to the hooded man. "We're honored, my lord."

Bruan risked another look at the hooded man. He was nothing like how he imagined the Ebon Crow. He stared into the black veil, trying to make any features of the man's face.

The Ebon Crow folded his arms and stepped towards Bruan, forcing the captain to step aside.

"Where are the rest?" the Ebon Crow said.

"The rest?"

"—Of the guild," the Ebon Crow snarled. "I've waited long enough for you all to arrive. Surely this can't be all?"

"Oh, no my lord." Guile bowed his head. "Come, follow me."

Harrot, Edwin and Garth followed Guile to a back room. Bruan took the chance to leave. He was far too outnumbered.

Lyle should have listened. Had Barret brought men as Bruan suggested, this would already be finished. What could the Ebon Crow hope to achieve with this ridiculous plan?

"Where do you think you're going?" the Ebon Crow grabbed Bruan's shoulder and pulled him back. "Go."

Bruan tried to look through the Ebon Crow's veil. It was like staring into the midnight sky. "Who are you?"

The Ebon Crow said nothing. He pointed to the back room.

Bruan cursed his luck. Alone with the remaining Syndicate. Lyle had promised to keep an eye on him, but he left when Harrot got too close for his liking. The Ebon Crow gently prodded Bruan along.

"Lyle?" Bruan spoke to the black veil. "Is that you?"

"Move along captain," the Ebon Crow said with a gentle prod.

Bruan breathed a sigh of relief and forced down a laugh. He thought he was alone. "I should have known better," he whispered to Lyle.

The back room was the storage place for dry goods. Four people were filling large sacks of food and dried meat.

"Here, my lord." Guile pointed to four people, stuffing bags with jerky and preserved produce. "My four remaining officers: Finch, Pickweed, Hedmare and Cressida. Finch here was able to round up the others. Hedmare and Cressida used to run the granary hideout. Pickweed is good for nothing… except for maybe a good ole tavern tussle. The rest are waiting in the cellar."

"You're the remaining officers?"

"Well, since Davrian was captured, I've taken it upon myself to keep the guild running."

"Have you now?" the Ebon Crow said. "Tell me, who orchestrated this escape? Who convinced Kvrual you could be of some use and negotiated your release? And who has funded the guild with more coin than you've seen in your miserable life? You're a vulture, Guile—Nothing more. Just waiting to pick through the fallen and ready to claim the kill. This is my guild."

Guile lowered his head. "Yes, my lord. I've only managed, is all."

"Take me to the rest, I've waited long enough. The Itihasians gave us only until the storm passes to clear the city."

Bruan did his best to keep unnoticed. Lyle's ability to command a room was the makings of a fine officer, yet it was all an act. The actor truly was the Syndicate's bane. He was there at the beginning of King Alderman's campaign and was now at the end, fooling one guild member after another and leading them to justice. Still, there was the question of how the two of them would be able to arrest eight guild officers, with more in the cellar. Bruan studied the shop for a way to capture the Syndicate. Perhaps there is a way to lock them in, but then again there is the underground passage.

As Bruan looked around he saw movement in one of the windows. A hand waving to come closer. The hand vanished, then the top of a head bounced up. Someone was trying to look.

Bruan whispered to the side of Lyle's hood and pointed to the window. "Looks like another is wanting in."

The Ebon Crow looked to the window. Two hands grasped the window sill and pulled up, revealing the outsider. To Bruan's horror it wasn't another Syndicate member. It was Lyle, waving for Bruan to run away.

Bruan looked to the Ebon Crow; it wasn't Lyle after all. He made for the door. Guile and Pickweed drew swords.

"Leaving so soon?" Guile pointed to Bruan, "Kill him."

Pickweed lunged at Bruan. Bruan batted the attack away while drawing his own sword. He parried Guile's blade and backed to the door. Lyle rushed by the captain's side. Pickweed stayed on Bruan, hacking in careless blows. Bruan patiently parried each attack, waiting for Pickweed to make a mistake. Lyle had less control over Guile. Where Lyle had skill, Guile had brute force.

Guile caught Lyle's wrist and squeezed in a crushing grip. Lyle dropped his sword. Guile swung a haymaker. It caught Lyle's chin, forcing him to the floor. Guile raised his sword with both hands.

"To me!" Bruan bellowed to Guile. Pickweed stumbled away, bloody hands grasped at his throat. The captain's eyes were afire with fury.

Guile turned in time to block Bruan's attack. By now more Syndicate came from the cellar, all armed. Lyle reached for his sword, but his broken hand couldn't support it. Guile's strength prevailed again. Bruan landed an attack on the giant, but Guile blocked it with his forearm. With a fierce roar Guile backhanded Bruan with the same arm, knocking the captain off his feet.

Lyle grabbed his sword with his left hand and crawled to Bruan's aid. He shouldn't have convinced Bruan to come alone.

The windows and door crashed open. Barret, Ingran and a dozen soldiers flooded the room. Illiott and King Alderman followed. Guile darted downstairs to the cellar. Harrot, and Finch crawled out of the broken windows.

"They're getting away," Lyle cried to Illiott. Lyle jumped to his feet and ran outside. Finch and Harrot were already at the well.

Illiott held his breath and fired a shot. It landed square in Finch's back. The man tumbled to the ground. Harrot stopped only for a second then continued to run. Determined, Lyle continued the pursuit. Harrot ran down the alley between the tanner and saw mill. Lyle would have stayed on him, but he saw movement out of the corner of his eye.

Scurrying along the saw mill, the Ebon Crow climbed a wood pile to reach the building's roof. Harrot vanished into the rain and dark. The Ebon Crow was the greater prize.

"Illiott!" Lyle pointed to the Ebon Crow.

Illiott quickly shot. The arrow pinned the wood pile, catching the Ebon Crow's cloak. Lyle was on him before he could rip free from the arrow. Lyle hacked with his bad hand, missing the last man's leg. The Ebon Crow fell from the woodpile. He grabbed a dagger, clasping it with both hands. Lyle swiped across with his blade, knocking the dagger out of the Ebon Crow's hand.

"I yield! I yield!"

Lyle cocked his head. "Yield?" He yanked the hood and veil free. Lyle dropped his sword. Illiott rushed in with an arrow drawn, ready to fire. Lyle waved him off.

A sheepish face flashed across the Ebon Crow.

"I can explain," Kit said with his hands up in the air.

*   *   *

Guile hurdled over the broken hutch that once hid the underground passage. The Syndicate was gone, but he wasn't going down with it. Kvrual won't be happy with him returning empty handed. He would have to escape to the north. He crawled through the mud, growing more at ease as the sounds of battle faded in the back. He made his way through the tunnel quickly, even in the pitch black. After a tight squeeze through the last narrow passage, he saw light from the torch he left at the end. As he neared the end he noticed two men waiting with their swords drawn. One held the torch.

"It ends here, Guile," Athan said.

Eamon tossed the torch to the ground and drew his sword. "You have only one option if you want to get out of this alive. Drop your weapon and come with us."

"I guess my luck ran out..." Guile said as he crawled free from the tunnel. "You know, you two were some of the guild's finest. Athan, I hated to see you go... However, your brother made up for it. Until he betrayed us back in the camp."

"Drop your sword," Eamon said.

Guile didn't move. "It's not too late. I can forgive. Come with me to the north. I have work lined up with Marquis Eelton. I'm sure he'll have a job for you two as well."

"Make your decision," Athan said. He spun both of his short blades in his hands.

Guile stared at the torch's glow. He sheathed his sword. "That first mark you took, old Melchoir the merchant. No hard feelings anymore is there?"

Eamon said nothing. He gripped his sword tighter.

"No hard feelings between Eamon and I," Athan said. "He has forgiven me."

"Has he?" Guile laughed. "Perhaps he is softer than I thought."

Eamon watched as Guile stepped closer to the torch. "You will pay for what you've done, Guile."

"We'll see," Guile said, taking another step to the torch.

"Athan," Eamon said, his voice cool and calm. "After his next step, he plans on kicking the torch in the river. He knows he can escape without it. Perhaps even try to kill us."

"I've been hoping this whole time he'd try." Athan said.

Guile stopped scuffling to the light. "I know better than to fight you," Guile said to Athan. "You're the killer...How quick did you kill that merchant?" Guile said. "Wasn't even a challenge, was it? A pointless kill. Proved nothing. Right Eamon?" He studied the brothers for a moment then raised his hands over his head. "I surrender."

Eamon stuck his sword in the ground. He pulled a pair of cuffs from his belt and approached Guile. "This might be the best decision you've ever made."

Guile held out his hands. Eamon looked back to his sword, his last gift from Melchoir. "I have forgiven my brother," Eamon said as he clamped the first cuff around the giant's bloodied wrist. Blood poured down Guile's arm from Bruan's attack. Eamon reached for Guile's other hand. "There's nothing you can say to make me turn against him."

Guile jerked away. He used the free cuff as a flail and struck Eamon's face. As planned he kicked at the torch. Eamon stepped on the torch's shaft, just short of the river's edge. Guile drew his sword and slashed at Eamon, but Athan was there to block the attack.

Athan stared past the crossed swords into Guile's eyes. "I really hoped you'd try."

Guile pushed Athan away and charged. Athan sidestepped and clipped Guile's ankle with one of his blades. It didn't slow Guile down. Guile spun with his arm extended. His reach nearly hit both Athan and Eamon. Eamon dodged the attack. Guile arched his blade and brought it down towards Athan's head. Guile was quick, but Athan stayed ahead. Athan stepped into the attack and parried Guile's blade to the ground. It clanged against the marble floor, sending sparks in all directions. Athan riposted his blades in Guile's chest.

Guile collapsed, gasping for air. He tried to lift his sword, but Athan kicked it out of his hand.

Guile held his chest. "Led astray... That... Crow."

"The Ebon Crow led us here," Athan said. "We've been waiting for you."

Guile wheezed and hissed as he laughed, "I'm a fool. You are too... to follow him."

"You said you were fleeing north. The Marquis has a job for you. What is it?" Eamon said.

Guile spat a mouthful of blood at Eamon. A blood-lined smile curled across his face. His eyes rolled back.

Eamon picked up Guile's sword and looked to his brother. Guile killed many in his days with the Syndicate. No one had seen or heard of him losing a fight. For years he eluded Captain Bruan and King Alderman, fighting his way free every time. Athan defeated him in a matter of seconds.

"If we hurry we can get him to the healer," Eamon said.

"He's dead," Athan said. He wiped his swords clean on Guile's shirt. "Haven't you seen a dead man before?"

Eamon stared at Guile's still body. "You know I have."

"Are you alright?"

"Yes. Thank you." Eamon couldn't pry his eyes away from Guile. "He's dead."

"And Melchoir is avenged," Athan said. "Forgive me. I should never have joined the Syndicate then. I should never—"

"Athan," Eamon smiled. "I have already forgiven you. Melchoir did too. Thanks to you it's over. The Syndicate is no more."

Athan nodded. "Let's head aboveground and make sure."

"I pity him," Eamon said. "There's no doubting how wicked the man was, but he was always just a piece in someone else's game."

"Guile is no victim. The Ebon Crow may have double crossed him, but it was only a matter of time for Guile. What goes around comes around," Athan said.

"I just hope we don't suffer the same fate. Hopefully we are done dealing with the Ebon Crow."

Athan sheathed his swords, "Here's hoping."

CHAPTER SEVENTEEN
RELIANCE AND RECONCILIATION

CHAPTER SEVENTEEN

RELIANCE AND RECONCILIATION

FADRIEN PLOPPED his book, *Magic in it's Entirety*, on his desk. "This is it. Just about everything I've learned came from this book."

"You mean tome," Bratheon laughed. "It's enormous. Where did you find it?"

"It came from our library, a gift from the king."

"Father would have loved this book," Freja said.

"He did well with what little he had," Bratheon said.

"And what about the books you are sealing away?" Freja said. "Have you read those?"

"No, I haven't. I've yet to finish this book—Tome, I mean." Fadrien hid his embarrassment with a laugh.

"Did you bring any books with you?" Lurie said.

"Just our journals," Freja pulled a weathered, leather book from her pocket. "We use these to record our thoughts. Everything from wishes and desires, to struggles and heartaches."

Bratheon opened a similar book. "It helps us keep in touch with our heart and mind. We use them to identify habits, both bad and good. It's all about keeping a loving and selfless heart. These journals help us do just that," Bratheon said.

"It just seams impossible," Nalinda said. "I mean... If I am honest with myself. I do something selfish daily... maybe even hourly."

"As do I," Bratheon said. "We're not perfect—Far from it. But it's one thing to live selflessly with no intention or drive to change as opposed to identifying selflessness and working to become more altruistic."

"So you don't have to be perfect to cast a spell," Lurie said.

"No," Freja tried to hold back a laugh. "No, not at all. I think... Father said—"

"He said, just the sincere desire to become selfless and loving is enough. It's a gift really—To be able to see the wrong in our lives. We then have the choice to change it. For example, a sincere effort to become more giving, even though we struggle with possessions, is a selfless act in of itself. You find that though you may have setbacks, you will grow more altruistic if you are diligent in your effort to change. There will be signs of progress, or fruit that people will notice. You will notice it too!"

"How encouraging," Illiott said as he slammed the door closed. "Everyone play nice and the world will brighten up. Even the Itihasians will pack up and go home, perhaps leave us a parting gift."

"Morning, headmaster," Bratheon said.

"Good morning, indeed," Fadrien said, drumming his fingers across his book. "You've come to listen in on Bratheon's lecture about a selfless heart?"

"No," Illiott said.

"Then, I'm afraid I'm going to have to ask you to leave, sir," Fadrien said.

Lurie and Nalinda froze. Their eyes met in utter disbelief.

"Seems like you started without me," Illiott shrugged. "That I can understand, but why without Eamon? Isn't he as much of this class as any other?"

"We waited, but he never showed up," Fadrien said.

"That's because he and I were involved in a raid last night. The Syndicate is no more."

Fadrien's eyes widened. "You are serious?"

"As serious as our enemy," Illiott said.

"That... That is wonderful. I mean, are you certain? We have all of them?"

"Well not all. All were killed but an old man. And the one-handed man escaped, but we can handle one thief on our streets. We even caught the Ebon Crow. The Syndicate is over."

"Gracious—the Ebon Crow?" Fadrien held his head. "Who? Who was it?"

"That is why I am here. King Alderman has summoned the Elite... And the school."

"The king?" Nalinda's jaw dropped. "What need does he have with the school?"

"That's for us to discuss there," Illiott said.

"Perhaps Bratheon and I should be going?" Freja said.

"Or we can wait for you here. If you want to continue when you return," Bratheon said.

"No, I think you all should come. It's about the manaist treasure, isn't it?" Fadrien said to Illiott.

"I didn't ask. I was just told to find you and my students."

"If the king is need of the school, then it would be foolish not to bring them. They are just as much of our school now as any of us. We will need them."

"Need them? What we need from them is to tell the truth," Illiott eyed Bratheon. "—To admit *he* is the Prince of Itihasia."

Fadrien slammed his book. The room paused. "Nalinda, Lurie... pack my things. Make sure we have all of the medallions. Lead Bratheon and Freja to the barracks. I'll meet you all there."

The girls left for Fadrien's desk. Bratheon and Freja stepped outside and waited. Illiott's eyes never left Fadrien. He tightened his fists.

"How dare you?—Override me in front of everyone—My students. Last I checked, the king made me headmaster of this school."

"And the king appointed me as his councilor," Fadrien retorted. "It's my job to bring to him those who can help. He trusted me to form the Elite. And he trusted my proposal not to accept the position of the headmaster, but to select you instead. Proof, that even I can make mistakes, I suppose.

"I suggested you lead the school, not only because I saw a bright and determined mind, but a temperate heart as well. I saw a young man willing to own up to his mistakes and burdened with a desire to make this world a better place. Now... I see a child. A child threatened when instead he should be encouraged and grateful for our fortune. A real manaist, someone who can guide us, has arrived. Rather than welcome them with open arms you've done nothing but push them away and I've had about all I can stomach of it. I won't risk the future of this school, of this kingdom, so I can coddle your pride. Bratheon and Freja are coming and that is final."

"I don't think it is wise to have such powerful strangers close to the king," Illiott said.

"Ah, so noble of you," Fadrien said.

"I'm serious. We still don't know if Bratheon is the Prince of Itihasia or not."

"And what danger is there in that? An enemy of our enemy is our friend, are they not? Especially when they heal and protect our own? With such power I'd imagine if they meant the king any harm they would have laid waste to the keep by now."

"Or perhaps they have been patiently waiting for an opportunity?"

"I don't think that is the case. Think of what we know of Manaism. One can't heal and cast such wonderful magic and have evil intent in their heart. They mean well."

"Did the girl not admit to evil after burning those men at the gate?" Illiott said.

Fadrien crossed his arms in an exasperated fashion. "Come," he said. "I have something I need to show you."

Illiott rolled his eyes.

Fadrien opened the bottom drawer of his desk and pulled out a red book with an envelope tied around its cover. "This was given to me by the Ebon Crow—"

"The Ebon Crow?" Illiott said. "We need to go to the king now before you continue. There are some things you need to know."

"There are some things you need to know," Fadrien thumped his finger against the book. "I'll make it quick.

"This book is an account of the Arbiter's Conclave. Are you familiar with them?"

"I've heard of them," Illiott said. "But please come with me now. There is something you must understand about the Ebon Crow. This book will have to wait."

"It cannot wait." Fadrien said. "Do you not listen? When have I led you astray? There is something you must know. I need your help, Illiott. Things have gotten more complicated, more urgent. This book changes everything."

"How so?"

"There were five arbiter's in the conclave. Each had a specific job. There was the Grand Arbiter, the head of law. After him the Guardian, he protected the kingdom's secrets and assets. Then there was the Master, the most powerful manaist in the kingdom. His responsibility was to teach and write curriculum. The final two were of nobility. Though they held the political power in the kingdom, they were the least powerful of the five. The first was the Marquis of the Northern March; the second was the King of Averlace."

"The king?"

"Each had not only a chair in the conclave, but—"

"A medallion as well," Illiott said. He pulled his medallion from under his shirt.

"And," Fadrien continued. "Do you know of the primary purpose of the medallions?"

Illiott shook his head, "No."

"Together, they unlock a chamber that I believe holds the Manaist treasure."

"Let me guess, you need all five?"

"No, you need the king's medallion alone, or you can use all four of the others."

"The king has a medallion?" Illiott said.

"I'm not sure if he has one now or not, but according to the book he used to carry one."

"Is there a way for us to tell which three we have?"

"I don't know. So far they all look identical."

"Perhaps the king's and marquis' medallions look different than the other three?" Illiott said.

"Perhaps. This is why I want Bratheon and Freja present. They can help."

"Can they?"

"They recognized the medallions didn't they?" Fadrien said.

"More reason for me to think they are lying about their identity."

"We will see," Fadrien said. "I believe they are here to help. Together with their knowledge and this book, I believe we can find this treasure."

"I wouldn't put too much faith in the Ebon Crow's book," Illiott said.

"Why not? He led you to the last of the Syndicate did he not?" Fadrien furrowed his brow. "Who is he?"

"I'll let you find out for yourself," Illiott said, his voice reticent.

CHAPTER EIGHTEEN
REGAL PRESTIGE

CHAPTER EIGHTEEN

REGAL PRESTIGE

KIT SQUIRMED on the floor, trying his best to get comfortable. His hands were cuffed above his head to the wall; they went numb hours ago. The sun rose in a cloudless sky. Kit hung his head low. With the storm gone, the Itihasians would surely attack today. He started to nod off when he heard Lyle's voice in the hall.

"Of all the dumbest things—This tops them all!" Lyle slammed Kit's cell door open.

"Did you find it?" Kit said. "Was it where I told you?"

"Yes," Lyle said. "Why would you hide a letter in a chamber pot?"

"Because I knew you wouldn't look there. Worst case, you would stuff your laundry or something in it," Kit smiled, but Lyle wasn't laughing.

"Kit this is serious. The king is furious."

"Have you read my letter from the Ebon Crow?" Kit said.

"No."

"Why not? It explains everything."

"Does it look like I can even open it right now?" Lyle raised his right hand. It was wrapped in a splint. His fingers were black and blue.

"You can't open an envelope with one hand? It's not even sealed," Kit said.

"I still disarmed you with a bad hand last night, didn't I? Who holds a dagger with two hands anyway? I should have known it was you."

"Would you read my letter? You must believe me."

"I already believe you," Lyle joined Kit on the floor. "I just got it as evidence for King Alderman."

"Is he really as mad as you say?"

"Furious. When he first heard you were the Ebon Crow he shouted, 'His prophecy came true after all! He has betrayed his companions.'"

Kit rolled his eyes.

"Let's take a look at this before everyone arrives. I need an idea how I'm going to sell this to Alderman," Lyle said. "When did you get this?"

"Weeks ago. There's two in there actually. The first one came maybe two weeks ago. The second came the same day you received your letter at my house."

"Stupid—Stupid, stupid, stupid. Kit you could have been killed."

"It wouldn't have been the first time," Kit said, smug.

"What were you thinking running off alone? In the middle of the Syndicate? What if something happened to you? I would never have known. Think of poor Josie!"

"I did this for her... To end the Syndicate. Will you not read the letter?"

Lyle grumbled as he opened the envelope. It took a combined effort between the two of them. Lyle tugged on it with his left hand while Kit held it in place with a cuffed hand.

To the Master Thespian,

"Whoa, wait a second." Lyle said. "Master Thespian? He just called me Lyle."

"We always knew he was smart," Kit smiled. "Read on."

To the Master Thespian,

Times have changed. Contrary to what you may believe, I am your ally. I aim to destroy the Syndicate. Seeing how we want the same thing, I have a role for you in the guild's downfall. I am a wanted man, both my allies and enemies seek an audience with me, but my identity must remain hidden. That is why I need you. You will stand in my place and bait the trap I have set against them. I realize your trust in me may be lacking, but I assure you in time I will garner some credibility. Keep quiet, watch and listen. I will earn your trust. Look for another letter soon. Specific instructions to follow.

The Ebon Crow

"Why didn't you tell me?" Lyle said.

"I didn't want you to know I was working with the Ebon Crow. I thought the longer I acted interested in helping the more clues I could gather. Then you received your letter and Bruan found the one to Davrian. Just like King Alderman said, we had no choice but to trust. Turns out the Ebon Crow was honest. We have all of the Syndicate."

"Save Harrot."

"The Syndicate is gone," Kit said.

Lyle nodded, "You're right... What did the second letter say?"

"Mainly just tips on how to act like the Ebon Crow. How to dress and where to meet. I didn't know for sure, but I had a feeling others would show up to help. I was so relieved when I saw Bruan enter."

"Then King Alderman and Illiott. Athan and Eamon guarded the tunnel exit."

"Everyone received a letter?"

"I believe so," Lyle said. "I guess we'll find out when we all meet."

"Will King Alderman believe me?"

"I think so," Lyle said. "Especially, if he received a letter too."

"I guess that was quite a surprise for you. Seeing me as the Ebon Crow."

"I should know to expect the unexpected with you," Lyle said. "Please, no more surprises for a while. Tell me I know everything there is to know about you, Davrian and the Syndicate."

"I'd say you're caught up by this point," Kit said.

Lyle rested his head against the wall and rubbed his eyes. He stuffed the letters under Kit's tunic. "I'm not sure what to do with myself now with the Syndicate gone."

"Have you thought about a career in acting?" Kit said, his face serious.

Lyle batted his brother's face away.

"You can always man a post on the wall," Kit said.

"I think I may," Lyle said.

* * *

King Alderman listened to Kit's defense, chin resting on his hand. Kit's heart pounded inside his chest, but one would never have guessed by watching alone. From his first letter to the moment Lyle struck the dagger free from his hands, Kit told his story as if performing on stage. At the close of his tale the room roared in laughter, King Alderman loudest of all. Even Illiott stifled a laugh, forgetting his differences with Bratheon, Freja and Fadrien.

"You thought it was Lyle the whole time?" Alderman slapped Bruan's shoulders.

"Until I saw his head peeking through the window," Bruan said.

"Worse yet, he pointed me out to all of the Syndicate," Lyle said, joining in the laughter.

"It appears the captain gave you too much credit brother. He thought you were beside him when instead you let him march in the center of the hideout alone."

"Me against twenty!" Bruan said.

"Twenty-seven to be exact," Athan said.

"You weren't alone, you had me. Bravest of them all," Kit said. "I never left the captain's side."

"Most foolish of them all," Lyle said. "What he failed to share was how easily I disarmed him with my left hand." Lyle held up his splint. "One swipe and his dagger must have flown a dozen yards."

"One! No I blocked the first," Kit said.

"Oh, excuse me. Two strikes."

King Alderman stood from his chair. "What I failed to share with everyone is that I too received a letter from the Ebon Crow. It told of the Syndicate meeting at the butcher's shop. All I had to do was lead my men there."

"Why didn't you tell us Your Majesty?" Bruan said.

King Alderman raised his eyebrow. "The question is, Captain. Why didn't you tell me about your letter? Why didn't Kit, and Athan? As for me I didn't have the time. I received my letter shortly before the raid."

"Forgive me, Your Majesty," Bruan said. "I should have let you know."

"I don't care to hear any apologies or excuses now. Nor do I want to hear anything about the Itihasians. This morning, for just a moment, all I want to do is bask in the here and now; And right now the Syndicate is no more!"

Kit raised a mug and cheered. A chorus of cheers and applause followed. King Alderman raised his hand, the room fell silent.

"It's all I've known since I've been king. You lads... You've all done the impossible. Bringing the Elite together may be the greatest thing I've done for Averlace. Without you all... without Owin—The Syndicate would still have a hold in the kingdom.

"I know we have our greatest challenge ahead, but I am certain the King's Elite will lead Averlace as a shining beacon."

Fadrien rose from his chair and led the room in another round of applause. Bratheon and Freja looked on as all of the Elite shouted King Alderman's name. Kit, still in shackles, stood on the table and made a toast in the king's honor. Davrian sat in his corner, indifferent. King Alderman slumped back in his chair and stared off while his men carried on. He ran his hand down the handle of his war hammer.

"Something is wrong," Freja whispered to Bratheon and Fadrien.

Fadrien went to Alderman's side. The others hardly noticed. They all laughed as Kit talked into an empty mug, impersonating Bruan surrounded by the Syndicate.

"My king, is everything alright?" Fadrien said.

Alderman took Fadrien's hand. "No, councilman. The Syndicate is gone, I fear Averlace will soon follow." Alderman ran his fingers through his hair. "The King's Elite... they will defeat the Itihasians will they not?"

"Or die trying," Fadrien said.

"No...That is fear speaking, councilman. We can't afford any more fear in this city. Do you hear me? The King's Elite will defeat the Itihasians. I need every man on the wall to hear it, every squire to believe it. I need every woman singing our victories or mourning the death of a loved one to hear it. Word must get out, the Elite destroyed the Syndicate—The blight of Averlace!"

The cheering laughter faded. The men took their seats. Athan approached the king.

"Is it time, Your Majesty?"

Alderman pursed his lips and scratched his beard. "I heard this morning, that another wave of reinforcements marched into the Itihasian camp last night. Fifteen thousand Itihasians camp outside of Averlace. We are outnumbered, fifteen to one. It's been my hope that we could outlast their siege, but it is time for me to think more realistically."

Bruan breathed a sigh of relief. Had Alderman come to favor magic? Would the school have permission to pursue a resolution through Manaism? Fadrien and Illiott exchanged glances.

Alderman nodded to Athan. "Prepare your team. Coordinate with Captain Bruan before you ride out."

"Ride out?" Eamon said. "You can't be serious? To where?"

"To Marquis Eelton," Athan said, his voice reticent. "We believe the army he sent was destroyed before they arrived. That is how the Itihasians came armed as if from the Northern March. It's likely the Marquis doesn't even know Averlace is under attack. We must get to him, so he can send his army.

"Even with the Marquis' army, we would still be outmatched. Fifteen thousand? We might have half that with the Marquis and his men. We don't even know if the Marquis is behind it all," Eamon said.

"Behind it all?" Fadrien said.

"Captain Picus would've died before betraying the king," Bruan said.

"Perhaps that's why he was murdered," Lyle said.

"Either way, we must get to him and find out," King Alderman said. His voice silenced the others.

"How?" Eamon said. "How is he to ride past an army of fifteen thousand, travel for five days while under pursuit, talk to a military leader who may or may not be loyal then ride back to Averlace and fight through the army of fifteen thousand a second time."

"He will, because he has to," Alderman said.

"Then I'm going with you," Eamon said to Athan.

"No," Athan said. "I'm sorry Eamon, but I won't allow it."

"Your Majesty!" Eamon said. "With your permission, I want to ride out with my brother."

"I'm sorry Eamon," Alderman said. "I promised Athan I wouldn't allow it."

"He can't go alone. It's impossible enough as it is. He'll never make it alone."

"He may have a better chance sneaking past the army alone," Alderman said.

"He is right, Your Majesty," Bratheon said. He stepped forward and leaned on his staff. His bright red hair was matted to the right side of his head.

"Who are you?" Alderman said.

"The manaist riders from Evertide, Your Majesty," Fadrien said. "Bratheon and his sister, Freja."

Bratheon pointed to Athan. "This man has no chance, but I can help."

Freja tugged on Bratheon's sleeve. He batted her hand away. "My sister and I rode past the army once already. I am sure I can do it a second time."

"You must discuss it with Athan. The decision is his to make," Alderman said.

Eamon sat in his chair, seething at Athan. Freja didn't look any happier with Bratheon.

Illiott also had a problem with the plan.

"Your majesty," Illiott said. "There is still much we don't know about this man."

Alderman raised an eye. "What do you mean?"

"He believes Bratheon is the Itihasian Prince," Fadrien said.

"Do you agree?" Alderman said to Fadrien.

"No, I don't. Bratheon denies it and I believe him."

"He was chased to the city gates. Shortly after they demand we give up the Prince of Itihasia, powerful enough to wield a manaist treasure. Illiott's suspensions makes sense to me," Alderman said. "What say you boy?"

"I'm not the Prince of Itihasia. My sister and I come from Evertide. The Itihasians destroyed our homes. We are here to stop them," Bratheon said.

"You can be honest with me boy," Alderman said. "If the Itihasians have to demand that we give their prince up, then it sounds to me as though the Prince of Itihasia doesn't want to cooperate with them. Perhaps we can work together?"

"I promise, Your Majesty. It's not me. I know nothing about this," Bratheon said.

"Why would we lie about it?" Freja said.

"Because you're afraid we will turn you over," Illiott said.

"Leave the boy alone."

All eyes turned to Davrian's corner. The guild master plopped his feet to the ground and sat up. "It's not him," Davrian said. "He's not the prince."

"Oh, so now you are the authority on this matter?" Illiott said.

"Can you not take my word for it?" Davrian said. "I've been nothing but honest since I've joined your ranks as an Elite."

"You are nothing like us," Lyle said.

"Perhaps not, but I have been honest. At least I haven't kept any secrets about the Ebon Crow."

"We only know about your letter from the Ebon Crow because Bruan found it."

"Doesn't that strike anyone as odd?" Davrian said. "Why write so many letters to different people. Each one baring a small piece to the puzzle. Why not just tell everyone at once?"

"So we can learn to trust him?" Kit said.

Davrian tapped his nose, "That's it. It also shows we can trust each other. If any one of you had not done your part just as the Ebon Crow instructed, the raid last night would have failed. That's how the Ebon Crow has always worked. That is why I've learned I can trust him. You all already know you can trust one another, hopefully you know you can trust me. I've worked hard to earn your trust. I sacrificed my guild for it."

"Speak clearly," King Alderman said. "We don't have time for your games."

Davrian straightened his posture and looked to Bratheon. "This young man is not the Prince of Itihasia. That loathsome title belongs to yours truly." Davrian bowed.

The room went silent. Bratheon and Freja exchanged glances. King Alderman fidgeted in his chair. He didn't know whether to be angry, grateful or disgusted.

"Impossible," Illiott said. "You...the Prince of Itihasia?"

"You... scheming snake!" Alderman yelled. "The Itihasians, they're coming for you. This war—It's all about you."

"No! This war is about the treasure. It has nothing to do with me."

"The Itihasians said their prince is the key to the treasure. What does that mean?" Fadrien said.

"The legend is that only royal blood can open the chamber that holds the treasure," Davrian said.

"If that is the case, why won't the king of Itihasia come himself and open the door. Why must it be you?" Fadrien said.

"Well... He'd rather someone else do his dirty work. You know how king's can be," Davrian smirked at Alderman.

Alderman's eyes narrowed. "Why wait until now to tell us?"

"You wouldn't have believed me had I told you. Leading you to the old under-city, helping you find the last of my guild—All of this was so I could build your trust."

"Why?" Lyle said. "If you are one of the Itihasians, why betray them?"

"Because I don't see eye to eye with their king."

"Your father?" Lyle said.

"That man isn't my father. He doesn't know me apart from anyone else. To him I'm just another pawn—A piece he's willing to sacrifice to take the board."

Lyle folded his arms as he studied Davrian. The guild master looked sincere, but Lyle knew better.

"I believe now, Lyle, you will realize that you and I are quite alike. Years ago, when I first created the guild I started taking on jobs. Contrary to popular belief, I didn't want the guild running rampant, mugging the next easy mark. I wanted us to act as a unit, taking on big jobs that paid more and came with less risk. Eventually we came across an offer. We were to hunt down five manaist medallions and bring them to an old man out in Havenwood."

"Gredulous?" Eamon said.

"Yes," Davrian nodded. "As you know, Eamon. We came close to obtaining all five of them."

"We only had three," Eamon said. "Fadrien's, Illiott's and the one I stole from Gredulous. All three are back at the school now."

"We had a fourth," Davrian said. "I kept a medallion as well. One I had stolen before. All we needed was the fifth medallion..."

"Where is your fourth medallion now?" Fadrien said.

"The Itihasian camp. They took it from me when they captured me, along with my sword."

"Do you know where the fifth one is?"

"I have an idea," Davrian said, his eyes shifted back to the king.

Alderman returned the glare. "Who was it that hired you to collect the medallions?"

"The Ebon Crow," Davrian said.

"Why would the Ebon Crow want all of the medallions?" Athan said.

"I might have the answer to that question," Fadrien said. "The Ebon Crow sent a book to the school. It was about the Arbiter's Conclave, a group of five arbiters. They oversaw the kingdom's use of Manaism. There was the High Arbiter, the Guardian, the Grand Master and then the two final positions were held by the Marquis of the Northern March and the King of Averlace. Each had a medallion, they are the same five Davrian was hired to collect. The medallions had many purposes, but the most important use, at least the most important concerning us today, is that they could open the sealed chamber that housed the manaist treasure. There are two ways to use the medallions to open the chamber. The king's medallion alone could open the chamber or the four others combined."

"We almost had all four," Davrian said. "But now, we are down to three. Kvrual has mine, and the king's medallion remains hidden. For now, Kvrual has no way of getting into the chamber, even if he takes the city."

"Neither do we," Fadrien said.

"Does that book say anything about where to find the king's medallion?" Athan said.

"It doesn't," Fadrien said. "That was a secret kept safe with the king."

All eyes went to Alderman.

"I don't know where it is," Alderman shrugged his shoulders.

"Marotte didn't either," Davrian said. "When we had him acting as king, we searched high and low."

"Perhaps you didn't have the right people for the job," Lyle said. "I'm sure between you, Fadrien and Illiott we can find the chamber."

"Even if we were to find it, what next?" Fadrien said. "Would we open the chamber ourselves? Use it to negotiate peace?"

"The manaists sealed away the chamber for good reason," Davrian said. "It would be foolish of us to think we could wield the weapons inside."

"Hah, something we agree on," Alderman said. "What then do you suggest?"

"Whatever it takes to keep the Itihasians from getting in that chamber. Once they are in, there is no telling what Kvrual will do with the treasure. If the weapons there are anything like my sword... Then there is little the world could do to stop the Itihasians."

"Just what does your sword allow you to do?" Illiott said.

Davrian's lips curled into a devious smile, "Win." He said with an empty laugh.

"How do you suggest we keep the Itihasians from finding the chamber?" King Alderman said.

"Find it ourselves first. Then we will know how to keep it hidden... or defend it."

"Do you have any idea where it is?" Fadrien said.

"Below us. I've spent a great deal of time before searching for it, but like Lyle said; I may not have had the right people looking."

"How long do you need to find it?" Alderman said.

"As much time as you can give me," Davrian said. "You have bought yourself a tremendous amount of time by eliminating the rest of the guild. I'd imagine Kvrual had some plans for them. Spying, assassinations, starting fires, poisoning food and water—We've eliminated many risks when we took out the Syndicate. Now Captain Bruan can focus on just keeping the wall."

"We also eliminated the hidden passage into the undercity. Plus we have two powerful manaists. I'd say with a little more fortune, we may just hold out yet," Bruan said.

"Hopefully long enough for the Marquis to arrive with his army," Athan said.

"We will hold," Bruan said.

"Athan, may I suggest you travel through Havenwood." Davrian said. "It may behoove us to pay old Gredulous a visit. Plus the Run may prove a viable way to lose the Itihasians, if you are able to ride past their camp."

"The Run?" Athan said.

"It's the way you came when you were supposed to meet me at the tree to collect the medallions," Eamon said. "It's a secret Syndicate trail."

"I doubt I could find my way through that," Athan said. "There's enough twists and turns to get lost even with a map."

"Then I'd suggest you bring someone along who knows the way," Davrian said as he shot a subtle wink to Eamon.

CHAPTER NINETEEN
FORLORN HOPE

CHAPTER NINETEEN

FORLORN HOPE

ATHAN SNUCK OUT of the meeting before Eamon could follow. Eamon would try everything he could to convince him to come. It would only be a waste of time. Athan made up his mind, he would ride for the marquis alone. He needed the afternoon to plan and prepare for his ride, not argue with his brother.

Athan took the most direct way home, cutting through Manadon Square and walking alongside the Carper's Vale wall. He looked for Eamon from his periphery. He'll never forgive me if I leave without speaking to him, Athan thought. Nor could I forgive myself. Athan sighed as he opened his door. How could he say goodbye? When? He locked the door behind him.

"This is childish," a voice said from behind.

Athan turned from his door. Eamon leaned forward on a chair, elbows resting on his knees.

Athan's eyes flickered "... How did you?"

"Why not tell me?" Eamon said.

"Eamon... Surely you can understand why I wouldn't have you come with me."

"No, actually I don't. And why leave without even speaking to me?"

"That's not true," Athan said.

"Then why avoid me after the meeting?"

"I need time to prepare and to think clearly."

"Thinking," Eamon huffed. "It hasn't been a gift of yours."

"I know why you're here. The answer is no. You might as well leave. The king won't overrule it. The decision is mine."

"What were you hoping to achieve? Ride out at night without me knowing? Leaving me behind because you know we would argue? Just like you did years ago."

"This is an entirely different matter, Eamon. I must go!"

"And I must go with you!"

"It's too dangerous."

"Ah. Too dangerous. Then what am I to do without big brother here to protect me? But no you're right, I'll just stay behind Averlace's walls—safe and sound."

"That's not what I meant."

"Have you forgotten what I've done since Melchior's death? I'm no stranger to risk. I can help. You are a fool if you think you can make the journey on your own. This ride may be the only hope Averlace has. If you fail, Averlace is gone, and I'd go down with it. So much for protecting little brother," Eamon folded his arms.

"I have a better chance on my own. I can easily sneak by."

"If you can find your way. You said it yourself, you'll lose your way before you leave Havenwood. I can help."

"This is suicide, Eamon—Not some heroic jaunt."

"You think I don't know that? You think I'm only interested in glory?"

"I didn't say that."

"You are all I have—If I lose you what is left for me here? A fallen kingdom? I'd rather die by your side than alone on Averlace's wall. Averlace needs you to succeed, I can help you. "

"I know you can," Athan said.

"Then you will have me come?"

Athan looked to Eamon. There was no doubting Eamon's cunning and finesse. Still, when he looked at his younger brother Athan couldn't help but see the helpless boy that watched in horror as Melchoir was murdered. That day changed Eamon. He saw evil and vowed to fight against it. Eamon hid himself in the Syndicate, waiting for the perfect moment to strike. It took patience and cunning to survive within the Syndicate. It will take the same to ride out for Marquise Eelton.

Athan closed his eyes. Already he regretted what he was about to say.

"While separated you and I both vowed to fight against the Syndicate. It wasn't until we were together that we prevailed. Now that Melchoir has been avenged, I suppose there shouldn't ever be a time that we find ourselves apart from each other..."

"That may be the smartest decision you've ever made. Though you still needed me to help you make it."

"Let's hope that wasn't your worst decision." Athan said as he grabbed a bag from under his bed. "Let's get one thing clear, you will do exactly as I say while we're out there."

"As long as it's nothing stupid."

Athan looked up from his bag. His stare was icy and sincere.

"Fine," Eamon said. "As you say."

"Then pack light. Meet me at the stables at dusk."

* * *

Athan and Eamon arrived at the stables just moments apart. They were greeted by the stable boy, who had prepared additional supplies. Three bags each filled with food, waterskins, simple tools, maps and charts. The center bag also held a sealed envelope.

"That's the letter for Marquis Eelton, so I'm told," the boy said.

"And the third bag?" Eamon said.

"That belongs to me."

Athan and Eamon turned to see Bratheon. Freja and Illiott were by his side. The young man wore a new tunic and trousers. Without his rugged cloak and leather vest, he looked half the size he was before. His wiry hair and scruffy beard looked as wild as ever.

"I don't believe you are," Athan said. "I want as few as possible for the ride. A third man will only get us caught. Besides, your magic is best here, defending Averlace."

"I've already ridden past the Itihasians," Bratheon said. "It would be foolish not to take me on such an important mission."

"I'm afraid you have no choice," Illiott said. "The king has requested that Bratheon lead you to Fargaible. From there he will return back to the kingdom."

"Fargaible is twenty miles west. It's out of the way," Athan said.

"The king is interested in hearing from Gredulous. Your orders are to take Bratheon with you and learn what you can. From there you will continue on to the Northern March and Bratheon will return alone."

"We had thought of the possibility of using the Syndicate trail," Eamon said. "Fargaible is not far from there. If anything it may be the safest route, even if out of the way."

"What's at Fargaible that is so important?" Athan said.

"Clues for the king's medallion," Illiott said. "We must know where to find it."

"The ride was going to be difficult enough as it was. Riding to Fargaible won't make it any easier," Athan said.

"But having Bratheon with you will," Illiott said.

Freja and Bratheon exchanged looks, both surprised by the compliment. Illiott lifted the third bag and slung it over his shoulder.

"Please forgive me. I doubted and mistrusted you. I'm sorry for mistaking you for the Prince of Itihasia," Illiott said.

"I can't say that I didn't fit the description," Bratheon smiled through his beard. "All is forgiven. I look forward to serving your school upon my return."

"We will be honored to have you."

Freja threw her arms around Bratheon's chest and squeezed. "Take care of yourself."

Bratheon kissed her head. "You too. Promise me you will continue to love, no matter what happens."

Freja wiped the tears from her eyes and nodded. She hugged him again; her small hands clinched his shirt. Bratheon rested his cheek on her head. Eamon looked away. He couldn't help but wonder if they had the same argument that he had with Athan. They could use Freja's magic on the road.

Illiott helped the stable boy saddle a third horse. He strapped a small satchel behind Bratheon's saddle.

"A small gift from the school," Illiott patted the satchel. "I hope it serves you well." He lifted the satchel's flap. A red manastone blade glowed inside.

"I've been blessed with a new friend, now he leaves me with gifts?" Bratheon said.

"An apology isn't enough," Illiott said. "Come back to us safely. Freja needs you—Averlace needs you."

A bright red spark popped overhead. It crackled as it drifted to the ground, illuminating half the city in a crimson light. A moment later another flared above the slums.

"What is that?" Freja said.

Illiott and Athan stared on. Watching as the two lights fell behind the horizon.

"I don't know," Athan said.

Another shot up in the air, higher than the keep. It floated above Carper's Vale then landed in the Numen. Athan cursed as a hundred streams of fire arched in the air.

"Cover!" A voice from the wall shouted.

A thunderous chorus of explosions erupted in every direction. Wave after wave of fire landed in every corner of the city. Only the keep was out of reach.

"Do we ride?" Eamon shouted to Athan.

Athan looked to the western wall. The banners were still down. The enemy wasn't moving. "This may be our only chance."

Bratheon rushed Freja under the ramparts for cover. He gave her one last hug then ran for his horse. Athan and Eamon led him to the western gate. As he rode away he saw Freja climbing a ladder to the top of the ramparts. Illiott held his medallion, deep in concentration.

Eamon rode ahead, wasting no time. They had to ride out before the enemy marched against the city. More blasts fell. A home exploded in a ball of fire. Rock and wood blasted across the road. Eamon barely held on as his horse reared back. He followed behind Bratheon around the rubble, while a second blast hit the home again.

A banner rose over the barbican. It was too late. The enemy was marching against the western wall.

"Open the gate," Athan ordered the gatekeeper.

The gatekeeper recognized Athan, but he waved the riders on. Black bolts smacked against the stone merlons. The enemy was close. Opening the gate would be disastrous.

"Hurry," Athan shouted to Eamon and Bratheon. "The south gate is our only chance."

Bratheon ducked is head low and rode as hard as he could. His horse darted down Bollarow's roads in an effortless sprint.

Bollarow was getting hit the hardest. Every row of homes had at least one home in flames. Townspeople scrambled to fight the fires, risking their lives in the open streets. Columns of fire sprouted up in the night sky. The ride from the west gate to the south took only a matter of minutes. It felt to Athan an hour was lost. The south gate's banners were down.

"Open the gate," Athan shouted. He raised his hand showing his signet ring.

"The army is massing in the field," a guard shouted. "They are waiting for us to reinforce the west wall."

"Open the gate," Athan shouted again. "We are riding for help."

"They'll attack once they see the gate open," Eamon said to Athan.

"Are we riding out or not?" Athan snapped at Eamon. He pointed his sword to the guard. "Raise the gate before I open it myself!"

The man vanished in the gatehouse. A moment later the portcullis lifted off the ground.

"I'll lead," Athan said. "Make straight for the woods and stay near the river. If we are separated ride northwest. Stay clear of the Arata Road, they will no doubt search for us there. Meet up at Fargaible."

Another eruption exploded overhead. Athan expected to see fire and smoke, but instead a flash of lightning followed by a clap of thunder. A heavy storm cloud rolled over the city. It floated above the Numen River, its shape tumbling and converging with more clouds. Lightning bounced between the thunderheads, each with a deafening roar. The storm cloud grew until it covered all of Averlace.

Bratheon marveled at the storm. Raindrops started to fall on his face. "This is Freja's work," he told Athan and Eamon.

By the time the portcullis raised enough to ride underneath, Freja's rain fell in blinding sheets. The way was clear, but Eamon was right; the enemy moved toward the open gate. Athan spurred his horse into a sprint. If they were fast enough, they could make it to the forest's edge before the enemy could cut them off.

Eamon heard the Itihasians yelling orders. The army was on foot and all were clad in heavy armor and held long pikes. They were in no position to give chase. Halfway across the field Athan pointed behind the marching army. A group of riders moved fast to intercept them. Bolts whizzed overhead.

Athan looked back, Eamon and Bratheon were still with him. The hail of bolts increased. The party of riders looked to be geared specifically to cut off deserters. These weren't the slower, stronger war horses Athan fought against in Havenwood. They were white Averlacian horses. Athan looked to the forest, they weren't going to make it.

Athan drew his sword. He could slow them down while Eamon and Bratheon rode past. He turned back to give his order, but Eamon's horse fell hard, struck by a bolt. Eamon tumbled to the ground. Athan reared his horse back and made toward his brother. Eamon wasn't getting up. Bratheon rode ahead, waving his staff in the air.

"Up, up—Get up!" Athan shouted. He jumped to the ground and lifted Eamon onto his horse. The enemy bolts continued to fall. If they didn't move soon, even the foot soldiers would reach them.

"Bratheon!" Athan yelled for help, but the young manaist was too far to hear.

Athan jumped on his horse and pulled Eamon onto his lap. He looked back at the gate, it was closed. Their only hope was to outride the Itihasians. Bratheon rode ahead towards the enemy. Athan cursed and made for the woods. He watched as Bratheon veered back. The manaist reached in a pouch and waved a glittery powder in the air. Sparks shot off his horse's hooves. As he rode on, a wall of flame grew, leaving a trail of fire and embers. The enemy horses panicked. Bratheon stood in his stirrups, his cloak waving in the air as fire leapt from the ground behind.

"Ride," Bratheon waved Athan on.

Athan continued alongside the river's bank. The bolts stopped. Bratheon had the enemy's attention. Athan smacked the reigns and spurred his horse into the woods. Bratheon rode westward, his wall of fire diverting the riders from Athan and Eamon.

"The fires," Eamon mumbled. He pointed back to Averlace.

Rain poured over Averlace. One by one the dotted lights went out until the whole city went dark. Bratheon's trail of fire lingered, though he was nowhere to be seen. Athan stopped on a hill covered with thickets. They were safe for the moment.

"Are you hurt?" Athan said.

"My head is ringing... I'll be fine. My horse?"

"She's gone."

"I'm sorry, Athan. I'll only be a burden now. I shouldn't have come."

"No, you shouldn't have, but here you are." Athan jumped to the ground and led his horse by foot. "You best ride until you get your wits back. Hopefully Bratheon was able to stay ahead."

Eamon held his head low and rubbed his neck.

"I'm sorry about your horse," Athan said. "There was nothing you could do."

"I'm only going to slow you down."

"Perhaps," Athan said, "but I'm still glad you came."

CHAPTER TWENTY
TEN DAYS

CHAPTER TWENTY

TEN DAYS

BRUAN STRADDLED a crate, sharpening his sword. He overlooked the city from the north wall. The first morning light revealed the extent of the destruction. Thanks to Freja's storm, the fires were extinguished, but the barrage still managed to smash homes and buildings from Bollarow to Manadon Square all the way to the keep.

The catapults and siege towers hadn't moved. Bruan counted forty altogether. The bulk of the Itihasian army camped before the them. As long as their machines were out of reach, the Itihasians could pound Averlace into submission... or rubble. For Averlace to survive the catapults must be destroyed. But how?

Bruan ran a whetstone along his sword. His mind raced from one plan to the next, each more ludicrous and impossible than the one before. Finding the treasure and using it against the enemy was Averlace's only hope, but would Alderman condone the use of magic? Would Freja's storm change his mind?

A woman's cries stole his attention. He dropped his whetstone and looked over the ramparts. He saw her on her hands and knees, moving stones and dirt with her bare hands. A few others helped her search through what was left of her home, but there was nothing to be done. Her loved ones were lost, along with everything else she owned. Bruan could hear more cries and screams. It would only get worse. Averlace was running out of time and the enemy was just now getting comfortable.

Bruan reached for his sword and went back to work. His eyes stayed on the catapults, cursing them. The king's cavalry was the only force that could come close, but even they would be overwhelmed. Averlace had no infantry that could withstand the sheer numbers of the Itihasians. Though the marksman on the walls were skilled, they would be decimated in an open field. Freja wasn't even a viable option, Fadrien insisted that she would never agree to a direct attack, even if it was against the enemy. That left Averlace's hope in Marquis Eelton. Bruan knew nothing of the man, except the Northern March had been in his family's domain longer than any dynasty reigning in all of Averlace.

Though he had never met Marquis Eelton, Bruan's opinion was unfavorable. The Northern March and its wall bordering the Foreign Lands was governed more by the generals. Anyone unwilling to ride out from his chambers and join his men in battle was unfit to lead. Yet the marquis sent out Captain Picus to aide King Alderman, while he remained on one of his couches, growing softer and rounder.

"Captain."

Bruan's eyes were drawn from the catapults. It was his lieutenant, Barret.

"Morning," Bruan said.

"A good morning it is, sir." Barret handed Bruan a scrap of parchment. "One of the men found it earlier this morning. A raven carried it from Havenwood."

"Havenwood?" Bruan squinted his eyes to read the small letters. He jumped to his feet. His sword fell from his lap. "They made it to Fargaible?"

Barret smiled.

The Itihasian ranks at the west and south extended across a quarter of the field. Bruan shook his head, he could hardly believe it. With luck they could be in the Northern March in three days.

"The wall is yours, Barret. I must meet with the king." Bruan said. "If Athan made it through then perhaps Averlace may yet have a chance."

"Your orders?"

"Keep the men rested. The Itihasians may be against the clock. We just need to hold out."

*   *   *

"You called for us?" Lyle said, kneeling at the king's throne. Kit knelt by his side.

King Alderman's hand rested on the pommel of his war hammer, the other reached out to Valice. Prince Vance tugged on his father's robe, begging for attention. Fadrien paced behind the throne. Alderman's shoulders sagged and his eyes were weary.

"I need you to speak with Davrian," Alderman said.

"About?"

"The Prince of Itihasia. I don't trust him, Lyle. He is hiding something, I need you to find out what it is."

"Your Highness... I don't see what I could accomplish."

"It's the key to the hidden treasure. I believe he knows more. I must know if it is real."

"May I ask, Your Highness, what you intend to do once we find the treasure? Will we give it and Davrian to the enemy as they demand or do you plan on using it against the enemy?"

Alderman clasped his son's hands. With heavy eyes he looked to Valice. "Right now I need options. Is the treasure even obtainable? Where is it? Can it be defended?" Alderman said. "Can you help me?"

"I don't know, Your Majesty." Lyle said.

"You don't know?"

"Davrian is a step ahead. I can't catch him in a lie. He is running circles around Kit and I."

"But you know it is all a lie," Alderman said.

"Lyle, if not you, then who?" Valice said.

"A mere man cannot control so much. Surely something happened that caught Davrian off guard—Something he didn't prepare for. Perhaps there is a question you can press that will force him to tip his hand," Alderman said.

"I believe there is," Kit said.

Lyle's brow raised. "Is there?"

"Queen Valice is right... If Lyle can't figure out Davrian's plot then who can?—No one can, and Davrian knows it," Kit said.

"What are you saying?" Lyle said.

"Davrian has you compromised. You've said it yourself. The fight between you and Davrian is personal, my guess is more personal than Davrian prefers. I imagine that if you confront Davrian about Erisa, something will crack."

"Something will crack alright..." Lyle said. "I don't think that is a good idea."

"You believe Davrian's secrets involve Erisa?" Alderman said.

"She's been involved since the beginning. Lyle and I have often wondered about her involvement with the Syndicate... Something doesn't add up."

"Do what it takes... Davrian knows more than he says and it may make the difference between survival and defeat," Alderman said.

The throneroom's door clattered shut. Bruan stood at the entrance, waiting for the king's permission to enter.

"Captain Bruan. What brings you here?" Alderman said.

"It appears my timing couldn't be any better," Bruan said. He took off his golden, winged helm as he entered.

"News from the wall?" Alderman said.

"Indeed. A message sent by a raven; Athan and the others have made it to Fargaible."

Alderman's shoulders lifted from the news. He leaned forward from his throne. "I believed I had sent them to their graves... This is wonderful news."

"With a little more luck we may yet see Marquis Eelton's army crest the northern plains," Fadrien said.

"Yet the enemy army continues to grow," Alderman said. "Twenty-thousand I last heard. The marquis' army, though formidable, may not be enough to turn the tide."

"Why so fearful?" Valice said. "Is there no hope?"

"No, there is hope," Alderman said. "Victory will be costly. We must be ready to join Marquis Eelton on the field. A combined attack may be our only choice."

"Your Majesty, even with the best circumstances, we may not see the Northern Army for another ten days. I fear Averlace won't last. The catapults must be destroyed, we won't be able to withstand too many attacks like last night."

"What do you propose, Captain?"

"Permission to lead your cavalry on a night raid."

"Are you mad? Two hundred horsemen against—" Alderman shook his head. "You would never make it to the first catapult."

"They would never expect it."

"Because they don't have to. Even if it were a surprise, their camp surrounds their weapons. You would never make it through and even if you did, you would be cut down before you could destroy them all. I won't allow it. We need those men defending the walls, fighting fires. They are mighty men, their presence alone in the city brings peace and courage. What would it do to our morale to watch them die and rot in the fields?"

"Something must be done," Bruan said. "Morale would suffer more to do nothing while our homes are destroyed. People want to take action, even if it's a losing fight. Better to die fighting than cowering behind a wall."

"Cowering?" Alderman lifted his war hammer. "Tell me, Bruan. Who is the coward in this fight? The army with overwhelming numbers throwing fire and rock on our families, or the people who remain—defiantly standing and refusing to give into the demands? For now we wait. We will hold out until we can learn more about the manaist treasure and help arrives."

Bruan lowered his head. "Yes my king."

"Lyle and Kit will speak with Davrian now. Hopefully they can learn more. I want to meet with the Elite afterwards. Fadrien, I want your students to attend. Bruan, bring your officers. Afterwards I want to hear a contingency plan if the Marquis never arrives… Something other than a brazen charge against the heart of the army."

"Yes, Your Majesty." Bruan said.

"Bruan," Alderman called out. "I denied you permission, not because I doubt you. It's because I trust you on the wall. I need ten days and I believe you can make that happen."

Bruan stuffed his hand in his pocket and felt for his signet ring. The Aegis of the Elite. *Does the king trust me more than magic?* Bruan thought.

Bruan strapped his winged helm on his head and saluted the king. "Ten days, Your Majesty. I swear it."

CHAPTER TWENTY ONE

TALES, LIES, AND PROMISES

CHAPTER TWENTY-ONE

TALES, LIES AND PROMISES

LYLE TOOK A deep breath before turning the key.

"You alright?" Kit said.

"No," Lyle said.

"Should I go alone?"

"I'm afraid I'll either kill him, or what I learn will kill me."

"Well that answers that," Kit pulled the key from Lyle's hand.

"No, I'll be alright. Just being dramatic."

"Which is why I'm concerned. I get nervous when you're not your usual stoic self."

"This needs to happen. I've known it for a while, but I've been afraid to face the truth. I should have confronted Davrian about Erisa long ago," Lyle said.

"And that will give you peace and the king answers?" Kit said, his voice incredulous.

"You're the one that suggested it."

"Right, just wanted to make sure I was going to get credit for this," Kit smiled.

"Regardless of what happens in that cell, I'm going to kill you first," Lyle said. Kit turned the key and pushed the door open. Davrian sat on his cot. The guild master's pearl hair was tied back in a ponytail. His leggings were rolled up to his knees, his arms folded as if he had been waiting.

"Greetings," he said.

Lyle said nothing. He pulled a chair from the hall into Davrian's cell. He sat across from Davrian, clasping his hands and leaning on his knees. Lyle stared at the guild master, unsure what to say or how to begin. Kit hesitantly closed the door.

"Waiting for me to break the silence?" Davrian said. "Hoping I'll just talk? Give into the pressure?"

"Seems to be working," Kit said.

"It's not necessary," Davrian said. "I've been wondering when we would have this conversation."

"And what conversation is that?" Lyle said.

"The Syndicate," Davrian said.

Lyle smiled, his eyes unmoving. "That's it then? You have it all figured out?"

"Haven't you learned that about me yet?"

"I'm not here about the Syndicate. They are finished."

"And you are fine without knowing why or how?" Davrian said. "Have you added it all up, Lyle? …I know you better than that. You can't help but wonder. You're wondering now, if Davrian really has it all figured out, then why sell out his guild for just a chance that the Ebon Crow will bail him out of prison."

"It has me puzzled, I will admit." Lyle said.

"It's because you misunderstand me, Lyle. You misunderstand my guild."

"Oh I think I figured out your guild years ago. As for you… You're not nearly as complicated as you'd like to think. You're crafty, but you also give yourself too much credit. I'm not here about the Syndicate, I want to know about Erisa. She is the piece of the puzzle that I can't seem to place. She helped us trap and capture so many of your guild mates, only to turn on us."

Davrian's smile shrunk to an unsettling grin. Lyle couldn't tell if it was confidence or an act.

"Erisa," Davrian's voice was endearing. "Solving Erisa is solving the Syndicate."

"Then what do you have to say about her?"

"Oh do I have tales and promises for you Lyle—"

"And lies? More of those too?" Kit said.

"Not for you..." Davrian snapped to a more rigid demeanor. "If we are going to have this conversation you must agree to believe everything I tell you, Lyle."

Lyle laughed. "Oh alright. Easy enough. I don't sense anything wrong with that."

"Sure," Kit said. "We prefer to be vulnerable and have our trust abused."

Davrian narrowed his eyes. "Everything I've said, everything I've done has been to build your trust."

"Try me," Lyle said. "You share your 'tales and promises,' and leave me to decide on my own."

"Fine," Davrian reclined in his chair and propped his head with his hands. "First, you tell me about the Syndicate. What comes to mind when you hear of my guild?"

"Murderers, thieves, rapists—They've cut throats for pennies and sport, and robbed the helpless."

"Cowards," Kit added. "Unable to answer for their crimes."

"Agreed!" Davrian shouted. "A thousand times I agree! Before the Syndicate, the thieves and murderers, everyone you described, they're all the embodiment of unchecked evil. Like a pack of rats, they devour what they can at night, terrorizing the streets. They had a leader, but Guile lacked ambition. When I first came to Averlace I marveled at the potential of greatness, so

I took action. I rallied the most foul and corrupt and promised them a greater life. I dared them to find more to serve. I found sponsors to pay for jobs, corrupted guards and lawmen to turn their eyes. I even found men in the palace court and won over King Marrote himself. Within weeks the Syndicate was born. An entire network of like minds, working together to obtain a utopian kingdom."

"Your Greater Good?" Lyle said.

Davrian gave an empty laugh. "While I was forming my guild. I ran across a young lady. A daughter of the street… Erisa was a battered, angry girl. She had no vision for herself and settled for a life less than what she deserved."

"But you had a vision for her?" Lyle folded his arms. His face reddened.

"That I did. At the height of the guild's prominence so too came it's opposition. It seemed as though every night I learned that more members abandoned the cause, were killed in a raid or fled the kingdom. I was losing members daily. The Syndicate demanded that I do something about the noble, Rhett Alderman, who rallied the kingdom against the guild, but I knew better. Though Alderman was a thorn in the guild's side, it was the young actors who were bleeding us out…"

Davrian shook his head and laughed. "You two spied on the Syndicate and lured them into Alderman's snares. I needed you to cooperate, so I sent Erisa to spy on you. I wanted to know your next move. I wanted to know your next setup."

"Yet still you lost more men to us," Lyle said.

"That I did… and a young woman too. I remember the night she fell in love with you Lyle."

"I bet it ate you alive," Kit said.

"You have no idea…"

"So how long did it take you to figure out you were still losing men even after you sent Erisa?"

"Immediately," Davrian said.

"Yet you did nothing?" Lyle scoffed. "You played along. Erisa would lie to you about the king's next move and your men would be captured or killed. You kept sending her, even though it was costing you more men?"

"The guild was still serving its purpose… Tell me, Lyle. Do you know what that was?"

"The Greater Good?" Kit said.

"And do you know what that was?"

Lyle cocked his head, unsure of his answer.

"Of course you don't know. No one has ever known save but one." Davrian said. "The guild had one purpose—To be destroyed. The potential I saw of this kingdom was not of the evil or its growing power. It was the heritage of its people. Averlace was a fertile field yearning for the teachings of Manaism to reap a harvest of good, peace and love. But years of abandoning Manaism had turned the fertile garden to a field of weeds. When love, peace and altruism are eliminated, evil will fill the void. That is what precisely happened to Averlace. Evil was unchecked. It had to be destroyed. I used the Syndicate to unite all of the monsters that plagued the land. Every thief had a name and home and I knew each and every one of them. The sponsors I speak of were wealthy and corrupt men within the Syndicate. The jobs I gave were jobs I created that pitted sponsor against sponsor. The guild was tearing itself apart, but it was easy enough to cover. The winners received the spoils and the losers were eliminated. As long as the richer were getting richer, they didn't mind.

"I knew it wouldn't last, eventually an external force would have to finish off the guild. Thankfully, I had you two, Alderman, Bruan and the others. By the time the Syndicate and remaining sponsors tried to dispose of me, it was too late. They were already finished. The Itihasians arrived and I had the pleasure of having a hand in eliminating the last of the guild."

Lyle looked indifferent. He sat quiet. Kit knew Lyle was brooding. Davrian's story was convincing, but it lacked one detail. One hole in the story had yet to be filled, and Lyle didn't know how to ask for the details.

"But what about Erisa?" Kit said.

"Erisa is my greatest regret."

"Sorry to hear that," Lyle said.

"Truly," Davrian said. "When Erisa first came to me to join the Syndicate I denied her membership. It wasn't for her. She had anger in her, but there was good also. I watched her for days. The street is no home for a young lady... It is hell. It's a nightmare. A nightmare Erisa lived every night alone. I decided the only way to protect her was to claim her as my own."

"Claim her?"

"Let me finish!" Davrian said. "She stayed by my side, but I never touched her. She had food and shelter and a safe place to sleep at night, still it was no life for her. I used her to help set up more Syndicate for capture. Like I said before, that is how she met you Lyle. One night, her eyes told me she was in love. I acted angry, but I wanted to push her away and have her grow loyal to you. It seemed to work. She spent more time with you and the number of setups against the guild increased. Eventually she stopped coming back and I learned afterwards she was married. My heart was relieved, but then the unthinkable happened. She returned."

"And she never came back," Lyle said.

"And that's what happens to a young girl who believes she has no value, who believes that no one has ever loved her. They can't accept love. She refused you Lyle, not for any reason other than she believed the lie that she didn't deserve you."

"And you were all too happy to have her back." Lyle said.

"Lyle, I tried everything I could to lure her back to you."

Lyle thought back to the night on the balcony. Davrian pushed Erisa away. It was her choice to return to him.

"And the fire?" Lyle said.

"It was over for the Syndicate. I knew we were finished. I also knew she would follow me to the end. I broke her leg and left her to be rescued. The king's men were just behind."

"Instead she died in a prison," Lyle shouted. "Was that better!"

"A broken heart... Truly my deepest regret. I should have guided her more, but I was too caught up in the act I had to play out. I was the ruthless guild master of the Syndicate, set on destroying King Alderman and fighting for the Greater Good. I couldn't show sympathy."

"You said she was cursed," Lyle said. "What do you mean?"

"Cursed and angry... I should have poured wisdom in her; instead she cursed you with one of the medallions. If she couldn't have you, no one would. She cursed the next woman you kissed to die, unfortunately for Erisa, she died from your kiss.

"I..." Lyle shook his head. "Tales and promises... I—I wasn't expecting this..."

"There's more," Davrian said.

"I'm done," Lyle stood from his chair. "You're either a liar, a fool with a heart of gold, or a madman with the best intentions. Either way, I'm done," Lyle barked as he left.

Kit chased after Lyle, being sure to lock the door behind. Davrian never moved. The guild master looked at the remaining list of names and maps that littered his floor. Each name was marked off. Davrian rested his head on his pillow.

"The Syndicate is no more," he whispered to himself just as he had a hundred times before. A smile crept along his face, but then it faded. He rose and collected the maps and papers from his floor and wadded them all up. He threw the wad of paper to the corner of his cell.

"But was it worth the cost?" he whispered again.

He took a fresh sheet of paper and dipped his quill in the well. His work was far from over, but with the Syndicate gone he was closer to his goal than he had ever been before. He flattened out the paper on the stone floor and scratched out his next assignments.

Find the treasure

Unmask the Ebon Crow

Dethrone the King

CHAPTER TWENTY TWO

LOOMING DEATH, UNENDING PEACE

CHAPTER TWENTY-TWO

LOOMING DEATH, UNENDING PEACE

ILLIOTT RESTED HIS head in his hands. He held back a yawn as he read through a short stack of papers. Each sheet documented every improvement or extension made to the city sewers for the past century. Everything had to be read; blueprints and contractor quotes, even the council chamber minutes that approved the phases of building. Fadrien had retrieved the documents in the library archives, hoping they would offer clues to the hidden treasure.

The evening marked Illiott's second day without sleep. Illiott fought to stay awake, but the council's minutes weren't helping. The words and lines jumped out of turn, and he found himself reading each sentence twice.

"You should sleep," Fadrien said. The councilman took the top sheet from Illiott's pile. He pulled a chair up to Illiott's desk and started to read.

"No one else has that luxury," Illiott said.

"Captain Bruan forbids it?"

"No… it's just impossible under the ramparts. Like sleeping with someone breathing down your neck. Besides, I have work here that needs to be done."

"Just an hour," Fadrien said. "Even that could make a difference."

"You have a boring job," Illiott turned his paper over and laid it down. "Is this what you do every day, listen to old men argue about money and land?"

"It is, but being at the head of the table has its advantages. I just need to look like I'm paying attention. A nod here, another there; maybe a 'yes' or 'no' if necessary."

"I know you better. You're listening to every word."

"Maybe so, but it works well during class."

"You sleep during class?" Illiott eyes widened.

"It's so quiet in here when the students read. Then Nalinda will ask one of her long questions… She doesn't wait for me to wake up. It never fails she is halfway through her question before I realize she is talking to me. What can I do?" Fadrien smiled, "I nod my head and say 'yes,' 'no' or 'I'll think about it.'"

"What exactly am I looking for anyway?" Illiott rubbed his eyes and picked up another sheet.

"Anything about underground structures ordered to be cleared or built around."

"I've found nothing so far. These papers are eighty years old, roughly around twenty years since magic was outlawed. It's like they've already forgotten about the old city. It doesn't seem possible."

"It's amazing how quick people forget," Fadrien said.

"When did Averlace make the move from underground to above ground?"

"I'm not sure."

"It must be documented somewhere."

"It may have happened years before magic was outlawed. I doubt everything changed overnight. It was gradual."

"I try to imagine what it must have been like. Everyone practicing magic—Magic as powerful as what Bratheon and Freja have displayed. It's beyond me… But I find it even harder to believe our forefathers were willing to give it up."

"I've often wondered if they could see Averlace now, would they have still outlawed magic. Is this what they wanted?" Fadrien said.

"A kingdom unable to defend herself…" Illiott said.

Fadrien tapped his fingers on the desk as he thought. His eyes slanted to Illiott. "Freja told me you helped her send off Bratheon."

"I did."

"I hope you meant well."

"I did."

"You weren't too eager to have him gone?"

Illiott blushed and turned away. "I'm ashamed. I regret my words and actions. He came to help, and I was threatened by his skill."

"He has what you want," Fadrien said.

"Indeed. But I was reminded that it will all come with time… An old man reminded me of my selfishness." Illiott said with a smirk.

"An old man…" Fadrien looked indignant, but a smile soon followed. "You didn't trust Bratheon?"

"I just knew he was the Prince of Itihasia. I knew he was hiding it from us, that he was using us."

"Instead it was Davrian."

"Can you believe it?" Illiott said. "All this time."

"And you trust the guild master? You believe him?"

"I trust you… I'm sorry for doubting your judgment about Bratheon. I believe you are right about him."

Fadrien smiled. "I was worried about you. I didn't want to see your anger and jealously grow. But now I see patience and peace; I believe you are walking in the right direction and that soon your heart will be in a position to cast magic."

"I've had a good example to lead me," Illiott returned Fadrien's smile. "Thank you for not giving up on me."

"Giving up? I said I was worried, not despairing. I knew you would temper your emotions."

"They are still there," Illiott said. "I still feel my anger."

"They will always be there. That's why I said temper. You just have to desire the selfless path over anything else."

"There is something I don't understand," Illiott said.

"What's that?"

"You are so wise, slow to anger, quick to listen and patient. Why haven't you cast a spell yet?"

The old councilman folded his arms and stared in the distance. "I suppose I haven't tried."

"You haven't tried?"

"No reason to I suppose," Fadrien said.

"No reason? The Itihasians haven't given you a reason yet? Perhaps you should join me on the wall. I'm sure you'll see things differently."

"Perhaps, but then again I'm not on the wall. I've been where I've been needed. Just as you have been where you are needed."

"I don't understand."

"So far I've won all the battles that I've encountered. Love and compassion has sufficed."

"Then what are we doing here? If there is no need for magic?"

"I never said that. I said love and compassion have sufficed. I believe they always will. Never underestimate the power of the most humble acts of service. When you think of magic, you think of calling fire from the sky, dividing rivers and moving mountains, but can a small act of kindness not do the same?"

"I don't see how. That seems like nonsense to me."

"That is why you struggle Illiott. You don't believe. The other day, I was angry with you, but still I showed you love and compassion. I was patient with you. Did I move a mountain?"

"Not hardly."

"I disagree. You see a mountain has no will. It has size, strength and weight, but no will. If we wanted to move a mountain it may be tiresome and hard, but given enough time we could move it. But what about a man's heart? Man has a will. He may have no strength, but if he has a will that opposes me, I will never move him. He can only move himself."

"You're making little sense."

"Let's say a man robs me and forces me to walk with him; perhaps he is holding me ransom and wants the king to pay for my release. I could send fire from the sky to destroy him; did I remove the threat? Did I move the mountain that was between me and my freedom?"

"I want to say yes, but something tells me I would be wrong."

"Yes you would be. I removed the threat by killing him, but I never moved the mountain. I never changed the man's heart. But what if I noticed the man was hungry and gave him food. What if I gave him my robe? What if I decided to go as far as he wanted, serving him all along the way. Not because I fear him, but because I had compassion for him? Will that move the mountain? Will that change his heart?"

"It may."

"You're right; it may. I can't control the outcome, but I can play my part. In the end, I can choose to make strides towards killing a foe or making a new friend. Each has consequences. There is no telling what wonderful things may happen from sparing the man's life."

"What if you are forced to kill him?"

"A loving heart would do that as a last resort, and it would have to be a selfless act. Perhaps out of love for another. A wife and child to defend or return to, preserving the life of another—There could be hundreds of reasons, but trusting love and wisdom will help you make a decision if you are ever in that position."

"I'm in that position every day, Fadrien. I've no idea how many I've killed."

"Out of love for king and country, defending your fellow man? You must remember that the enemy brings destruction upon themselves. You can't carry guilt for destroying wickedness. It destroys itself."

"I just don't know if I can always tell the difference. It's hard when you are on the wall, or raiding the Syndicate, or in the presence of the man who murdered your family. Was attacking Sullion a mistake?"

"What do you think?"

Illiott said nothing. The anger and rage he felt the day he attacked Sullion resurfaced. Sullion deserved to die; he had crimes to pay for... Illiott then remembered the arrow he shot at Bruan. He almost killed Bruan, all because of a misunderstanding. Was he any different from Sullion? Did he deserve death?

"The king spared you," Fadrien said. "He could have thrown you away in prison for treason or had you killed, but he spared you. Now you serve him and serve him well."

"I don't know about that," Illiott said. "I've made mistakes since."

"And you and I will make more. The question is: are you satisfied with your mistakes, or do they motivate you to do better—Do they motivate you to change?"

Illiott slowly nodded.

"Did King Alderman move a mountain?"

"I don't know."

"I believe he did." Fadrien stood from the desk and took what was left of the stack of papers. "Remember that an act of love and mercy may change the course of a man's life for the better. Perhaps even a man like Sullion… I'll finish up here. You get some rest and think about what's been said."

Illiott didn't argue. He cleared his desk and laid down his head.

Fadrien moved the work to his own desk. He made short work of the papers. He glanced over to Illiott between each sheet. Illiott's eyes had dark bags underneath, but they were still open, lost in thought. By the time Fadrien finished Illiott was still awake. Fadrien left without saying a word. He blew out the candles, hoping Illiott would sleep.

With Fadrien gone Illiott raised his head and picked up a smoldering candle from his desk. The tip of the wick glowed. Illiott concentrated on the small ember, willing for it to catch flame again. Nothing.

Illiott directed his focus. He thought of Sullion and the day his parents were murdered. Did Sullion deserve forgiveness? Would he have changed had Illiott forgave him instead of attacked?

Illiott remembered the night he sat with the Elite at the Kettle and Dove, each man receiving the king's blessings. Illiott was named Headmaster of the new School of Manasim and better yet, pardoned for his treasonous act against the throne. Did he deserve the king's forgiveness? He thought of last night, killing Syndicate during the raid. His heart and mind jumped from one emotion to the other, conflicted in deciding between right and wrong. Still he focused, yet the candle did nothing.

Illiott reimagined the night he attacked Sullion. Instead of reaching for chains, Illiott knelt beside Sullion. Rather than curses, Illiott told Sullion that he was forgiven. He tried to imagine Sullion's reaction, but he could only remember the murderer's laugh.

Illiott gently spun the candle between his fingers, waiting for a warm feeling to overcome the loss of his parents. Forgiving Sullion wouldn't have brought his parents back. Illiott pounded his fist against his desk. At that moment the candle erupted. A blinding light flashed in the school then disappeared. The room went dark. Illiott waved the smoke away and coughed.

Hot wax ran down his face and hands. What happened? What did he do to cause the fire? He tried to remember what he was thinking when he pounded his fists, but instead he started to laugh. It didn't matter what he was thinking. He finally cast his first spell. Illiott could hardly contain his excitement. His hours of study had paid off. All of the books and long sleepless hours of practice came to this moment. Too bad Fadrien wasn't around to see.

Illiott searched for the candle to try again. With enough practice he could show Fadrien, Eamon and the others. He patted around the disk to find the candle, but his hands landed in a puddle of melted wax. The candle was gone.

CHAPTER TWENTY THREE

THE CARRION KING

CHAPTER TWENTY-THREE

THE CARRION KING

ALDERMAN TAPPED on the glass panes of Fadrien's council chamber. In the distance he could see thousands of fires glittering in the Itihasian camp. An ominous sight. The edge of the camp moved closer to the walls. Inch by inch they would come, build shelters for protection against Averlace's arrows then dig under the curtain wall's corners. The southwest corner was the tallest and the heaviest. It would be the sappers' first target.

Despite the siege, Averlace was fortunate enough. The news Athan and Eamon made it past the enemy line brought much needed hope. Mandel tested the Numen River's water, it was still good; and Bruan's lieutenant, Barret, brought estimates that the city's rations could last another thirty days.

Averlace has a chance, Alderman thought. We can outlast the Itihasians. When enough have died at our walls... they will lose their resolve.

"Everyone's here, Your Majesty," Fadrien said.

Alderman snapped out of thought. Slowly his hand relinquished its grip from the window sill.

Lyle and Kit sat at a pedestal table. Students from the school of magic huddled around a burning brazier. Captain Bruan whispered with two of his officers, Ingran and Barret. Behind them Davrian sat on the floor near his own brazier, his feet shackled to its stand. Illiott leaned against a pillar, alone with a complacent smile.

"We're ready when you are." Fadrien said.

Alderman nodded. He looked back at his window.

"Are you well, Sire?"

"I am." Alderman narrowed his eyes then tore them from the enemy fires.

"Shall we begin? Bruan is eager to return to his men."

"Then I'll begin with you, Captain," Alderman said. He sat at the center table and sprawled his hands across a map of the city. "Last we spoke I asked for a contingency plan if the Marquis never arrives."

"Yes, Sire. Barret told you of the city's rations?" Bruan said.

"He did."

"I've since planned with my officers. We have thirty days of food for every home in Averlace. That is a conservative estimate accounting for three meals a day for every mouth. I am confident that we can outlast the enemy based on provisions alone. Our scouts say there are not enough supplies coming into the enemy camp. They'll starve out before us at that rate. However, we can't outlast their catapults and trebuchets. I propose we move all our non-combatants to the under city and prepare the keep as an inner cloister. There my men can fall back when the enemy takes the curtain."

"Every home must be stripped of supplies and food. Nothing can remain that could aid the enemy," Barret said.

Ingran pursed his lips. "The city would become a killing ground. We'll cover the city in pitch and oil. Once the enemy has settled and starts its attack on the keep, my archers will set the city aflame."

Alderman stared at his map. He said nothing.

"Surely it won't come to that?" Nalinda said. "We'd lose everything—"

Fadrien glared at his student and raised a finger over his lips.

Lurie held Nalinda's hand. She had seen the wounded soldiers and heard cries of battle from the walls. Lurie never doubted Averlace would prevail, but the view from the keep and Captain Bruan's contingency plan changed everything. Averlace's future was on a knife-edge.

Bruan's eyes met with Lurie's. "We need only to hold out. Once help arrives, the Itihasians will scatter. The Marquis will come."

"The Marquis," Davrian scoffed. "You don't know who've you placed your faith in... The man's grown soft. Hasn't lifted a sword since he inherited his father's march, nor has he rested his goblet."

"It is true that Eelton isn't the warrior like his fathers before him, but he hasn't forgotten his heritage, or the traditions of the Northern March," Alderman said. "They say he's the smartest man in the kingdom."

"Crafty maybe, but smarts? That's a different thing altogether," Davrian said.

"Spare us your idle annotations. I haven't the time nor the patience," Alderman said into his map.

"I'm only saying you're wise to have a 'contingency plan' in place. I'm surprised to see you so trusting of the Marquis, seeing how your experience of late has found him less than dependable."

"You underestimate the Marquis. His father was an honorable man. Eelton has served the kingdom well since his father passed."

"Do I really underestimate him?" Davrian said. "He sends an entire battalion of troops to help you finish the Syndicate. Apparently he didn't think it strange when none of his men returned. You sent word to him about General Picus, did you not? One would assume the kingdom is in peril if an entire battalion was destroyed within its own borders. Not Marquis Eelton. What does he do? I imagine he ordered another plate and held his goblet up for more wine. Any 'honorable' man would have assembled the Barons and marched the grand armies of the north to the kingdom's capital."

"We have no idea what is between us and the Northern March," Bruan said. "Anything could have happened to our runners."

"Yet you hold out that Athan and Eamon will make it through?" Davrian glared at Nalinda. "Like I said, it's best to have other plans, but I agree with the lady here. Burning our homes sounds a bit ludicrous."

"Are you proposing an alternative?" Fadrien said.

"I doubt Athan and Eamon are prepared to deal with the Marquis. Few men know how."

"And you do?" Alderman said.

Davrian gave an empty chuckle. "I've had past dealings with the Marquis, but what does it matter? I'm chained to this brazier. I won't be visiting the Northern March anytime soon."

"If you are making a point I suggest you get to it," Alderman said.

"I understand Bruan's reasoning for his plan. The Itihasians would lose many to the fire and there is a good chance their siege weapons will be destroyed. Hiding your women and children in the under city, however, is dangerous. It too is a killing ground. They will be lost in the labyrinth of twists and turns or caught in an old manaist trap. I suggest the library. It is safe behind the inner cloister and large enough to house them all."

"With a wood roof and hundreds of thousands of books inside—We would be one fire pot away from disaster," Lyle said.

"The library and keep are high enough. They won't have an angle to attack the vulnerable roof."

Bruan thumped the map with his finger. "They would from Carper's Vale. The hill rises just enough. Worst yet, I've ordered homes cleared to make room for our own catapults for the city's defense. The grounds are already prepared for them. If they take the city they will stage their siege from there. I am sure of it."

"Then we mustn't let that happen." Davrian said.

"Of course not," Bruan said. "Like the rest of the city, Carper's Vale will be covered in pitch. It will burn.

Alderman folded his arms. He didn't care for Bruan's plan, but there weren't any better options. He looked to Fadrien, "The under city is as dangerous as he claims?"

"It is." Fadrien nodded.

"And you still believe the hidden treasure lies there?"

"I am afraid so. Sealed and guarded by old spells," Fadrien said.

"Even if we were to find it," Illiott said, "we wouldn't be able to open it. We need either the king's medallion or the fourth lesser medallion."

"The Marquis'?" Alderman said. "I assume you have no idea where to find either one."

"No," Fadrien lowered his head.

A raspy cough came from Davrian's corner. Alderman sighed. "I suppose you know?"

"I have a story." Davrian's eyes cut to Lyle. "I began it earlier, but was unable to finish."

"Lyle told me your story about the Syndicate," Alderman said.

"And do you believe me?" Davrian said.

Alderman leaned his chair with an incredulous laugh. "I'll let your story speak for itself."

Davrian clapped and rubbed his hands. "What a tantalizing invitation… You see, I too had a medallion. It belonged to the Marquis. It was a family heirloom passed down through the generations. I remember the first time I saw it. The Marquis wore it with such pride. It dangled from the outside of his shirt."

"You had to steal it," Kit said.

"I did," Davrian smiled. "But it may not appear as you think. Years ago I was always on the hunt for work to help fund the Syndicate. My list of employers, or sponsors, grew week by week. Eventually I had the luxury of declining jobs that didn't strike my fancy. Some were too risky, sometimes I just didn't like the employer. One day I was offered such a job. It had trouble written all over it, and the foreigner that contacted me couldn't be trusted. His name was Sullion."

"The foreigner Owin executed?" Lyle said. "What did he want?"

"He said his master was interested in collecting five magical medallions. He wanted the Syndicate to find them. Seemed easy enough at first, until I learned that two of the targets included the Marquis and the King. There was another stipulation to the job; I'd have to induct Sullion into the guild… I declined. As we parted Sullion told me that if I changed my mind I could find him in the Northern March.

"Several months passed without giving Sullion's proposal another thought, until I was contacted by one of the guild's most trusted sponsors, Gredulous. Gredulous wanted to hire the guild to collect the same five medallions. I realized then there must have been more to these medallions. I did a little digging and learned Gredulous was collecting them for the Itihasians. The old manaist himself already had two of the medallions. Turns out his family came from the line of masters. His great, great grandfather held the chair of Master in the Arbiter's Conclave when Manaism was outlawed. The medallion stayed in his family ever since. The second medallion Gredulous bought for his wife at an auction, when such trinkets were quite a commodity. Gredulous, being a manaist himself, told me the history of the medallions. That's when I was able to add it all up. The Itihasians were interested in collecting all of the medallions to open the hidden treasure buried deep beneath Averlace.

"I contacted Sullion. We met at the Northern March and I accepted the job, unbeknownst to Gredulous. Reluctantly, I enlisted Sullion in the Syndicate. He was there just to keep tabs on the guild's progress.

"I remembered the Marquis' medallion. I took the next several weeks befriending him and working my way in the inner circle of nobles he entertained. When the time was right, I stole his medallion. I never told Gredulous I had the Marquis's medallion. That made three medallions total between the two of us. We lacked the King's and the Grand Arbiter's.

"There isn't much good I can say about Sullion, except that maybe he was skilled in gathering information. Within three weeks of moving to Averlace he learned of a practicing manaist who had a medallion. He told me where the man and his family lived and requested that he be given a team to steal the medallion. I refused. I didn't want anyone in the guild other than myself taking possession of the medallions; besides, I knew Sullion would use violence to take it. Turned out I was right."

"You're talking about my family?" Illiott said.

"I am," Davrian said, his voice stoic. "I planned on going to steal the medallion myself, but Sullion beat me to it. He never found the medallion, but he killed the man who owned it and his wife. I am sorry."

Illiott said nothing. He folded his arms and stared at a nearby brazier.

"I was infuriated," Davrian said. "I kicked Sullion out of the guild and ordered Guile to dispose of him. Unfortunately, Guile was already planning on supplanting me. With Sullion's help, the two were able to set me up, and I was captured by the virtuous *Bear of Arrata*." Davrian smirked at King Alderman. "Shortly afterwards I was sent to Davrian's Tomb to wait for my trial. The rest of the story should be quite familiar to you."

"Where is the Marquis' medallion now?" Lyle said.

"In the Itihasian camp, along with my sword. Taken from me when I was captured at Havenwood."

"And the king's?"

"I'm not sure," Davrian looked to Alderman.

Alderman drummed his fingers against the table. "Say we find the king's medallion, what would you have me do?"

"Then I'd say it's time to search for the treasure." Davrian said.

"Then what? Open it?" Alderman said. "Open the vault hiding the weapons Averlace buried more than a hundred years ago?"

"If you want any hope of defending your kingdom."

"And if we fail? What if Kvrual gains access to the treasure we opened?" Alderman looked to Fadrien. "Perhaps it's best to keep it hidden and locked away."

"Kvrual has come all this way. If he takes the city, he'll leave no stone unturned until he finds the manaist treasure," Davrian said. "He isn't leaving without it."

"Our ancestors believed Manaism would destroy Averlace. That's why they buried it. Even if it were to save us from our enemies, would we destroy ourselves, just as our ancestors feared?" Alderman said.

"Don't you see, Your Majesty? That is what I have desired," Davrian held out his cuffed hands, imploring the king. "Such power in corrupt hands will destroy. Averlace has forgotten its heritage. I'm not talking about magic itself, but magic's very essence—Selflessness. It's without magic that Averlace corrupted itself. People did away with the standard that kept them selfless and moral. Ever since Manaism was banished crime has been on the rise. The kingdom almost destroyed itself without Manaism." Davrian shifted closer to the edge of his chair. "That was the purpose of my Syndicate—Band together the criminals, then eliminate them, giving Averlace a clean slate to start anew. Fertile soil for the teachings of Manaism to grow and ripen. Now all we need is Manaism itself. The hidden vault is the answer. With it we'll not only prevail over the Itihasians, but we can foster a future of White Magic. A kingdom where selflessness is celebrated and altruism praised. That, Your Majesty, is the Greater Good I've wanted for Averlace."

"It's not that simple," Lyle said. "There's more to the story."

Davrian held out his hands. "I'm an open book."

"Why try to assassinate the king?" Lyle said.

"That was Guile's doing," Davrian said. "I accepted responsibility because I still had a role to play—I was the evil guild master doing what he could to stop Alderman."

"Then what about the trial? You obviously knew of Womack's attempt to murder Queen Valice and Prince Vance."

"Ransom," Davrian said. "Womack was there to kidnap. I wanted them as ransom for my own release and for King Alderman to step down."

"Why have Alderman step down?"

"Because I knew of the coming Itihasian invasion. That was the whole purpose of putting a puppet king on the throne. I wanted to prepare the kingdom for war without prematurely provoking the Itihasians to attack. And I wanted to find the King's Medallion."

"That is why the Itihasians are here now. Kvrual believed Averlace had grown weak. He didn't fear you, Your Majesty. Itihasia was hoping for more time to find all of the medallions and then take the treasure with more subtle measures, more than likely with the guild's help. They believed with the Syndicate so strong, Averlace wasn't in a position to defend herself. But as the guild fell apart and as Alderman grew in power, Kvrual realized he had to act. Kvrual attacked much sooner than he wanted."

"Which explains why Kvrual wanted you," Lyle said. "He wasn't getting any more medallions, and Averlace was only getting stronger."

Davrian nodded.

"Where does the Ebon Crow fit in with all of this?" Lyle said. "He's the last piece on the board to move."

Davrian laughed. "The Ebon Crow isn't a piece to the game. He's the master. We're the pieces. I'm the queen, I guess you could say."

"Enough of the analogies," Bruan said. "I say we look for the vault, but I fear the Ebon Crow is the one who wants the treasure more than all."

"Helping ourselves is helping him," Kit said.

"I agree," Alderman said as he eyed Davrian. "Can the school verify all Davrian has claimed about the medallions?"

Fadrien and his students nodded. "Yes, we have material that can back up his claims."

Alderman shifted in his chair and looked away from his men. "Then take the guild master as a guide and search for the vault. See to it, Fadrien. Once found I'll decide what needs to be done."

"As you wish," Fadrien said as he stacked his papers neatly against the table. He watched the king loom over the map. Alderman wasn't one to be indecisive.

"Decide?" Davrian said, his voice skeptical. "Are you not convinced? The treasure is Averlace's only hope."

"I've made myself quite clear about my reservations, guild master. So long as I'm king, I'll see to it that the power of the treasure is respected. It was buried and hidden for a reason."

Davrian's neck strained. "I've made myself clear as well. Kvrual isn't leaving without it. You may be king, but without the treasure you will be nothing but a carrion king, ruling over a ruined city of corpses."

Alderman pushed himself from the table. He fixed his eyes on Davrian. "Bruan, prepare the city to fall back to the keep. Every soldier, woman and child—Every dog must be ready to retreat at a moment's notice."

"Absolutely, Your Majesty."

Alderman mindlessly rasped the table with his knuckles. "That will be all," he said.

Lyle observed the men as they dismissed. Fadrien extended his gait, excited about the king's permission to find the vault. Bruan held his shoulders back and walked as if a ram rod supported his back, yet he wore a subtle glower and stared at the map as he left. The captain's faith was in the treasure, not his battle plan. Illiott too seemed dismayed. His eyes shifted between Alderman and Fadrien with a nervous twitch, his thumb circled his medallion. Alderman sat straight-faced. Was he afraid? Often Alderman would clasp his hammer when angry, pace in circles when stressed, but the king's lifeless stare was new. Even Davrian was in rare form. Rather than his characteristic confident smug, he bit at the corners of his lips. Perhaps frustrated?

Lyle left without a word, leaving Alderman alone with his map. Alderman shuffled on his feet and walked to the window, relieved to have the room to himself. The enemy fires still flickered in the distance.

All for a hidden treasure...

CHAPTER TWENTY FOUR
WRITING A STORY

CHAPTER TWENTY-FOUR

WRITING A STORY

LYLE AND KIT stared at the canopy of stars overhead. Kit laid across half a cord of firewood. Lyle stood with his head cocked back trying to focus on the sky alone. They'd been stopped on their way home by two foremen collecting firewood to heat the tar and pitch for the city defenses.

Any that could be spared, one had said.

Splitting wood wasn't how Lyle hoped to spend the evening, but it had to be done. Kit had only a cord of wood left to his home. With Josie's parents staying inside, a small fire was needed at all times in the kitchen hearth. They offered to split a rick of wood if the men carried it off themselves.

Lyle and Kit made short work of it. As arranged, two soldiers came to collect the wood. They looked haggard and withered. It concerned Lyle. With Davrian at the foremost of his thoughts, Lyle had little time to think of the Itihasians and the fight at the wall.

"There is something I want to talk to you about," Lyle said. He turned his head to look for the girls. They were inside. "It must stay between the two of us. Not a word to anyone, do you understand?"

"Don't worry, you're too boring to repeat."

"Kit, I'm serious."

"What is it?"

"You must promise me you won't say a word of it to anyone."

"Lyle," Kit smiled. "I haven't seen you like this for some time. This might actually be good."

"Kit."

"What if I guess it? Do I have to keep it a secret then?"

Lyle's eyes straightened into a glower.

"Oh my!" Kit said. "You looked for the girls didn't you? Before you asked—It's Adeline, isn't it? You love her!"

"Forget it," Lyle waved Kit off.

"What is it?" Kit said.

"The king. I wanted to ask you about the king."

"Boring… just like I said."

Lyle lifted his hands, defeated. "Why is everything a game with you?"

"Because if I pretend it's all a game, I can solve it. There's a trick to every game. Once you figure it out, you can win."

"I have a serious question about the king. I need you to be…"

"Not myself."

"Serious, just for a moment."

"You think the king is hiding something?"

Lyle nodded. "You too?"

"I hadn't, at least I didn't want to think."

"Well let's pretend that he is," Lyle said. "What would he be hiding?"

"By heaven… I don't know. It could be anything. I am not sure this is safe to speculate, Lyle."

"Davrian said something tonight. I haven't been able to get it out of my head."

"The chess game reference?" Kit said.

"You caught it too?"

"Davrian referred to himself as the queen."

Lyle held his chin. "He also referred to Alderman as a carrion king."

"Nothing left but ruins and corpses," Kit said.

"Like a carrion crow," Lyle said.

"You think Davrian referenced the Ebon Crow? You think Alderman is the Ebon Crow?"

"I think Davrian at least believes Alderman is the Crow... So let's pretend that Alderman is, indeed, the Ebon Crow. What would he be hiding and why?"

"He'd be waiting for someone else to make a very specific move..." Kit drummed his fingers on his lap. "I shouldn't have doubted you. This is more interesting than I thought. Do you think Alderman already has the King's Medallion?"

"It's possible."

"Then why not come out with it and help Fadrien find the hidden vault?"

"Too risky?" Lyle said. "Alderman may be waiting on the school to find it first, then he will open it. If everyone knows he has the medallion, it would be harder for him to keep it safe."

"Davrian seems confident the Ebon Crow will find a way to release him when all is said and done. That makes more sense now assuming the king is the Ebon Crow," Kit said.

"I agree."

"So what do we do? Do we confront him? Does this change anything?"

"We do know that the Ebon Crow was a sponsor of the Syndicate. What we don't know is what role he played in the

Syndicate. Davrian claims he and one other are the only ones to have known the guild's true purpose... which supposedly was to cleanse the kingdom of its crime. As an investor I doubt the Ebon Crow would have supported the guild had he known it was doomed for failure. If that's the case, we must assume the Ebon Crow has dark intentions. Or at least no moral compass."

"So what are you saying?" Kit said.

"I'm afraid the king may not be who we think he is."

"I'll say it again, Lyle. This is a dangerous speculation."

"Now you know why I wanted to you keep this just between us?"

"Yeah... But allow me to flip the coin and discuss the obverse. We can't forget what we've learned in the past. We must trust one another."

"I believe it was said that we must trust one another if we were to overcome our fear and doubt. Which I agree, but those were the king's own words." Lyle leaned forward. "What if the king has primed us for this precise moment; building our trust and indoctrinating us to remain steadfast when the evidence stacks against him?"

"You're playing a dangerous game."

"I thought you liked games?"

Kit chortled through his nose. "This is different...so what do we do?"

"Nothing for now. We look for more evidence before we act. We must try to understand the king's motives if he is indeed the Ebon Crow."

"I'd like to learn more of our little Prince of Itihasia too... Davrian's been swept under the rug. Regardless of who the Crow really is, there is an obviously strong connection between him and the Itihasian prince."

"Fadrien is leaving first thing in the morning to search for the vault. I suggest we accompany him, I want to keep a close eye on Davrian."

Kit looked to Lyle. "Speaking of Davrian—"

"I know what you are going to ask… Don't."

"So you believe him? You think he created the Syndicate just to destroy it?"

"I do."

"So Erisa—"

"I said not to say it."

Kit shrugged his shoulders and sat on the ground. Lyle grabbed the woodpile axe and ran his thumb across its edge. The silence grated Kit's nerves.

Kit let out a dramatic sigh. "It's a beautiful night."

"I hate idle talk," Lyle said.

"Give me a second," Kit raised his hand. "It's called a segue… You've really lost your artistic flare as of late."

Lyle rolled his eyes and struck the chopping block with his axe, leaving it in place. "You were saying?"

"There is something I want to talk to you about," Kit said. He turned his head side to side. "It must stay between the two of us. Not a word to anyone, do you understand?"

Lyle tried to hold back a smile, but he couldn't. He knew when he was being imitated. "I guess my next line is to say, 'I won't share anything, you're too boring.'"

"Oh come on," Kit said.

"What is it?"

"Promise," Kit crossed his chest with his finger.

"I promise."

"Would it be a mistake to propose to Josie? Right now? During all of this?"

Lyle's eyes squinted from a serene smile. "Did I hear you right?"

Kit nodded.

"I can't think of a better time."

"Really? You're not telling me what I want to hear? I'm drawn to the romantic and dramatic... For once I'm interested in the practicality of it all."

"Ah, practicality. So you ask me?" Lyle laughed.

"Well, you are my brother... And a bit pragmatic."

"That I am, on both counts... Honestly Kit, you do have to be practical and realistic in your marriage, but it goes hand-in-hand with the romance... I doubt you'll have a hard time remembering that. You're not like I," Lyle said. "You and Josie have a wonderful relationship. Erisa and me... We seemed perfect, but I knew she was troubled. Looking back, I'm not sure I tried hard enough to reach her. Davrian said she believed she could never be loved... Yet it's my love that killed her. It's all my fault."

Kit lowered his head.

"All that to say, don't let the romance die." Lyle stood up and looked to Kit, who sat pensive. Lyle sighed, "I'm sorry, Kit."

"Sorry? For what?"

"Making the moment about me. I apologize. I'm thrilled for you and Josie."

Kit puffed out his cheeks. "It's alright. I am thrilled too," he chuckled.

"No, I shouldn't have been so—"

"Lyle, it's fine."

Lyle shook his head and sighed. "So when are you going to ask?"

"That's the thing," Kit said. "She's a good girl. Loyal, hard working, creative and affable. She deserves more. I want to give it to her, but I don't see how that's possible... not with Averlace..."

"What do you mean?"

"Averlace isn't long for this world," Kit said. "I've been thinking. Athan and Eamon escaped, I believe we can do the same."

"They also had a manaist with them. I haven't seen Josie summoning storm clouds out of thin air."

Kit rubbed the back of his head. "You think I'm a coward?"

"No. I think you're in love and you want to protect the girl holding your heart."

"What should I do?"

"Averlace is home, Kit. Even if it were to fall, where would you two go?"

"Port Camden?"

"Then where? I doubt the Itihasians will stop with Averlace, especially if they acquire the treasure."

"I suppose not."

"You are invaluable, Kit. The king needs you. I need you. Josie won't leave her parents or Adeline."

"No," Kit looked away. "No, you're right."

"The best thing you can do for her is stay here and help us find the vault."

"Lyle, I am no fighter... What good am I once the walls are breeched?"

"More reason to stay with us," Lyle laughed. "Though I think a wedding might do this kingdom some good."

"Ah, a practical incentive for the good of the kingdom. Is this keeping the romance alive?"

"I'd say it's going hand in hand," Lyle said. "I doubt I could write a more romantic scene—Two hearts determined to begin their lives together though their home lays under siege. Their wedding day raises the morale of the people and with new vigor the kingdom defeats the wicked invaders."

"Sounds more romantic when you don't have to live it."

"On the contrary, I think it makes it all the more beautiful," Lyle said.

Kit smiled as if lost in a daydream. Lyle hadn't spoken like that in years.

"And where do you fit in this fairytale?" Kit said. "Does the epilogue tell of a bitter and depressed brother, or does it say that he too was inspired to pursue love again?"

"That depends on the villain." Lyle said.

"Ah, the villain," Kit said. "Behind every great protagonist lurks a great villain in the shadows. I doubt I could write a better story. Your nemesis turns out to be a powerful ally. The hero needs only to forgive and together the two may possibly save the kingdom, perhaps even themselves."

"Now that does sound like a fairytale. One much easier to believe when you're not living it."

"On the contrary," Kit said with an antagonizing smirk.

"Davrian may not be who we once thought he was, but I still hold him responsible for Erisa's death. He may have had the best intentions, but he still hurt a lot of people. When this is over, I will make sure he pays."

"It won't bring her back."

"No, but…"

"But what?" Kit folded his arms

Lyle shook his head. "Nothing."

"Erisa believed no one could love her. It was nonsense, was it not?"

Lyle said nothing. He slowly nodded.

"And now you believe you could never love anyone else—"

"Enough, Kit."

"That is nonsense as well, is it not?"

"What do you know about this?" Lyle shouted.

Kit lowered his head. Never had Lyle raised his voice at him.

"You can't possibly imagine," Lyle said. "Try loving someone else now as you fawn over Josie, planning your future wedding. Death makes no difference. She may be gone, but my love for her remains. Love again," Lyle scoffed. "I can't possibly do that to Erisa. It would only confirm what she died believing."

Kit opened his mouth to speak, but decided against it. He reached for his front door. "Thank you for your blessing," he said as he slammed it behind him.

Lyle rose to go after Kit. Instead he dropped to the ground. He didn't know why he had lashed out. Kit had only tried to help. He leaned against the woodpile. *Give him some time*, he thought.

The door opened again. Lyle expected Kit, but it was Adeline. He'd forgotten she was inside. She held her apron to her eyes and ran from the door, tears streaming down her face.

CHAPTER TWENTY FIVE

ANXIOUS HEARTS

CHAPTER TWENTY-FIVE

ANXIOUS HEARTS

LURIE AND FREJA watched as Mandel shook a vial in the air. He held it still and studied its swirling contents.

Lurie could barely hear him counting down. "It should stay clear, right?" she said.

"Yes," Mandel said as he tried to count.

"What are you testing for?"

"Shh," Mandel finished counting. He tapped the glass a few times. "I'm testing for poison."

"I know that," Lurie said. "But what exactly?"

"The water turns an amber color if there's a high level of necrotic material in the water. Dumping the dead in the water is one way to poison it."

"Are there others?"

"Yes, but I don't know how to test for them, other than have you taste it."

"Not funny," Lurie said.

Mandel raised an eyebrow. "I wasn't trying to be. I'd do it myself, but when you get to my age, taste and smell are nothing but memories."

"You need me to taste it?"

The old physician nodded. He handed her another vial.

Lurie took it and gave it a skeptical glance. "Is there a particular taste I'm looking for?"

"Anything other than water. A strong, rancid taste I suppose. Like meat gone bad."

Lurie's stomach churned. She held the vial up. Now wasn't the time for fear. Men watched the walls and fought off invaders day and night. The least she could do was taste the water for poison.

"It's just water," she said, staring down the vial, refusing any fear to win over.

Freja held her breath as she watched Lurie lean her head back then down the vial.

Mandel's eyes widened as he waited. "What does it taste like?"

Lurie closed her eyes and savored the taste. "I don't taste anything different."

"Oh no."

Lurie cracked her eyes. To her horror Mandel held up an amber vial.

"The water," he said. "It's turned color."

Lurie gasped and covered her mouth. She did the first thing that came to mind and started spitting to the ground. She reached in the back of her mouth with her finger, but stopped when the old physician started to cackle.

"Funny girl," he said. "He uncorked the amber vial and swallowed the water himself. "It's supposed to change blue if poisoned."

"You..." Lurie's mouth hung open. "I believed you!"

Freja's cheeks raised and reddened into a conspicuous smile.

Mandel bit his tongue as he held back a laugh. He poured the rest of his vials and test water to the ground. "It is safe to drink."

"But your water wasn't amber until after I drank it. How did you know it was safe?"

"If poisoned, the water turns blue immediately after adding the solvent."

"I've never known you to be a jokester."

"I've got to keep you young ones guessing," Mandel said. "You were so brave. Didn't even give it another thought. I'm proud."

"Here I thought I was doing Averlace a great service. Nope, just humoring you."

"I apologize, but you must admit, it made for a good laugh."

Lurie shot him an incriminating glare as she collected his test kit. "How likely is it that they poison the river?"

"The Numen is a large river and flows quite steadily. It would be quite an undertaking, and if they plan on taking the city I doubt it would be in their own interest. Still, I'll continue to check it twice a day just to be safe."

"Twice a day? Doesn't that seem a bit excessive?" Lurie said.

"To poison the Numen, they would have to spoil the water south of the dam, not even a mere two miles from here. It would travel quickly to us."

"I could help you test. No need for you making two trips each day." She stuffed a vial and packet of solvent in her pocket. "Why only south of the dam?"

Mandel closed his eyes and rocked his head back. Lurie couldn't tell if he tired of standing in the river, or answering her questions.

314 | THE KING'S ELITE & The Prince of Itihasia

"Because," he said, "if the enemy were to poison the river anywhere north of the dam, they would poison the reservoir which serves as their own source of water... This city," Mandel shook his head, "it's a perfect target. Thin, low walls, surrounded by open fields, built on a modest hill—The Itihasians will learn our weaknesses and will soon exploit them."

Freja stood straight and stretched out her back from hunching over the river bank. She took a deep breath and savored the morning's brisk air, doing her best to ignore Mandel's pessimism. The fires from the last attack had died down. The only smoke in the air came from chimney stacks, baker's ovens and smithy's shops. Without looking over the walls one could imagine all was as it should be, but Mandel was right.

"It's been quiet too long," Freja said. "I'm afraid something big is about to happen."

Mandel stared down the river to the city's southern wall. "I am too, dear. I'll be honest. Don't just fear that something bad is coming. You must plan on it. It's just a matter of time; else they would have left by now."

"I've been meaning to tell you," Lurie said, hoping to change the subject, "Fadrien requested that I go with him to search under the city."

"For the treasure?"

Lurie nodded.

"I need you here. I can't possibly tend the wounded on my own."

"What if I were to stay in her place?" Freja said.

Mandel sighed. "I was hoping you would stay with me, but it sounds as though Fadrien could use your help below as well.

If only you could be in two places at one time..." He eyed her suspiciously. "Or do you have another surprise for us?"

"No," Freja laughed. "That's impossible." She offered her hand for the old physician. Together they stepped lightly out of the river's marshy bank. "I think it's best for me to stay with you. There is little I know about the hidden treasure. I will be more useful here helping you with the wounded. And there is Bratheon. I want to be here when he returns."

"So be it," Mandel said. He turned to Lurie. "When do you leave?"

"Noon," Lurie said.

"Fadrien tells me it's dangerous below the city."

"It is, but I'll be with good company."

Mandel nodded, but his brow furrowed. "You are bright and resourceful. Your gifts will serve you well. I'll miss them until you return."

"Freja will do more for you than I ever could. You won't even notice I'm gone."

"I doubt that," he said.

"You have a calming presence," Freja said to Lurie, thinking back to the night they first met. It was Lurie who had encouraged and calmed her while Bratheon barely held on to life. "You have a sweet and gentle spirit. It heals the wounded as well as any medicine or spell."

Horns blasted from the west wall, startling a flock of birds. The king's green standard rose above the barbican. Each wall returned the call with their own blasts.

"They're calling for the king's cavalry," Mandel said. He turned to Lurie. "You best hurry along and find Fadrien. You may need to leave sooner than planned."

Lurie and Freja helped Mandel walk up the river's bank. Before crossing they yielded the bridge to a small troop of soldiers. Bruan was with them. Lurie waved to him as the men rode toward the king's rising standard. She wished she had a medallion on hand to bless the captain, whether it was keen senses, courage, strength or leadership. She closed her eyes and concentrated on Bruan.

"He'll be fine." Freja said, reaching for Lurie's hand.

"I'm sure your brother is well too," Lurie said.

"Take cover!" Mandel shouted. He grabbed both girls and pushed them towards the bridge.

Lurie froze with her mouth gapping, staring at the sky. She couldn't believe her eyes. Mandel grabbed her arm again and tugged on her. They stumbled to the ground and rolled underneath the bridge.

*   *   *

"They're still outside!" Josie yelled, but Kit couldn't understand.

"They're outside!" Josie tried again, pointing at the window.

Splinters and straw fell from the ceiling as hundreds of arrows shredded Kit's thatched roof. An arrow ripped through. It landed with a thud on the kitchen table. Kit looked outside as thousands upon thousands of arrows fell from the western sky.

"Everyone's outside," Josie screamed. She tried to break free, but Kit held her under the table.

Razor-tip points broke through the ceiling. The joists and beams quaked and moaned as the arrows hammered overhead. Josie cried as she reached for the door. Kit held a pot over her head and waited for the pummeling to die down. A few eternal seconds passed and the storm of arrows ended. Kit and Josie listened, afraid to move from safety. More stray shafts rattled outside, bouncing against the cobblestone and down the roof.

"Let me go!"

"Not until it stops."

"They may need us."

Kit released her; not because of the silence, but the smoke.

"Hurry!" He said. "Get to your parents!"

Gray clouds seeped through the thatch. Kit couldn't believe it held as well as it did. If he was fast enough, he could stop the fire from spreading. He grabbed a bucket and ran for an outside vat. Lyle stopped him at the door.

"Back inside!" Lyle said.

"The roof's burning," Kit tried to push by.

"Back inside." Lyle shoved Kit to the ground. He held the door open and Adeline rushed in.

"Bring your parents down," he ordered Adeline. "Is there anything to fight the fire?"

"That's why I need out."

"They are waiting for everyone to come outside. There'll be more!" Lyle said.

"Or burn alive?" Kit said. He squeezed past Lyle and ran to a nearby trough.

Rather than fight him, Lyle grabbed blankets from Kit's bed. He ran out with his eyes on the sky.

Any moment more will come.

Lyle plunged the blankets into the trough. Kit tossed his bucket onto the smoldering roof then bolted back. Before he made it to the water he could hear the scream of tens of thousands of arrows whistling and slicing through the air.

"Run," Lyle held the door open for Kit.

Arrows struck the ground all around. Water sloshed out of his bucket as he ran and he ducked his head. Kit made it in with a half-empty bucket. He threw it at the ceiling. Sparks and embers fell with the splinters and straw as the roof took another beating.

Josie and Adeline led their parents, Caren and Esra, down the steps and hid them under the stairs. Lyle batted at the flames with a wet blanket. The ceiling started to bend and the beams cracked as bit by bit chipped away.

Knowing it was lost, Lyle pulled Kit away from the fire. They joined Josie and her family. Together they all watched as a portion of the roof collapsed. Smoke and debris filled the house. Kit hunched over Josie's head while Lyle continued to bat the smoke away with his blanket. By the time the arrows stopped, the smoke cleared away. Lyle could see the extent of the damage. Though Kit's roof collapsed it had also smothered the fire.

Lyle crawled from the steps. He pulled an arrow out of the floorboard. "These arrows are different than before. Their shafts are longer and hollow, designed for tearing through flesh."

"You were right," Kit said. "They waited for people to leave their shelter."

"Will they attack again?" Adeline said.

"They will," Lyle said, "but I doubt soon."

Josie helped her mother up. Esra coughed on the lingering smoke. Her chest heaved, trying to catch a full breath. "Help," Josie said. Adeline rushed to her side.

Esra's lips turned blue. Her mouth opened and closed with empty gasps.

"No, No," Josie cried. "What is wrong with her?"

Kit brought a ladle of water. He brought it to Esra's mouth, but she turned away. Lyle ripped part of his wet blanket and laid it over her face.

"She need's air," he said.

Kit helped him carry her outside. The air wasn't much clearer, but it helped. Caren hobbled to his wife's side and held her hand. Tears streamed down his face. With each breath she struggled less and less. At first Josie thought it was being outside, but then she realized, her mother was dying.

Adeline moved the rag from her mother's face. Esra lacked the strength to speak or hold her daughters, but her eyes told of her love. They held a placid gaze. Caren nuzzled his head next to hers and kissed her one last time.

Lyle couldn't bare to watch. Caren's sobs broke his heart. Josie wept on her father's shoulders. Kit sat behind her, rubbing her back, her tender heart broken. Adeline was silent. She held her mother's hand up to her lips, kissing it over and over. This was the second time poor Adeline's heart was broken today, Lyle reminded himself.

More cries wailed in the smoky air. Thousands of arrows poked and jutted all the homes from the Artisan District to Manadon Square. Kit had read of armies so vast that their arrows could blot out the sun. He never thought it possible, but the Itihasians gave him reason to believe it could be done.

"Averlace doesn't have any time," Kit whispered to Lyle.

"No," Lyle said. He looked to Adeline as she held on to her mother. Her world was falling apart. Could he save it?

Lyle knelt beside Adeline and reached for Esra's hand. Adeline buried her face in his shoulder and wept.

Kit and Lyle's eyes met. Each knowing the other's thoughts.

The vault must be found.

CHAPTER TWENTY SIX

THE NORTHERN MARCH

CHAPTER TWENTY-SIX

THE NORTHERN MARCH

EAMON ROSE with a startle. He jabbed at the night with his knife, shouting unintelligibly. A man grabbed Eamon's wrist and forced the weapon down.

Eamon struggled for control of the knife. He cried out again and shifted to his side, trying to break away.

"Eamon. Eamon," Athan said as he muffled his brother's mouth. "Quiet; you're alright. It's alright."

The flickering campfire revealed Eamon's attacker. With an exasperated gasp Eamon released the knife. "I'm sorry," he said between breaths.

"It's your watch," Athan said. "If you can't stay awake then wake one of us up."

"It wasn't long I swear it," Eamon said, his heart still racing. "I can't sleep out here. Not after the other night."

"Everything alright?" Bratheon said; his head rose above the fire.

"Yes, fine," Eamon pulled his blanket over his shoulder and laid his head back down.

"There's no shame in that," Bratheon said. "No one thinks less of you."

"Though I for one would appreciate it if the watch wouldn't doze off," Athan said.

"I know, I apologize," Eamon said.

"We are fine, I promise," Bratheon said. "They've lost track of us."

Eamon stared at the fire. He couldn't tell if it made it harder or easier to sleep. It was their first night with a fire since they rode out. Bratheon promised the enemy was far enough for them to make camp. Still, Eamon couldn't shake the feeling of an Itihasian creeping by as he slept.

"Your friend there hasn't seen anyone?" Eamon said.

"No," Bratheon smiled. He reached out from his blanket and rubbed a red fox behind its ears. "She'll let us know."

"Thank you for accompanying us," Eamon said. "I know you'd rather have returned to your sister."

"There was nothing to report from Fargaible. At least nothing that couldn't be trusted to the raven." Bratheon smiled. "My place is here, with you two."

*   *   *

Bratheon packed the camp before sunrise. The fire was extinguished and dismantled. Athan covered the sopping wet ashes with leaves for added measure. By the time they left, their site looked no different than the rest of the forest floor.

"We'll ride past Ranon today," Athan said.

"I would like to visit again some day," Eamon said. "Though Ranon doesn't quite feel like home anymore."

Athan lowered his head. "No I suppose it doesn't."

"Are we taking the Rim or do you plan on going east through the wilds?"

"I know which you'd prefer, but we haven't the time."

"The Rim is what still feels like home."

"The Rim?" Bratheon said. "Are you talking about a place?"

"A bluff with a view unlike any other. It swoops down to Ranon, overlooking the wilds. Just north is the glistening Lake Naya which thunders down the Rim's steep face. From the top you can see both the Naya and Manon rivers before they conjoin and make the Numen."

"It sounds beautiful. And perhaps even more so with fond memories?" Bratheon said.

"Melchoir, our caretaker brought us up there occasionally," Athan said.

"I see. How far is the ride to the Rim?"

"To the top? I'd say a full day's ride, if we push into the night. We should be in the wilds by noon, once we cross the Naya," Athan said.

"And the wilds are safer?"

"Safer and quicker," Athan said. "Don't let the name fool you. The Wilds are nothing but rolling hills. They stretch out towards Port Evertide; I'm surprised you're not familiar with them."

"I've never seen the River Manon," Bratheon said. "My family never left the woods."

"That secluded?" Eamon said.

"Much has changed since Alderman became king. My family and those who practiced with us had been hunted for generations. We never left the wood's safety."

"After what we've been through, I'd hardly describe the woods as safe," Eamon said. "It's a miracle we've made it as far as we are."

"A miracle or providence?" Bratheon turned in his saddle, his smile inviting a philosophical discussion. Eamon wasn't in the mood.

"Either way. I'm amazed we're coming to the end of Havenwood at the cost of only one horse."

"Speaking of which, I'm sure we'll be asked why three riders with desperate news from the king come with only two horses," Athan said. "What should we tell the marquis?"

"The truth?" Eamon said, his voice puzzled. "That we were attacked as we rode past the enemy camp."

"And what about Fargaible?" Athan said. "Do we tell him what we found there?"

Eamon shuddered as he remembered approaching Gredulous' quaint cabin. It was the most frightened he had ever been. Bratheon was still missing after riding away to draw the Itihasians. Though the manaist diverted most away from Athan and Eamon, a small party followed them to The Run's trailhead. With Eamon's guidance, Athan lost their pursuers in the trail's twists and turns. Eamon knew better than to seek shelter with Gredulous, not without returning the medallion he stole. Though Gredulous was nothing more than an old, heartless manaist with a nose for profit, Eamon never wished evil upon him or his wife, Idella. Yet evil already found them.

The open door and dark windows were the first signs something was wrong. Dried blood ran down the front door. Discarded to the side was Gredulous' discharged crossbow. The living room's singed upholstery told of a continued struggle. Broken glass and battered furniture cluttered the floor. Gredulous' body had been left where he died, pinned against the wall and fireplace mantle by a wicked halberd. Athan found Idella dead in her bedroom. Every drawer and closet was open, their contents spilled out on the floor.

Athan and Eamon stayed the night in a nearby cabin. They hid their lone horse in the woods behind. Eamon volunteered for the first watch, knowing he shouldn't sleep after striking his head in their flight. Shortly after Athan fell asleep, Eamon could hear the forest stir with life. Rustling leaves, chirping crickets, hoots and growls kept Eamon's nerves at edge. He disregarded the sounds as he fought to stay awake, listening for laden steps or opening doors. Without knowing, he drifted to sleep.

Eamon woke to Athan calling his name. He apologized for sleeping, but it was too late. As his eyes focused he caught sight of a sword held at Athan's neck. Two Itihasians held Athan's arms back and walked him to the door. A blade rested at Eamon's neck as well. Two more men hoisted Eamon to his feet. It was over.

The leader of the four asked Athan about the old manaist's magical weapons. Athan said nothing. They tied Eamon's hands behind his back and forced his head against a chopping block used for splitting firewood.

Again the man asked Athan. Eamon listened for Athan's response, hoping his brother could think of something. Nothing, there was only the forest rustling and scurrying. Cold steel scraped the back of Eamon's neck as his executioner lined up his strike. Then came the fox. It ran beside Eamon and barked at the Itihasians in defiance. From the darkness a pack of timber wolves leapt at the Itihasians. A horned owl swooped from the treetops, its talons ripped at the face of one of the men holding Athan. With blinding speed, Athan dispatched the other with his own sword. The other Itihasians were at the mercy of the wolves, but the beasts' ravaging hunger left them without grace. Bratheon emerged from the brush and helped Eamon to his feet. The fox led the three from the grizzly scene to a large barrow where they stayed the night.

"I don't know," Eamon said as he remembered that night. "It's not like we found anything at Gredulous' cabin... We might as well tell the marquis all that happened, if he asks. Though I doubt he'll believe us anyway." He looked from his horse down at the red fox following behind Bratheon.

"It's the fact that we were looking for something that may be suspicious to him," Athan said.

"I don't understand why we must be so secretive," Bratheon said.

"Simply put, we don't know for sure who our allies are. Fadrien and Lyle find it highly suspicious that Marquis Eelton hasn't contacted the king since his first battalion went missing. Surely, he'd suspect something, or assume the king may be in peril."

"If we don't trust him, then why bother asking him for help?" Bratheon said.

"Because he is our only hope. Besides it's his duty! As the marquis of the northern march it is his duty to defend the kingdom," Athan said.

"Only hope," Bratheon said with disdain.

"You think there is no hope?" Eamon said.

"Far from it!" Bratheon said. "There is no reason for Averlace to be at its knees, facing defeat at the hands of an inferior enemy."

"Inferior?" Athan said. "We are vastly outnumbered and were surprised. They clearly have the upper hand."

"They've never had the upper hand. Averlace has forgotten what it once was—What it still has! We are a legacy of insurmountable power and providential wisdom. Peace, power, wealth and growth was our inheritance, but we threw it aside in exchange for... nothing!"

"Nothing? I don't understand."

"I'm talking about magic! It was given up for what they believed would bring us peace."

"The kingdom gave it up in fear of what magic was becoming. A powerful tool abused by the wicked. After seeing you, I understand why magic was feared," Athan said.

"The power of magic and the wisdom to wield it goes hand in hand. People wanted the benefits of magic, but did not want to make the sacrifices it required to remain selfless and good. But that wasn't the biggest mistake. The gravest mistake came from the ones who gave in to the fear of evil and agreed to give up Manaism altogether. They didn't stand up against the evil practices of black magic. They didn't try to disciple those who had strayed from the selfless path. It required them to be vulnerable in difficult relationships, or to spend time teaching the young. So they settled for no magic at all… And now the kingdom trembles as an enemy knocks at their gates. An enemy that demands what they gave up!

"Can you imagine what Averlace would be now, if every man and woman fought with the magic my sister and I possess? The enemy, if not retreating, would be burning and its ashes scattering in the wind… That was Averlace once. That is what Averlace is destined to be. That is why I ride with you all now. Not to help you obtain some false hope, but to show you what hope truly is!—A power beyond understanding that is simply here for the taking. It's ours to claim, and then to give."

Athan continued to ride. He lowered his head, pressed his lips and swayed his head side to side. Eamon knew he was thinking.

"I have faith in Manaism, but none in people. So long as there is power, there will always be evil," Athan said.

"No," Bratheon retorted. "So long as we fear power and prefer numbness over selfless love, evil will grow."

Eamon rested his head on Athan's back as they rode. He closed his eyes and imagined one of the manaist medallions back at the school.

For the giving and the taking. The inscription read around its rim.

Eamon opened his eyes and stared at an angry and annoyed Bratheon. Ours to claim and then to give. For the first time in his studies, the inscription made sense.

Few words were exchanged the rest of the day. They found a shallow ford and crossed the River Naya with ease. The rest of the day's ride was uneventful. Bratheon found a cove nestled between a set of rolling hills. They made camp for the night and rode out by daybreak the following morning.

*   *   *

Bratheon found The Wilds tamer than the name implied. Hill after bald hill rolled on as far as the eye could see. Though covered with a verdant blanket of lush grass, the land felt barren. Small streams babbled from spring to spring between the hills. Water was easy to come by, but little wildlife inhabited the wilderness. As food became more and more scarce, Bratheon was surprised the red fox continued to follow him.

"Does it have a name?" Eamon said.

"I don't know," Bratheon said.

"You haven't named it?"

Bratheon shook his head. He ripped apart a dried piece of jerky and tossed it to the fox. "No, I haven't named her."

"Ask him if he has a name," Athan said.

Bratheon laughed, "I can't talk to her. Who do you think I am?"

"Oh, right... what was I thinking? I just assumed since you could, you know, throw fire and call thunder and lightning that perhaps you could speak fox."

"Wait a moment," Eamon said. "What do you mean you can't speak with it? How else have you... You know, communicated?"

"We haven't communicated. She just knew to help."

"Oh she, my apologies," Athan said.

"She just knew to help... I've never seen, or even heard of an animal helping someone like what happened back at Havenwood."

"Have you ever stopped to help a stranger in distress? You just had a feeling, you know? They didn't have to ask for help. You just knew," Bratheon said.

"This is a bit different," Eamon said.

Bratheon chuckled and winked at the fox. "I suppose so. How about Eago?"

"How about what?" Athan said.

"Eago. You implied we should name her, Eago it is.

Eamon cocked his head. "Eago? I've heard that name before. Where?"

"Oh?" Bratheon raised a curious brow. "Now that is interesting. Where have you heard it?"

"I'm not sure... It's a foreign name right? Itihasian?"

"Itihasian? No, not hardly. Though I guess you could say it is foreign to you. It's an old manaist name. A common name for pets. It means to follow."

Eamon snapped his finger. "That's it. Davrian named one of his horses Eago."

"Ah, see. It's quite a popular name. Not surprised to see the Prince of Itihasia was familiar with it. I guess now I know why you thought it was Itihasian."

"It still baffles me," Athan said.

"What's that?"

"That Davrian… the guild master of the Syndicate turns out to be a manaist as well."

"It make sense to me," Eamon said. "I told you about the quotes and manaist proverbs he'd have the Syndicate memorize. Sayings like the greater good, and the road to a thousand woes is paved with good intentions."

"Out of the Elite, you spent the most time with him."

"But a good manaist? He is hiding something. There is still an end goal. Something he hopes to achieve… How else can you explain all of the secrets?"

"Perhaps he's not hiding anything at all," Bratheon said.

"You obviously know little about the man," Eamon said.

"I know enough."

"What do you mean?" Athan said.

"Dishonesty and greed; those aren't characteristics of a manaist. One could never practice Manaism with such selfish ambition," Bratheon said.

"That's just the thing," Eamon said. "We've yet to see him cast a spell."

"Certainly nothing like what you and your sister have done," Athan added.

"Perhaps your preconceived judgments have left you blind about his character?"

"I'm not even sure I know what that means," Athan said.

"You expect him to act a certain way, so he can't do anything to convince you he acts otherwise."

Athan chuckled. "I appreciate your optimism, Bratheon. But only Davrian can be responsible for his reputation."

"Then I suppose only time can tell."

"That's what I'm afraid of," Eamon said.

CHAPTER TWENTY SEVEN

THE WEIGHT OF THE WORLD

CHAPTER TWENTY-SEVEN

THE WEIGHT OF THE WORLD

ILLIOTT OFFERED Fadrien a helping hand. Fadrien looked over the edge and studied the climb. He handed his staff to Illiott then eased himself down feet first. The councilman landed on the marble floor with a spring in his step, moving as if twenty years younger.

Fadrien was better prepared this time for the under city. He left his white, court robe behind in exchange for a simple tunic, jerkin and a pair of trousers tucked in leather boots laced up to his calves. Slung over his back was a brown satchel filled with books, maps, candles and the three medallions.

Kit released a loud sigh as his feet reached the marble tile.

"Something wrong?" Lyle said.

"Back sooner than I had hoped," Kit said.

"You prefer the war above?" Davrian said as he worked his way down with cuffed hands.

Kit didn't answer. His thoughts were with Josie.

Lyle could read his brother's eyes. "Come on," he clapped Kit's back, "the sooner we start, the sooner we can leave."

"At least she is safer, for now," Kit said. "Thank you again, Fadrien."

Fadrien opened one of his books from his bag. "They should be comfortable in the library, though they'll have their work cut out for them."

"They're hard workers, and Josie managed the Kettle and Dove for years. Preparing the library for refugees should come easy."

"It's the least I could do," Fadrien said. "I need you lads thinking clearly down here; but enough of that. We have work of our own that needs to be done." Fadrien grabbed three stacks of paper and a goose pinion for each to write. "First things first." He handed the supplies to Lurie and Nalinda to pass to the others. "Our primary objective is to learn what we can about the vault's whereabouts and what steps must be taken to open it. We'll split off into three groups. Lurie and I will make the first group. Illiott and Davrian will be the other and Lyle, Kit and Nalinda will be the third. Your job is to find any evidence of a well-guarded tomb and take notes on anything that may be a clue. Look for inscriptions, reliefs, statues, doors with peculiar markings. If you think it looks interesting or promising then take note."

"Remember this place is dangerous," Illiott said. "Though we are in a race against time, you won't be doing us any good if you get yourself killed. Be cautious, and don't venture too far alone."

"Do you have anything to add?" Fadrien said to Davrian.

"Stay out of the rooms," Davrian said.

"Ah," Illiot said, his voice cynical. "Don't want to end up like the top officer you tried to reward... Still trying to see how that fits in with this crusader story of yours."

Davrian gave an amused laugh. "I knew the home I gave him was cursed. He was evil, without doubt. The man needed to be stopped, so I 'rewarded' him for his contributions to the Syndicate. He can't do any more harm trapped behind stone walls."

Lurie shuddered. "What else is down here?"

"Who knows?" Davrian said. "You must keep in mind one thing while you're here. The Averlacians didn't want anyone finding the vault, not even their descendants; and if we just happen to find it, your ancestors took certain precautions to make us think twice before opening it."

"But you can help? Right?" Nalinda said. "Being the Prince of Itihasia, you can lead us there and open it?"

"Yes, and grant you three wishes if you'd like. My hands are practically crackling with power," Davrian twinkled his fingers. He grabbed a torch from Illiott and marched ahead.

Illiott tucked his paper and pen under his arm. He shot Fadrien a disconcerted glance. "This should be fun," he said as he followed Davrian.

*   *   *

The three groups split apart but never strayed out of sight. Hours passed before they crossed the river. Fadrien studied every statue and relief with unabated scrutiny, making remarks and observations which Lurie jotted down on paper. Lyle, Kit and Nalinda took a different approach. Kit copied key characteristics in doodles and sketches. Lyle worked with Nalinda, taking notes on whatever she pointed out. For intricate engravings he'd lay paper across the stone and rub it with a lead ingot, creating perfect copies for Fadrien's investigation.

Davrian and Illiott covered less ground. They started at the pedestal previously used to control the aqueducts. From there they crossed all three bridges; crisscrossing the river until they made it to the final relief of the gigantic stag drinking from the Numen as it vanished below in a furious whirlpool. Davrian studied the relief for hours.

"You've found something?" Illiott said.

"Not yet," Davrian said. "He waved his torch over the final bridge's rails and peered down to the rushing water below.

"Where does it all go?" Illiott said. "It just vanishes at the cave's wall."

"And where does the water come from?" Davrian added. "That's what I would often wonder when I came down here. The Numen River flows above ground and divides the city, yet it does the same below. The river is just as strong leaving Averlace as it is coming in; yet this is arguably the strongest portion of the two… It's a mystery we don't have time for now." His chains rattled along the marble tiles as he worked his way across the final bridge to the river's edge.

The Numen was lined with cut stone, with steps that dipped into the river's bank. The stone banks led to the base of the relief. Illiott followed Davrian to the towering monument. Approaching the stag's hooves offered Davrian a new perspective. The stonework took on a different dimension. The path led underneath the stag's head and wove behind chiseled rocks and tree trunks that depicted a tranquil glade. Hidden in the center, behind one of the stag's hooves was a pedestal similar to the one Fadrien used to control the flow of water. It had five settings for the medallions. Four of the settings circled around the raised center.

A devious smile flashed across Davrian's face. "Now I've found something."

Illiott peeked over Davrian's shoulder. "Does it say anything? Any instructions?"

Davrian's smile widened. "For the Giving and the Taking."

"We need Fadrien," Illiott said, his voice giddy. "This may be it. Stay here." He ran across the bridge and shouted over the river's roar for the others to come.

Davrian did as he was told. In the distance he could see the others' torches bob up and down in a line as they made their way toward him. Davrian lowered his torch.

"I've found you," he said as he ran his fingers along the pedestal. "I should've known you were hiding it," Davrian said as he patted the stag's head. He raised his torch and admired the relief. A masterpiece of art and engineering, the stag looked like it was walking out of the wall. Its head and limbs along with the trees and river rock provided not only a third dimension when viewed by the bridge, but also provided support to hold the cavern's ceiling.

Davrian looked to the stag's head from behind. This time it appeared different. Davrian dropped his torch. He scrambled to pick it up again. With trembling hands he raised it up, unsure of what he saw. From the center looking out, the relief had an obverse image. It was no longer a stag drinking from the water, but that of a throne. The stag's leg's when viewed behind were the legs of a coronation throne. Most intriguing was the pedestal, when viewed as part of the obverse image it was clearly the throne's foot rest.

"Alderman's stag..." Davrian whispered to himself. For the giving and the taking..." Davrian read the pedestal again. "I found it," he whispered to himself. "By the greater power..."

Fadrien was the first to join Davrian, Lurie followed close behind. Davrian lowered his torch, hoping not to reveal the obverse image.

"Amazing," Fadrien said. "We should have started here."

"The path wasn't easy to spot," Davrian said. "I assumed the base was inaccessible due to the river. A closer look proved me wrong."

"Yes, yes indeed," Fadrien said, his face beaming. "Show me the pedestal."

Davrian pointed with his torch, being sure to keep it low and drawing their attention only to what they wanted to see.

"A setting for five?" Fadrien said. "The elevated one... I suppose for the king's medallion?"

"I believe so," Davrian said.

"If only we knew where to find it."

Davrian said nothing.

"Should I take any notes for you sir?" Lurie said.

"Do you remember how we used the pedestal last time?" Fadrien looked to Davrian.

Illiott joined them. "We inserted a medallion into one of the three inlets, simple as that. You don't suppose this would work as easily?" Illiott pulled his medallion from Fadrien's bag.

Fadrien shook his head. "Why go through the trouble of making four settings if only one is required to work?"

"Should we set one in, just to see what happens?" Illiott said, his medallion dangled over the setting.

"Don't be foolish," Fadrien pulled Illiott's hand from the pedestal. "We have no idea what may happen."

"Still it could give us another clue," Illiott said.

"I'd be willing to have you do it," Davrian smiled. "So long as I can watch from a safe distance."

"Funny," Illiott said, "I had the same idea for you."

Davrian's smile faded to a musing grin. "You'd have me place the medallion?"

"What better way for a remorseful prisoner to serve the kingdom?" Illiott said.

"Unlock my hands and we have a deal."

Illiott didn't even pretend to entertain the idea. "Seeing you bound reminds me of the last time my hands were cuffed... You just stood there while your men beat me."

"Couldn't show my hand," Davrian said. "Don't take it personally, just playing my part."

"And you will continue to do so with your hands bound," Illiott said.

"I don't think that is wise," Lyle said as he snatched the medallion from Illiott's hand.

Illiott's eyes narrowed. "Give that back." He opened his hand.

"We don't know where the fourth medallion is. Of all of us here, Davrian is the one to have seen it last. The last thing we need is to have him send it off to the unknown. I don't think handing the guild master one of our medallions is the right choice here."

"Especially now that we know he's the Prince of Itihasia," Kit added.

"Don't be so insistent about finding the treasure that you cast all caution aside." Lyle met Illiott's eyes with a stern stare.

"Then what do you suggest?" Fadrien said.

"Leave it alone," Lyle said. "Surely some instructions are written on the wall, or in one of your books."

"We haven't the time," Illiott said. "Taking a stab may tell us much in a short amount of time."

"If we survive it."

"Feel free to leave," Illiott held his hand out to Fadrien. "The other medallions please."

Fadrien, Lyle and Kit exchanged looks; their concerned glances ended at Davrian who stood uncharacteristically quiet.

Fadrien dug the remaining two medallions from his bag. "Girls, wait for me at the tunnel with Lyle and Kit."

"This is insane," Lyle said. He grabbed the medallions from Fadrien.

"Give me those," the councilman demanded.

"I'll place them," Lyle said. "No need for you and Illiott getting killed. We'll never learn how to open the vault without you two."

"Lyle this is my responsibility," Fadrien said.

"Which is why you need to be out of harm's way," Lyle turned to the pedestal and waved Fadrien and the others away, it was then he realized the medallions were missing. "What? Where'd they?" He held up his empty hands. His eyes darted to Davrian, who looked just as surprised.

"Right here," Kit dangled the medallions for all to see. "You're far too slow."

"What are you doing?" Lyle said.

"Helping."

"Give me those and head to the tunnel with Fadrien."

Kit didn't listen. He walked to the pedestal and waited for the others to leave. "Take notes," he smiled to Illiott.

"I'm not leaving," Lyle said.

"I never assumed you would. You didn't think I was going to do this by myself did you?"

"You're a fool," Lyle said. "If you are serious about Josie it's time to start considering her when you make these decisions."

"What do you think I'm doing down here?" Kit said. "I'm not here to sightsee. Besides, when have you ever gotten yourself out of trouble?"

There was no point in arguing. Lyle joined Kit at the pedestal. "Well there was the time I—"

"The bar fight doesn't count," Kit said.

Davrian walked to the pedestal. "I'm helping too."

"Good," Kit looked to Davrian's shackles. "I won't feel bad out-running you."

"Just place two medallions on the side inlets. Leave the center," Illiott said. He started back, wringing his hands. He stopped and dropped the bag he was carrying. "There's rope and oil and candles if you need... for whatever reason"

"We'll be fine," Lyle said. He watched with Kit and Davrian as the others walked to the muddy tunnel.

"Whatever happens," Davrian said. "Think twice before you act."

Lyle said nothing. In the distance he could see Fadrien waving his torch. They had reached the tunnel. He looked to Kit. "Ready?"

Kit nodded. He set the first medallion in place. The second he palmed and hovered over the pedestal's left inlet. He hesitated for a moment, then dropped it in.

Nothing.

Kit drew in a deep breath. He held the third like the one before.

"Wait," Davrian said. His eyes scanned the stone relief behind, trying to spot any changes and listen for new sounds.

"The medallions," Lyle said, his voice calm and intrigued.

Their red stones came to life. Light swirled inside with a soft glow. The three waited, still as the statues surrounding them. Once convinced nothing else would happen, Kit looked for Lyle's approval to place the third medallion.

Sweat beaded up on Lyle's brow. His head dipped with a subtle nod. Kit dropped the medallion.

Heavy clanking whirled nearby. The sound was so deep and resolute they couldn't tell where it came.

"Gears?" Lyle said, his head darting in every direction.

Davrian stared at the stone stag hovering overhead. Nothing changed. Kit ran to the relief's edge that met the river.

"The water," Kit had to yell over the clanking. "It's dropping."

Lyle and Davrian met him at the edge. They watched as the whirlpool's angry torrent died to a steady stream.

Lyle pointed. "The bridge!"

Beneath the bridge, a dam rose out of the water, blocking the Numen from the whirlpool and the base of the relief. The water continued to drop to where the stag's head no longer lapped up the river.

Davrian ran to the bridge. The blocked river spilled over the edge onto the marble tiles. By now the dam had risen all the way from the river bed to the bridge's underside.

"It's flooding the city!" Illiott shouted from a distance.

Davrian stopped midstride. Water flowed over his feet. "Run!"

Kit and Lyle didn't wait to second-guess. Kit leapt from the relief and splashed onto the tile. They didn't make it far when they realized they had left the medallions. Lyle tried to catch Kit from turning back, but he slipped on the wet tile. Without a proper hold the water swept him down the marble road.

Davrian washed up beside Lyle, and the two found themselves caught against a grated drain. Their heads poked just above the water. The current pulled them down as it escaped through the drain at their feet.

Lyle knew not to panic. He looked for a way to escape. A sidewalk elevated above the water's level was just out of reach, at least for now. Kit made it safely to the pedestal and frantically searched for the rope in Illiott's bag.

"Lyle," Illiott shouted from the sidewalk above. Fadrien, Lurie and Nalinda were with him. They held onto Illiott has he stretched out with Fadrien's staff. Lyle couldn't reach it.

Illiott cursed, wishing he'd kept his bag for himself. Lyle tried to stand, but each time the water knocked him down. He'd swirl around in a small circle then end against the drain again. Still his head remained above the water.

Fadrien's staff waved agonizingly close. No matter how he tried, Lyle couldn't manage to reach it.

"It stopped rising," Davrian yelled. A wave washed in his face. "The water isn't rising."

Lyle scanned the scene. Davrian was right. The water leveled off thanks to the drains.

"Throw me the staff," Lyle shouted.

Illiott tossed it upstream and it floated against Lyle. With it Lyle had enough support to stand. Davrian managed to keep his head up, but with a great effort. Lyle toyed with the idea of leaving him. Before he moved on, he found himself reaching in the water for Davrian's hands. After several attempts the two were able to stand. Working together they forded the water and made it close enough to the relief for Kit's rope to reach them.

"Why not just pull the medallions off the pedestal?" Lyle said as he wrung water out of his sleeves. "Surely it would reverse it."

Kit sheepishly looked at the pedestal. "What a great idea. Lyle, I'm impressed." He pulled a medallion from its setting. Nothing happened. He pulled out the second. Again nothing happened.

Kit glared at Lyle. "A brilliant idea, that's why I pulled them off the moment I got here. As you can see nothing changes."

Davrian pulled himself out of the water. His chest heaved as he tried to catch his breath. He crawled to the edge of the relief and rested his back against the short wall.

"Thanks," he said to Lyle.

Lyle said nothing. "How do we get out of here?"

"Let me show you something," Kit said. He stood at the edge beside Davrian and pointed to a deep chasm. "This is the whirlpool."

Lyle looked out across the city. The dam blocked the water from pouring into the chasm, the redirected water flowed out of the city through the series of aqueducts. The homes and buildings remained unharmed. Lyle prepared a torch and dropped it down the chasm. It fell only twenty feet or so before rattling down a series of steps that spiraled down the chasm's side. Davrian lifted himself above the wall and looked below.

"I think we found Fadrien's vault," Lyle said.

"Or a deathtrap," Davrian said.

Davrian's tone sent a shiver down Lyle's back. "Do you see a way down?"

"There," Kit pointed at the bridge. Steps like a ladder once hidden below the waterline worked their way to the chasm's spiraled staircase.

In the back of the relief Kit found a tunnel that led to the elevated sidewalk. Lyle could now see the sidewalk circled the entire city. Fadrien already discovered the connection and nearly ran into them as he made the last turn to the base.

"Is everyone alright?" Fadrien said.

"Fine, you?" Lyle said.

"We felt so helpless," Nalinda said.

"The water is emptying out of the aqueducts. A new pathway has opened," Lyle said.

"Unbelievable," Fadrien's eyes gleamed as he looked down the spiraled stairs. They were close. He clapped and rubbed his hands together. "Illiott and Lurie took off in the other direction. They believe they saw another passageway open. They'll be back shortly."

"I think the aqueducts we opened last time are what allows the water to empty through the drains," Kit said.

"Are you certain?"

"No, but I wonder if we would have flooded the entire under city had we not opened the drains before."

"We are terribly fortunate if that's the case," Fadrien said.

"Fortunate indeed," Lyle said. He stepped behind Davrian. "You knew, didn't you? That we had to open the drains before we could open the vault," Lyle said.

Davrian shrugged his shoulders. "You don't even know if this leads to the vault."

"But something tells me you do," Lyle said.

"Shall we explore it together then?"

Lyle's lip curled and his fists tightened. He grabbed Illiott's bag and pulled out the lamp oil. He prepared another torch.

"You're going down there?" Kit said.

"Yes, and you are staying up here."

"I don't think so."

"I need you to," Lyle said. He tied one end of the rope around Kit's waist then the other end around his own. "I won't be long. Just having a look."

"You're going alone?"

"I am, unless Davrian wants to brave it without a rope." Lyle didn't wait for a response. He started down the stone ladder and stepped on to the slick tile. Water trickled down the stairs. He reached the torch he first dropped when Davrian started down the ladder. Kit, Fadrien and Nalinda looked over the edge. Kit's coiled rope unwound over the wall as Lyle traveled deeper down the chasm.

Lyle left the torch for Davrian. The spiraled stairs made five turns before it leveled out to a long tunnel. Statues of men holding the cave's ceiling on their backs lined the hall. Ten men could walk the hall side by side and it extended twenty feet before reaching a dramatic end. The hair on Lyle's neck stood on end as he approached a thin bridge that spanned a gap. Lyle threw a rock as far as he could, but he could not hear it hit a wall on the other side. Moments passed until he heard the faintest crash echo from the depths below. He started to cross the bridge, making it only a few steps before his rope went taut.

Davrian's chains rattled along the tile as he descended the last few steps. Warily he walked the hall like a cripple. Lyle waited for the guild master before crossing.

Davrian started across the narrow bridge, moving as fast as his shackled stride allowed. Lyle followed. He untied his rope and stepped onto the bridge.

Even if Lyle had thrown his stone twice as far, it would never had struck the other side. Lyle felt as if the earth had swallowed him whole. The bridge was suspended in a dark void. Above there was no ceiling his light could illuminate, and below a depth the Numen could never fill. There was only the next step ahead and Davrian walked it with an unsettling vigor.

At last they came to a vast wall. The bridge ended at a door as wide as the previous hall. Its height reached at least thirty feet, but Lyle couldn't be sure in the dark. At the center, another pedestal stood. Atop it was a single setting.

"The king's medallion," Davrian said. "It's all that remains to open the door. Then we'll see all of Averlace's wonders from its glorious past."

Davrian turned to see Lyle's sword gleaming in the torchlight. Lyle grabbed Davrian's throat and held him over the pedestal.

"Averlace and all its glory—Is that the work you still have? To claim it as your own?"

Davrian struggled to stay balanced. He said nothing, but his eyes never left Lyle's sword.

"Listen to me guild master. You've painted quite a picture with this story of yours. Creating the Syndicate just to destroy it. Plowing fertile ground for Manaism to take root."

"I've never lied to you," Davrian said.

"Perhaps, but don't think you've me fooled. I know you're working another angle."

Lyle pressed his sword against Davrian's throat. "You've hurt a lot of people to obtain your 'Greater Good.'" Lyle shook Davrian's head. "When this is over, when the Itihasians are gone, I will come for you and I will make you pay for what you've done."

Clanking, similar to the rising dam, sounded in the walls and ground. Lyle and Davrian heard gushing water overhead.

Lyle sheathed his sword and ran across the bridge. Davrian straggled behind. As he came close to the other side, he could hear water falling from the cliff. Above the rushing water Lyle could faintly hear Kit's voice calling out.

Lyle grabbed the rope and tied it around his waist and made for the hall of statues. Water poured from the spiral steps. The clanking sound grew louder.

"Lyle, run!" Kit and others cried out.

Halfway through the hall water surged forward, knocking Lyle back. It pushed him down the hall and towards the cliff. The rope's slack tightened before he reached the bridge, where Davrian was standing.

Lyle stood and held on to the rope. Little by little it pulled him down the hall. Kit and the others were hauling him out. If the river reached its full strength before they made it up the steps, they'd be trapped below. Lyle saw Davrian standing helpless on the bridge, water rushing at his feet. His first step off the bridge would surely sweep him over the cliff.

"Davrian," Lyle reached out to Davrian, surprised by his own attempt to save the man he just swore he'd punish.

Davrian ran and jumped for Lyle's hand. Lyle grabbed the chain between Davrian's wrists. They worked to keep each other upright and walked down the hall. The water rose fast. Another loud clank rumbled in the hallway, followed by a white tide of foam and surf. It knocked Lyle off his feet. He lost his grip on Davrian's chain. The water pulled on him, keeping his head submerged and rendering his arms and legs useless. Lyle's only hope was in Kit and the others. The rope tightened around his waist in an agonizing synch. He tried to bring his legs back under him, but the current churned harder, bashing him against the hall's ceiling. Lyle got one last breath before being tugged under. He reached for the rope to gather the slack, but the water was too strong. Lyle could feel his lungs begin to burn. His head bumped against the first step. He was never going to make it. With one last push he tried to bring his legs underneath, but the water won and continued to thrash him about. His head grew heavy and the cave's darkness began to grow from all around.

*   *   *

"Pull. Pull!" Kit yelled as he and the others heaved on the rope.

The whirlpool was in full power now. Had Illiott and Lurie come any later, it would have been futile, but they were getting close.

"I see him," Nalinda called out.

"Pull!"

Lyle rose out of the water. Nalinda reached over the wall and brought his head and arms over. Kit wrapped his arms around Lyle's chest. He barely had the strength to pull him over. Illiott grabbed Lyle's shoulders and tugged. They toppled over the wall, yet Lyle's leg remained pinned against the ledge.

Lurie turned Lyle to his side and compressed his chest, while Illiott finished pulling him over. Lyle erupted in a series of violent coughs. Illiott stepped back, amazed Lyle was alive.

"He's fine. He's fine," Illiott said.

Lyle's eyes rolled open. His head was bruised and bleeding and his chest felt crushed and battered.

Kit wrapped his arms around his brother. His face still strained with fear.

Lyle looked around, trying to find his bearings.

"You're alright, you're alright. You're safe now." Kit said.

"Of course I'm alright," Lyle said, annoyed. He tried to stand but his leg was still snagged.

"How?" Kit said. "It took us forever to pull you up."

"Davrian is lost," Lyle said as he pulled on his leg.

"Help," Illiott called out, leaning over the wall.

Illiott, Fadrien and Lurie freed Lyle's leg from the edge. Cuffed to Lyle's ankle was one of Davrian's shackles. At the other end hung Davrian. The guild master crashed to the ground beside Lyle, his lungs heaving in air.

Lyle shook his head. Davrian had been lost, swept away in the current. Now he lay beside him, and they were shackled together.

Kit rolled up Lyle's legging. "How did you unlock the cuff down there?"

"I don't know," Lyle said. "I never unlocked them."

Kit sat Lyle up. He looked at Davrian and studied the chains, unbroken and untampered. "Prince of Itihasia indeed."

CHAPTER TWENTY EIGHT
THE MARQUIS

CHAPTER TWENTY-EIGHT

THE MARQUIS

THE WILD'S expansive plains came to an abrupt end. Eagles soared above the snow covered peaks and mighty rams jumped about the mountain cliffs that rose over the barren, green steppes. Athan, Eamon and Bratheon traveled ancient pathways which started at the foot of the mountains, dividing the plains in half with smooth river stone, the beginning of Manadon Road. Homes were scarce along the border of the Wilds, but as they came closer to the March's pass, farm houses and plotted fields were more commonplace.

A lonely peak emerged from the mountain range into the plain. A timber palisade circled the low mountain, protecting a farming village nestled in the valley. Manadon Road veered eastward. As they approached the town, they could see terraced fields running across the mountain's face. Storehouses, several stories tall, loomed over the homes and stables. Herds of cattle roamed the open fields to the north and flocks of sheep grazed the southern pastures.

"I believe I could live here," Bratheon said.

"Here? Here in Gillian?" Athan said. He gave his horse a soft kick and never looked away from the road.

"It's quaint, yet the people here must be a sturdy folk. They live in wonderful harmony with the land."

Eamon buried his face in Athan's back to stifle a laugh.

"Something funny?"

"No," Eamon smiled. "I just knew you were going to say something like that."

"Like what?"

"Perfect harmony with the land... Who says that?"

Bratheon didn't answer. His head rocked back with a subtle laugh.

"Perhaps when it's all over you could move up here," Athan said. "Marry you one of these quaint, sturdy girls, build a quaint, sturdy house on a quaint, sturdy farm... Oh and kids, you'll have quaint—"

"I get the idea," Bratheon said. "I think I just may... It suits me."

"Well, I hope the best for you," Athan said as he brought his horse to a halt at the town's palisade.

"No gate?" Bratheon said.

"Or guards," Eamon said.

"Why should they?" Athan pointed ahead.

The bordering mountains in the north looped along the countryside then sloped down to a narrow pass at the base of the southern range. Wedged defiantly between the two ranges was the marquis's fortress city, Drowl Crag.

"Gillian lies in Drowl Crag's shadow," Athan continued. "If ever threatened, the town would retreat there."

"If ever threatened indeed," Bratheon said with a bewildered stare.

The fortress city was a mountain in of itself, guarding the only entrance to the continent. The road through the pass was narrow and the mountains jagged and ruthless. Drowl Crag stood over the road with a series of twelve gates underneath it.

From a distance one couldn't tell where the mountain ended and the city began. Its thick walls towered above the road, challenging any invading force to do its worst.

"I see now why the Itihasians didn't bother to come through here," Bratheon said.

"So then how did they manage to take Evertide?" Eamon said. "I thought no ship could survive those shoals."

"Questions for another time," Athan said. "Right now I'm more concerned about Marquis Eelton."

"Right, tact and etiquette... Not necessarily your strengths."

Athan couldn't argue, he faced Eamon and grinned. "That's why I brought you along. I just hope we're not too late."

Eamon patted Athan's back. "We've done everything we can to get here, and it's no small miracle that we've made it. Just another hour's ride and we'll be speaking with the marquis in his hall. The hardest part of the journey is behind us."

"Maybe so," Athan said, his voice somber.

*   *   *

The marquis' hall was not how Eamon imagined it would be. Drowl Crag's enormity couldn't be overstated. The fortress city belonged to the landscape as much as the impassable mountains. Marquise's Eelton's hall was plush, streaming with color and filled with melody and incense. Satin curtains draped from the ceiling. Hundreds of candles flickered from the hall's columns. Tables were surrounded with red and purple pillows and covered with rich cakes, savory ham and ewers of wine lined the walls. If Drowl Crag's impenetrable wall was the city's bulwark, then the hall was its soft underbelly.

Athan, Eamon and Bratheon followed an armed escort through the hall, refusing food and drink offered by Eelton's maidservants. The escort clicked his heals before the marquis' throne and pummeled the ground with his polearm.

"Guests, my lord, from the capital," the man announced as he turned aside with a high step.

The marquis rose from his throne. He brushed his blonde, curly locks of hair from his face and studied the men with questioning eyes.

"Word from the king?" Eelton said as he adjusted a large, satin bow back under his collar. "I feel like it's been nearly an age since I heard from His Majesty."

"The king feels the same," Eamon said.

"Does he?" Eelton's voice was incredulous.

"The king's land—"

"Have you already forgotten to whom you speak?" The escort flashed his polearm before Eamon; at its end was a polished iron glaive with a sinister edge. "You stand before Marquis Eelton, Lord of the Northern March."

Eamon clinched his fists, "My lord, Averlace is under attack."

"Under attack?" Eelton raised his voice. "What? Rebel rousers from Arata? Brigands? Surely we've put an end to the Syndicate? General Picus—"

"Picus is dead, my lord." Athan said.

"Dead?"

"My lord, as we speak Averlace is held at siege."

"How?" Eelton's voice trailed off. He braced his weight on his throne. "Dicun, clear the hall."

"My lord," the escort spun and reached for a curtain. He pulled it free from the ceiling across the two inner columns. Its folds loosened and fell to the floor, dividing the hall into two separate rooms.

"What's happened to my men? General Picus?"

"Picus was murdered, my lord." Eamon said.

"By whom? The Syndicate?"

"No, the Syndicate was framed. We believe it was the Itihasians."

"Itihasians, here? Impossible. None have made it through the mountain's pass. Drowl Crag's gates are closed and have been for years."

"Your army was intercepted and destroyed by an invading Itihasian force."

"Impossible!"

"They came from Evertide. The port was overrun, and for a fortnight the enemy has grown as more march to the siege. Averlace will surely be taken if your armies don't aid the king."

"What size of a force are you talking about?"

"Averlace was outnumbered twenty to one when we left," Athan said.

"Twenty to one?" Eelton fell back into his throne and slumped his head. "Picus gone... How did you manage to ride past such an army?" Eelton said.

Athan and Eamon looked to their companion.

"Bratheon here," Athan said as he clasped the manaist's shoulder. "He led us past the enemy with magic like you wouldn't believe."

"Magic?" Eelton's eyes widened. "A manaist, here?"

Bratheon lowered his head. "At your service, my lord."

"It's been some time since I last hosted a manaist in this hall." Eelton glanced at his throne and tapped his chin. "You're hungry, no? ...Come, eat. We must hurry and discuss what needs to be done."

Athan raised his hand to object, but noticed the relief in Eamon's eyes. Dinner wouldn't take long. Eelton brushed the curtain aside then clapped for his maidservants. Eight women darted from behind the curtains. Before the men sat at the table the pillows were fluffed, wine poured and food plated.

Eelton lowered himself to the floor. His joints popped and cracked. "Have Dicun send for Rayghar." He pulled his plate to the edge of the table and tucked his bowtie away from his chin.

"Rayghar?" Athan said, still standing. He looked at the food and pillows, unsure what to do.

Eelton sipped some wine and cleared his throat. "Aye, Rayghar, the Wolf. That's what the men call him. He's my captain. I suppose general now. He'll join us shortly."

Eamon looked at the table. Not even Alderman enjoyed such lavish meals. The ride from Averlace had taken its toll, but Eamon couldn't bring himself to eat such fine food.

"Come, eat. I'm not the only one hungry," Eelton said.

"Once our work is done here," Athan said.

"Suit yourself," Eelton grabbed the plate he patiently waited on, being sure to at least wait for his guests.

"You host guests here often?" Bratheon said.

"Yes," Eelton said. "Nearly every day."

"For business?" Athan said.

"Yes, business," Eelton said.

"You've had manaists here before?" Bratheon said.

"One," Eelton said. "No offense to you, Mr. Bratheon, but one was enough for me."

"Were they here for business too?" Bratheon said.

Eelton grabbed his wine and gulped it down; his eyes peered over his cup at Bratheon. He placed the cup on the table with a thud. "Camaraderie—Fellowship was our business. It seems the more power you gain, the fewer friends you have—Genuine friends at least. Everyone wants a share of the food and entertainment offered at my hall."

"I can imagine," Athan folded his arms.

"That wasn't the case with him. He seemed authentic. There was something different about Davrian."

"Wait who?" Eamon said.

"You heard me," Eelton grunted. "Beginning to understand my prejudice?"

"What happened?" Bratheon said.

"He was a traveler. Came with a few others from the foreign lands in the east. I was intrigued when my gatekeeper came to me to grant access for such a small party. I didn't think it was possible to make the journey without the protection of a caravan. My gatekeeper brought him to me for questioning. That is when I learned he was a manaist. Magic was illegal then, but he gave me no reason to distrust him. He and his men stayed with me while they waited for King Marotte's permission for entrance into the kingdom. That is when we became friends.

"He'd do some of the most puzzling things with his magic. I'll never forget that first night he joined me and the rest of my guests for dinner. He lit a candle without holding it to a flame, pulled a napkin out of thin air and moved objects without touching them. Everyone loved him. I kept inviting him. He livened up the halls; it was fantastic entertainment. Every night was something new. At first I thought they were just cheap tricks, like what the traveling troupes do for children. Until one night..."

"One night he made a sword dance—Dance, I swear it. It's the only way to describe it. It floated about the air then spun so gracefully. It was the most amazing, and terrifying thing I ever saw. I wasn't afraid, mind you. We were all awestruck. The control he had over the sword... He was a master."

"What happened?" Eamon said.

"I obsessed over the magic. I wanted to know how he did it. I wanted to use it. He offered to teach me. Day and night we talked magic and practiced. This went on for several weeks until I gave up. I was terrible at it. It seems as though there is much you must sacrifice in order to use magic. My lifestyle didn't really permit it," Eelton gave a guiltless chuckle. "I love my food, wine and couch too much to be interested in the more conservative life Manaism demands. The history and culture, though, it still fascinates me. They say our kingdom was once riddled with magic. Davrian and his men taught me much, from the trinkets and secret orders to the Arbiter's Council. That's when I learned about the history of the marquis and their past role as an arbiter."

"I had a medallion it turns out," Eelton continued. "For years I sat on my throne, growing fat and complacent, unaware that I was sitting on my legacy—My heritage! How Davrian knew about the medallion hidden just under my throne's seat I'll never know, but he opened the tray for me and out it fell. When I held it, something stirred in me like a fire which I've never felt since. Power, a good power. A calling to be a better man, a warrior for good. That was the legacy of my family. Now look at me..."

"What then?" Eamon said.

"He stole it," Eelton tossed his plate back on the table, his appetite gone. "He stole it and ran away. Months later the Syndicate was born and the kingdom plummeted to its darkest age yet. There's no telling what Davrian's done with it now."

Athan and Eamon eyed each other, unsure what to say. Athan took a bite of the ham and poured himself some wine.

"He no longer has it," Eamon broke the silence. "He was captured by the Itihasians. Their commander, Kvrual, now has it."

"Lost to the enemy... At least Davrian went down with it," Eelton said.

"Davrian is now King Alderman's prisoner," Athan said.

Eelton raised his eyebrow.

"It's a long a story," Athan. "Perhaps another time."

Rayghar entered the hall. His presence demanded recognition. Black hair with course, white tufts flowed from his helmet. His unforgiving eyes looked down from his long slender nose.

"Riders from Averlace?" he said with a spectral voice.

"Bearing bad news I'm afraid," Eelton said. "Averlace is under siege, and General Picus is dead. Summon your officers. I need you to rally all of the banners and lift the siege."

"My officers?"

"You're general now, Rayghar," Eelton said.

Rayghar gritted his teeth into a lupine grimace. "It will be done."

"It seems that you have an opportunity to reclaim your medallion," Bratheon said to Eelton.

"You mean take it back from this... Commander Kvrual?"

"When you crush the invaders with your army."

"Bah," Eelton masked his shame with a laugh. "I'm too fat to lead an army. No hauberk could fit around this paunch. I'd have to go to the stables to find any armor to fit me. No, Rayghar is your man. I just give the word."

"The king gives the word," Bratheon said. "He's called you to defend Averlace, not delegate to another."

"Keep speaking, young manaist, and I'll have another reason not to like your kind," Eelton said.

"That fire you spoke of; that was not stolen from you. You lost only a medallion not your ardor. Seize this opportunity. March against the enemy and I promise you, you'll come alive."

"I never said I was dead, boy."

"I beg to differ," Bratheon said.

Eelton rose from his pillows, his face reddened. "Gentlemen, I strongly suggest your friend leaves before we continue with the general."

Athan didn't hesitate. With a subtle glance he directed Bratheon to the door.

"I'll accompany him," Eamon said. "Tactics and logistics have never been my area of expertise."

Rayghar waited for the two to leave. He bowed before Marquis Eeleton then took off his helmet.

"My lord?"

Eelton twirled his mustache as he spoke, still glaring at Bratheon's empty seat. He reached for a napkin and dabbed at his brow. "How soon can the whole army of the north move?"

"By morning. But preparing for a siege is different. It's not like quelling some makeshift rebellion. Two days at best."

"Not soon enough," Athan said.

"I agree," Rayghar said. "But my best is all that can be done. I assume we are dealing with a sizable force, seeing how

Averlace has called the Northern March—All of the Northern March at that. We'll require more than a few day's rations and arms for a light raid."

"It will be a battle unlike anything other in our time," Eelton said. "A war, like what my father's fathers fought." Eelton walked to his throne and stared at its cushioned seat. Below it hung an empty tray that he never cared to push back into place.

"Do what can you tonight, Rayghar," Eelton said. "We ride out tomorrow."

Rayghar gave Athan a skeptical glance.

"We, my lord?"

"Yes," Eelton drained another cup of wine. "We."

CHAPTER TWENTY NINE

APOLOGIES

CHAPTER TWENTY-NINE

APOLOGIES

LYLE'S HEAD throbbed. Burning pulses shot up his neck and swirled at the back of his head. He was in a darkened room with the curtains drawn, lying with his head turned away from the window. The bed only made the pain worse. It took him a moment to find his bearings, but the stale air and musty smell gave it away.

"Getting any reading done, brother?"

Lyle cracked his eye and followed the sound of Kit's voice. At his feet Lyle saw Kit leaning against his bed with a book in hand, reading from a small candle's light.

"What am I doing here?"

"Sleeping?" Kit said, his voice quizzical. "At least you're supposed to be."

"Not on this bed I'm not," Lyle said as he leaned up.

"Sorry it's the best we could do."

"We?"

"The girls and I."

"Are these books?" Lyle reached under his blanket and pulled out a handful of ripped pages.

"It was either that or the cold stone floor," Kit said. "Don't worry, they're just the romanticisms. I figured you wouldn't mind."

"Ugh, I feel worse sleeping on them than if I had stayed up reading one."

"Oh, humor." Kit clapped. "Are you feeling well?"

"No."

"Should I be concerned?"

"Why am I in the library?"

"They moved the infirmary to here now, along with all of the displaced," Kit said.

"The infirmary? Why here?"

"It was destroyed."

"Destroyed?"

"Most of the artisan district is gone," Kit closed his book.

"Another barrage?"

Kit nodded.

"How long have I been gone?" Lyle tried to rise, but his pain brought him back.

"Just a day, but it was a long one."

"How are the girls?"

"Wonderful," Kit smiled. "Josie is a miracle worker. She's transformed this library into a haven. People are finding a home here. She's finally asleep now. The girl won't stop."

"That's good," Lyle said. "What about my home?"

"Gone," Kit said, his voice thin. "As is mine."

Lyle said nothing. He tossed and turned in the pile of books. Doing his best to get comfortable.

"Adeline wouldn't leave your side," Kit said.

Lyle stopped his fidgeting. "Help me up?"

"You shouldn't Lyle," Kit said. "Your leg isn't well."

"My leg?" Lyle lifted his blanket. White bandages blotched with red wrapped his leg from heel to knee.

"Davrian's shackle... Ripped you pretty good."

"Mandel didn't dress my ankle... He'd make sure I was in a good bed," Lyle glared at Kit.

"I wouldn't be so mean, those are good books. It's like you're really in them." Kit did his best not to crack a smile.

Lyle threw a book at Kit, missing entirely. He held his hand, forgetting it was still in a splint. Lyle closed his eyes. "Blow out that candle. It's killing me. Shouldn't have an open flame in the library anyway."

"You're right, bad idea," Kit's eyes never left his book. "I guess I shouldn't read next to your... book-bed." Kit chuckled. "Seriously, what would you do if your bed caught fire right now? You can't even run!"

"Where is Mandel?"

"Unavailable. So is Freja. She hasn't been seen for some time now. Are you in pain?" Kit's voice was raised.

Lyle held and clinched his eyes. "Unavailable?"

"Unavailable," Kit repeated as he slammed his book shut.

Lyle grimaced and cupped his ears with his hands. "What's wrong with you?"

"Oh, nothing... Well, nothing an apology can't fix."

"An apology? What for?" Lyle chanced a glare, but recoiled at Kit's candle.

"I guess the water got in your head, seeing how you don't remember our talk at the woodpile."

"Kit, you're being childish."

"Perhaps, but I'm not the one withholding an apology."

"Kit—" Lyle held his temple. "I'm sorry, but—"

"Ah, no but's. They only cast blame elsewhere."

"Fine then... I have a lot on my mind."

"And I don't?"

"It's not that, it's just—"

"Ah, no just's. Their only *just*-ifications." Kit said.

"What do you want me to say?"

"I came for your blessing to marry Josie. Instead I got an earful of lamentations and about all the self-pity I could stomach. I'm sorry about Erisa, truly I am. You know that I am. I've never left your side. I still won't. But we've reached a point now, brother. It's time to move on."

"It's not that simple."

"Yes, it is."

Lyle sighed and rubbed his eyes. "Listen, Erisa—"

"I'm not talking about Erisa," Kit lowered his voice. "Why Davrian? ...You forgave Alderman for imprisoning me; you forgave Owin for killing me. Why not Davrian? Your bitterness is poisoning you, Lyle. You spoke to me as if I was an imposter; you're pushing Adeline away. What will you sacrifice to exact vengeance on Davrian for what happened to Erisa? No matter what you do you can't bring her back... And now it seems she was responsible for her own death, not Davrian."

"All her life, she was a victim," Lyle said.

"She dropped the letter into Davrian's Tomb that almost got me killed. She spoke a curse against you and whomever you loved. Victim or not, she is still responsible for her own actions... and her own undoing. Stop second guessing yourself, Lyle. You loved her. It's time to stop blaming yourself for whatever it is that drove her away from you."

"And what about Davrian?"

"It's time to forgive."

Lyle sat up from his books. "What happened in the under city?"

"I knew for sure you had drowned. When you came up over the ledge you started breathing immediately, no water, no... nothing. It was the same with Davrian. He chained himself to your leg. If you don't remember doing it yourself, then only magic can explain it. Which answers the question if Davrian can practice magic or not."

"You think he saved me?" Lyle said.

"You were under water for a long time. He must have done something to keep you from drowning."

"He saved me?" Lyle said.

Kit nodded.

Lyle leaned back into his pallet of books. He covered his face with his hands. "You really thought I was lost?"

"Yes," Kit said.

"Yet you still pulled me up?"

Kit could see a hidden smile beneath Lyle's hands.

"Well, I'd be lying if I said the thought of dropping the rope never crossed my mind. It started to get heavy."

Lyle chuckled, "I'm sorry, Kit." He muttered. "I shouldn't have talked to you the way I did."

"I apologize for being a nuisance, but I had to make my point."

"I thought you said no but's?" Lyle said.

"That I did. Are you still hurting?"

"In great throbs. Every word you say hurts my head... More than normal."

"I'll find Adeline."

"No, please don't."

"Why not? She's taken excellent care of you. She can help."

"Kit... Not now, just. Please. She's angry with me. I upset her."

"Great, you'll have a chance to apologize to her too."

Kit was out of the door before Lyle could protest. Lyle braced himself for what was sure to be an awkward moment. He reached behind and opened a book. The soft pages made for a better pillow than the hard cover. A book corner jabbed at the small of his back. He reached to pull it from the pile, but the books started to avalanche. Just as Adeline entered, Lyle spilled onto the floor with a hundred books.

"Oh, Lyle!" Adeline bit her lip to keep from laughing. She pulled his arm over her shoulders and lifted him to his feet.

"Are you alright?"

"I'm fine," Lyle said, wishing he was asleep; free from pain, awkward conversations and embarrassing moments.

"You shouldn't try to get up. I'm not sure your head can—"

"I wasn't trying to get up," Lyle said, his voice harsher than intended. "I was trying to get comfortable."

"Here, let me help."

Adeline sat him next to the books and stacked them back into a stable pile. She was right about his head. The few seconds on his feet felt no different than the churning whirlpool. He closed his eyes and listened as she worked. When she stopped he cracked his eyes open.

"Kit was supposed to give you this," she said as she spread a woolen blanket across the books. Adeline transformed the pile into a pallet, with an elevated rest for his head and feet, and a modest dip for his back. The woolen blanket absorbed the hard covers and rough edges. It wasn't his bed at home, but certainly better than how Kit left him.

"That reminds me," Adeline said. She pulled a thin book with a green cover from her satchel. "Not that you need another, but it was given to Josie. It came with this letter addressed to you."

Lyle read the letter. It was short, the handwriting all too familiar. He flipped the letter over and to no surprise found the black crow stamped on the back. "Who gave Josie this book?"

"A soldier delivering supplies from the barracks."

"Wiles and Wagers," Lyle read the title aloud. "Why send me this?"

"What does the letter say?"

"A rulebook for a game you should learn. Tread lightly, not for the faint of heart."

"Is it important?" Adeline said.

"Perhaps, but who knows for certain? I know I don't feel like reading."

"Worry about it later. You need to rest," she held his hands and lowered him into bed. "Better?"

"Much," Lyle said. He opened a book like he did before and rested his head on its pages.

"That won't do," Adeline said. She unwrapped a maroon shawl from her shoulders and balled it up. With tender hands she stuffed it under his head. Her cold fingers felt good on his throbbing head. She made more adjustments to the bed, talking only when necessary. She straightened his room and filled a pitcher of water and brought it within his reach. Lastly she checked his ankle.

"I'm sorry about your mother," Lyle said, risking another peek.

"I am too," Adeline said, playing with her apron. "Its better this way I suppose. She may be one of the luckier ones."

"Lucky?"

"This siege..." Adeline sighed. "I'd rather her pass, surrounded by her family than fleeing as the enemy sweeps the streets. At least there was some peace."

"She was fortunate to have you and Josie. You took wonderful care of your parents."

"Father...," she said as she worked, her voice exasperated. "There isn't much I can do for him now. I can't mend a broken heart. He is afraid for us too. He knows Averlace's days are numbered."

"He also knows Kit and I will be there for you two."

Adeline smiled, unsure how to respond. She thought she knew what Lyle meant, but things had turned out different than how she dreamed. Her straight lips and burdened eyes was enough for Lyle to read her thoughts.

"Averlace's days aren't numbered," he said. "Before it's all over, I'll see you on a new stage, perhaps a rebuilt Kettle and Dove. You'll be moving the crowd to tears and then to laughter-touching them like you always did."

Adeline blushed. "Mom said that every night after the fire. Seems like you two think the same."

"It's because I promised it to her."

Adeline shook her head and crossed her arms. "Lyle... I apologize for putting you in a position you never intended to be in. I am grateful to know you, and my family is blessed to have friends like you."

She squeezed his hand and walked for the door. "Let me know if you need anything."

Lyle tried to say goodbye, but a lump had grown in his throat. He picked up the Ebon Crow's book and thumbed through the pages. After a minute he tossed it aside. There was no concentrating now. He drank from the pitcher and closed his eyes. His head hurting more than ever.

CHAPTER THIRTY
RISING FLAMES

CHAPTER THIRTY

RISING FLAMES

HE ARMY OF the Northern March was on the move.
Rayghar promised Marquise Eelton the army could
move by morning. He bested his promise and by
sunrise the last of the army's supply wagons passed the farming
town, Gillian. Athan remembered General Picus boasting about
his army's discipline, but even his own praise fell short.

Three thousand spears trotted down Manadon road on
mighty Averlacian warhorses, another five-hundred footmen
marched behind. Even the draft horses pulled the supply
wagons and machines of war at astonishing speeds. However,
despite the might of Rayghar's force, there was one wagon that
casted doubt and apprehension and it smelled of fresh fruit,
costly perfume and wine.

"He doesn't plan to actually lead this expedition, does he?"
Eamon said as he goose necked back at Marquis Eelton's private
wagon.

"Turn around," Athan said. "Between you and Bratheon the
marquis may very well change his mind."

"The Wolf would never abandon the king," Eamon said.
"He has more honor than that."

"But not enough sense to refuse giving up command,"
Bratheon said.

"You need to be quiet," Athan said. "You've obviously never traveled with soldiers. Talk of mutiny won't be tolerated. The army is strong and moving fast. We can't ask for more."

"I beg to differ," Bratheon pointed at Eelton's entourage. "Look at him, war isn't on his mind. I hear music, women laughing and merry-making from that wagon. He's not here to serve the king; he's here to bolster his own name, to bring some sort of peace of mind."

"Quiet," Athan scowled. "We know who's in charge here, don't worry yourself about Eelton. If he wants to parade himself around the battlefield then I say let him, so long as his army shows up. Besides, these men aren't here for the marquis; they march for King Alderman."

Bratheon clinched his teeth and gave the wagon one last resentful glance. "How long do you expect?"

"Rayghar says three days," Athan said. "I didn't believe him at first, but now..."

"Will we break the siege?" Eamon said.

"Do we have a choice?" Athan said.

"Of course we will," Bratheon said.

Athan raised his brow. "So confident? I wouldn't have guessed a moment ago."

"I don't doubt the army, Rayghar, Averlace or my friends. We will break the siege, that I have no concern. It's when the war is over that troubles me, when Averlace rebuilds. When men like Eelton go back to their thrones and lead... Its leaders like him that are responsible for this invasion. I've said it before and I'll say it again; there's no reason for Averlace to be threatened by the Itihasians. Unless Eelton changes, the Northern March will remain soft and unguided. Men like Picus and Rayghar are the only reason there is strength here."

"Until then you best keep your opinions to yourself," Athan said.

"Maybe it's a good thing Eelton is coming along after all that," Eamon said to Bratheon. "Perhaps you stirred a fire in him."

Bratheon let out an empty sigh. "That's what I hoped. We will see. We'll have to wait and see."

*   *   *

Farvré purred on Fadrien's lap, oblivious to the chaos outside. Townspeople scurried to evacuate Manadon Square. Whinnying horses, screaming children and yelling men kept Illiott from delving into his books. Fadrien, on the other hand, seemed impervious to the interruptions.

Cracking timber from a nearby collapsing building served as the final straw. Illiott tossed his book to the floor, defeated.

"I'm going out. There's nothing I can do here."

"No, I need you," Fadrien said, his voice strained, but composed. "Our work here is just as important."

"Should I carry the books we need to the library? They can't stay here, Fadrien. It's only a matter of time before the school is hit. They've pushed their catapults closer, we're in range."

"Are we correct about them?"

"Correct about what?"

"The medallions. Are we sure they can unlock the manaist vault like we first thought?" Fadrien said.

"Did you hear me?" Illiott said. "We need to leave. We can continue this on higher ground, out of range."

"The way opened, though only temporarily," Fadrien said.

"Fadrien, we must make for the keep. What do you want me to gather?"

Fadrien looked from his book. "Leave the school?"

"Yes, I believe it is time to move."

"The medallions…"

Illiott cursed, "We put them in wrong. They still opened the way, but only for a short amount of time. It's all rigged as a trap; we must set the medallions in correctly for safe passage. And we must have all four."

"But, why the final pedestal? Lyle said there was one more at the vault's door. Perhaps we need all five of them. Not just the four like we thought. We may need them along with the king's."

"Either way, we don't have the king's or the fourth. Davrian said the Itihasians have it."

"How did Davrian come by the fourth medallion in the first place?"

"We'll have to figure that out later," Illiott said. "Right now we have to get out."

"How did Davrian cast a spell without his medallion? How did he and Lyle survive the water? You can't cast a spell without a medallion or trinket, right? You must have access to manastone."

Illiott was about to pull Fadrien from his chair but stopped. "You're right."

"You don't suppose he still has his medallion?" Fadrien said.

"No, we've searched him. He doesn't have it." Illiott thought back to the night he lit his candle. He didn't have his manastone knives, they were tucked in his drawer, along with his medallion.

"Perhaps you can…" Illiott mused. "I lit a candle the other night with magic."

Fadrien's eyes widened. "You did what?"

"I lit a candle. I would have told you, but I thought you would have been concerned."

"How?" Fadrien said.

"With magic... My will. I imagined the candle aglow so it happened. Well, in a way. It actually erupted."

"Erupted?"

"I was so excited that I didn't realize at the time that I didn't have my medallion with me. I did it without any manastone."

"That's impossible," Fadrien said. "All of the text is clear. You must have manastone to cast a spell, or altercation."

"Nothing, I promise. I didn't have it with me. Perhaps there is an exception, something we overlooked?"

"No, there is no exception."

"What if you are in close proximity to manastone?"

"No you must be mindful of the source," Fadrien said.

"Fadrien I'm not sure that is the way it works. I'm telling you I had nothing and Davrian had nothing on him that could have given him power... Do you realize what this means? We must get to Davrian now; if he can use magic without the use of manastone then he is dangerous."

Fadrien couldn't move. His eyes drifted to an unfocused stare. "Something is wrong."

"Either way," Illiott said. "We must inform the Elite. Davrian is dangerous."

"The Elite..." Fadrien petted Farvré faster and harder as he thought. He stopped and looked at his signet ring. "The King's Elite... Did you have your ring on?"

"My ring?"

"Were you wearing your ring when you lit the candle?" Fadrien held his breath.

"Yes," Illiott held his hand up. "You don't think?"

Fadrien slid his ring off and held it for both to see. The onyx stone looked nothing like manastone. Fadrien strained his eyes as he observed the ring's intricate details. Engraved on the onyx was an image of a sword piercing a glowing stone. Just below the sword's pommel was a notch. Fadrien fuddled with the ring, trying to pry the notch open. After a few attempts the setting popped off the ring, revealing a glowing red stone.

"Manastone," Illiott gasped. "Our rings... Who knew?"

"These were once manaist rings," Fadrien said. "Infused with manastone."

"You were right," Illiott said. "You must have a source to cast a spell. I had the ring, but that doesn't explain Davrian."

"No, you forget," Fadrien said, his voice grave. "Davrian is wearing the king's signet ring."

"He knew. It's why he insisted he have one!"

"Yes," Fadrien said. "Hurry, we must go to him now and obtain the ring."

Fadrien knelt down for Farvré who jumped into his inside coat pocket. Illiott started gathering the books and scrolls needed to continue their research when the shouts and screams outside grew more desperate. A moment later, Bruan barged into the school. His sword and tabard dripped with blood.

"Get out of here," he yelled. "The wall's breached!"

Illiott ran outside with a satchel loaded with books. The northern wall was engulfed in flame. Fiery arrows rained down. Itihasian soldiers scaled over the gate. A few brave men stood their ground, but were eventually overcome by the enemy or fire.

"Fadrien," Illiott tossed the satchel to the councilman's feet. He ran back into the school and returned with his bow and a near empty quiver of arrows.

"Don't be a fool," Bruan grabbed Illiott. "Follow me to the keep. We're gathering at Astrannax bridge."

Bruan's voice bellowed for retreat as he ran down Manadon. He stopped at every distressed townsperson, helping the injured back to their feet or guiding the lost and confused. Officers knew where to find their captain, and many reported to him as he led the evacuation to higher ground. Though the northern wall fell, Bruan remained poised and composed.

Fadrien and Illiott made it to Astrannax Bridge, the last chokepoint before the keep's gatehouse. Fadrien slipped on the bridge's planks, bringing him to his hands and knees. Black pitch covered his hands. Bruan was going to burn the bridge. Fadrien's heart sank, Averlace was slipping away.

Illiott helped him to his feet and they continued to the keep with the rest of the retreating townspeople. Illiott joined Ingran and the Falconers, who waited with fixed bows at the keep's barbican. From the gatehouse Illiott could see the entire might of the Itihasian army fall onto the northern wall. He watched as the forces defending the south, west and east walls worked back to the bridge.

Manadon Street crossed the Numen River at Astrannax Bridge then climbed a steep hill before reaching the keep. A few farmhouses lined the road before the ground sloped to the foot of the keep's walls. The steep and open road made for a perfect killing ground.

"Arrows!" Ingran ordered, his gruff voice carried from the barbican.

Illiott drew an arrow and scoured the streets. Bruan led the last survivors of the north wall to the bridge. Manadon Street flooded with Itihasians, hoping to overcome Bruan and his men.

"Fire!"

Illiott let an arrow fly into the mass of enemy soldiers. He notched another arrow and watched as fifty Itihasians fell.

"Fire!"

More of the enemy fell. Barret led a small force to meet Bruan and the survivors on the bridge. Together they made a phalanx and backed down the bridge. The Falconers' arrows rained death on any foolish enough to pursue the Averlacians. The enemy had enough. They had taken everything north of the Numen River.

Bruan waited as long as he dared. He raised a red streamer overhead and led the last of his men across the bridge. Once over, Ingran launched a fiery arrow at the bridge's far end. Within seconds the structure was engulfed in flame.

The enemy lined the opposing shore, raising curses and threats to Bruan and his men. Ingran and his men picked off a few more of the enemy. The Itihasians retaliated with a few stray arrows then fell back to the city's ruins.

Bruan watched safely from the river's bank. Barret stood beside him.

"How many made it across?" Bruan said, bracing himself for the worst.

"Eight-hundred," Barret said.

Bruan couldn't believe the number. It was more than double what was planned for the retreat. Bruan's plan worked as well as anyone could have hoped. Evacuating the townspeople to the library days before made for an easy retreat, though costly. The bridge wasn't completely burned. Bruan looked down Manadon Road to the north wall. It burned from the gatehouse to the eastern tower.

"Why burn the walls?" Barret said. The plume on his helmet and ratted green cape smoked and smoldered. "They mean to destroy everything?"

Bruan nodded. "They are making way for their catapults and towers. They know this is far from over."

He looked at Astrannaxian Bridge with forlorn eyes. Though the retreat was successful, Bruan couldn't help but feel defeated as he watched the walls burn.

When the enemy army sounds the retreat, then you may wear your ring.

CHAPTER THIRTY ONE

PARLAY

CHAPTER THIRTY-ONE

PARLAY

T HE MORNING report was promising. Of the twelve-hundred fighting men, a thousand remained. Bruan couldn't believe the resilience of his men. Even more encouraging, one of Ingran's scouts witnessed the collapse of the western wall. The gatehouse fell as the Itihasian forces passed, crushing an estimated hundred men.

The retreat wasn't without its shortcomings. Bruan ordered his men to oil homes, bridges and roads as they fell back to the keep. Most were successful, but the fires caught prematurely as the Itihasians raised the walls. Bruan had hoped to burn the city today, once most of the Itihasian force occupied the lower Averlace. Had it worked, it could have devastated the Itihasian army. Instead, the Averlacians watched throughout the night as their homes and businesses burned for naught. But the effort wasn't in vain. Though burning the city came sooner than planned, it slowed the Itihasians as they overran the wall, allowing more of Bruan's men to retreat.

More survivors presented a new problem. There were more than enough men to man the keep's walls. Perhaps too many. Two men were assigned to each merlon; even still, the numbers spilled out into the keep's courtyard. The road was blocked, and the staggering numbers were of little benefit. Most were boys or older men, unarmed save whatever they could throw over the wall. The walls, ramparts and roads were overcrowded. Bruan dismissed the young and the old to the library. Without sufficient shelter at the wall, they would only be killed in the coming barrage.

Bruan looked out from the barbican. The Itihasians were quick at work, fortifying Carper's Vale and moving their catapults into position.

"Carper's Vale rises just enough…" Bruan mumbled to Illiott. "Their catapults could reach even the top of the keep."

"We can still outlast them?" Illiott said. "The Marquis should be here in two days."

"With no small amount of courage or without a great deal of luck," Bruan said. He pointed to the catapults. "The keep and its walls rise just enough above Carper's Vale to allow them to fire their catapults at full strength. Rather than lobbing them at a great distance, they'll pummel the wall's sides until it crumbles. Something must be done about Carper's Vale."

Illiott sighed. From the barbican he could see most of the city. Averlace was overrun. Barret spent the greater part of the morning calculating the enemy's strength.

Twenty-two thousand.

"Carper's Vale is out of reach," Illiott said.

Bruan nodded. He remembered Kvrual's parting words at the parlay.

If you want to protect your people you better do what you believe to be best and take matters into your own hands.

Kvrual meant for Bruan to surrender, King Alderman forbade his cavalry to attack. Neither option was acceptable. Bruan knew what was best, but Alderman had his doubts about the manaist armory.

"There is no other way," Bruan said. "We have to destroy those catapults."

"Even if we emptied the keep, we'd never reach the top of Carper's Vale," Illiott said.

"Is there nothing?" Bruan said. "The girl? Can she do something?"

"I'm afraid it doesn't work that way," Illiott said. "She's vowed never again. Attacks like that... it's all from anger."

"Right," Bruan folded his arms. "Can't become what we're trying to destroy."

"Something like that..." Illiott said. He looked down on Carper's Vale as the Itihasians' prepared their siege weapons. *When is it justified?* he thought. If I had the power I would save my city.

Illiott imagined fire raining from the sky and consuming Carper's Vale. He could see men fleeing from the catapults as an unquenchable fire swept the hill. Just as he reached for his medallion a horn blasted from the bridge's ruins.

It was Sgoravon and Kvrual with his body guard led by the towering man, Mruav. They climbed the hill up to the gatehouse with shields above their heads. Mruav carried a white banner. He stuck it in the road and cried out to the gate.

"Captain of the wall. Aegis of the King!" Mruav leaned on the banner and laughed. "Where are you?"

Bruan and Illiott peeked through a set of murder holes at the gigantic Itihasian.

"What does he want with you?" Illiott said.

"He promised to pour my blood," Bruan said with a forced smile. "I'm half tempted to let him try his hand."

"You could barely reach the top of his head. What does he have against you?"

"Sport. He wants the glory of killing the enemy captain."

"Will the Captain of the Wall not answer the King's emissary?" Another voice called out. It was Sgoravon. He observed the portcullis as he waited. It was thicker and stronger than those on the outer wall.

Bruan never answered.

"This is madness," Sgoravon looked to the barbican ceiling overhead. He could see dozens of eyes peering through the murder holes. "Look at you all. You're backed into a corner. Trapped. You will all die, cowering behind your walls. The entire might of Itihasia will fall upon you. I come now peacefully, offering you terms of your surrender. Will the Captain of the Wall not answer?"

Bruan had scoffed at Sgoravon's terms on the field; that was before the Itihasian army nearly tripled in size. Now he could feel the eyes of his men. He could see it on some of their faces, hoping he would accept the terms of surrender. Others were ready to fight to the death. All were afraid.

"Give up our prince, and grant us access to the manaist treasure. Those are our demands. Comply, and not another drop of Averlacian blood will be spilt."

Illiott whispered to Bruan, "He lies. What else would they want with a magical armory? If they are willing to take it by force, surely they have no intentions of using it for peace."

"They come now because they know they can't take this keep easily," Barret said. "Perhaps we can last until the marquis arrives."

"But can the marquis overcome the Itihasians?" Bruan said.

"Will you not answer?" Sgoravon's voice called out.

"You must say something," Illiott said. "At least address the men."

"Our terms remain the same," Bruan yelled. "Leave our land, and no more Itihasian blood will be spilt against our wall."

"So be it," Sgoravon said. He reached out for one of his escorts and hobbled back to Mruav.

Bruan watched Mruav with contempt. "He doesn't seem to be an officer," he said to Barret.

"Perhaps a champion?" Illiott said.

Bruan nodded and looked to Barret. "When the catapults attack I want the men pulled from the wall. They will only be crushed. Leave a few volunteers to keep watch, no more."

"Where should the others take cover?"

"The keep is nothing but stone. I doubt they will send a volley. Nothing will catch fire. They will bring down the wall then storm the keep. The inner courtyard may be as safe as any place."

"Shouldn't we evacuate into the undercity?" Illiott said.

"Not if it's as dangerous as you say."

"No more dangerous than up here."

A boy wearing a leather cap entered the barbican. A short sword hung from his belt without a scabbard. "Captain, a message."

The boy stepped aside and Freja entered. She held a small note, her face beaming.

"It's from my brother," she said. "He's here."

"The marquis is here?" Illiott said with a start.

"Soon," Freja said.

Bruan reached in his pocket for the signet ring. He lowered his head. "The wall is yours," he said to Barret. "Illiott, Freja, come with me. We need to speak with the king."

* * *

Alderman's face glowed as he read Bratheon's letter. Marquis Eelton's army would arrive by evening. Even more encouraging was a strategic plan devised by the new general, Rayghar.

"He intends to raid their supply camps." Alderman said. "With most of the enemy inside Averlace's gates, their supply camps and caravans are practically unguarded. If they strike fast and hard enough, the enemy will lose its capacity to wage a long siege. They will have to withdraw."

"Unless their catapults can level the keep's wall fast enough," Bruan said.

Alderman furrowed his brow. "What is wrong Bruan?"

"My men are afraid, most are unarmed. They can do nothing now, but watch the enemy as it builds the catapults that will destroy them. Even if General Rayghar is successful, will it be enough to stop Kvrual? He will try to take back their camps. Rayghar will be overrun."

"What do you suggest?" Alderman said.

"We must be ready to destroy Carper's Vale when that happens."

"Impossible," Alderman said. "I'd rather take my chances behind the wall."

"We may have a chance if we attack when Kvrual leads his army against the Marquis."

"Kvrual's army is large enough to fight two fronts," Alderman said. "Besides, you said it yourself. Most of your men aren't sufficiently equipped for war."

"Unless we open the manaist treasure." Bruan cleared his throat.

Alderman drew a deep, slow breath. "From what I understand it's not even an option until we find the medallion. It's time to think of a way of winning this war without the treasure."

"But we can't win without it," Bruan said. "This treasure is involved in the war whether we want it or not. If we don't claim it the enemy will use it to finish us off. There is something Davrian isn't telling us. He knows where the medallion is hidden."

"Then why not tell us?" Alderman held out his hands. "He claims he wants to help, but why not tell us? Don't you see, Bruan? He's waiting. Davrian's waiting for the Itihasians to liberate him. He will then lead them to the vault and open it."

"Then why would Davrian run from Kvrual in the first place?" Bruan said. "We have to trust Davrian."

"Since he's been so cooperative in the past?" Alderman said.

"Your Majesty," Fadrien's voice trickled between Alderman's echoing bellows. "Perhaps Davrian has been more cooperative than it seems. Illiott and I stumbled across a discovery concerning the guildmaster. I would have told you sooner, but time hasn't permitted. The signet rings are imbued with manastone, which allows manaist to cast spells."

"And Davrian is wearing one..." Alderman said. "This allows him to do what exactly?"

"Cast a spell, altercation, curse. Anything magical," Illiott said.

"You fools!" Alderman said. "Must you seek my permission? Retrieve the ring from him. He's dangerous."

"Is he?" Bruan said. "Is he really dangerous? To me this proves we can trust him. How long as he had the ring? Surely he would have used it against us by now if he wanted?"

"He did save Lyle's life," Fadrien said.

Alderman lifted his crown from his head and wiped his brow. He grabbed his hammer and stood from his throne. "Where is Lyle?" He said as he made for the door.

"Recovering in the library," Fadrien said.

"Find him and have him meet us in the council chamber. Prepare Davrian for my arrival. He won't have any secrets when I'm done with him." Alderman rested the hammer on his shoulder, "Or my ring for that matter."

CHAPTER THIRTY TWO
WILES AND WAGERS

CHAPTER THIRTY-TWO

WILES AND WAGERS

LYLE HADN'T slept for long when Fadrien and Kit woke him. They were walking down the library steps before Lyle was fully awake, and crossing the courtyard before he thought to ask where they were going.

"Alderman has asked for you," Fadrien said as he led the brothers through a maze of soldiers, tents, horses and wagons. "We've learned our signet rings have magical properties, and we must confiscate Davrian's."

"You need Lyle to talk Davrian out of his ring?" Kit said. "What if Davrian refuses."

"Bruan, Illiott and King Alderman will also be present. Let's just say I hope you are successful. King Alderman isn't leaving without the ring and the whereabouts of the king's medallion."

"Surely, Davrian knows the ring is magical," Lyle said.

"Of course, that's how he was able to save your life," Fadrien said.

"If that's the case, I doubt he will offer it freely."

"And if he hasn't already told us the whereabouts of the medallion I doubt we'll persuade him to do so now," Kit said.

Lyle snapped his fingers. "Perhaps we may."

"What do you mean?" Kit said.

"I was given a book from the Ebon Crow. It taught me how to play a game."

"A game?" Kit's eyes scrunched together. "How does that help us?"

"I'm not sure, but I have a feeling we are about to find out."

Fadrien led Lyle and Kit to his council chamber. Lyle went silent. Kit knew not to ask any questions. His brother was on to something and was best left alone.

Alderman, Bruan and Illiott waited outside the council chamber, weapons drawn. The king's rigid face told that he'd exhausted all patience already. He cleared his throat with an angered growl.

"Don't let him toy with you, Lyle," Alderman said. "I won't tolerate it. He either tells us where to find my medallion and gives us his ring, or dies."

"Assuming he's still inside," Fadrien said. "He may know we've learned about his ring's power. He may be long gone."

"Or waiting for us," Illiott said. "Be ready for anything."

Bruan closed his eyes, hoping for the best and preparing for the worst. He gave everyone a short nod then opened the door. Alderman rushed in first, his war hammer at the ready.

Davrian was in the corner of the chamber, seated next to an unlit brazier. His ankles and wrists still cuffed to the wall. He nearly fell out of his chair at the sight of the king.

"Your Majesty," Davrian smiled. "How may I serve you?"

"Don't speak," Alderman said. He held out his hand. "We're here for the ring."

Davrian recoiled his hand and jumped to his feet.

"Allow me, Your Highness," Lyle said. He stepped between Alderman and Davrian. "It's over, Davrian," he said. "We know about the signet rings. It's time to hand yours over."

"Hand it over?" Davrian turned his hands away. "Or else?"

"Don't be a fool," Lyle said, spreading his arms to keep Alderman from passing. "The kingdom is at its breaking point. You claim you want to help, and earn our trust? Then give us the ring."

Davrian tightened his hand into a fist, hiding the ring. "You are wise not to take it by force," his voice was thin. "But your trust is no longer important to me."

"What do you mean?"

"The enemy is here. It's too late. The king's medallion and the manaist treasure can't help you now."

"Stand aside, Lyle," Alderman shouted.

Lyle refused, his eyes never leaving Davrian's ring. Fadrien pulled at Alderman's shoulders.

"Listen, Davrian. This can end peacefully. We just need you to give us the ring and tell us where we can find the medallion," Lyle said coolly.

"What makes you think I know?"

"Just a hunch. I doubt you would have played us the way you have unless you knew everyone's hand," Lyle said.

"Perhaps I know," Davrian said.

"Then why not tell us? Why not help, like you claim."

"That's a lot of questions..." Davrian sneered. He spun the ring on his finger. "Most I refuse to answer, unless it could be of some benefit."

"Saving this kingdom isn't a benefit enough?"

"What of my freedom?"

"Granted," Lyle said, knowing Davrian's pardon was beyond his power.

Alderman said nothing.

"I'm afraid it won't be that easy," Davrian said. "You see, I'm at an advantage, I'd like to keep it that way. I'll wager my ring for my freedom and challenge you to a duel."

"This isn't just about the ring; we need to know where to find the medallion," Lyle said. "Besides I'm not fighting you. I'm trying to help."

Davrian laughed. "I don't want to fight you either. If you want to help then play a game with me."

"He's toying with you," Kit said.

"I said no games, Lyle," Alderman said.

"If you want this to end peaceably, then you have no choice." Davrian clutched his ring in a tight fist. "You want the ring and the king's medallion?"

Lyle nodded.

"Are you familiar with Wiles and Wagers?"

Lyle was right about the book Adeline delivered. He'd only read the introduction and flipped through the rest; part rule book, the rest theory. At the time resting was more important than studying an ancient manaist game of questions, wagers and answers. Now he thought differently.

"I know of it," Lyle said.

"Let me explain the rules," Davrian said. "Under oath and spell, both players make an agreement of two or more wagers. Then they each take a turn asking a question. The first to tell a lie or refuse to answer, loses. Simple, no?"

Lyle only flipped through the pages, but he knew enough to know the game was far from simple. Questions are dangerous, and before playing one must know what secrets they're willing to pay to win their opponents wager. Consequently, there was more to win than just Davrian's ring; the questions could prove just as valuable. But Davrian would also never suggest such a game unless he was trying to learn something himself.

"How will we know you aren't lying?" Alderman said.

"The most common way is to alter a candle to light when one tells a lie. That is why it's a game played by manaists, or the foolish." Davrian's eyes taunted Lyle.

"The brazier then? Seeing we are without a candle." Lyle pulled an empty chair beside Davrian.

Davrian rolled the ring across his knuckles. "Here's a tip from a master... Remember the winner often loses more than what his wager is worth." Davrian looked to the brazier then closed his eyes, concentrating as the ring tumbled down his fingers. His eyes opened with unnerving confidence. "Your wager?"

"Your freedom," Lyle said.

"And I wager my ring and the whereabouts of the King's Medallion," Davrian said as he waved his hand at the brazier. "The board is set."

"Shall I begin?" Lyle said.

"Naturally, you're the challenger," Davrian said.

Lyle wasted no time. This was the opportunity he needed, a game to freely pry into Davrian's mind, and the guild master was more than willing to play.

"Where is the king's medallion?" Lyle said, folding his arms.

"Ah, a question that will award you one of your wagers win or lose," Davrian said. "Well played."

"Where is it?"

"Underneath the king's throne. The footrest I believe. You'll find a drawer. It's in there."

"You lie," Alderman said.

"No, Your Majesty. I speak the truth. As you can see the brazier is still unlit."

"You never altered it, or whatever it is you're supposed to do to make it work," Alderman said.

Davrian stood erect, his eyes stern. "I've never led the Syndicate!"

A flame popped to life in the brazier's cold ashes. Alderman's face changed from anger to bewilderment. He held his hand over the fire then quickly brought it back. The flame was no illusion.

"You try, Lyle," Davrian said.

Bruan was just as amazed. He reached over Alderman's shoulder and suffocated the flame with his leather glove.

Lyle watched as a wisp of smoke puffed in the air. "I have no brother."

The flame returned, burning on nothing but powdery ash.

"Shall we continue?" Davrian said. "I believe it is my turn."

Bruan patted the second flame out. Alderman pulled a chair beside Lyle and sat down. Kit, Illiott and Bruan followed suit. The scene was reminiscent of the night they heard their prophecies.

"King Alderman accused me of lying about the medallion's location. I doubt he would have accused me had he not already searched there himself. Sounds like he already looked under the throne, but didn't think to look under the footrest. Interesting, no?" Davrian said.

Lyle smiled, believing Davrian made a mistake. "That must be your question."

"It is indeed," Davrian said. "I'd like to know what you're honest thoughts are about Alderman searching his throne for the medallion."

Lyle stared at the brazier. To be honest with his thoughts may offend the king. Still, he had to answer the question honestly.

"I think it is interesting," Lyle agreed, keeping his answer vague. If Davrian wanted to know more, he'd have to ask.

Davrian gave an approving nod. "You're careful with your answers."

"It's your turn to answer," Lyle said. "Why not tell us where the medallion was, if you were sincere in helping?"

"Because I wanted to know if I could trust you with it first," Davrian said without a moment's hesitation.

Alderman, Bruan and Illiott wanted to laugh, but the brazier never lit. Davrian was as serious as death when he spoke. It was now his turn to ask. He tapped his chin for a moment then faced Lyle.

"Are you going to survive the siege?" Davrian continued rolling the ring down his knuckles.

"How should I know?" Lyle shrugged. "Is this some sort of trick? What if I guess wrong?"

"Play the game," Davrian said.

"I can tell you in honest what I hope, but I have no way of knowing what's to come."

"Is it a lie if you answer wrong in ignorance?" Kit said.

"I gave him a question," Davrian said. "He must answer it."

Kit lowered his head. The game was more than just a battle of wits, but a terrifying joust of nerves and courage.

Lyle tapped his chin. Not only was he at a loss for an answer, he didn't know if he dared try. He hoped to survive the war. Something told him he would. Was it a lingering feeling of invulnerability from his youth? Or a desire to overcome the odds? Either way, he had to answer the question, unfair or not.

He decided to go with what he hoped. He will survive... but what if he was wrong? Not only does he lose the game, he will learn his fate.

"I'll survive," Lyle said. His voice wavered. He looked to the brazier, afraid to see the flame.

Nothing.

Both brothers breathed a sigh of relief. Lyle knew he had to be more intentional with his questions. Davrian was playing a certain strategy, perhaps one he perfected. It will take more than cunning to stump or scare Davrian into forfeiting. Still, there was more to learn from Davrian if Lyle had the courage to stay in the game.

"Will you survive this war?" Lyle said. The question was more of an attempt to buy time to think. If anything he could play using Davrian's own questions against him.

"Yes," Davrian said. He didn't even bother to look at the brazier. "How did you learn about this game?"

"The Ebon Crow," Lyle said slowly, studying Davrian's eyes and face. The guild master's face remained neutral, his pupils never dilated. Davrian wasn't surprised by the answer, he expected it.

Lyle was at a loss, what was Davrian trying to accomplish? Every question Davrian asked seemed strategic. No matter how hard Lyle tried, he couldn't get under Davrian's skin, but then the perfect question came to him.

"What's your strategy to winning this game?"

Davrian wasn't as quick this turn. He was more impressed than concerned by Lyle's question. He thought for a moment.

"A strategy to win?" Davrian mused. "...To search for a series of questions that will pull out a secret, a secret more valuable to you than my freedom. Which leads me to my question... How is it that the Ebon Crow, the one who introduced you to this game, could be confident enough to promise my freedom?"

"I believe that was an empty promise and that the Ebon Crow is using you. You're nothing more than a tool."

Alderman shuffled in his chair. "This is going nowhere! We already know where to find the medallion... What else do we need?"

"We can't leave him with the ring," Lyle said. His mind raced to find a challenging question. Lyle knew Davrian was hiding something, but what?

"Why do you feel like you must trust us with the treasure?"

"I'm not concerned with what you will do with the treasure, but what you won't do."

Lyle rolled his eyes. Alderman was right. They were getting nowhere. He knew better than to ask such a question.

"Now tell me," Davrian said. "Do you think Averlace should use the treasure to fight the enemy? Or do you fear it?"

"I do have concerns," Lyle said. "Our ancestors hid the treasure for a reason, yet I have faith in Averlace to be responsible with the power."

Davrian wore a smug look and pointed to the brazier. Smoke started to rise.

"No, I was honest!" Lyle protested.

"Perhaps you should be more specific," Davrian said. "Do you think Averlace should, or shouldn't?"

"Yes, I fear it, but I believe we should use it." Lyle hated that his voice sounded so panicked. He had to change the pace of the questions.

"Did you care for Erisa?"

Davrian folded his arms. "As though she was my sister."

Lyle and Kit exchanged looks. Still no flame.

"Do you finally accept that I am not your enemy?" Davrian said.

The answer came to Lyle quickly. He checked it in his mind to make sure it was true. It came to him so naturally, yet a part of him still couldn't believe.

"Yes," Lyle said. "You are not my enemy." He thought back to Davrian's second question… "How did you know the Ebon Crow introduced Wiles and Wagers to me?"

Davrian looked amused. "A similar game was popular within the Syndicate. Now tell me, why won't the king use the treasure against the enemy?"

"What does this have to do with me?" Alderman roared. "You are delaying."

"Answer the question!" Davrian stood from his chair.

Lyle sunk his head into his hands and rubbed his temple. Davrian read him. The guild master knew what Lyle suspected Alderman planned to do with the treasure, and with the question worded as it was, Lyle had to be specific.

"I believe he would fight to the death, before taking a risk to open it. He's afraid that even with the treasure Averlace could not hold back Itihasia and the enemy would then have access to the manaist weapons."

Alderman scoffed at the question, and his mood darkened even more after Lyle's answer. Davrian nodded in agreement.

It was Lyle's turn.

"What does the Ebon Crow want with the manaist treasure?"

"He wants it for himself. I am not certain what he may do with it," Davrian said. He faced Alderman though his question was for Lyle.

"To never use the treasure would be dangerous, would it not?"

"Possibly," Lyle said, grateful for a chance to be vague. He could hear Alderman's laborious sighs. He had to put the pressure on Davrian. "How would you describe your relationship with the Ebon Crow?"

"Strictly business, but the old crow's been known to throw me a bone." Davrian ran his fingers through the brazier's ashes, taunting the fire to come alive. He made Lyle and the other's wait for his next question.

"...You've already said that Averlace will need the treasure to win. So here is my question. Since you believe the king won't open the vault, then you believe the king may be dangerous, don't you?" Davrian sat back down. His face smug and victorious.

Lyle knew the honest answer, but to say it before the king might not be worth the ring's wager. He could feel Alderman's eyes pressing into his back. Either way, the question has been asked, the damage now done. To refuse to answer it would be just as destructive as telling the truth.

"Yes," Lyle said. "I believe the king may be dangerous."

Davrian had no reaction to the answer. Even Alderman kept quiet. Did they both believe he would forfeit?

"I believe it is your turn," Davrian said.

Davrian's questions were becoming more and more dangerous. If the game continued, there could be fissures between the king and his men. Davrian was using the game to stir the king's anger, but why? Lyle needed one question to end the game, one question that Davrian wouldn't dare answer. Lyle sat at the edge of his seat and leaned towards Davrian.

"You know who the Ebon Crow is… Don't you?"

Davrian's smug face grew even more complacent. He pinched the ring with his right hand and tossed it to Alderman.

"The game is over," Davrian said. "I refuse to answer the question."

Silence hung in the room. The king and his men exchanged questioning glances.

Illiott clapped Lyle on the back. "Well done."

Lyle said nothing.

Bruan kept silent, keeping the ring in sight as Alderman slid it back on to his finger. He pondered over Davrian's questions about the king, wondering if the ring went to someone less trustworthy.

Alderman turned the ring on his finger. "I can agree with you on one matter, Guildmaster. The game was quite simple, but a waste of time."

"Thank you for humoring me, Your Majesty."

"What now?" Fadrien asked. "We have the ring and the medallion. Do we open the vault?"

"I know what Lyle would have me do," Alderman said. "But this is a decision I will make with full council."

"Then let us not waste any more time," Fadrien said, eager to move on.

Kit sensed something was wrong. Lyle should be basking in his victory over Davrian, not stooping in his chair, eyes locked on the brazier.

"What of Davrian?" Bruan said.

Alderman scowled, "What of him?" He rested his hammer on his shoulder and made for the door. He left his men with no choice but to follow him to his throne room.

CHAPTER THIRTY THREE
AEGIS OF THE ELITE

CHAPTER THIRTY-THREE

AEGIS OF THE ELITE

ILLIOTT AND FADRIEN searched the throne for the medallion. Their fingers probed around its carvings, fiddling the spindles and gilded carvings. Bruan, Lyle and Kit kept their distance as they waited in anticipation. Alderman propped his foot on the steps leading to his throne. Resting an elbow on his knee, he eyed Fadrien and Illiott like a hawk.

"You don't think he lied to us again?" Alderman said, his impatience growing.

"No, Your Majesty," Lyle said.

"Then why haven't we found it?" Alderman snapped at Lyle.

"We are close," Fadrien's voice carried from behind the throne. "We see a medallion engraved underneath."

"Yes, I've seen it too, but it won't open," Alderman said.

Illiott slid on his back under the throne. Centered beneath the seat was the engraving. He ran his fingers across it. Nothing.

"You don't suppose it's locked by some spell?" Illiott said.

"Possibly," Fadrien cracked open one of his books. He turned a few pages then closed it shut, rolling his eyes. How could he forget? "Which side of the medallion does it show? Does it say anything?"

"For the giving and the taking?" Illiott's muttered as he read.

The throne clicked and clanked. A small tray popped underneath the foot rest. Inside the King's Medallion lay, identical to the others save its purple lanyard.

"Ha," Illiott's eyes lit up. "It's here. This is it!" He grabbed the medallion and held it out for all to see.

Alderman snatched it from Illiott's hand. "Where are the others?"

"Here, Your Majesty," Fadrien said. "We only have the three. The other is with Kvrual, presumably."

"And we need it to open the vault?" Alderman said.

"No, just yours," Illiott said.

"Davrian should have told us long before," Fadrien said. "We may not have lost the city if we had the treasure."

Alderman draped the medallion around his neck. "Tell me, Fadrien. Can we use it?"

"What do you mean?"

"Do we have the time to train our men with these weapons? Would they be able to face the Itihasians?"

Illiott lowered his head. For months he studied Manaism, only to be able to light a candle, even then he wasn't sure if it was a fluke. Fadrien had yet to show any signs of casting a spell or altercation.

"It would take some time," Fadrien said.

"How long?"

"There is no way of knowing, Your Highness. There is much more to it than just learning phrases and words. It requires a change of heart. A selfless heart at that."

"How soon?" Alderman's face demanded an answer.

"...Months. Maybe years."

Alderman observed the medallion. It seemed insignificant, good for nothing save its precious metal.

"War is no time to search for selfless hearts." Alderman clasped the medallion in his hands.

"I disagree, my king." Kit said. "Think of all the love we have for our families and fellow man?"

"Enough of your romantic ideas. This is war. Over twenty thousand men camp outside this keep, each hoping to bring back my head to their king. Do you think they'll stop to discuss a change of heart?—They'll run you through, just like the hundreds before that died protecting these walls. What act of love can we have for those here to destroy us... If that's the type of power and commitment it takes to wield the Manaist treasure then I won't risk opening it. We may be concerned about its power, but I can assure you the enemy is not. They don't want it because of their love for us. We owe it to the rest of this world. The vault will remain closed."

"Then what will you have us do?" Bruan said. "You know just as well as I that they will overcome us. They'll find the medallion and open the vault once we've been conquered."

"Can it be destroyed?" Alderman said.

"I'm sure it can," Fadrien said. "Many things were destroyed after the ban."

"Then make it happen. It stays with me until then."

"My king," Bruan said. "I—It's not in me to give up the fight."

"Nor I, Captain. I'm not giving in. It's what must be done. The medallion can't fall into their hands."

Bruan gritted his teeth. "I think this is cowardice. You've lost faith in your people. Marquise Eelton is only hours away. We can defend ourselves, our homes and families—Our heritage. Think what we've stumbled upon. We are a mighty people. Is that not worth defending? Are we to give up and let the world devour what is ours?"

"Dangerous and a coward... That's what you all think of me? Tell me," Alderman roared. "Is it not courage to stand up and fight against an enemy twenty times our strength? Don't mistake my decision as fear. It's conviction. We owe it to the rest of the world not to let it fall in the enemy's hands. I don't see it as cowardice. It takes no small amount of courage to forgo the only weapon we have against them.

"Fadrien said it himself. We don't have the time to train our men to use the manaist weapons. They won't avail us now, nor will they for the enemy if we are to be conquered. The medallions are to be destroyed."

"Then what should I tell the men?" Bruan said. "That our king has lost all hope?"

"This is a safeguard, Captain. That is what you will tell the men. Now if I were you I'd get back to the wall before I regret my decision of making it your command."

Bruan clenched his fists. He would have crushed his ring had he the strength. He stormed away from the throne. Lyle tried to stop him, but Bruan shrugged him off. None of the others dared to speak. The tension in the air was suffocating. Lyle could see the disappointment Fadrien and Illiott felt; to come so close to the king's medallion, only to have them all destroyed. There was nothing to be done. As the guards closed the doors behind Bruan there was a hopeless finality to the king's decision.

Fadrien lowered his head and whispered to Illiott. "Even if we survive the siege, Averlace is already lost."

*   *   *

Davrian looked from the council chamber's lone window. From his vantage he could see Carper's Vale. Dark shapes hustled around the towering catapults, gearing them for the coming onslaught. Arms were lowered and slings loaded. An attack was imminent and Averlace was not prepared. It was a sobering thought.

Davrian rested his head against the glass. At any moment there will be more cries and screams. A cold tingle worked up his neck. Someone else was in the room.

"What do you want?" Davrian said, unsure who it was.

"I don't know," a broken voice answered.

Davrian turned around. It was Bruan. The captain approached with a weary gait. Instead of a sword he held his winged helm against his side.

"You don't look like a captain ready for war," Davrian said.

"I think that is why I'm here," Bruan said.

"I see," Davrian stepped from the window. "You come to a prisoner for help?"

"You were right about the king."

"Was I?"

"He's ordered the medallions to be destroyed. He means well. He does! But it's wrong, Davrian. I won't stand for it. We have a means to win this war. We must use it."

"So why are you here?" Davrian said.

"Because I believe you are the only one who can do something."

"What would you have me do?"

"I don't... Is there anything that can be done? Help me. Fadrien won't say anything against the king. Even if he did, the king wouldn't listen. His mind is made. Lyle, Kit and Illiott can't speak any reason to him. The heavens know I've tried," Bruan said.

"He has no faith in his people."

"Yes, that's what I told him."

"He has no faith in you." Davrian's eyes were compassionate.

Bruan froze. Davrian was right. How else could everything be explained. Alderman never trusted Bruan; but could he be blamed?

When the enemy army sounds the retreat, then you may wear your ring.

"He never believed I could hold the wall," Bruan said. "That's why I wasn't allowed to wear my ring. He trusted you though... He let you wear his own."

"Do you trust me?" Davrian said.

"I don't know."

"Oh, I think you do. Why come to me? You're at the end of your rope. You're burdened with an impossible task. You can't hold the wall with your men alone. You need a weapon, an advantage."

"Can you give that to me?"

"I can," Davrian said as he held out his hand. "But I'll need something in return from you. Your ring please."

"I've trusted you before. It brought me nothing but shame and it imperiled the king."

"Bruan, have you heard nothing I've said? The Syndicate was designed to destroy itself. I never lied to you in that prison. I needed Alderman off the throne, surely by now you can see why. That is why I chose you. You would make the decisions Alderman is too afraid to make."

"Why the ring?"

"Opening the vault, and collecting the medallions will require no small amount of magic." Davrian extended his hand and opened his palm.

"I can get the ring myself. Illiott and Fadrien can lead me to the vault. Why do I need you?"

"Though the medallion is required. The vault can only be open by royalty."

Bruan grunted. "That's why the Prince of Itihasia is necessary."

"Unless you think you can make Alderman cooperate," Davrian smiled. "There's also the Queen and Prince."

"I won't stoop to that," Bruan said.

"Then I'm your man."

"What then? Once I give you the ring? The king will be furious."

"I doubt he'll oppose you once you're armed to the teeth with the finest weaponry ever created."

Bruan shuddered. Davrian's words sounded like a rebellion.

"What's in it for you?"

"Freedom?" Davrian tugged at his chain.

Bruan looked out to Carper's Vale then to Davrian's lock. He stepped back.

"I've been in this game long before the first Itihasian stepped foot in this kingdom. I'm a step ahead of everyone... Everyone!" Davrian said.

"What of the Ebon Crow?"

"Even the Ebon Crow."

Bruan heard enough. Averlace's only hope without the treasure was with the Northern Army, but even then victory seemed out of reach. Trusting Davrian wasn't so much of a gamble. He pulled the key to Davrian's lock from his belt. He couldn't believe what he was doing.

Bruan shook the key at Davrian. "Once the vault is open, you're to leave immediately and Averlace is to have no future dealings with the Prince of Itihasia."

"Understood," Davrian held out his hand. "So we have a deal?"

Bruan held his breath. He remembered the time he first met Davrian in the crowded prison. The guildmaster's words were promising. Had Davrian never led him astray? Or was he about to agree to another lie? Was it all a lie?

If you want to protect your people you better do what you believe to be best and take matters into your own hands.

Bruan cleared his throat. It was decided. Davrian was Averlace's only hope. He shook Davrian's hand, leaving his ring in the guild master's palm. He opened the lock and slung the chain aside.

"If you fail us, I'll kill you. I swear it! So help me..."

Davrian bent down and rubbed the aches out of his ankles. "I appreciate your faith, Bruan." He slid the ring onto his thumb. "Now how about a little magic?"

CHAPTER THIRTY FOUR

THE BEAR AND THE WOLF

CHAPTER THIRTY-FOUR

THE BEAR AND THE WOLF

ALDERMAN PULLED a small purse from his belt. He shook it in the air, the coins jingled inside.

"My work is free, my lord," a grizzled man said. He draped a leather apron over his neck and tied it behind his back.

"The gold is to keep quiet," Alderman said, his eyes penetrating.

The blacksmith reached for the bellows of his makeshift furnace. "Might be best if the job was done by another. I haven't experience repurposing such fine metal."

"I want the medallions destroyed. What you do with metal is up to you," Alderman said. He plopped his medallion on the blacksmith's anvil and motioned Fadrien and Illiott to do the same.

"An odd chore to take such priority with the kingdom under siege," Valice said from her throne, her voice cynical.

Alderman pretended he didn't hear. "On with it," he said to Fadrien and Illiott.

Fadrien laid his medallion next to Alderman's. Its cold clatter against the anvil was finite. Fadrien was losing more than his cherished medallion, he was sacrificing the last vestige of his hope to abrogate the king's fear. This wasn't the purpose of Manaism.

Illiott sat the school's medallion atop of Fadrien's.

"There is no need to destroy all of them." Illiott said; he held his father's medallion against his chest. "Without the king's medallion, all four are needed to open the vault. May my father's be spared?"

"The enemy will find some use with your medallion, will they not?" Alderman said as he pointed to the anvil. "Destroy it with the others."

"I understand your fear, but we're just now beginning to understand the power of manaist magic."

"As am I!" Alderman said. "One girl rode past the army, casting fire and summoning wind, nearly ripped the gates from the wall. Armed with what? A bracelet I'm told! Imagine an army of our enemies armed with the finest weaponry. I won't leave a single scrap of manaist metal intact so long as the enemy demands it."

"This is the last I have of my father."

"He'd understand. He'd give up his medallion without question."

"I'm not sure he would," Illiott said. Without a choice he obeyed. He set his medallion on the anvil and stepped back.

"This is a mistake," Illiott whispered to Fadrien.

"Perhaps, but it's the king's orders."

"I feel responsible."

"Responsible? What for?"

"I've failed the school. I've failed Averlace. I haven't grown as I'd hoped. Much would be different now if I could defend the city with magic and teach others to do the same," Illiott said.

"You've done all you could," Fadrien said. "Perhaps I am to blame. I was far too cautious. I held you back."

Illiott said nothing. The embers in the brazier started to turn white. The fire was ready.

The blacksmith strapped on his leather apron and reached for his tongs.

Illiott inched closer to the medallions. He knew where to find the vault and where to place the medallion. If he was fast enough he could swipe them. Perhaps with a powerful manaist weapon he could do more. Was it worth the risk? Was it worth the wrath of King Alderman?

Fadrien grabbed Illiott's hand. "Don't," he said. The old man's eyes were firm and unwavering. "There is another way."

The selfless path. Illiott thought. He walked to the anvil as the smith worked the billows. Lightly, he ran his finger over his father's medallion.

"Bless the King's Medallion," he muttered under his breath. "May it see no end this day."

"Step back," Alderman said, suspicious of Illiott.

The blacksmith grabbed the king's medallion first. He looked to the king and queen for certainty before starting his work. Alderman said nothing. He folded his arms; his stalwart countenance hinting at his impatience. Valice gave a regretful nod. The blacksmith tossed the medallion on an iron pan. He lifted the furnace lid with his tongs and shoved the pan on the coals. The purple ribbon caught fire within an instant. Illiott looked away, it was over.

"By fire?" the blacksmith said. He started beating his bellows again.

Smoke stopped pouring from the furnace chimney.

"The fire's gone cold." The blacksmith opened the furnace with his tongs. The coals were black. Puzzled, the man dropped his tongs to the ground. He reached barehanded and grabbed the medallion off the pan.

"Cold to the touch," he said.

Illiott and Fadrien exchanged baffled glances.

"Again!" Alderman said. "This can't wait any longer."

The other braziers blew out, as did the chandeliers, leaving the throne room shrouded in darkness. A cloaked figure jumped from behind the smithy's worktable and made for the portable forge. It grabbed the medallion from the blacksmith who tried to seize the man. The blacksmith's large, calloused hands slid down the man's arm, unable to take hold. They crashed into the furnace, spilling out the coals which had returned to fiery red.

"Thief!" Alderman shouted. "Stop him."

Illiott drew an arrow, but couldn't take aim in the dark. He made a blind shot. It rattled against the stone floor. The shadow moved quickly, sliding under the smithy's table then bolting for the main entrance. The cloaked shadow snapped his finger and the doors flung open. The hall's light illuminated the throne room. Illiott focused on the man, trying his best to note any detail the darkness allowed.

He had only one hand.

"Stop that man," Alderman shouted as he ran.

The thief jumped through a stained glass window then made for the keep's courtyard, recently transformed to the soldier's prepping area. The one handed man weaved through the workers and soldiers, all oblivious to the chase. He reached the ramparts and started up a ladder, slowing just enough for Illiott to take a shot. The arrow sailed through the air and landed in the thief's back, bouncing away. One last guard stood in his way. With two precise blows the thief knocked the man down. He stepped over the guard then jumped over the wall.

Illiott cursed. The medallion was lost. The thief gone as quickly as he came.

"Find him!" Illiott shouted. "Stop the one armed man!"

Soldiers flocked to the gatehouse, throwing torches over the wall in a desperate attempt to spot the thief. Illiott ran inside the barbican and looked out. Ingran and Barret were already there. A series of shouts erupted just outside on the ramparts. Two guards spotted the thief crossing the Numen. More men came to help. Arrows flew from the wall.

"Hold!" Barret cried out. "Hold"

It was too late. With a heavy presence on the wall and arrows flying, the Averlacians appeared to be taunting the enemy. A few Itihasians shot back with their bolts. Despite Barret and Ingran's attempts to cease fire, the fighting escalated. Within moments the enemy army rose and the streets swarmed with angry footmen. A few moments later the first of many volleys peppered the barbican.

"Take cover!" Barret ordered.

Wave after wave of bolts landed against the wall, most bouncing harmlessly against the stone. A few struck soldiers who could not find cover in time.

Illiott hoped the attack would die down, but the bolts continued to strike the barbican. He risked a glance between each wave, finally he saw the enemy crossing the Numen.

"They're charging the wall!"

"Where is the captain?" Barret shouted.

No one knew. Barret cursed and lowered the visor of his helm. "Brace the gate!"

Ingran and his men fired at the bridge's ruins. The Itihasians took heavy losses, which seemed to only fuel their determination.

The two-man shields the Itihasians used earlier raced to the forefront. Crossbowmen fired from behind, providing cover for teams of battering rams as they approached the portcullis. Clay pots sailed over the wall, exploding into curtains of fire. Patches of the courtyard's cobbled road ignited.

The Falconers exhausted all their arrows within minutes. The Itihasians paid dearly to cross the river, but now Ingran and his men could do nothing to slow their advance. Within seconds the enemy swarmed the killing ground unchallenged. Grappling hooks and ladders assaulted the walls while the volley of black bolts never ceased. With each bolt stuck in stone the enemy had a new hand hold to scale the wall.

Illiott stayed in the barbican, hurling stones through a murder hole. An older man, years past fighting age, worked to bring a vat of pitch to a boil. The sight of fire reminded Illiott of the smithy's fire. He'd already forgotten about the thief and the stolen medallion. Averlace's hope was lost. And worse, it was now in enemy hands.

"Where's Freja?" Illiott shouted, but no one answered. He looked back at the old man fanning a small fire under the vat. It would never boil in time.

Horns blasted from the field. Large red banners rose above the ranks. The marksmen ceased fire, dropped their crossbows and drew swords. In unison the horns blasted a sustained note. The Itihasians swarmed the wall.

Below the barbican, the battering rams pummeled the portcullis. The iron bars bent against the oak doors they protected. Barret and a hundred men braced the gate with wooden beams. Others lowered their shoulders and pushed against the oak doors with all their might. Two battering ram teams alternated their strikes. The barbican shook with each relentless blow.

Illiott heard screams and scraping swords from the ramparts. The Itihasians were on the wall. He drew his sword and made for the door, but the floor shook violently underneath, causing him to stumble. The wooden gate was breaking apart. Three Itihasians stormed the barbican. Illiott faked a thrust then swiped the first man's neck. Ingran shot the second with his last arrow then tackled the third, allowing Illiott to drive his sword in the man's chest.

Another violent shake.

"We need to fall back to the library now!" Ingran said. "We can't hold this wall."

The barbican rumbled. Illiott could hear the timber beams cracking as they gave way. He looked down on the enemy below.

"The gate's been breached!" Ingran yelled.

Itihasians crawled over one another past the door's twisted wood. Barret and his men waited with long spears. Illiott rummaged through the room for anything to throw. The old man's vat was just starting to warm. There was nothing else the barbican could do to help.

A final blow to the gate sent Illiott to the floor. More Itihasians crawled over the wreckage. Illiot was just about to call for retreat when he saw the first shoots of leaves growing thought the floorboards. It was Freja. She pushed against the splintered beams as the men fought to keep the enemy from passing. Her fingers turned the hardened oak doors to a verdant color. Roots grew out of the base and planted themselves deep into the earth. Strong, healthy vines shot from the top until it reached the barbican's stone ceiling above. They curled and twisted then returned back to the ground, entangling and crushing the enemy as they tried to crawl through the gateway.

"Stand back," Freja yelled to Barret and his men. She pressed harder against the door. The men stepped back in awe as the door came to life, not only mending damage, but growing twice as thick with gnarled bark and merciless thorns.

The battering ram continued to pound, but the door's lush wood flexed with each blow. The rams and their crew were overcome by the foliage, rendering them useless. Most abandoned the charge against the gate. The few that pushed on were cut open and strangled by the thorns and vines. The door's growing weight crushed the rams. The gatehouse was now secure.

Barret led his spearmen to the ramparts where they engaged the enemy. The Itihasians were slow up the wall; still their numbers overwhelmed the Averlacians. The fighting was brutal and unforgiving. Illiott hacked at a pair of grappling hooks, sending their climbers screaming back to the ground.

A pack of Itihasians gained ground in the center of the ramparts, parting the king's men. They pushed in both directions as reinforcements climbed. Ingran batted a man over the edge with his bow, shielding Illiott who struck from behind at every opportunity. Together they pushed against the massing Itihasian foothold.

Ingran's bow split across an enemy helm. The enemy pushed harder as more scaled the walls. They were taking the wall without razing the gate. Illiott, Ingran and their fellow soldiers were pushed back into the barbican. From there the Itihasians tried to gain ground onto the bailey, but met stiff resistance. King Alderman had joined the battle, rallying the rest of the spearmen.

The enemy pushed into the barbican. A shield bashed into Illiott's chin. Dazed, he held himself against the window. Ingran stood in cover. Looking out he could see enemy archers climbing the wall. Once on the ramparts they would rain death on Alderman and his men. He looked to his ring and imagined a strong wind knocking the Itihasians from the wall.

Nothing.

A swordsman stabbed at Illiott as he concentrated, nearly catching his thigh. He parried the next strike. With each deflection the Itihasians forced Illiott and the others deeper into the barbican.

Another series of horns blasted across the battlefield. Illiott dispatched his attacker and chanced a look outside. He expected more red banners to rise, instead he saw more soldiers pouring into the lower city through the remains of the northern gate. It was over.

Illiott faced his enemy. He wasn't going to die in retreat. A bolt hissed overhead. The archers were on the wall. Ingran fell forward, the tip of a spear pierced through his back. He rose to his feet and wrapped his arms around the man before him, pushing against the enemy until he reached the door. Swords, bolts and spears ripped at his mail. With his last breath he spun and toppled over the wall, bringing the swordsman with him.

Illiott's sword shattered. It served one last block before snapping at the hilt. An axe caught his forearm. He cried out in anger and defiance. With no weapons or armor he held out his hands. He was about to charge like Ingran, but he remembered the pitch. The old man tending the vat lay dead at the fire.

The medallion was stolen, the wall taken, Itihasian reinforcements swarmed Manadon, Ingran and many others were dead. All he wanted was a fighting chance. Illiott reached for the vat of pitch in a desperate attempt, he focused on his ring, but most of all—He felt his anger and contempt.

The vat leaned to its side then floated over the fire. Illiott lowered his hand. Did he move it? The vat wobbled as he lost concentration. Illiott couldn't believe it, yet it felt so natural. He focused harder. The vat launched into the air then crashed into the nearest enemy. Hot clay, and bubbling pitch exploded over the enemy. Many jumped over the wall. Others ran wildly, writhing and screaming. Illiott rose and stared at his ring. Quickly he looked for something to use against the enemy.

Alderman ordered his men to take cover from the enemy archers on the wall. A blast came from the barbican's right door. A cloud of fire raced across the rampart, engulfing the enemy. The Itihasian archers were gone.

"To the gate!" Alderman ordered all of the men in the bailey.

The enemy worked to free the battering rams from the foliage. They hacked at the door with their axes and halberds. Freja remained on the other side, willing the door to remain.

A curtain of fire burned on top of the ramparts. No one dared scale the wall or defend it. Illiott never felt more alive. He single handedly destroyed a hundred men. The few remaining spearmen in the barbican weren't sure what they had witnessed.

"The marquis!" a spearman yelled.

Cheers sang out. Illiott looked. He had mistaken the Northern Army for enemy reinforcements. It was a mounted cavalry, charging the Numen and dividing the enemy army in two.

*   *   *

Athan feared they were too late. The wall left of the barbican burned, but fighting continued on the right. Rayghar led the charge. The same discipline that promptly delivered the army to Averlace excelled in battle. Upon their arrival, Rayghar ordered that the enemy's supply camps be taken first; from there he led the cavalry through the city.

Having focused their strength against the wall, the Itihasians were caught off guard. Athan, Eamon and Bratheon rode beside Rayghar. They rode from the destroyed wall to the artisan district with little resistance, trampling the enemy beneath. Those that stood their ground were cut down. Still, the size of the Itihasian force was staggering. For as much ground as they covered, Athan knew the fight had just begun.

Bratheon held his head low as he rode. His thoughts with his friends and fellow soldiers, but mostly with Freja. Eago, the red fox, followed from a safe distance.

Their charge halted at Astrannax's bridge. Rows of halberds lined ahead of the bridge's charred ruins. The Itihasians were now divided into two separate forces; a few remnants were trapped between the keep's wall and Marquis Eelton's army and Carper's Vale.

Archers lined the short wall surrounding Carper's Vale and fired upon Rayghar's cavalry. They were pinned. The halberds were a perfect counter to the fast moving cavalry, but to linger under fire would prove disastrous. The general waved his sword towards the halberds guarding the bridge and kicked his horse into a charge. His men followed without question.

Athan saw first hand Rayghar's ferocity in battle. He was a patient combatant, waiting for the enemy to make a mistake before striking with devastating and precise blows. Not to be outdone, Athan jumped from his horse, preferring to be on foot in such close quarters. The halberds length had no advantage against Athan's short blades. Athan disrupted the front line, giving Rayghar and his men enough of a wedge to push deep into the enemy ranks. Eamon kept close to his brother, bearing a shield overhead to block the Carper's Vale arrows. The marquis' cavalry crept to the Numen's shore as one unit until they overcame the halberds.

Enemy arrows continued to fall on Rayghar and his men. They had to cross the river to escape the archers' range. Rayghar gave the order to dismount and wade across.

A creaking and crashing sound came from the gatehouse. The gate was torn from its foundation. Bratheon feared the worst. More screams and cries followed as the enemy swarmed the gate. Despite the chaos, Bratheon could make out a distinct voice.

"Freja!"

"They're attacking the gate!" Her voice carried in the smoky wind.

Bratheon charged ahead of Rayghar's men. The enemy advanced, clashing against Alderman, Barret and the spearmen. He reached in his saddle for Illiott's satchel. The red dagger glowed inside. There had to be a way to act in love.

Illiott held his head, his ears rang. Below he could see the enemy overwhelming Alderman and the others. He had to act now. The vat of pitch was gone. What else could he use? He focused on his ring, hoping something would come available. His mind flooded with his family's last moments before Sullion killed them. The foreigner, the Itihasian had killed them. More were killing his friends below. He could feel power seething within. Freja summoned fire without aid; surely he could do the same. He held his hand towards the enemy. It trembled and started to burn. Horrific images of burning corpses took hold of his mind. More terrifying was the delight he found. The power was there, the spell envisioned, all was left was the desire.

Illiott looked one last time as the Itihasians attacked Freja's living gate. Fire swirled from his fingertips towards the enemy. Pillars of red flame broke the earth, engulfing the men and the surrounding area.

"Stand down!" Rayghar ordered his men. The earth before them cracked open with steam and fire.

The few Itihasians caught between Rayghar's cavalry and the inferno continued to fight. Athan neared the fray, but the heat was too intense. His horse reared up, refusing to advance. A crumbling sound came from the gatehouse. Parts of the barbican collapsed from the extreme heat, avalanching over more of the enemy and extinguishing the fire. A cloud of dust and smoke covered the battle.

All was still at the gate.

As the smoke cleared, Eamon could see King Alderman standing in the gap with his men behind; all unharmed.

The remaining Itihasians made one last push into the keep's bailey. Rather than dig in and hold ground, Alderman advanced against the enemy.

"To the king!" Rayghar shouted.

Athan and Eamon joined their voices with the Northern Army's war cry. The cavalry crushed the remaining row of halberds guarding the shore. All that remained between the Northern Army and King Alderman was a hill of crossbowmen, hiding behind their large shields.

Alderman swung his hammer in giant, sweeping arcs. He mauled his way from the gatehouse and started downhill. Rayghar tripped in his advance, brought down by a lone halberd. A swordsman leapt in for the kill. Rayghar rose and stepped into his attacker with a feral strike. He sliced his way uphill. Athan whirled his blades between the broken ranks, making short work of the infantry.

The marquis's cavalry flanked the hill, herding the last of the Itihasians to the barbican's smoldering rubble. Alderman and his spearmen made a tight phalanx, crushing the Itihasians between the two forces.

The Bear of Arata and the Wolf of the Northern Army met in the center. Swords, spears and lances rose in the air as the victors cheered and embraced one another. The battle was won, but celebration would have to wait.

"Form ranks!" Alderman shouted.

The vast majority of Kvrual's forces retreated safely to Caper's Vale. The war was far from over. King Alderman ordered his men to fall back to the keep. General Rayghar left a third of his cavalry to reinforce the keep. The rest of the Northern Army needed to regroup and prepare for the enemy to counter. Athan and Eamon remained with Rayghar, but Bratheon was nowhere to be seen.

Victory came at a great price. The loss of life was overwhelming. Fire raged across the parapet, the gatehouse was destroyed.

Illiott stumbled across the rubble. He couldn't believe what he had done. Singlehandedly he incinerated hundreds of enemy soldiers, but the fire also destroyed the barbican.

"Help," a voice called out.

Illiott followed the voice, waving off smoke as he searched the rock. He could hear coughing.

"Help," the voice was weaker.

Illiott worked his way to the edge of the rubble. There he found Bratheon. A forlorn fox overlooked the young man's broken body. An oak joist pinned him against a jagged rock. Illiott pushed against the beam then recoiled. His hands throbbed with burning pulses. He looked at his hands. White and yellow blisters bubbled his skin, making his hands unrecognizable. Was it from the spell? He pushed again, but it was no use.

"Help," Illiott shouted. His head started to spin.

His voice was lost in a chorus of voices, all calling out in anguish. Illiott thought of the signet ring. He concentrated on the joist, but it wouldn't budge. Bratheon fought to breathe.

"Help!" Illiott cried out.

"Freja," Bratheon whispered.

Illiott crawled to Bratheon's side. "Stay with me. Help is coming."

"Tell, her I love—" Bratheon gasped.

"She knows," Illiott shushed. "She knows."

"Averlace... Can defend. Herself." Bratheon's lungs rattled, his eyes kept open.

"Help!" Illiott raised his hands to his mouth to call out. His stomach churned at the sight of his blisters. He stopped the enemy advance, but at what cost?

CHAPTER THIRTY FIVE
THE PRINCE OF ITIHASIA

CHAPTER THIRTY-FIVE

THE PRINCE OF ITIHASIA

FOG COVERED the Numen like a death shroud. Harrot waded between dozens of floating bodies, hiding in the reeds and cattails. Every few steps he patted his pocket, making sure he still carried the King's Medallion. Quietly he worked his way north, searching for a lone man, his contact. He reached a stone bridge with a farmhouse built at its western bank. Water babbled past a jetty, funneling to the farmhouse's creaking watermill. Straddling a rock sat a cloaked man, tossing pebbles into the river. Pearl strains of hair fell from the man's hood. Harrot had found his contact.

Harrot crawled out of the bloodied water. "I hope you had an easier time than I crossing the Numen."

Davrian cocked his head and pulled down his hood. A relieved smile parted his mouth. "Well done." He tossed his cloak onto Harrot's wet head. "Are you alright?"

"Fine." Harrot rubbed his head dry. He looked across the river to the keep. "I'm alive and well... I fared better than most." He opened his jacket and pulled out the King's Medallion.

Davrian eyes widened. "You have it!"

"A moment later and it may have been too late."

"And the ring?"

Harrot slid the signet ring from his finger and placed it in Davrian's open palm. "I've known you to cut it close, but last night was pushing it."

"Information comes slow these days," Davrian said. "Comes with killing off the guild I suppose."

"I found it where you said to look. A blacksmith was about to melt it down."

"Lucky us."

"Luck?" Harrot scoffed. "Don't sell yourself short. "I doubt we'd be here with luck alone."

Davrian gave a faint laugh. "I prowled around Carper's Vale while you were out. Kvrual's in trouble. He may have a mutiny on his hands."

"Does that change things?"

"I don't know, but one thing's for sure. We can't forget that Kvrual wants us just as bad as Alderman." Davrian gave a subtle nod with his head.

Harrot looked behind. Two Itihasian archers were watching from the Caper's Vale wall.

"They're waiting for you?" Harrot said.

"No, they're waiting for the medallion."

"Hopefully we'll have a warmer reception." Harrot held the medallion out.

"You keep it," Davrian said. "It's safer with you."

Davrian faced the guards and pointed to Harrot. "He has it! Just as I promised."

Harrot raised the medallion for the men to see. One whispered to the other then waved for Davrian and Harrot to come.

"Give it to me," the first archer said. He drew his sword and held it against Davrian.

"This is for the commander," Davrian said. "Take us to him."

"Kvrual said nothing about you bringing the medallion," the Itihasian hissed. "We were told our prince carries the medallion."

"You have more resemblance to a plucked bird than an Itihasian," the second said. He twisted Davrian's arm. "Perhaps you hand me the medallion now and I'll bring you to Kvrual alive." He pressed his sword deeper into Davrian's back.

"Unhand him," Harrot ordered. He pulled back his hood.

The two men fell to their faces.

"My liege. A thousand apologies."

"We did not know." The second man tugged on Davrian's shirt, trying to bring him to a bow.

Harrot extended his one hand to Davrian. "This man is my champion. He walks beside me."

The two men said nothing. They pushed their faces into the ground, not daring to look up.

"Run ahead," Harrot said. "Tell Kvrual the Prince of Itihasia has returned and he carries the Manaist King's Medallion."

Keeping prostrate the men backed up and turned without looking to their long-lost prince. Slowly they stood then ran as ordered.

"I have a confession to make," Davrian smiled. "I hope your highness will forgive me."

"What is that?" Harrot's brow raised.

"I told Alderman and the Elite I was the Prince of Itihasia."

Harrot laughed. "For shame. For shame."

*   *   *

Lyle met Kit at the library's steps. Both were dressed in leather helms and tunics. Kit felt uneasy with the sword he carried. During the battle they were ordered to guard the library. Josie and Adeline spent the night helping Freja, Lurie and Mandel tend to the wounded. Kit was grateful for the assignment; it allowed him to be at Josie's side. Now the king had new orders for them. Find Captain Bruan.

"What do you mean find him?" Kit said.

"He wasn't seen last night during the battle," Lyle said.

Kit looked concerned. "Bruan wasn't happy with the king. You don't suspect anything funny do you?"

"We'll keep it simple for now," Lyle said. "We can speculate once we know more."

"Something must be wrong for Bruan not to show during the battle," Kit said.

"Protecting the wall was everything to him," Lyle said.

"He disagreed with King Alderman about the Manaist treasure."

Lyle nodded. "But he wouldn't have abandoned the fight. Bruan's no coward."

"I'm concerned, Lyle," Kit said. "What if we find him dead? Murdering leaders during a siege is not unheard of."

"I'm concerned too," Lyle said. "But not of that."

"What then?"

"Follow me."

Lyle headed to the council chamber. Kit didn't have to ask.

"Davrian didn't lose... He forfeited the game we played," Lyle said.

"Why?" Kit said.

"I believe it had more to do with him being done with the game than refusing to answer the question."

"He was just tired of playing?"

"No, he accomplished what he had hoped to do," Lyle said.

"What was that?"

"Plant an idea," Lyle said as they approached the council chamber. He slowly pushed the door open.

All of the furniture had been pushed to the sides. In the center of the room they found Bruan chained to a chair, gagged. A sign hung from his neck. Bruan didn't look relieved to see help had arrived. He lowered his head.

"We'll need someone to break these chains," Kit said. He pulled the gag from Bruan's mouth. "Are you alright?"

Bruan shook his head and started to sob. "What have I done?"

"Where's Davrian?" Lyle said, fearing the worst.

"I let him go. I'm such a fool."

Lyle could barely understand Bruan as he cried.

"This is what he wanted," Lyle said. "Davrian wanted us to trust him over Alderman. He didn't care about his freedom or the ring… He played me."

Kit untied the sign from Bruan's neck. "He's played all of us," he said as he pointed to it.

Davrian's handwriting couldn't have been mistaken. In large, lavish letters he wrote a parting mockery.

Long live the Elite. Long live the Elite. Long live the Elite.

THE END

About the Author

JOHN ELLIOTT KAY attended school at Union University in Jackson, Tennessee, earning degrees in history and psychology. He is a former teacher and he and his wife make their home in Tennessee. He is also the author of "The Kings Elite," Book One of THE KING'S ELITE series. He believes biblical truth can be found anywhere, expecially in a great story.

Proof

Made in the USA
Charleston, SC
14 May 2016